THE GOOD DAUGHTERS

THE GOOD DAUGHTERS

A NOVEL

BRIGITTE DALE

PEGASUS BOOKS
NEW YORK LONDON

THE GOOD DAUGHTERS

Pegasus Books, Ltd.
148 West 37th Street, 13th Floor
New York, NY 10018

First Pegasus Books cloth edition November 2025

Interior design by Maria Fernandez

ISBN: 978-1-63936-987-4

10 9 8 7 6 5 4 3 2 1

Printed in the United States of America
Distributed by Simon & Schuster
www.pegasusbooks.com

For my mother

AUTHOR'S NOTE

E verything in this novel is based on real people, places, and events. These truths were buried, dusty, and crumbling, in storerooms of libraries or forgotten in the footnotes of men's stories.

Until now.

12 July 1913

THE TIMES OF LONDON

WOMAN'S MAD ATTEMPT:
Militant Throws King's Derby Colt

Hundreds of spectators were gathered at Epsom today for the annual running of the horses, when a rogue woman sprinted in front of the leading steeds. The scene was already a tense one, as onlookers hung dangerously over the wooden rails at the point where the jockeys hug the final turn. Amidst this commotion, a woman slipped under the rails and rushed forward onto the course. She held her arms wide open and dashed in front of the king's horse, as if in a desperate effort to seize its reins.

To stop a racehorse in full flight is not a safe or easy proposition, and in a moment the horse had fallen and was rolled onto its back, throwing its unfortunate jockey clear, while the woman herself was propelled violently to the ground. Shrieks erupted throughout the stands as the woman lay unconscious.

"She was bowled over like a ninepin," a gentleman standing by observed. "The horse stumbled over her and eventually turned a complete somersault."

It was hardly a surprise to onlookers that the woman wore a tricolor sash, striped with the violet, white, and green of the militant suffragette union. This paper condemns the suffragettes' hysterical and anarchistic demonstrations. The woman's identity and present state of health are not known, and she was last seen being carried into an ambulance.

"His poor Majesty," said an anonymous onlooker, acknowledging the king's disappointment at the results of the race. Readers shall be buoyed to learn that the king's horse appeared not to be seriously hurt. Another steed, the thoroughbred bay horse Aboyeur, won the race at record odds.

PART ONE

ONE YEAR EARLIER
AUTUMN 1912

CHAPTER ONE

CHARLOTTE

C harlotte Evans has exactly one day left at home, and she is determined to spend it wisely. For years, nothing mattered more to her than getting out—out of her brooding stepfather's house, away from her mother's criticism and her sisters' squabbling. And out, most importantly, into the world, where ideas matter and intelligence is valued. When the day finally arrives to pack her bags, her fingers quiver with nervous energy each time she places a folded blouse in the valise. Months of studying by candlelight after her chores, books stacked high around her like a fortress, followed by weeks of begging, arguing, and pleading with her parents, earned her a spot at Girton College. She will not squander this chance at freedom.

Still, it's been a long summer. A reckless summer.

"Charlotte," says Sarah, lips pursed. "Come upstairs for a moment."

Charlotte's stomach drops with a low, deep sense of dread, as she follows her mother up the creaky wooden staircase and into the master bedroom. The faded blue curtains are still drawn, even though it is almost midday, and they stand in near darkness. Even so, Charlotte can see the apprehension etched upon her mother's face. *Does she know?*

She wills her face to stay impassive, her voice to remain steady. She reminds herself to breathe.

"What is it, Mother?"

Sarah wrings her hands and exhales. "Just . . . be careful. Be good and be careful."

"Mother—"

"I mean it, Charlotte. Your virtue, once lost, is—"

Charlotte sighs, cutting off her mother's last words: *gone forever.*

"I know, Mother." The usual sarcasm returns to her voice as her body floods with a warm rush of relief—she has not been caught.

From the time Charlotte was five years old and permitted to cross the street on her own, her mother has repeated the importance of virtue. Sometimes she used other words, like *purity* or *honor*, but the message was always the same, delivered with frantic fervor. Charlotte has long considered the warning melodramatic, and she and her sisters used to joke about it behind their mother's back.

"Careful," they'd say when Sylvia began to knead dough, or as Anna left for school. "Your virtue, once lost, is gone *forever.*" It became a running joke, a game: Who could attribute warnings about promiscuity to the most mundane or absurd activities?

Still, Sarah is tense as they stand together in the dark bedroom. "Please, Charlotte," she says, her voice a hair higher than usual, a violin string tuned too tight.

"Yes, Mother." Charlotte bends to kiss her cheek. Sarah remains stiff.

The irony, of course, is that Charlotte has not been virtuous at all this summer. When Sylvia walked into the root cellar last week, Charlotte had needed to cover Jack's face with her palm to stifle his laughter. She had been almost certain that her younger sister heard them down there. But after an excruciating moment, holding her breath in the dark and jabbing Jack in the ribs as he fumbled with her skirts, Sylvia had turned on her heel and climbed back upstairs. Charlotte avoided her sister's gaze for days afterward, a million insufficient explanations at the tip of her tongue should Sylvia decide to confront her.

She'd been so worried that Sylvia would tell their mother, that somehow Sarah already knew and would pounce at the excuse to prevent Charlotte from leaving. This last week home, she lived in a constant state of anxiety. Charlotte swore off Jack and promised herself perfect propriety until, at last, she boarded the train bound for Cambridge. Jack was no one; it didn't matter. They were children, neighbors, friends running around their tiny village unsupervised and sneaking private moments together. Over the years, Charlotte had struggled to find the words for the raw desire she disguised, the feelings she could not quite express. Not that she dared to speak them aloud. Though she and her sisters used to poke fun at their mother's dire prognostications, sometime in the last few years they had stopped. Charlotte cannot quite remember when or why they ceased joking together, but she knows she can never, ever tell them about Jack. Sylvia and Anna wouldn't understand.

There is a distance between herself and her sisters, and not just caused by age, although the four years between Charlotte and Sylvia feel more like a chasm lately. It is that Sylvia and Anna breathe propriety. They have no interest in running through town on mad escapades alongside Charlotte, following whatever impulsive whim left her skirts muddy and her heart pounding. They are inexplicably content to stay home and help Sarah with the chores. Charlotte, on the other hand, had to beg for George and Sarah to consider her plea to attend Girton College. But most of all, Sylvia and Anna are younger, so they love George, their stepfather, who feels more like a father than anyone they've ever known. Charlotte, however, remembers her real papa, a man gentler and lovelier than George Penfield could ever be.

Naturally, Charlotte never told Sylvia and Anna about what she did that summer, about what she allowed Jack to do in those final weeks before she escaped that stifling life forever. There had been years of touches, stolen kisses, chaste but curious. Then, at last, in the waning days of August, when each blade of grass was verdant and singing with life, she had said yes and yes and yes.

Charlotte had thought it might hurt. *Lie back and think of England*, the girls at school had whispered. But it hadn't hurt. Nor had it been particularly pleasurable. The damp chill of the root cellar hadn't much contributed to a sense of romance. But unlike the tacit warnings she had internalized over the years, Charlotte did not feel ruined or violated or dominated. She felt, in fact, oddly powerful. She had consumed him, taken his most vulnerable piece inside of her. If that wasn't power, what was? She didn't love him, of course. But she wanted him. And that felt like enough.

Still, whether or not her summer with Jack meant something or everything or nothing at all, if she had been caught, there would be no Girton College. There would be no future. She would have been married off, if she was lucky. Otherwise, she'd have been ruined. Thank God for Sylvia's naïveté. On her last night at home, Charlotte keeps her hands busy, leaping at every chore placed before her. She knows how close she came to missing her chance.

With a puff of black smoke and a short, sharp whistle, the train jostles into motion. George sits across from her, his nose, as usual, in his newspaper. It was kind of him to accompany her, she supposes, though she'd have preferred her mother. But Sarah doesn't travel alone. Or at all. Charlotte can't remember the last time her mother left Fulney. Through the plate-glass windows, she watches brown fields and tiny, pinprick villages blur in the setting sun. The countryside rolls past as Charlotte travels farther from home than she has ever been in her life.

Like indigo dye in a vat of cotton, the horizon grows darker and more beautiful with each shift in light as day descends to darkness.

The train jolts into the Cambridge Railway Station, and George folds the paper, then straightens his cravat. Charlotte's cheek is numb from the cold window. She still wears her stiff traveling cloak, the one her mother sewed herself on candlelit evenings this summer, sacrificing her own eyesight to save the few extra shillings it would have cost to buy the cloak new in the village. Girton was, Sarah reminded Charlotte at every opportunity, costing George a fortune. Beneath the cloak, Charlotte wears a starched blouse, buttoned up to her chin, and under it, a tightly laced corset. The whalebone cuts into her ribs from sitting too long in one position. Her heart thrums against it as the yellow lights of Cambridge come into view. Wordlessly, George stands and gestures for a porter to retrieve their bags.

Charlotte's rooms in Girton College feel like pure luxury. Unlike her sisters, Charlotte still remembers the days before they moved in with their stepfather, before they had a cook and a housemaid to light the fires every morning. Her younger sisters have forgotten what it was to wake up cold. George is not rich, no—he hunches over the expenses each month, and when Sarah thinks he won't notice, she pores over the bills, too, performing her own calculations to determine how best to scrounge and save. They are comfortable enough, but always, it seems, teetering on the edge. Back home, all three sisters shared a bedroom.

Now, Charlotte discovers that she has a bedroom and an adjoining sitting room all to herself, with a narrow bed frame, a small wooden writing desk with an inkstand, a chest of drawers, and even a simple mantel surrounding her very own hearth—all of it is hers and hers alone. A thick though faded carpet covers most of the floor, and the windows, which look out on to manicured gardens, are curtained in cream-colored lace.

She hasn't brought anything with which to decorate the room, though she notices girls and their parents dragging in extra furniture and paintings and spare blankets. Out in the hall, mothers instruct the porters on how to hang drapes and where to store furs. George stands in the doorway fiddling with his pocket watch.

"I think I'm settled," Charlotte says. She'll unpack her simple valise on her own. George slips an envelope of folded bills into her hand before he leaves. Perhaps she has judged him too harshly. He had helped her fill out her application to Girton back when her mother was against it. Sarah thought that a university education meant a long, expensive road to spinsterhood.

"You'll ruin yourself for marriage," Sarah had fretted. "Why do you need to learn more than you already know?"

"Because," Charlotte had said, "I don't know what I don't know. And I'll never be satisfied unless I find out."

Charlotte and George had teamed up for the first time in her life in order to convince Sarah that her fears of the masculinizing effects of university were unwarranted, and that the pursuit of an education was not incompatible with Charlotte's future life as a wife and mother. Though he probably just wanted his overambitious eldest stepdaughter out of the house, Charlotte had been grateful for George's support. His only true flaw, she knows, is that George is not her real father. Papa would have been proud; she remembers how his eyes crinkled when he laughed—the same wide brown eyes she had inherited. Charlotte has not seen her mother's real smile since Papa died. She wishes Sarah could have come to drop her off at Girton, could have exhibited some pride, or at least some support, instead of acting the ever-gracious, frugal housewife, demurring to George's every whim, making herself small within their home.

All that is behind Charlotte now, thank goodness. She watches George putter down the stone pathway out her window before he disappears onto the street. And then she is alone. How exhilarating it feels to be entirely, wonderfully solitary! Each patter of the floorboards comes from her very own feet. The air smells like paper and ink, and the whole place hums with possibility. She explores the building, noting the stairs that creak and the ones that don't, the intricate molding where the corridors meet the ceiling. Ghostly faces of long-dead benefactors grimace at her from their gilded frames.

The stern housemother, Mrs. Pennington, has the face of a trout and lives at the end of the hall. "Girton College," she intones on their first night, all the girls gathered in the library for prayers, "is one of the few institutions intended solely for women that has ever been built in England. It is, in fact, among the few such institutions in the entire world, with the exception of convents, created to educate women. You must endeavor to embody all the superior qualities of womanhood and good breeding, so that you may go out into the world and improve it through manners, femininity, and grace."

Charlotte scans the room, noting the huddle of first-year girls who hang on Mrs. Pennington's words. The second-year cohort is rather smaller, but the third-years, she realizes, are reduced to only a handful. She doesn't mean to be cruel, but all she can think, as she looks at the oldest students, is how awkward most of them seem—all but a few dress in outdated clothes and hover near the corner in their small flock.

Charlotte quickly learns that Mrs. Pennington is even more obsessive about virtue and chastity than her mother. Known for regimental surveillance of her charges, Mrs. Pennington makes it her mission to put a stop to any behavior that might associate her girls with unfeminine bluestockings. Education, she insists, won't take Girton girls off the marriage market.

As Charlotte comes downstairs for seven o'clock breakfast on her first morning, Mrs. Pennington pokes out her metal-tipped cane, nearly causing Charlotte to trip.

"Young lady, how dare you present yourself in this state of undress?"

Charlotte flushes red—has she forgotten her knickers? But after a quick assessment, she's certain she is fully clothed.

"Your hair," Mrs. Pennington continues, pointing a knobby finger at the single braid that winds down Charlotte's back. "Girton girls must wear buns at all times."

"I'm just going down to breakfast," Charlotte protests. "I'll pin it up later."

"You'll do it now," Mrs. Pennington admonishes. "And do not let me see you in such a state of dishabille again."

Charlotte hurries back upstairs, her neck hot. It takes far longer than she would like to do her hair properly. Back home, she rarely had reason to wear it up, and for the odd formal occasion, she and her sisters helped each other. Now Charlotte huffs into the tiny looking glass, pins between her lips like a porcupine. She's done it all out of order—already dressed, she can hardly lift her arms high enough to manage her hair.

When at last she's succeeded in fashioning some semblance of a chignon, she rushes back downstairs. She steels herself to enter the dining room full of strangers, hoping there will still be a seat free at a friendly table. The door creaks as she pushes it open, and the room falls silent, eyes greeting her with cold stares. Charlotte is acutely aware of the loose strands in the back that she couldn't reach, of the beads of sweat dripping between her breasts and dampening her chemise. She cannot find a seat, and her footsteps are too loud. The girls turn back to their plates, heads bowed as they laugh and whisper together. Mrs. Pennington sits at the head of the table, unperturbed.

Over the next several days, Charlotte observes her classmates but speaks to almost no one. Or, rather, almost no one speaks to her. It appears that most of the girls are from London, and they all know each other already. They've been to the same finishing schools, attended the same parties, and seem to have little interest in meeting anyone else. Charlotte tries to participate when the conversation presents even the slightest opening. "Pretty dress," she is quick to compliment, or "Have you read Wollstonecraft, too?" The responses are usually concise—thank-yous, and yeses or nos—before backs turn and Charlotte is, once again, on the outside.

At teatime she overhears fellow first-years, all dressed impeccably, whispering about the men at King's College.

"Will you stay next year?" Flora St. Clare, an earl's daughter, asks the beautiful, raven-haired Georgina Fernsby-Bryce.

"I haven't decided," says Georgina, batting her black lashes conspiratorially. "The engagement, though unofficial," she mock whispers, "is set for spring. I suppose it depends if I've had time to prepare my trousseau."

Flora nods emphatically. "Well, if you leave before our second year is finished, so will I," she says. "My father has a third cousin I'm meant to meet soon, but even if that doesn't work out, I'd rather be back in town than here alone."

"Pardon my interruption," says Charlotte. "But what do you mean, here alone?"

The girls turn to her but no one responds. It's as though she asked her question in a foreign tongue. At last, Georgina explains, in a voice one would usually reserve to communicate with a child or someone hard of hearing, that *no one* stays for their third year at Girton College. "Unless," she adds, as an apologetic afterthought, "she has no marriage prospects." The diminished cohort of third-years suddenly makes sense.

Soon Flora and Georgina swish away in their silk skirts, leaving Charlotte in the wake of their whispers about the London season, wondering just what sort of world she's landed in.

No matter, she tells herself. *Be patient*. Charlotte explores the charming Cambridge streets on her own, counting the spires of medieval towers that pierce the gray autumn skies. And when the clouds open up and the air is dense with cold rain, she finds squashy chairs in the library and reads undisturbed for hours at a time. She feasts nightly in the dining hall, enjoying pudding at every meal and rich roasted chicken that she is never required to pluck or prepare herself. She hopes—no, she *knows*—it is only a matter of time before she finds friends. She must hold on.

At night, she hears girls clamoring down the halls, doors opening and closing as they visit each other. She leaves her door propped open, but though laughter trills through the corridors, no one knocks. Charlotte breathes deeply, reminding herself to relish each moment. She's here, isn't she? In her very own room at England's premiere college for women.

How dare she feel lonely when her dreams have come true?

CHAPTER TWO

EMILY

E mily plunges the mop into the murky water of her bucket, the hallways of Holloway Prison quiet in the fading afternoon light. She'd left school in a hurry, as always, rushing home to do her chores. Her father, Thomas, is tucked in the warden's office on the first floor, hunched over intake forms strewn across his small desk. Her mother, Marianne, is somewhere within the labyrinthine passageways of Holloway, cranking open windows caked with rust to air out the odor of unwashed bodies. Emily grips the wooden handle of the mop with strong hands, her skin perpetually chapped and her mind anywhere but here. Swirling water onto the floor in patterns and shapes that fade gently as the streaks dry, she cannot quite pretend that she is painting, though her fingers itch to find the charcoal pencil tucked into her skirt and return to her drawings. Maybe later, when the work is done, she'll find a spare moment, though lately it feels like the work at Holloway is never over.

The prison was built in the radial style of the previous century, a fact that Thomas Brown proudly repeated to his daughter countless times in the decade since they had moved into the small warden's cottage adjacent to the jail. "Six wings, 435-prisoner capacity. Optimal surveillance," he explained. "From the observation post, one guard can see into every wing, but the inmates cannot see anyone outside their cell."

As a child, Emily had found that idea disconcerting. The hivelike hold, with its tight cells packed side by side and one atop the other, connected by clanging metal railings and narrow winding stairs, reminded her of the old abolitionist postcards she had seen in school, the images of enslaved people packed into the berth of a ship. Her father thought the prison was the pinnacle of scientific efficiency. But she couldn't shake the image of human sardines.

The screams of women in fear and in pain used to terrify her, but over time she'd grown numb. Holloway could never be considered home—with its blood-red brick façade, fierce winged griffin gargoyles, and cold corridors that felt even more bitter in winter than the streets outside—and yet it was where she had lived for most of her life. She grew up playing make-believe games with her rag doll, Geraldine; sneaking silently through the corridors; and listening in on half-understood conversations of grown-ups. Hardly anyone took notice of the small child playing in the nooks and crannies of the jail; she was silent, docile, invisible.

"Hello, sweetheart."

Emily cranes her neck over the metal railing to locate her mother's voice, and there she is, a floor below.

"Come on down. I need your help."

Emily stows the mop and clatters down the stairs, sliding into her mother's sideways hug.

"What is it, Mama?"

A rumble of footsteps and the sound of Thomas's voice echo from down the hall. Emily raises an eyebrow.

"A new charge," Marianne says with a nod. "Let's go."

Down the hall and past the entryway, the gate to the prison like a sharp-toothed mouth, in the second-degree D wing where prisoners are held in solitary confinement, Marianne and Emily arrive as two guards drag in a young girl, barely older than Emily.

"Gentle," Marianne hisses as one of the guards wrangles the girl into the cell.

Emily turns away out of politeness while Marianne strips off the girl's street clothes and dresses her in the itchy brown prison uniform. The girl resists, clinging to her own clothing and throwing the standard-issue boots against the bars. Marianne clicks her tongue. Later, when the guards are back in the main hall, Marianne walks quietly into the hold. As ever, Emily follows two steps behind.

"Do you need anything?" Marianne whispers. The girl looks up, her eyes brimming with tears. "First night in jail?"

She nods.

"It'll be alright," Marianne says. "Here." She slips a thick slice of home-baked brown bread in through the grate. The girl hesitates and then takes it with a trembling hand.

"Thank you."

"My name is Marianne, and this is my daughter, Emily. We'll be right around the corner, dear. You're not alone."

Marianne knows just what to say to reassure a woman in panic. Emily tries to mirror her mother's kindness, her generosity, but she is often tongue-tied and worried she'll say the wrong thing. She tries to imagine herself in this young girl's shoes, the rattling, jangling cells of the jail unfamiliar and frightening, a long, dark night ahead of her.

"You'll be alright," Emily whispers as they leave.

Seated on the stiff cot in the corner of the cell, the girl nods.

"The damn suffragettes," as Thomas Brown calls them, have changed the composition of Holloway Prison in recent years. More women than ever enter her father's cells, younger ones, too, admitted for strange crimes Emily had never before heard of. It's never anything objectively violent, and always shrouded in strange jargon—inciting agitation, unlawful assembly, conduct likely to provoke a breach of the peace. Emily ponders over those words. *Likely to provoke*, as a phrase, seems rather too insubstantial to warrant a jail sentence.

Over dinner that evening, she broaches the subject.

"Papa, will you please supply me with a list of illegal deeds?"

"What's that, Em?"

"It's just that there are so many young prisoners these days. It seems as though a person could accidentally commit a crime without even realizing it."

"I don't have a list," Thomas says, breaking off a crusty corner of bread. "There isn't one."

"Then a law book," Emily says. She keeps her tone inquisitive, but she can't help smiling at her father's flustered expression. "How can I be sure that I'll never commit a crime?"

Marianne, to Emily's surprise, bursts out in bitter laughter. The laugh, as usual, devolves into a rumbling cough.

"What, Mama?"

"You can make no such promise," Marianne says. Her eyes flicker with something Emily does not recognize. "Crimes are constructed at the government's will. Who knows what they'll criminalize next?"

"But when people do bad things—"

"Of course, murder and thievery are wrong. But the rest of it . . ." Marianne waves her hand, as though conjuring the litany of absurd misdeeds she has encountered in the halls of the jail in recent years. "Crimes make criminals," she says. "Not the other way around."

"Marianne," Thomas warns, his voice taut.

"I don't sympathize with the suffragettes. You know I don't. What use is the right to vote when women are struggling to feed their families?"

"Don't you think there's more to it than that?" Emily asks.

"I just don't think locking teenage girls in jail does anyone any good," says Marianne. "They're all someone's daughter."

"That's enough, I think," Thomas says.

Marianne stands and begins to clear the table. There is a pregnant silence, and then Marianne lets out a small laugh. "Little Martin's become quite the looker, hasn't he?" she says, prodding Emily with her dishrag. Martin is a guard in training with sandy-blond hair, whose cheeks ruddy whenever Emily is near. Emily feels her ears grow hot.

"My Martin?" Thomas teases. "My training guard?"

"I daresay he fancies you, Em."

Emily buries her face in her palms, laughing. Her parents so deftly skirted an uncomfortable subject, and once more, their kitchen, though tiny, is full of laughter. She often wonders about crimes and criminals, and the girls her age who occupy the cold cells across the courtyard. But she doesn't dare ask again.

Later that night, Emily lies in bed with her sketch pad and falls into a rhythm with flicks of her wrist across the page. The underside of her right hand turns silvery with charcoal. Marianne knocks lightly on the door, then sits on the edge of Emily's bed.

"It's nearly your birthday," Marianne says. "I have a feeling this is going to be a very special year for you, love."

Emily bites her lip.

"Eighteen," Marianne continues. "I was your age when I married your father."

"I can't imagine being married. Not now."

"Nor should you. You've got your whole life ahead of you. And you're so very bright, my love. You won't work at Holloway forever, no matter what your father says."

Emily shudders at the thought of working at the jail for the rest of her life, though her father seems to think the best job available is the one she already has.

"I'm going to continue with school for as long as I can," she says.

"That's my girl," Marianne says, squeezing Emily's knee. "Promise me, darling, you won't follow some fellow down the aisle before you've got your teacher's certificate. Men, they come and go. But your own cleverness will open doors you've never even dreamed of."

Emily grins, indulging her mother in a hope that feels as impossible to pin down as the stars outside her window. She has known what tomorrow will look like for her entire life: school, chores, repeat. It's at once tantalizing and laughable to imagine a future beyond.

"I mean it, Emily. Promise me?"

"I promise." She strokes the soft skin of her mother's wrist. Though Marianne's hands are calloused and rough, her wrists are petal soft.

"And then, the future is yours for the taking."

"Alright, Mama."

Marianne gazes into Emily's eyes as though seeing her anew. "Goodness, you've grown up in the blink of an eye. It feels like yesterday that you were turning six years old. That was the year of the village fair. Do you remember?"

Emily conjures that year in her mind, the memories of childhood veiled with hazy nostalgia and half-remembered images. It had been their last year in Oldham, nearly twelve years ago. She had seen the signs fluttering around the village all week, believed that the fair had come to town for *her* sixth birthday. At last, the day arrived. There were games and musical instruments, cakes and contests. And best of all, the mysterious traveling exhibition: the Invisible Lady. Marianne had stayed home with a hacking cough. But Emily and Thomas approached the tent together.

The carnival barker's breath reeked of gin as the man and the little girl approached. He held open a curtain, and the pair stepped into the hush of the dark tent. Emily gripped her father's hand. There, in the middle of the tent, sat a large glass box. It was empty.

"Shall we walk 'round it then?" Thomas asked. Emily released his hand and stepped forward. They tapped the side. Through the glass, Emily's reflection flashed back at her, translucent. On one side of the box, an ear horn sat at the ready.

"This is the Invisible Lady," the barker droned. He was bored, hungover, perhaps even still a bit drunk. But children clung to his every word. Emily was no exception. "You cannot see her, but she can see you," he continued. "The Invisible Lady knows everything, all the secrets of the universe. You may ask her any question, and she will tell you the answer."

Thomas raised an eyebrow, impressed, and smiled at his daughter. Emily, age six, looked from her father to the glass box and back again. She was certain that the box was empty.

"Ask her a question," the barker instructed.

"Go on," Thomas said.

Emily leaned in and pressed her ear to the horn. It felt cool against her cheek. "Er . . . who are you?" Emily asked. A moment's pause, and then her eyes widened. "How do I know you're real?"

"What's she saying?" Thomas asked, grinning.

"She says—" Emily gasped. "She says I've got brown hair and a . . . a blue dress." Emily looked down at her dress as though to check that it was indeed blue. Of course, besides her brown muslin, Emily had no other dresses. And the blue one was getting old. Marianne had mended it just that morning and added new trim to the collar to spruce up the faded fabric. Thomas protested the trim, but Marianne insisted. "It's scrap," she whispered, thinking Emily couldn't hear, as Thomas bent to kiss her cheek.

"Ask another question," Thomas said. Emily flushed with excitement.

"How far away is India?"

The carnival barker flipped open a rusty pocket watch. "One more question," he drawled.

Emily furrowed her brow, considering her final question gravely. She had about a million at the tip of her tongue, concerns she had been too afraid to voice before, worries and wonderings that had long swirled in the recesses of her mind. *Are unicorns real? Why does Peggy Kemper have two pairs of silk stockings when I have none? What happens to Mama when her eyes turn soft and watery?*

The man cleared his throat and Thomas nudged his daughter. "Go on, now," he said.

Emily stepped closer, pressing a palm against the empty glass. "I would like to know," she said slowly. "How do you make yourself invisible?"

A voice, tinny but clear, rang in her ear, as near as a whisper. Emily shivered in the stifling tent. She replaced the ear horn as the carnival barker gestured toward the way out. As Emily floated in and out of sleep that night, tucked into her little cot, something at the fair burrowed itself in her mind. A few weeks later, when the Brown family left Oldham for the last time and made their way on the clanging train to London, Emily would replay that moment over and over in her memory. If Thomas and Marianne noticed that their daughter was quieter than usual, they didn't mention it. But the little girl had grasped the magic, the mystery, of the Invisible Lady. That strange and susurrus whisper rang in her ear for years after she uncurled her fingers from the smooth metal of the ear horn.

"I am invisible because you choose not to see me. You see nothing. And in turn, I know everything."

It was a promise.

Marianne coughs, her eyes misty.

"It's getting late," Emily says. And she has so much to think about before she falls asleep: the girl in the dark cell across the courtyard; the life she imagines for herself outside the prison walls; her future as a teacher with her own salary and a room in a boardinghouse where she can paper the walls with her sketches; and maybe, some very distant day, a home of her own.

"So it is. Good night, my good girl." Marianne kisses the top of Emily's head.

CHAPTER THREE
CHARLOTTE

Charlotte slips into her favorite navy wool skirt and buttons up her best blouse, the one with the imitation pearls at the neck. She rolls her shoulders back and makes her way to the classroom within the Girton College library. The courses she's sampled so far are standard fare, literature, Latin, and history classes in which the students are expected to sit in silence as the professor lectures for two hours and the chaperone dozes in the corner. Charlotte tries to absorb all the information, but finds herself restless. Today should be different: a visit from Matilda George Foster, the Girton alumna and women's rights advocate. She intends to discuss real ideas and things that matter—no offense to ancient history and dead languages.

About a dozen students sit around the room. The dim, rain-mottled afternoon light filters through stained glass windows, lending the space an underwater appearance. Charlotte spots a few fellow first-years, though some of the girls present must be upper-years, as she doesn't recognize them. There's a pretty blond paging through a book in the corner, and there at the center of the room is Mrs. Foster, her graying hair knotted at the nape of her neck.

Charlotte grins—her first woman lecturer!—as Mrs. Foster makes her way to the front of the room.

"Students, it is my sincere pleasure to speak to you today. It seems that not long ago, I was in your very seats, though, of course, you must look at me now and think I am about a hundred years old," she says, her voice gentle and grandmotherly. "When I left Girton, my mission was to help women win the vote. And tonight, I ask for *your* help."

Charlotte studies the aging woman before her. Everything she's ever heard about votes for women seems stodgy and old-fashioned—the bland petitions that circulated in Fulney every few years and ended up in the gutters, the tea parties where, she assumes, old ladies served overbaked biscuits and complained about their rheumatism. Mrs. Foster looks as prim, conservative, and, well, old as she imagined a suffragist to be. But she cannot say she isn't curious. A few students begin passing around sheets of paper and pens.

"Thank you, ladies," Mrs. Foster says, once everyone has the writing materials. "Today, we write letters to members of Parliament, asking for their support of our women's suffrage bill. If you know your local MP, please feel free to address him personally. Otherwise, I suggest directing your letter to Prime Minister Asquith. Any questions?"

"What should we write?" someone asks.

"Introduce yourself," Mrs. Foster says. "The art of letter writing should be maintained even in political correspondence. *'Dear Sir, my name is Mrs. Edward Foster,'*" she dictates. "*'I am a graduate of Girton College, in Cambridge, and I wish to convey to you my support for the issue of woman suffrage.'* Then, you may add your own opinion. Perhaps explain why women's innate ability to nurture would benefit the state. Or quell his concerns that voting would keep women from the housework—we all know that to be untrue!"

Charlotte stares down at her paper and begins to write. *Dear Sir.* In the past, if she ever briefly thought about women's suffrage, the subject seemed as boring as its presenters. Women like Mrs. Foster were accomplished, no doubt, but they were of another generation, of petticoats and candlelight, not the electric twentieth century. But yes, Charlotte thinks, women *should* get the vote. *We are intellectual equals, as demonstrated by the very fact that women at Girton College excel in identical coursework to the men studying at the University of Cambridge, though we are not permitted to prove ourselves in official examinations or earn proper degrees.*

When she's finally finished writing, her hand is numb. She flexes her fingers and brings the letter up to the front of the room, where Mrs. Foster is collecting them. Charlotte's letter looks much longer than most of the others.

"Thank you, my dear," says Mrs. Foster. "Are you interested in learning more about women's suffrage?"

"Yes, I am," Charlotte says. "I think we need more young women as suffragettes."

"We are law-abiding suffragists," Mrs. Foster corrects sharply. "Not wild *suffragettes.*"

"Sorry," Charlotte says. "I didn't know there was a difference. I just mean, it would be nice to see more women my age represented. We would get to be voters, too."

"Perhaps," Mrs. Foster says.

"Perhaps?"

"Our proposed bill would give the right to vote to unmarried women over the age of thirty. And widows, of course."

"But why?"

Another student comes up behind Charlotte to hand in her letter. "Our husbands will vote the same as us," she chimes in.

"But that's not necessarily true. And it's not fair or equal," Charlotte says.

"Parliament will sooner support gradual woman suffrage, and votes for some are better than none at all," Mrs. Foster explains. "A slow and steady approach will win the day."

"But if we're bothering to write letters, we should demand what we really want, not what we think the MPs want to hear," Charlotte protests.

"Patience is a virtue, young lady," says Mrs. Foster. "We work like a glacier: slow but unstoppable. Trust me, I've been doing this for over twenty years."

"Twenty years of writing letters? If that's the case, shouldn't we try something else?" Charlotte feels a clammy hand on her shoulder and turns around to see Mrs. Pennington.

"Perhaps, Miss Evans, you ought to take your leave. Further conversation with our guest can take place when you are less"— Mrs. Pennington pauses, her palms templed together as though in prayer—"agitated."

It takes Charlotte longer than usual to find her words. Giving up, she turns on her heel and weaves her way out of the room. So much for discussing ideas that matter. Her eyes prickle, though, as her breath comes up tight in her throat.

Why has it been so hard? Why is nothing and no one as she had hoped? She swipes at a tear, ducking her head. At the door, the pretty blond catches Charlotte's gaze. Her green eyes flicker with mirth as Charlotte runs out.

Charlotte crawls straight into bed with her clothes on. She shuts her eyes, buries her face in the pillow, and breathes deeply into the poky feathers. It is just like before, she can't help but think, just like back home, where no one understood her and she never fit in. She chose then to blame the place, but here everything was supposed to be different. She was finally meant to find friends, to meet young women who share her desire to make meaning of the world. But even something as clear as women's voting is muddled in propriety and etiquette, and she's made to feel like she's wrong when she points out that something isn't right. A question creeps into her mind and for once she cannot find the excuses to will it away: What if the problem is Charlotte herself?

Out in the hall, girls walk toward their rooms, chattering happily, pausing sometimes in front of Charlotte's door to lower their voices to a whisper. She knows what they're saying about her. *Charlotte Evans is cold and aloof. She is arrogant and supercilious. She thinks she's better than us.* Now would be the perfect opportunity to prop open her door and prove them wrong, to invite passing students in for tea or just to sit and chat. But Charlotte is spent. It has taken every ounce of effort, every day since she arrived, to try so painstakingly hard to fit in. She hasn't been warm enough, kind enough, genteel enough. But hasn't she tried?

What is wrong with her?

When she hears the first knock on her door, Charlotte thinks it must be a mistake. But the knocking persists, so she wipes her tears and twists her swollen face into a smile. There, in her doorway, is the pretty blond girl she'd seen in the library.

"I'm afraid the suffragist meeting was rather disappointing, wasn't it?" the girl says without preamble. "I'm Beatrice Piper. Do you fancy a cup of tea?"

CHAPTER FOUR
BEATRICE

B eatrice leads Charlotte up the stairs to the third-year suites, pretending not to notice Charlotte's sniffles or bloodshot eyes as they traipse down the corridors.

"Here we are," Beatrice says. "Home sweet home."

Charlotte's eyes widen as she takes in the space. Unlike the other Girton girls, with their frilly excess of velvet and lace, Beatrice took pains to make her room feel like her own sanctuary. The room is decorated almost like a country lodge, with miniature model horses positioned on the mantelpiece, and a painting of a hunt hanging in a simple gold frame above the fireplace.

"That's my horse, July," Beatrice says, pointing to the elegant chestnut mare in the foreground of the painting. "And this one's her foal, Brontë. I was there for the birth."

"Were you really?"

"I waited up all night," Beatrice explains. "Labor can happen so quickly, and I didn't want to miss it. When little Brontë was born, July was so protective. I've never seen anything like it." She sighs, turning from the painting. "Anyway, my mother absolutely detests my decoration." Instead of lace doilies on the table, she has left the wood bare. And on the shelf where the other girls keep delicate tea sets, Beatrice has stuffed the space with stacks of books, the thick spines of all her favorites on prominent display—Austen's collected works, the Brontë sisters, Shakespeare, Dickinson, and Emerson.

"I think it's lovely," Charlotte says. "Is that your family's home?" She studies the grand estate in the background of the painting.

"Champney House, yes. In Kent," Beatrice says, a little embarrassed by Charlotte's gaping expression. Not that she ought to be; most of the Girton girls came from families that are just as wealthy. *But I'm different*, Beatrice wants to say. *Trust me.*

"What do you study?" Beatrice asks instead.

"I haven't yet decided," says Charlotte. "I was thinking about politics or philosophy, because what I most wish to learn is how the world works. But Mrs. Pennington suggested poetry."

"Why learn something useful when your purpose in life is ornamental?" Beatrice says, her voice dripping with sarcasm. "You should have heard her when I announced my law degree. Her face turned purple."

"You read law? I didn't realize that was a possibility."

"I'm the first and only female legal scholar in all of Cambridge. Which makes it sound a lot more, oh, glamorous, I suppose. But in reality, I've got to be accompanied by a chaperone to every lecture, and I sit for my exams alone, separated from the young men."

"Why is that?"

"So I don't *distract* them," she whispers, rolling her eyes. "I don't mind. The only problem is that even after I graduate, I cannot actually *be* a lawyer, according to the law. At least, not yet."

"Not yet?"

"I remember my excitement about Mrs. Foster's guest lecture in my first year," Beatrice says, shifting from Charlotte's quizzical expression.

"Until I found out that all she's done is keep the stationery business alive for the past twenty years. It was more than a little disappointing."

"Yes," Charlotte says, "finally, someone understands! I came here wanting to learn about the world and make a difference, or at least meet people who had the same curiosity as me. But so far, I've just felt—"

"Lonely?" Beatrice finishes.

Charlotte nods.

"There are other young women like you—like us, who feel the same way and want to use our voices. But they can be difficult to find."

Downstairs the gong rings out, loud and low. It is nearly time for supper, and everyone will be gathering in the library to join Mrs. Pennington for evening prayers.

"I have an idea for you," Beatrice says, reaching for a folded piece of paper tucked between two books on her shelf. "Here." She presses the paper into Charlotte's hands. "Perhaps this will be of interest."

CHAPTER FIVE
CHARLOTTE

Charlotte has lost count of how many times she has reread the now-creased paper that Beatrice pressed into her hand. It is a leaflet for a women's suffrage meeting in the village. *Wild suffragettes*, she thinks, hearing Mrs. Foster's disdain in her head. Well, let's see.

With the leaflet burning her pocket, Charlotte uses both arms to push her heavy window open, just enough so she can slip through and land in the garden below. Mrs. Pennington would undoubtedly burst into hysterics if she were to discover her pupil's method of egress, but Charlotte knows that Mrs. Pennington enjoys a glass of sherry around seven o'clock each evening, leaving just enough time for her to escape unnoticed. She brushes herself off—landing in the prickly bushes was perhaps less graceful than she might have hoped, even from her ground-floor window—and dodges the glow of the porter's lodge. The night air is sharp, heady.

Girton College is located northwest of Cambridge proper, *so the young temptresses do not distract the gentlemen scholars,* Charlotte thinks. But she does not mind the walk. Huntingdon Road is quiet this time of night. When she arrives at the meeting hall, a simple stone building on the outskirts of the village, she finds the windows aglow and the front door propped open. Since arriving at college, Charlotte has grown accustomed to entering rooms of strangers. She straightens her spine and steps inside.

The hall is already quite full and lively, though no one of college age appears to be in attendance. Charlotte spies old ladies in long cloaks seated near the front and middle-aged mother types, some even with a child or two in tow, chatting animatedly with one another. The crowded space brings back a certain nostalgia for home. That same air of anticipation, the buzzing energy, unlatches something in Charlotte's memory. When she was very small, they used to attend church. They walked to the village chapel, full of familiar faces, every Sunday morning. The portly old pastor would give a sermon, and then they'd all return home for Sunday roast. Charlotte has not set foot in a church since her father's funeral.

She finds a seat in the back, hugging her shawl around her shoulders against the damp autumn chill. Someone passes Charlotte a handbill and she turns it over. The original leaflet from Beatrice simply said that all young women were welcome to attend. What exactly has she gotten herself into? She begins to read the handbill, but a clamor at the front of the room draws her eye.

"Good evening." A petite young woman climbs to the podium. Her hair is styled in the Gibson Girl fashion, a voluminous twist beneath a floral hat. "Good evening," she repeats as the audience settles. "Thank you all for being here tonight. My name is Isabel Hurston, and I am here as a representative of the Women's Social and Political Union."

Murmurs ripple through the crowd. Isabel appears to be a few years older than Charlotte. She is effortlessly glamorous. Already, Charlotte can tell, this is not Mrs. Foster's suffrage meeting.

"Why don't women have access to the ballot?" Isabel begins. Her voice lilts melodically, carrying through the room as though in song. It is strange, Charlotte thinks at first, though she cannot quite define why the sound of this woman's voice projected across a packed meeting hall is so jarring. "When we work, when we raise children, when we provide the spiritual and moral guidance for our families, why do we not have the same right to vote afforded to men? Men, I might add, who may well drink away the money they earn, beat their wives, and abandon their children?"

Isabel pauses and surveys the crowd. Someone cheers at the phrase "drink away the money," and Charlotte jolts. This no longer feels like church. And this woman, Isabel Hurston, with her stylish outfit and pretty voice, is nothing like the staid, potbellied pastor of Charlotte's childhood. As Isabel continues, Charlotte realizes what had niggled her at first. She has never heard a woman speak out like this. Not in a sermon, not in a speech, not in a lecture. It is dissonant to hear a woman's voice raised like this in a public space, outside the hushed halls of Girton College, commanding attention. It is intoxicating.

"We have embarked on a quest for equality among men and women. We do not ask for special privileges, merely for equal access to representation in our government. This fight has nothing to do with party or partisanship. It is about the moral obligation for our country to respect the women without whom it would fall apart. You all," she says, sweeping her hand over the crowd, "are here tonight because you *know* that our society, as it is, is not just. You *know* that a change needs to be made. But—" Isabel's cheeks glow.

Charlotte's breath catches. *But what?*

"But there is a difference, a distinct one, between thinking and doing. We must do more than complain amongst ourselves. We must be willing to act. Deeds, not words. And when we act—when we stand—we will change this country and the world."

The audience bursts into applause. Isabel smiles, poised on the tips of her toes and assessing the crowd. Charlotte's heartbeat thrums forcefully in her chest. She can tell that Isabel has more to say, and she stops clapping as soon as it seems appropriate, for she does not want to miss a single word.

"So," Isabel says, making eye contact with each woman in the back row. Charlotte feels steel-gray eyes lock with her own. "Are you going to play the woman, or are you going to play the coward? Are you going to stand aside and let others bear the brunt of the battle? Are you perhaps saying to yourself, 'I will be sympathetic; I will occasionally talk about it to my friends, perhaps I will give a little money, but I do not mean to do very much'?"

"No!" someone shouts.

Isabel narrows her sparkling eyes and continues.

"Are you saying to yourself, 'I do not mean to risk reputation or friendship or personal esteem by too prominently identifying myself with the cause of my sex'?"

"No!" comes another cry. "No!"

Isabel smiles.

"Are you made of sterner stuff than this?"

Over roars of *Yes! Yes, I am! Yes, we are!* she continues to speak, her voice loud and clear.

"Are you going to come forward and say, 'I will be a battle comrade in this great fight; I will share the difficulties and hardships; I will make the sacrifices that are required of me'?"

Charlotte finds herself standing, her hands on her burning cheeks. "Yes! Yes!"

"I will be a woman!" Isabel cries. "I will place myself in line with the great forces of womanhood that are stirring in the world today. And to all those who try to belittle us with the word *suffragette*, let it be known that we take on that name with pride. We are suffra*gettes*, willing to do whatever it takes to *get* the vote!"

The place rings from the rafters with whoops and cries and claps and stomps. "Votes for women! Votes for women!" The tips of Charlotte's fingers feel electrified from all the applause. Her pulse throbs as though she has just run a race against Sylvia in the garden, as though she is, once more, on the cellar floor with Jack. If she ever assumed that suffragists were dull old ladies, she knows now that she was thinking only of Mrs. Foster's type. These are not suffragists anyway—they're a new generation of women activists, the suffragettes.

Charlotte thinks of Beatrice's frustration at studying the law but not being able to practice it—at least, *not yet*. And suddenly, it seems a grave injustice that women have no say in the laws that govern them. Charlotte could kick herself for not realizing this earlier. But then again, people like Mrs. Foster used the word *suffragette* like a curse, uttered only as a pejorative. The phrase "votes for women" has never, in Charlotte's experience, been shouted in polite society. And yet voting is essential, isn't it? Voting translates to a voice, to equality in all facets of life. What if her mother had had a voice when Papa died? What if she had had another option? A widow with three daughters, Sarah had hastily married George just to keep her girls out of the workhouse. What if there had been an alternative, a world in which a woman could stand on her own two feet?

Charlotte is sweating. Her pulse pounds in her head. Perhaps she has felt this kind of intense inspiration once or twice in her life while reading a passage in a book—certainly never in public, never surrounded by others who feel it, too. One thought emerges clear in her mind, white hot and burning: *I must be a part of this.*

CHAPTER SIX
EMILY

Marianne Brown's long-dormant tuberculosis returns late that October. Feverish and weak, she takes to bed, unable to even swallow the broth Emily tries to feed her. Soon, Emily leaves school and spends all day pacing the cottage and acting as a nurse. And though their relationship with her has always been an unspoken secret, even the women prisoners dare to ask Martin, the young guard, what happened to Marianne.

He comes by the cottage to tell Emily. She is sitting on the stone stoop, wringing her hands, which have wrinkled like prunes after hours spent pressing damp cloths to her mother's forehead. The sky is robin's-egg blue, far too pretty for this late in the season. It is the kind of day when, in better times, Marianne would have insisted on a midday picnic in spite of the chill in the air. Now Marianne can hardly lift her head. They should have taken her to hospital when her symptoms began, but Marianne refused to leave her home. Now, Emily fears, it is too late. She rolls a pebble beneath her shoe, flattening the dusty earth under her foot. It feels better to look at the ground than at that tauntingly beautiful sky.

"Hello, Miss Brown," says Martin. He stands back from the house, from Emily, as though he does not want to get too close. There is fear of contagion, of course, but there's something else, too, something more pressurized. He shoves his fists into his pockets as he speaks. "The prisoners are asking after you."

"Oh?"

"And Mrs. Brown." He shifts his weight from right to left and back again. "How is she?"

"I don't know," Emily says. Thomas went into the city to fetch another doctor that morning. The prison doctor's prognosis had been grave, and Thomas wanted a second opinion. Such a statement from her dutiful father was tantamount to treason. But Emily did not object as he left. Marianne did not even seem to hear.

"I'm sorry," Martin says. "D'you mind if I sit?"

He crosses the invisible threshold that had divided them and sits beside her on the stoop, taking off his cap and running surprisingly slender fingers through his sandy hair. Their arms almost touch. His neck flushes as he catches Emily's eye. A few weeks earlier, Emily's stomach would have somersaulted to sit beside Martin, close enough that her skin tingles. Now she feels hollow.

"So," he begins. "I heard you've left school. Now that you're finished, are you going to keep working for your father?"

"I don't plan to," Emily says. Then she amends. "I don't know yet." She'll stay as long as her parents need her, though she longs to go back to school. It feels like every day she gets more and more behind, not only behind in her education, but behind on the chance to make a life of her own beyond Holloway's gates.

"Well, if you do decide to stay—"

"Martin!" The voice of another guard echoes from the main building into the courtyard.

"Damn, sorry," Martin says. "I mean, sorry, sorry—" His cheeks redden with the realization that he had cursed in front of Emily.

"It's fine." There is little she has not heard growing up inside a prison. When she was small, most of the women took care not to swear within earshot of Emily if they knew she was there. But Emily had a way of sneaking around so no one noticed her. And anyway, now that she is nearly grown—her eighteenth birthday is next week—the prisoners seem to enjoy tossing their most colorful curses around like confetti, regardless of, or perhaps especially in, her presence.

"Alright. I'll come see you again tomorrow, if you'd like," he says, standing and hurrying inside. She would like that. But Martin doesn't come the next day.

That night, the doctor stands helplessly in the doorway to the bedroom. Marianne's eyelids flutter and Emily grips her hand, tears rolling down her cheeks in silent sobs.

CHAPTER SEVEN
CHARLOTTE

Dear Charlotte,

 Your stepfather received a letter from Mrs. Pennington at Girton College. She reports that you have not been attending your classes over the past few weeks. We are gravely concerned. Mrs. Pennington writes that you are quite well, not ill or indisposed, though, apparently, you have been coming and going at all hours and flouting the college curfew. I assumed you were responsible and mature enough to attend university, but perhaps I was mistaken. An education is expensive and not to be squandered—you must take this seriously. Please, Charlotte, abide by Mrs. Pennington's rules. She is the model of proper womanhood to which I've always hoped you would aspire. This is your one and only warning. If we hear any more of your misbehavior, we shall be obliged to bring you home at once.

 Ever yours,

 Mother

The letter peeves Charlotte for several reasons when it arrives with the morning post at Girton Hall. First, it is not written in her mother's hand. Sarah obviously dictated to George, hence the condescending use of the royal "we." Charlotte detests the idea of her stepfather as the interlocutor of her communications with her mother. Shouldn't the correspondence between mother and daughter be private? Second, it isn't as though Charlotte *intends* to skive off classes or sneak home after midnight. It's simply that when the suffragettes give her assignments, she cannot say no.

Sarah, via George, writes that Charlotte needs to take this seriously. She wants to retort: I *am* serious. How can she expect to make use of her education if women haven't got the vote? Why should she bother studying mathematics or politics if she has no say in how the country spends its money or makes its laws? She came to Girton to find her place in the world, to make her mark. She is more serious about this than she has ever been about anything in her life.

But Charlotte cannot say any of that. Her mother would never understand. Why, her mother thinks that dour, old-fashioned Mrs. Pennington is the perfect model of womanhood. Anyway, neither Sarah nor George knows that Charlotte is working with the suffragettes at all. And despite her commitment to the cause—really, because of it—she does not want them to find out.

She crumples the letter and tosses it into the rubbish bin beneath her desk. Then she puts her hat on, the one she and her mother had purchased together specially for Girton. Tying the cream-colored ribbon beneath her chin, Charlotte tries to shake the image of her mother's face if she were to spy her daughter wearing this hat not to a college tea but to sell newspapers on a Cambridge street corner. She steels herself for a moment. But the day is clear and there's a job to do, and for the first time in her life, Charlotte is valued for her personality—not shushed or chastised or criticized for being too loud, for desiring too much, for taking up space. Charlotte, the women of the WSPU have told her over these last few weeks, is an asset. She is bold and quick and smart. It's the middle of the day, but more out of spite than necessity, she slips out her window once more.

Beatrice waves from the gate at the edge of the garden. "Come along, Charlotte!" she calls, tucking a bright blond curl up and away with a silver hat pin.

"My mother wrote to me," Charlotte says, linking arms with Beatrice. "She knows I've bunked off class."

"Oh, pity," Beatrice says blithely, and Charlotte laughs. They walk by the local Union headquarters to pick up stacks of *Votes for Women*, the suffragette newspaper.

"Good morning, Miss Piper, Miss Evans," says Polly Stevens, the local chairwoman. She hands over two hefty stacks of papers. "And good luck out there today."

The warm greetings, the friendly faces, all stand in such contrast to the deathly silent halls of Girton College, where girls don't deign to even greet Charlotte by name. She almost skips, giddy with the weight of the bundle of papers under her arm, as they approach the village center. It really is a lovely day, cold but clear. The autumn sun casts dancing flecks of light upon the ripples in the River Cam. Their boots click crisply on the pavement.

"Another beautiful day to get spat upon," Beatrice says with a grin, her green eyes sparkling as they step onto the raised curb at the corner of the main thoroughfare. "Shall we then?"

They rip the string from one of the bundles and each take a paper to wave overhead.

"Votes for Women!" Beatrice shouts.

"Votes for Women!" Charlotte echoes. "Pence for a paper!"

Although they send delegations almost every weekend, the suffragettes are still something of an oddity in the village. Until the WSPU came to town, women never stood on street corners selling anything—except the ones working in the market stalls, but these pretty college girls look nothing like the weatherworn farmers' wives. Whispers around town suggest, perhaps, that the suffragettes bear a more striking resemblance to the ladies of the night in Whitechapel. Charlotte has heard more than one mention of Jack the Ripper, uttered not quite under the breath of passersby.

Still, most villagers simply ignore Charlotte and Beatrice, which, frankly, is no easy feat on a busy Saturday. Every so often, though, a woman slips a coin into their hands and discreetly snatches a paper from the stack. Then she immediately rolls it up and slips it into her basket. Charlotte imagines her later in the day, unfurling the clandestine paper to devour in privacy, before burning the evidence.

"I heard Adeline and Isabel Hurston were arrested a few days ago," Beatrice says during a lull. "They were protesting outside a by-election campaign up north."

"Oh no, I didn't know that."

"They've both been jailed all around the country dozens of times now. I daresay Mrs. Hurston is as famous as Queen Mary."

"I've seen Adeline's photograph in the papers. She's so elegant. And when Isabel was here in Cambridge, she was . . . dazzling. I can't imagine women like that in a jail cell," Charlotte muses.

"That's the whole point, isn't it? Adeline and Isabel started the Union with just a handful of friends in their parlor back in '03. Ever since, they've been forcing the government to take women's demands seriously. A woman can be elegant *and* intelligent, a rebel *and* a reformer. And if it makes people uncomfortable to imagine proper ladies behind bars, well, let them be uncomfortable. We certainly are, without the franchise."

It's really quite amazing how Beatrice can turn anything into an argument and win each and every time. "You are going to be an excellent lawyer someday," Charlotte says.

Beatrice blushes, handing a paper to a young mother shuttling a red-faced toddler down the street. Charlotte offers a paper to an elderly woman who pretends not to see her and scurries along the pavement faster than a woman of her age ought to be able.

"Anyway, are you going to the ball?" Beatrice asks. The annual King's College ball is all anyone discusses in the dining hall these days.

"I haven't been invited," Charlotte admits. She has not spoken a word—truly, not a syllable—to a young man in weeks. Probably not a whole sentence since Jack, except, perhaps, for a perfunctory "pardon me" or "how do you do" in passing. At least her mother would be relieved to know that the limits of her eldest daughter's virtue have by no means been tested since her arrival at Cambridge. "Are you?"

"I have a family friend at King's," Beatrice explains. "Daniel Rosseter. He asked me to go with him."

"A friend? Or a *friend* friend?" Charlotte teases. To her surprise, Beatrice reddens to a deep scarlet.

"Not unless my mother has anything to do with it."

"Well, that'll be nice."

Beatrice smirks. "You don't sound very convincing. Isn't there someone from back home who can bring you, even just as friends?"

Now it's Charlotte's turn to roll her eyes. No matter how many times she tries to explain her modest middle-class upbringing, Beatrice doesn't seem to fully understand how a bright young lady like Charlotte doesn't have a posse of well-connected friends and neighbors at the ready.

"I don't know anyone here," Charlotte says simply, with a shrug to convey how little she cares. And in the grand scheme of things, she really doesn't. Charlotte would rather spend the night volunteering for the WSPU. Still—she wouldn't mind being asked to the ball.

"Well, I'll have much more fun if you're there. I'll see if any of Daniel's friends still need a partner."

"Thanks," says Charlotte. "Oh!" A boy who looks no older than twelve runs up and spits on Charlotte's shoe. "Excuse me!"

"That was very rude," Beatrice calls as he runs off.

The boy joins up with several friends who stand in a clump across the street, sniggering. Charlotte tosses her head with practiced nonchalance. It's nothing they haven't encountered before, and it's only boys. She tries to wipe her shoe against the curb.

"Watch it!" Beatrice cries. Charlotte looks up just as a small stone flies past her head. The boys are running away now, but she still feels her heart catch.

"Are you alright?"

"I'm fine," Charlotte says, straightening up.

"These boys are incorrigible," Beatrice says.

"And that one had unusually good aim."

"At least they didn't—" Beatrice stops abruptly.

"What?" Charlotte turns to see Mrs. Pennington striding in their direction. "Damn it," she whispers. The housemother's beady eyes and flat-lipped mouth appear even more troutlike than usual beneath the brim of her bonnet. Her neck bulges and bobbles against the black ribbon knotted too tight under her chin. In another situation, Charlotte might have laughed. Instead, she drops her arm to her side, no longer waving the paper overhead. Beatrice mirrors the movement, with a fraction of a second's delay.

"Miss Piper. Miss Evans." Mrs. Pennington's lips are so pursed it looks as though she swallowed them. "Come back to the hall with me at once."

"But—"

Beatrice stomps on Charlotte's foot as Charlotte begins to protest. With a sigh, she picks up the bundle of papers they have not sold.

"I think you'd best leave that there," Mrs. Pennington orders.

Charlotte relinquishes the bundle. Her stomach twists at the thought of that whole stack, all those vital fundraising papers, growing soggy in a puddle—or worse, pissed upon by those awful boys. She can only hope that Polly will return for them in time.

CHAPTER EIGHT
BEATRICE

A fire roars in Mrs. Pennington's office. She insists on maintaining a feverish temperature no matter the weather. She leads Beatrice and Charlotte inside and instructs them to sit on the stiff wooden chairs before her desk. Then she surveys her prey. Her stern bun stretches her skin unnaturally taut across her face, and her ears stick out against the slick bun like gills.

"Miss Evans. Absent in class, sneaking out . . . and now this," she intones, relishing each opportunity to slap her tongue across her teeth. "And as for you, Miss Piper, your mother warned me that you might cause trouble." Beatrice's stomach lurches.

"Do you care to explain yourselves? I presume you have a very good excuse for the inappropriate display I just witnessed on the street corner."

"Mrs. Pennington," Charlotte begins. "We were simply volunteering for a local branch of a women's club." Thankfully she doesn't dare say the words *political union*.

"And do you have anything to contribute, Miss Piper?"

Beatrice shifts in the chair. "I'm so sorry, Mrs. Pennington," she starts. Before she can utter another word, she bursts into tears. Charlotte

44

gives her a tight smile without Mrs. Pennington seeing, thinking, in all likelihood, that Beatrice's tears are faked. If only she were so clever. But Beatrice really cannot catch her breath. Her chest is tight as the hot tears continue to fall.

"There, there," Mrs. Pennington says. She passes a handkerchief across the desk and surveys her weeping pupil with barely masked pleasure.

"I needn't tell you both that the conduct you displayed today is unbecoming of a Girton girl. Should I become aware that either of you have chosen to engage in such improper behavior again, you shall both face immediate expulsion. As it is, I am placing you on probation, and your parents will be notified."

"But—"

Mrs. Pennington raises a knobby finger to her lips.

"Not another word, Miss Evans. You, especially, are on thin ice. You'll both go straight up to your rooms now. End of discussion."

Upstairs, Beatrice struggles to catch her breath, bracing herself against the closed door as she gulps for air. When her mother receives word from Mrs. Pennington that Beatrice is on probation, facing expulsion . . . The thought is a gut punch. She crumples onto the bed, still clutching Mrs. Pennington's sickly sweet perfumed handkerchief.

A few minutes later, there is a soft knock on her door. When she doesn't answer, Charlotte opens it anyway.

"It's alright, Bea," Charlotte whispers, placing a hand lightly on her back. Beatrice shudders. "Mrs. Pennington won't really expel us. As long as tuition arrives at the bursary on time," she adds with a little laugh.

Beatrice feels like an anchor is weighing her down from within. Charlotte, it seems, has not considered that order might surpass wealth as the most powerful currency.

"I can't get expelled," Beatrice whimpers. Her whole body is trembling, like a leaf in the wind. "My mother won't let me return home until I'm engaged to be married. That's why I've got to go to the ball at King's. And I can't be caught like this again."

"Oh, don't be silly," says Charlotte. "This won't change a thing." She strokes Beatrice's curls gently. "You'll go to the ball and we can still volunteer with the suffragettes. We'll just be more careful about Mrs. Pennington."

Beatrice exhales slowly, a quivering breath. She is humiliated and terrified all at once. How ridiculous Charlotte must think her for bursting into inconsolable tears over Mrs. Pennington's chastisement. If only she could explain why going home is not an option, not unless you considered a death sentence a viable alternative. "I can't get expelled," she repeats, beseeching, even desperate. Beatrice tugs her lace gloves from her fingers, twisting her gold bracelet around her wrist.

"I suppose you won't be coming to the meeting tonight, then?" Charlotte asks.

Sadly, but decisively, Beatrice shakes her head *no*.

CHAPTER NINE
EMILY

In the days after Marianne dies, Thomas comes home for a supper prepared by Emily, and they pick at their food in silence, their eyes instinctually glancing to, and then darting away from, Marianne's empty chair. Her eighteenth birthday passes, ignored by them both. It's for the best. Emily can't bear to acknowledge the day without her mother. It takes every ounce of her strength to simply wake up in the morning. How brutally unfair it is that the only person in the world who could soothe her in this wretched time is the one who is gone.

As the days turn to weeks, Thomas disappears for long stretches of the evenings, insisting that he must stay late at work. Sometimes he sleeps on his office floor, his hair rumpled when he staggers across the courtyard for a change of clothes the next morning. Emily knows it is too painful for him to sleep in the room where Marianne died, where her mother's shadowy presence remains etched upon every surface like flowers pressed in wax, and her scent still lingers in the stale air. Emily notices, too, the empty liquor bottles that Thomas trails with him. And the jar they used to keep on the cupboard shelf for spare coins now sits empty.

One day, Emily is certain she spots her mother at the end of a long corridor in Holloway. She pads after her like a child until she stops short and the new wardress turns around instead, the poor woman's face like a cruel mask. Emily doesn't bother to learn the name of the woman hired to replace her mother. She'll be gone soon enough. No one stays in this job long if they can help it.

Her eyes and ears play tricks on her, phantom footsteps and shadows that make her heartbeat speed up before she remembers the truth. The cottage is painfully silent. Every creak, every scrape, every swallow echoes loud in comparison to the never-spoken words between father and daughter, in the absence of Marianne's humming and laughter.

Emily has been too distracted by grief to keep track of the prisoners' names like her mother once did, but she wakes one morning and decides to amend that. Cell by cell, she introduces herself. And soon she feels so much less alone. Not only that, but the agony of her grief is quieted, at least momentarily.

"Do you need anything?" Emily asks, careful to whisper out of earshot of her father or the guards.

"Some tooth powder, if you please."

"Fresh cloths for my monthly, thank you, ma'am."

Her feet carry her down rickety metal steps and she returns with her arms full of supplies. She can almost hear her mother whispering, "Now, be a good girl and don't tell your father." Emily discovers that when she has a task to do, she can make it through the day without crying. The busier she is, the duller the ache in her chest feels. She bakes brown bread and slips slices to the prisoners. She brings her father tea.

"You're doing well," one of the prisoners whispers. Emily's face still cannot quite form a smile, but something inside her warms, just a little.

The woman's name is Jessie and she is a suffragette from Lancashire, not far from where Emily was born. Jessie's father died in a mine shaft when she was eight. The following year, she began working in the mill alongside her mother and four sisters. It was there that Jessie lost the pinky on her left hand. The accident, she explains, splattered blood all over the loom and sent shrieks among the women workers.

"It was gruesome," she recounts matter-of-factly. "Like the scene of a murder."

Emily stares at the stump on the end of the woman's left hand and wonders how she can be so blithe. When Jessie catches her looking, she tucks it behind her back.

"I know it isn't funny," she says. "But I can either laugh or cry, and I choose to laugh."

For the first time, Emily understands why her parents moved to London. For all her mother's nostalgia for country life, they were fortunate to get out. Marianne's tubercular lungs were already so damaged from her years inhaling the tainted mill air, the same mill, perhaps, where a few years later Jessie would spend her childhood. Marianne could not save herself, but she saved her daughter from the same fate. Jessie's story is like a mirror into what Emily's life might have been. That night, as she lies in bed, waiting for the sound of Thomas stumbling home from the pub, she wonders if maybe she, too, can choose to laugh.

CHAPTER TEN
CHARLOTTE

Charlotte has stopped using the front door altogether. It is dusk, early November. She climbs over the windowsill and traipses across the garden, shaking off the frustration of another one of Beatrice's limp excuses. It's maddening that Beatrice refuses to see the bigger picture, shirking the Union's activities to stay in Mrs. Pennington's good graces. But as soon as Charlotte arrives at the lecture hall, she no longer feels alone. The place is packed with women, some younger, others three times her age, hobbling and leaning on canes, everyone sporting some iteration of the violet, white, and green colors of the Union. Everyone has come out for this meeting; the Hurstons are in town.

Adeline addresses the crowd, flanked by her daughter, Isabel, and Cambridgeshire's ever-competent organizer, Polly. Their founder is as impressive as she appears in the papers, but even more magnetic in person, with her silver-gray hair swept into a hat, and a matching mauve velvet dress accented with a suffragette sash. Beside her, Isabel stands like a Selfridges fashion plate, doll lips and wide-set eyes, a youthful miniature of her mother.

"I am delighted to announce that next month, the Women's Social and Political Union will hold our annual Women's Parliament in London," Adeline says, her voice commanding. "As many of you know, this is an opportunity to unite our local branches from around the country and strategize our efforts for the coming year."

"For the first time," Isabel adds, "we shall host our Women's Parliament in the Royal Albert Hall."

Murmurs ripple throughout the room. Even Charlotte, though she has never been to London, has heard of the Royal Albert Hall, where operas and orchestras and world-class politicians take to the stage.

"We endeavor to sell six thousand tickets to fill every seat in the house," Adeline says. "It is a feat of which I have no doubt we are capable."

Charlotte cannot tear her eyes from Adeline Hurston. Unlike her own mother, who makes herself small in every social setting, Mrs. Hurston looms large, a presence. She speaks with certainty, stands her ground. Charlotte cannot imagine Mrs. Hurston hunched over her husband's dirty shoes or on her knees scrubbing a floor that will only get soiled again in an hour. Adeline Hurston, unlike Charlotte's mother, is a woman with *purpose*.

After the lecture, Charlotte takes a packet of ten tickets to sell, surreptitiously of course, at the college. Isabel waves to someone as Charlotte is leaving. It takes a moment to realize that Isabel is waving at her.

On her way home, Charlotte feels tipsy. She stumbles through the familiar streets, boots scuffing winding paths she has learned to navigate seamlessly in the dark. She replays the speeches in her mind, the voices raised in intelligent argument. She laughs, imagining Adeline Hurston in debate with meek Mrs. Foster. Even Mrs. Pennington would faint in the face of Adeline's inspiring oration.

In her pocket, she runs her fingers over the smooth edge of a metal button. She doesn't dare take it out this close to campus, but those three words call out to her even tucked away: VOTES FOR WOMEN, in bold black lettering. Charlotte is brewing a plan. She'll show the button and the tickets to Beatrice and convince her to join the next planning session for the Women's Parliament. It won't matter that Beatrice has missed a few weekends of selling the newspaper. And then the two of them could travel to London together for the event. Her first time in the city! It sounds like a dream.

She should have noticed the shadow across her bedroom window, but she did not. Not until she is positioned in a most unbecoming straddle, with each leg astride the windowsill and her skirts hiked up nearly to her hips, does she realize that Mrs. Pennington stands in the doorway, her narrowed eyes casting daggers upon Charlotte. She freezes, as though Medusa had turned her to stone—that is, if the goddess were an ugly, fishy woman who looks far too pleased about the evening's turn of events.

"This may well be the shortest probation ever recorded in Girton College's forty-year history," Mrs. Pennington mutters in a slow, self-satisfied tone. She must have rehearsed that line. "How efficient that you've gone from probation to expulsion so swiftly."

Charlotte's blood runs cold. She considers dropping to her knees and begging, though she cannot stomach feeding Mrs. Pennington the obsequiousness the housemother clearly craves. Charlotte's vision blurs at the sight of Mrs. Pennington's flat-lipped grin. The woman seems to relish watching her pupil squirm.

Head pounding, Charlotte weighs her options. She cannot be expelled, she just can't. How many years did she spend at her step-father's home, friendless and frustrated, desperate for an escape? When she discovered a university that admitted—miraculously—women students, her life finally had a purpose. She spent so many months buried in books to prepare for the entrance examination and catch up on the education she was certain she lacked from her ill-equipped local schoolroom with its overburdened teacher. And then, once she was sure she could earn her place, she had pleaded with her parents, convincing George and, at last, persuading her mother. God, what will her mother say?

Yet, Girton hasn't been all that she hoped. For a young woman used to loneliness, she has never felt quite so desolate as she has these last many weeks. She wondered what was wrong with her, why no matter where she went, she never seemed to fit in. *I fit in with the suffragettes.* But she cannot think like that. If she has to leave Girton, if she has to return home to her parents, then that part of her life is lost, too.

Charlotte does not want to lose her freedom. For all her eye rolls behind closed doors, she has a door of her own to close! And surely her life here is only just beginning to mean something. The what-ifs whir through her mind until a sudden clarity emerges. She mourns the loss of her freedom far more than the privileges of her studenthood. She doesn't want to fit in with the girls at Girton for whom the purpose of life is marriage and social climbing. The one thing keeping her here, the one thing for which she wakes every morning, isn't even at Girton.

And so, if she is no longer welcome here, it means there is nothing left to lose.

In truth, Charlotte hasn't paid attention to her coursework in weeks. Every waking hour is filled with work for the Union. And even at night, she dreams of one day giving her own speeches, of storming Cambridge, of showing up in front of all those self-important dons and wealthy young men and simpering girls, sporting a tricolor sash over her chest.

"You'll depart in the morning," Mrs. Pennington says, closing the door behind her. Charlotte slumps to the floor, but she does not protest.

The next day, Mrs. Pennington sends a telegram to Sarah and George, and Charlotte races into the village to send one of her own.

"I'm sorry," she writes, her mind abuzz with apprehension and a bit of excitement. "Please do not send for me. I'll let you know when I arrive in London." *London.* The word feels like an incantation on her tongue.

She knows they will be furious, especially her mother. But London—though she has never set foot in that city, never felt the soggy springtime or the breeze off the Thames—calls to her. As soon as she decided not to beg Mrs. Pennington to stay, London appeared in her mind's eye like a beacon; there is no alternative. The WSPU's headquarters at Clement's Inn is the only destination.

Charlotte still has the envelope of cash that George handed to her at the start of term. It's the last few pounds she will ever receive from him. But luckily, she has barely spent any of it, besides purchasing a few textbooks. Charlotte pulls her wool coat on top of her dress, and for the last time (and the first time in a while, if she is being honest with herself) she heads toward the front door of Girton Hall.

CHAPTER ELEVEN

BEATRICE

W ait." Beatrice hates the way her voice comes out like a croak. Her face is drawn and blotchy. Again, last night, she'd been crying. But nothing travels faster than gossip at Girton, and she had crept to the foyer early that morning, waiting to intercept Charlotte before it was too late to say goodbye. "I'm so sorry." Beatrice's eyes flash down the corridor, making sure no one else will hear her. "Where will you go?"

"London," says Charlotte. "I'm going to work with the WSPU on a full-time basis."

"This is all my fault," Beatrice whispers, gripping Charlotte's hand tightly.

"Your fault?"

"For introducing you to the Union in the first place. I never should have given you that pamphlet. I wish there was something I could do to make it up to you."

"Well, you know there is," says Charlotte, withdrawing her hand. "What?"

"Join me. Join *us*."

Beatrice takes a step back. "I can't do that."

"No?" Charlotte smolders. "Well, I should thank you, at least, for giving me that pamphlet. It's been worth a lot more than your friendship."

Heat rises to Beatrice's cheeks as Charlotte's gaze lingers over the strand of pearls she is twisting anxiously between her fingers. It's unbelievably easy to read her friend's face. In Charlotte's eyes, Beatrice is just another rich Girton girl; her interest in the women's cause was as fleeting as any debutante's fair-weather fancy. *It's more complicated than that*, Beatrice wants to cry. Instead, she lowers her gaze.

"I never fit in here," Charlotte says, "but it's clear you do."

"I'm sorry," Beatrice insists, and before Charlotte can respond, Beatrice hurries back down the hall, closing her bedroom door behind her. Through her window, she watches Charlotte step out into the sunlight and the startlingly blue sky, jumping down from the redbrick stairs as buoyant as a child. She digs the VOTES FOR WOMEN button out of her pocket and pins it proudly on her lapel.

Charlotte does not look back, but Beatrice watches until she disappears down the path.

CHAPTER TWELVE

EMILY

H ello, Emily," Martin says on a cloudy Tuesday. Martin is often hanging around, and Emily spots him now and then, grinning at her shyly or offering a feeble wave through an upper-floor window when he catches sight of her out in the courtyard. Sometime within the last month he stopped calling her Miss Brown.

"Hello, Martin," she replies, wiping her forehead. They stand near the courtyard entrance; he is heading inside and she is stepping out.

"I was wondering if you might want to take a walk into town with me this evening, perhaps stop for a cup of tea?"

"Oh." Emily's cheeks heat up. "I . . . I'll have to ask my father."

"I've already asked him," Martin says with a sheepish grin. "He said it was alright. My shift ends at six today."

For a moment Emily does not know what to say. Martin has already spoken to her father and Thomas agreed on her behalf. Is that charming? Is that normal? All she knows is her face is boiling.

"Well, then. I suppose I'll see you at six o'clock," she splutters.

Emily has never gone anywhere with a man before. And even though she's known Martin since childhood, he *is* a man now, isn't he? At half past five she slips into the cottage, takes off her apron, and stands in her bedroom, frozen. Emily has never cared much for her appearance. Her limp, light-brown hair never stays in place, and she's stopped trying to cure blemishes with useless boiled teabags. God knows Martin has seen her at her worst, sweaty from work or, more recently, choking back tears in what she mistook for an empty corridor.

But now she feels compelled to improve herself somehow. She pinches her cheeks and purses her lips in the looking glass. She feels wan and young and homely. As she smooths her flyaway tendrils into a braid, she nearly dabs on a splash of Marianne's rosewater, but then stops herself. It feels like a betrayal. She does not want to share that scent with anyone.

Martin meets her at the mouth of the front gate. He takes off his cap when she approaches, an uncharacteristic chivalry that makes Emily want to laugh. Unfortunately, it comes out as more of a snort. "Shall we?"

After a second's hesitation, Emily links her arm in his. As they walk down Parkhurst Road and toward the local tea shop, Martin talks on and on about his brother's farm, and Emily mostly nods. They pass the usual people on the street—workers, beggars, men in suits—but Emily feels an unusual surge of emotion. Is it pride? Perhaps these people think that Emily has a sweetheart. Or they might even think that Martin is her husband. She is mildly amused by the idea. This is her first walk arm in arm with a man. She finds herself almost as intrigued by the spectacle of it as by the man himself.

"Have you been drawing lately?" Martin asks after they sit down at a corner table and order a pot. It's pleasantly cozy, the air thick with an herbal aroma.

"I have actually," Emily says, pleased that he asked. "A bit." She places her hands on the table, folded, then changes her mind and rests them in her lap. In those first terrible weeks after Marianne died,

Emily couldn't look at a blank sheet of sketch paper without feeling her mother's absence staring back at her. But lately, she's begun to pick up her pencil again. The weight of it between her fingers feels grounding.

"I'm glad to hear that," Martin says. "You're very good."

Emily doubts that he has ever seen one of her sketches up close, but she appreciates the kindness of his words. At the pinkening of his face, she realizes that he, too, is nervous. Years spent in each other's orbit cannot erase the shyness that descends when they suddenly sit across a table from one another. Would it be too bold to suggest that perhaps, sometime, she could sketch him? Emily doesn't say it. But in the lingering silence, she imagines the arch of his brow on her page and the way his messy curls fall along his jaw.

"How is . . . how are you? At work, I mean?" Emily hates the question as soon as it forms on her tongue, but she doesn't know what else to say to fill the silence, and she needs to stop staring at the soft curve where his lips meet his chin.

"It's going well," Martin begins. "But it's not what I want to do forever."

"Oh?"

"I was never much of a schoolboy. I got out as soon as I could. But you know that. How old were we when I first started at Holloway? Fourteen?"

"I was twelve," she says.

"Right. Anyway, my work at Holloway is just the start. I talk with the police commissioner whenever he comes by, and he's said I could try for a job at Scotland Yard in a few years."

"Really?"

"That's right." He grins. "I won't be your father's assistant guard forever. No, sir. Just a few more years and then I'll join the force and rise through the ranks to support my family proper."

"Your family?"

"I mean, my future family." He rubs his forearm and looks down into his teacup. Emily realizes, rather belatedly, that the conversation has veered into a romantic direction. She hastily tries to shift them back on course.

"Yes, well, good on you. I don't want to work in the jail forever, either. My mother always hoped I'd be a teacher. But that would require college, or at least a training course. So I don't know—" She stops short, realizing she has said too much.

"Surely you don't need to worry about all that," Martin says. "Once you're married you won't need to work. My wife would never have to lift a finger if I was in the Met Police." They both sip silently, and Martin takes a large bite out of a scone. Emily tries not to read into Martin's slip of the word *wife*. She also tries not to notice the way her stomach flips as he licks the crumbs from the side of his mouth.

"I saw you chatting with that Jessie woman the other day," Martin says, his smile poised as though he is about to tell the punch line of joke. "She's a right mad one. They brought her in kicking and screaming."

"Jessie seems like a nice woman," Emily says tentatively.

Martin laughs, a short, sharp bark. "Apparently she flung herself in front of an MP at a by-election protest, shouting about votes for women, flapping about like a harpy."

"Is that so?"

"I thought you'd've known," he says, clearly pleased to have delivered the account. "Well, anyway, these suffragettes are all mad, aren't they?"

"Goodness," she says. "They can't all be."

"Not all mad? They're hysterical. Shrieking and throwing themselves about."

Emily forces a laugh. Martin isn't saying anything she hasn't heard her father say. Even her mother used to bemoan the women's insatiable demands. But coming from Martin, the words taste sour.

"I can't pretend I'm satisfied without the vote, myself," Emily says, mostly because she feels like being contrarian. Even so, the statement surprises her.

"What do you need the vote for? You've got a father, and you'll have a husband someday to take care of you."

"My opinion might differ from my father's," she argues, ignoring his bit about being a wife.

"Well, that'd only be because you don't know enough. Women don't know much about politics. Nor should they. It's a messy business."

Emily swallows such a large gulp of tea that she nearly chokes. It takes all she has not to remind Martin that unlike him, *she* is the one who actually finished school—well, all but her final term when Marianne got sick. Still, she could probably understand politics if she made up her mind to do it. She is the one who actually listens to what the prisoners say—women who came from nothing and taught themselves so much about politics that it makes her head spin. But she doesn't say any of that. She runs her tongue over her teeth. She isn't even sure why Martin's statement niggles her. His tone is kind, and he is gazing at her with nothing but affection.

It's not like Emily is a suffragette.

CHAPTER THIRTEEN
CHARLOTTE

London is the loudest place Charlotte has ever been. It isn't just the shouts, or the screeching of the omnibuses, or the clattering of horses' hooves on the cobblestones. It isn't just the throngs of bodies, or the blur of dialects, or the street musicians strumming strange instruments beside overturned top hats. It isn't any one of those things; it's all of them.

On the train ride, as she gazed out the window at the countryside disappearing behind her, she primed herself to face a hostile and imposing metropolis. She counted out her shillings and divided them between her various purses and pouches to avoid losing everything at once to a pickpocket. She even stuffed a spare hat pin down the front of her bodice—a small but sharp weapon should she need to defend herself. But now that she has arrived, now that she has inhaled the city's odd perfume of chimney soot and briny water and burning rubber, her trepidation is tinged with excitement.

There is so much to see, her eyes dart and dance left, right, down, and up. Mostly up. The buildings are taller here than in Cambridge, and it isn't just the church spires that unfurl toward the roiling gray sky. On Oxford Street, department stores tower three, four, even five stories high, with gleaming glass windows. She stops in front of a display of sumptuous silk dresses and buttery kid leather gloves, leaning so close that her breath fogs the glass.

She tears herself away, but not before catching sight, ever so briefly, of her own reflection. She must remind herself that the girl in the window is her—the girl whose dark curls are unraveling and whose hat is askew from hours of travel, the girl who hoists a valise full of everything she owns over one shoulder, the girl who looks worldly and glamorous despite the circles of exhaustion that rim her wide brown eyes, and who puts one dusty boot in front of the other as she makes her way through the looking glass of this strange city.

Overhead, rain begins to fall, cold, fat drops that make her bag feel much heavier over her shoulder. Its feeble strap cuts into her skin. Then her boots feel damp and tight, and Charlotte remembers she hasn't had anything to eat in hours. The knot in her stomach tightens. She must find the WSPU's headquarters before nightfall, and then hope—or pray or beg, whatever is necessary—that they will allow her to stay.

The map of London swiped from the pages of a Girton College library book depicts a rambling, intoxicating city, but now that she is here, each squiggly line of streets seems nonsensical. There are no straight lines, and half the streets don't have signs. When Charlotte finds herself on the same corner after trekking several blocks in what she thought was a different direction, she feels tears spring up in her eyes. She is impatient with her own limitations, and aware—from the prickles at the base of her neck—of eyes upon her. Eyes of strangers. Eyes of men. She folds the map and tucks it away, having offered her no help, and takes a turn at random, determined to get out of sight.

❧

She finally reaches 4 Clement's Inn at dusk. The small square of brick buildings is dark, except for the windows that glow from the top floor. There is a chance that they will turn her away. She has no idea how much it would cost to spend the night in a boardinghouse or even where to find one. Panic rises inside of her now that the sky is cloaked in inky shadow and the air grinds its teeth with a bitter chill. Taking a breath, Charlotte knocks on the lacquered front door.

A pretty, freckle-faced woman with a long auburn plait stands in the foyer.

"Who is it, Sadie?" a voice calls from inside.

"Who are you?" Sadie asks.

"I'm Charlotte Evans, a volunteer."

"Come on in, then."

Charlotte steps inside the warm and well-lit flat. The yeasty aroma of something baking nearly bowls her over as Charlotte registers her hunger. The entryway is sparsely decorated, but as Sadie leads her into the parlor, the atmosphere changes immediately. The room is like someone's great-grandmother's attic, stuffed with squashy chairs and littered with papers and books, sewing projects and half-used candles and old teacups.

Isabel Hurston sits on a rocking chair by the hearth, a bit of mending in her hands.

"Hello, Miss Hurston," Charlotte says. "I'm not sure if you remember me. I was at the meetings in Cambridge—"

"Of course!" Isabel stands and shakes Charlotte's hand heartily. "It's Isabel, please." She flashes a smile and her gray eyes sparkle like they do in her pictures in the newspaper. "Charlotte Evans, meet Sadie Lawrence, one of our best organizers."

"May I take your coat, Charlotte?" Sadie asks. Despite her freckles, Sadie has the arched cheekbones and elegant posture of a duchess. Her accent, though, sounds far from aristocratic.

"You're American?"

Sadie nods. "I'm an honorary Brit, by way of Boston."

"Come sit," Isabel instructs.

Charlotte shifts aside a stack of banners and sits down on the sofa. As Isabel puts down her mending, Charlotte realizes she's been sewing a tricolor suffrage sash—a silky twist of violet curls against streaks of pure white and leaf green.

"So, Charlotte, I seem to recall that you are a Girton girl?"

"I was," she begins. She does not want to say that it was the WSPU that brought about her expulsion, lest Isabel find her ungrateful or accusatory. But Isabel, somehow, already understands.

"I find there are better opportunities for young women to learn outside the university," she says, smiling. "London is, itself, an education."

Charlotte intends to speak, to offer gracious words and to request, as politely as even Mrs. Pennington would wish, for the possibility of a place to sleep tonight. But then someone in the kitchen opens the oven and the smell of warm bread renders her speechless. Charlotte's stomach grumbles audibly.

"You must stay the night," says Isabel. "And please, let me get you something to eat."

"Thank you," Charlotte whispers, her throat tight with emotion.

Isabel squeezes her hand and then hurries off to the kitchen. Later, Isabel finds Charlotte a place to sleep in a room upstairs. Three other women share the room and the two beds. They introduce themselves to Charlotte, but though she smiles, she cannot remember their names. Not tonight. Her limbs feel heavy, and each step puts pressure upon her blistered feet. As she climbs under the blankets beside a woman she's never met, the sound of three bodies breathing suddenly feels cacophonous. She squints her eyes shut, burying her face in the strange-smelling pillow. Charlotte swallows thickly, exhaustion and bewilderment forming a lump in her throat.

Someone blows out the single candle and the room goes dark.

The very next day, Isabel sets Charlotte to work. Speech-making, she learns, is an essential part of the job. The busy streets of the West End are nothing like the quiet alleys of Cambridge where she and Beatrice sold papers. Still, the suffragettes believe practice is the only way to improve, and so, by the end of her first day in London, it's Charlotte's turn to give it a go. It's sunny and the crowds are thick at Piccadilly Circus in the late afternoon when Isabel nudges Charlotte.

"You're up," she whispers.

Charlotte takes a deep breath and steps up onto the overturned soapbox, wielding the latest issue of *Votes for Women* overhead like a sword. Isabel purses her lips as she observes Charlotte, clearly assessing her as a volunteer.

"Good afternoon," she begins.

No one stops to listen. The day carries on, the bustling pavement in motion as always.

"Louder," Isabel instructs.

Charlotte closes her eyes briefly, remembering the rousing words she first heard Isabel speak in that little meeting hall in Cambridge. How jarring and electrifying it had felt to hear a woman project her voice so boldly.

"Good afternoon," Charlotte repeats. Her voice emits at a higher pitch than usual, sounding strange and a little shaky.

Isabel nods encouragement. Then something soars overhead. She sees the red stain before she feels the impact. A rotten tomato. The juices drip in teardrop streaks, sticky pink seeds on her borrowed white dress. Somewhere in the crowd someone gasps. Several more onlookers snicker. Her chest throbs, the impact of the flying fruit harder than she might have thought. Charlotte bites her lower lip, the sting of her teeth holding back the urge to burst into tears and run away. She can't cry, not here, not now. Isabel stands resolute and unflinching. Charlotte won't fail, not again, not like at Girton. She doesn't have that luxury. She takes another deep breath, exhaling slowly as she shakes the tomato chunks from her dress as best she can.

"Ladies and gentlemen," she says, her voice stronger than before. "To think the political outcomes in our country rest in the hands of people like that." She gestures toward the pink stain. "Why, we may as well let a chimpanzee run the country!"

A few people laugh. With her, not at her. Another few clap. Charlotte's shoulders unclench. Miraculously, she remembers the rest of the talking points: how women have been excluded from the vote on the same basis as children and the insane; how some men drink away their wages and leave their families with nothing; how, as wives and mothers, women are best suited to make decisions that impact the family; how, fundamentally, women and men should be treated equally in the eyes of the law. Charlotte prefers that last argument best.

As she continues to speak, the words flow more easily. A few women stop walking to listen. A man snatches a copy of *Votes for Women*, crumples it, and throws it at her face. Charlotte dodges it in the most dignified way possible, leading to more women's applause. As she descends from the crate minutes later—how long it's been, exactly, she isn't sure—her hands are trembling. Charlotte finds she cannot recall a word that she spoke. But the other volunteers cheer.

"You'll need some more practice, of course," Isabel says. "But you did a very fine job, indeed."

Charlotte flushes, her pulse dancing from the thrill of it all.

"That's high praise from Isabel," Sadie whispers in her ear.

Unlike most of the paid volunteers, many of whom bunk at Clement's Inn, Sadie resides on her own in what is rumored to be a grand house on Park Lane. Her father is a Boston newspaper publisher, and he apparently neither knows nor cares what his erstwhile daughter gets up to across the pond.

"Do you mind if I ask you something personal?" Charlotte asks as they walk back to headquarters.

"Of course," Sadie says.

"What brings you to London? I mean, why are you—"

"Willing to go to jail for the right to vote in a country that isn't even mine?" Sadie runs her finger over the little metal pin on her lapel, a prison badge. It looks like a small grate—prison bars—with tiny chains looping round. The many suffragettes who have earned these badges for their time in prison wear them proudly.

Charlotte nods.

"Well, I must admit it began with my older brother. Sam and I were thick as thieves when we were little, but as we grew up, Sam got everything I ever dreamed of: the best education, a place in the family business, the choice of whomever he wanted to marry. My younger sister and I got nothing except the message that we were meant to keep our mother company until we were married off to some steel tycoon. In case you hadn't guessed, I detest being told what to do.

"So when Sam decided to attend Oxford instead of Harvard, to our father's chagrin"—she feigns a dagger to the heart—"he and I devised a plan. I had to get away, you see. I couldn't . . . well, I had to find my freedom. Sam insisted he needed me to mind his flat here in London, though he hardly ever leaves Oxford. But that was enough of an excuse for our parents, since they'll do absolutely anything for dear old Sam. And it was enough for me. I get to do whatever I want here.

"I've always wanted to make a difference. Back home in Boston, I wasn't allowed to visit the tenements, but here I can visit the almshouses and try to help. That's how I first met Adeline. America may be the land of liberty, but I think England is rather more progressive than His Majesty might admit. If we can win votes for women here, it will set an example around the world. No one should feel less than because of their sex. Not here, not in America, not anywhere."

Charlotte studies the prison badge on Sadie's lapel. "Is it as terrible as it seems?" she asks. The assumption that suffragettes will go to jail for their beliefs is the one thing that has given Charlotte true pause.

"It is dismal," Sadie says simply. "Cold, damp, and so lonely you'll start to feel mad. Things are only getting worse, I'm afraid," she adds, "now that the warden's wife is dead."

"The warden's wife? Why was she any help?" Charlotte asks. "Her husband is the reason you suffered."

"It's not really his fault," Sadie says. "It's the law. And Mrs. Brown was kind. She'd slip us extra food. She treated us like . . . people."

Soon the beds at Clement's Inn are needed for new volunteers, and Sadie invites Charlotte to stay with her at Park Lane. Charlotte nearly bursts into tears at the realization that she's made a friend, a true friend, at last. The flat isn't terribly large, with only two bedrooms, but it is the grandest place Charlotte has ever lived. Plush Oriental carpets in rich jewel-tone hues cushion every floor, and all of the furniture is old and ornate. There are no servants or staff, since Sam is hardly ever in town, and a thin film of dust coats every surface because, as Sadie declares, a bit of dust never killed anyone.

"Are you sure?" Charlotte breathes as Sadie shows her to the guest bedroom. There are two narrow canopy beds with lace curtains and a wide window with a view of the square outside. Her room at Girton was marvelous because it was her own, but this luxury is beyond Charlotte's wildest imagination.

"Of course," she says. "I'm so glad you're here. I've been awfully lonely in the house by myself."

In response, Charlotte runs toward the nearest bed, and with a little yelp, she flops onto her back. Sadie falls onto the mattress beside her, laughing.

The work is hard, but Charlotte has never been happier. She is truly independent for the first time in her life, without even Mrs. Pennington peering around the doorframe. As a paid volunteer she makes a meager salary, but it's enough to keep her afloat. Her only complaint is the silence from her family. It hits her at night, when she is exhausted from the day's efforts but unable to fall asleep. Her body is fatigued, but her mind races. The soft hum of Sadie's snores down the hall are a comfort, but it still hurts to think that in all the time since leaving Girton, she has heard nothing from her mother or George or either of her sisters. She had sent them another telegram when she'd settled at Clement's Inn, but no one had replied.

Charlotte tells herself that she does not care; she does not need them. And in the daytime, she can convince herself it is true. But at night, she thinks of all she wishes she could say to explain herself to them, drafting letters in her mind that she knows she'll never send.

Now and then, a letter arrives from Beatrice. She prattles about the goings-on at Girton, the gossip and the parties. Charlotte realizes, happily, that she does not miss Girton at all. And she certainly does not miss Beatrice, or at least, that is what she tries to tell herself. Charlotte bundles the letters and places them in her drawer unanswered.

Adeline and Isabel give her frequent speech-making assignments. She traipses across Hyde Park, hikes along the Strand, and sets up her soapbox on street corners from the East End to Kensington, from Bond Street to Parliament Square.

"The government tells us that women's roles are critical to our collective society," Charlotte says one afternoon, projecting her voice along the busy lanes near Covent Garden. The crowds are thick today, and few faces pass by twice. There's one man, though, late forties and unshaven, wearing a rumpled suit, who's been circling. Charlotte keeps catching his eye. Something twists in her gut each time, but she quickly looks away and continues to speak. "That the home, the family, and civilization would collapse without our gentle touch. Why, then, if women are the caregivers of the family, if women raise their sons to be citizens, are we treated as children in the eyes of the law?"

"Go home!" a passing man heckles. "Back in the kitchen where you belong."

Charlotte ignores him. *Cue the chorus*, she thinks, and sure enough, other passersby, emboldened by the first man, join in against her.

"Ugly wench," one man yells.

Lazy, Charlotte thinks.

"Yer too pretty for politics," croons another, licking his lips.

The inconsistency of their criticism is almost amusing, but Charlotte focuses on her speech, ignoring the men and channeling her voice, as best she can, beyond the din. Then, suddenly, the man she's seen lurking all day is right beside her, grinning with bloodshot eyes. He looks younger up close.

"If you were my wife," he sneers, loud enough for the surrounding crowds to hear, and yet intimate—never breaking eye contact with Charlotte—"I'd never let you out of the house."

"If I was your wife," Charlotte replies, a smile plastered upon her face, "I would sooner die than share your bed."

The smirk melts off the man's face.

The other men crowded nearby begin to shove closer. The only woman in sight is a young wife, whose husband leads her by the arm to the other side of the road, away from the ruckus. Charlotte cannot catch her eye. The men elbow themselves right up against her soapbox. She can smell the faint reek of gin on their breath. And then, pushing through the crowd, two bobbies appear in uniform.

"Is there a problem here?" an officer asks.

The crowd disperses enough to make space for the police, and Charlotte steps down from her soapbox and onto the street. Immediately, the officers grab her arms, one on each side.

"What are you doing?" Charlotte demands, their fingernails digging into her biceps. "Let go of me."

"You're under arrest."

"What for?"

They're already pulling her toward the lorry.

"What for?" she repeats, trying not to allow the quiver of fear to enter her voice.

"Obstruction of traffic," the first officer says lazily.

Charlotte glances back over her shoulder; the unshaven man winks.

Jostling in the back of the lorry after a short sentencing at the Old Bailey, Charlotte tries to remember everything the suffragettes have told her about jail. Adeline, Isabel, and Sadie have all been there before. She knows what the uniforms look like, and she imagines the cells. If she knows what to expect, perhaps it won't be as frightening. When the red bricks of Holloway appear on the horizon, she steels herself. *I am not afraid*, she repeats, over and over. *I am not afraid. I am not—*

An unsmiling wardress with rough hands strips Charlotte naked in a cell so chilled her whole body bursts into goose bumps. Charlotte wraps her arms around her breasts, humiliated and freezing, until she is forced into the brown and mustard-yellow uniform. As the itchy starch scratches against her neck, she realizes that nothing at all could have prepared her for this. The door to the single cell, so narrow she can only take four steps in one direction, two in the other, clangs shut. A shoe-sized window at the height of her forehead provides the sole slat of light after the guards extinguish the feeble electric bulbs.

There are people everywhere, even though she cannot see them: women in their cells muttering to themselves or forcing out hacking coughs, and guards pacing across the rickety grates and through the narrow halls. Voices carry with the hiss of the water pipes, warped and warbled like a trick mirror. She has never been so surrounded and yet so alone.

It's a short sentence for a first offense, only two weeks, but that first night, Charlotte is gripped by fear. She doesn't sleep at all, kept awake by the sound of strange drips and the scuttling of rats. She tries to dream herself back to Park Lane, and when that memory isn't strong enough, she allows herself to revisit her childhood home. The faded quilt that always smelled of sweet grass. The creak of her father's rocking chair when he read her stories. How safe she felt curled up on his lap, her head nestled in his tobacco-scented shirt. Back then, she knew that if she cried out in the night, her father would come to comfort her. He would whisper songs in her ear and stroke her hair until she forgot she had ever had a bad dream.

But this is not a dream.

And her father is dead.

Charlotte indulges in one silent sob. Then, pulling the itchy blanket over her head, she resolves, she will be strong, impassive, and impenetrable until she is out.

CHAPTER FOURTEEN
BEATRICE

Girton seems duller in Charlotte's absence. Colorless. Autumn fades on campus, and every day, Beatrice notices the colorful leaves slowly seeping away, browned and deadened. Even the archaic language of legal philosophy fails to enchant her as it usually does. Dried leaves streak sideways past her bedroom window as the wind kicks up and she watches, wishing they were snowflakes—something cold and crisp to justify the iciness she feels clawing at her heart.

It's for the best, Beatrice reminds herself. It has to be. Daniel invites her for a cup of tea in town; she lets him pull out her chair and titters at his tales from the latest regatta. But in the dregs of her cup she sees her own betrayal. On the walk back to campus, they cross the Bridge of Sighs and Daniel kisses her on the cheek, hidden from sight behind an ancient stone pillar. She shivers at his touch.

Beatrice has not attended a WSPU meeting since Mrs. Pennington caught them on the street corner. It breaks her heart not to be a part of the fight for votes. For as long as she can remember, Beatrice had always been three steps ahead in every argument, demanding *how*, and *why not*, and *prove it*. When she discovered a world of women out there fighting to live their fullest lives, to be their truest selves, she couldn't *not* be a part of it. Votes for women meant giving voice to her own ambition. It meant not having to hide her innermost passions and desires and aspirations. But she had grown foolish, careless. She had been swept up in idealism and had forgotten the danger.

There was a reason why home had never been a welcome place; there was a reason why her mother, Helen, insisted through gritted teeth that Beatrice go to Girton to find a husband or else she would never see a shilling of her inheritance—or worse. The incident. Which, of course, is why Mrs. Pennington had kept such a close eye on her. Helen had warned Mrs. Pennington to restrain Beatrice, to prevent any unnatural behavior.

Beatrice had been so certain that distancing herself from the movement was the right thing to do, even though she hated to hurt Charlotte. Their friendship felt like everything Beatrice had been craving. And Charlotte was so smart, so funny, so bright and brave. Charlotte came perilously close to becoming someone Beatrice could trust. It is Beatrice's fault, therefore, that Charlotte got caught. Charlotte had come under scrutiny, guilty by association. The shame hits her anew each time the thought crosses her mind, sending a wave of nausea through her body. Beatrice blinks back the black splotches that appear in her vision.

If only she could have explained herself to Charlotte. But what could she have said? *I'm not the perfect aristocratic daughter you think I am. I am an outsider, like you, in more ways than you know.* Now that Charlotte has been expelled, they are more connected than ever, two young women sent away for being themselves. She'll make it up to Charlotte somehow. She must. If anyone knows what it feels like to be alienated, to be cast out, it is Beatrice.

Until then, however, Beatrice remains in her role. Her mother comes for a visit, wielding a box full of gowns for Beatrice to consider for the King's College ball.

"This color will bring out your eyes," Helen says, holding up a green satin dress. "Though the cream one may go better with your fair skin."

"Whatever you think, Mother," Beatrice says distractedly.

"Yes," Helen continues, "perhaps the cream. It makes one think of a bride. Don't give me that look, Beatrice."

"I doubt Daniel will be paying attention to the implication of the color of my frock. He's as oblivious as every other gentleman."

"Lord Rosseter—" Helen corrects.

"—is no more a fashion savant than my father," Beatrice quips.

"Will you never cease to cause me trouble?"

Beatrice bites her lip to keep from arguing.

"The cream gown it is." Helen lowers her voice to a near whisper. "*You*, Beatrice, know very well that you must secure a proposal from Lord Rosseter. As soon as possible. And if that means wearing bridal white, so be it. There is no room for failure."

How she wishes she could channel Charlotte now and simply say no, to her mother's utter shock. But in spite of everything, Beatrice has always tried her best to be a good daughter.

At the King's College ball, she admires the twirling couples, the women so dazzling in their dresses, the men so dull. Daniel and his friends are loud and rowdy, a pack of boyish hounds with too much energy. Beatrice downs every coupe of champagne within reach until she finds herself covertly and pleasantly drunk.

"You are simply gorgeous," Daniel whispers as they dance, his hand firm on her waist. Suddenly, the room feels like it is spinning.

"I think I need some fresh air," she insists.

He leads her outside, and she tries to clear the dizziness from her head, though it isn't easy with Daniel hovering over her, touching her shoulders, her back.

Later, he walks her home, stopping in the dark shadows beyond the lamplight that heralds the Girton College gate.

"Miss Piper," Daniel says. "I know I should talk to your parents first"—he clasps his hands around hers—"but I wanted to tell you myself that I should very much like to make you my wife. You are the most beautiful woman I have ever known. And I know our families would be very, very happy."

"Lord Rosseter, I don't know what to say." Beatrice's head feels fuzzy, and she knows she should smile, and demur, and somehow communicate both her ersatz elation with this proposition and her need to wait for her parents' permission. But the champagne is bubbling in her stomach, and the music from the ball is still ringing in her ears, and she's picturing Charlotte marching through these very front gates.

Daniel's face is suddenly inches from hers, his lips a breath from her own, and then Beatrice leans forward and vomits.

CHAPTER FIFTEEN

EMILY

W hat are you drawing?"

Emily jolts. She is seated on the cold stone floor, her charcoal and sketch paper propped against her knees. The prison is quiet this afternoon—in fact, Emily has not spoken to anyone all day.

"May I see?"

The new inmate peers through the bars of her cell. Emily locates the voice and then looks down the corridor, checking to make sure that no one else is around. The hall is empty. She stands, smooths her skirt, and walks to the cell.

"You're not supposed to shout," Emily says matter-of-factly. Her eyes are level with the prisoner's, and the bars that separate their two faces do little to mask the fact that the young woman is clearly around the same age as Emily. The prisoner's face is pale and cast partly in shadow, but her eyes glitter in the semidark.

"I wasn't shouting," she replies. "And I was only curious. You don't have to show me if you'd rather not."

"What's your name?" Emily asks.

"I'm Charlotte Evans." Charlotte pokes three fingers through the bars; not enough for a handshake, but the gesture is close enough. Emily can't help but smile and she takes the girl's fingers into her own. "So, are you an artist?"

"Oh no," Emily protests, feeling heat rise in her cheeks. "Not at all. I just . . . I didn't think anyone could even see me. I should have been doing my chores—"

"Well," says Charlotte, "I promise not to tell, if you let me see what you were working on."

Emily hesitates, less out of refusal than amusement. Then she shrugs and holds up the paper. "If you insist."

Charlotte leans so close that her nose flattens against the metal bars. Emily can see that she has been crying; the skin around her eyes is puffy and pink. Charlotte seems unfazed, though, and Emily knows better than to mention it. "That's really good!"

"It's nothing." Emily's whole face goes red. God, she hasn't shown anyone her drawings since her mother was alive. And this, well, it's hardly even a drawing. Just a sketch, an outline really, a figure in silhouette.

"It's brilliant," Charlotte insists. "You're Emily Brown, aren't you?" She nods.

"I've heard all about you. I'm sorry about your mother."

A thickness creeps into Emily's throat, though she is more surprised than sad to hear this strange girl mention her mother.

"Thanks," Emily says quietly. "Listen, I'd better go. But if you ever need anything . . ." She trails off.

Charlotte's wide-set brown eyes are searching her face. "Yes?"

"I was just going to say, if you ever need anything, you can let me know."

"I do need something," Charlotte says. Her expression is inscrutable. "I need you to come visit me again tomorrow."

Emily narrows her brows, but there is something in Charlotte's face that makes her agree. She walks down the corridor and folds her sketch paper into neat squares so it fits in her skirt pocket. Then the day is as it was. She sweeps. She mops. She flexes her aching knuckles until they crack. From the outside, everything looks the same. Like a pebble tossed in a pond, the ripples soon disappear and the surface returns to its smooth, mirrored façade. But something is different. That pebble is there forever, fixed and irretrievable.

The next day, as promised, Emily returns, this time bearing covert supplies: two slices of brown bread and a pat of butter, hidden between the layers of a scratchy, standard-issue blanket.

"Oh, thank you," Charlotte says, grinning at Emily as though regarding an old friend and not someone she'd met for mere minutes the day before. As though Emily had not spent the whole previous night turning over their exchange in her mind. And so it goes over the two weeks of Charlotte's sentence. She discovers that Charlotte is not only playful but whip smart. She hears snippets of stories about escapades with cyclists in Lincolnshire and tales of mischief at Girton College that send pangs of jealousy through her stomach. And there is something about Charlotte that makes Emily want to not just listen to her, but trust her, too. Charlotte's uncanny perceptiveness makes it easy to confide in her.

"You like him, don't you?" Charlotte says, one day, after Emily bumps into Martin in the corridor just outside the cell.

Emily instantly begins to sweat, shushing Charlotte until Martin is well out of earshot. To her own surprise, she tells Charlotte about Martin's invitation to tea, and his assertion that all suffragettes are hysterical.

"To be honest," Charlotte says, her arms crossed against her chest in an attitude that communicates her self-assurance and also keeps her warm in the drafty cell, "I'm fairly certain that my own mother agrees with Martin's assessment."

"So does mine," Emily says. "I mean, she did."

"I wouldn't have thought so." Charlotte drops to the floor so that she is seated with her legs crossed. After scanning the hall carefully, Emily joins her on the cold ground, knee to knee but for the bars between them.

"What do you know about my mother?" Emily asks. The question has been on her tongue for days now.

"I suppose not much," Charlotte admits. "But in my circle, Marianne Brown was known as a sympathetic presence here in Holloway. Someone dependable, at least, for fair rations and a kind word."

Emily's chest tightens. It hurts to talk about her. But considering the fact that her father hasn't even uttered Marianne's name since the funeral, it is a good kind of hurt. A healing pain, like the peeling of a scab—the skin beneath, as it turns out, is raw but clear.

"And when you say *my circle* . . . " Emily probes.

"The Women's Social and Political Union," Charlotte says, cocking her chin. "I'm here on their invitation."

"I see." Emily had guessed it was the WSPU. Almost all of their youngest prisoners are members these days.

"Want to join?" Charlotte asks, resting her chin in her hands.

Emily laughs. "I never said I disagree with Martin on that one."

"Ah well, I had to try," Charlotte says. "And, if I may, I think you do."

Emily pops by Charlotte's cell as much as she reasonably can without raising suspicion, a combination of loneliness and curiosity drawing her in. Emily has never met anyone so open, so self-possessed, and, most surprisingly, so interested in learning about *her*. Charlotte always perks up whenever Emily appears, clearing a hacking cough from her throat that seems to worsen with each day in jail, but always eager to chat nonetheless. Charlotte presumably longs for a distraction from her days spent staring at the wall in front of her. But she never blathers on, never speaks about the weather or the food; the mundane is of no interest.

"Tell me something I don't know about you," Charlotte insists. "Tell me your secret desire."

Emily would laugh, brush it off as silly that this woman she hardly knows is asking—or rather, demanding—to know her innermost wishes. Who *is* Charlotte Evans and why does she have the poise of someone twice her age? But in Charlotte's kind face and wide eyes, Emily sees the first person who has ever asked her anything about what is in her heart. And when she recovers from the shocking impudence of it all, Emily can't help but feel grateful.

"I have no secret desires," she says, almost wishing that she did. "I want to be happy. And make my father proud. What about you?"

"I want to win votes for women, of course."

"That's not a secret."

"No." Charlotte smirks. "But nor was yours. Really, isn't there something you want more than anything else in the world?"

She thinks about the last time she felt truly happy. It had to have been when her mother was alive. But no amount of wishing can bring Marianne back from the dead. Her wish, really, is not to be here, to build a life for herself far from Holloway.

"What do you love?" Charlotte prompts.

"To draw." It is instinctive. But it feels true when she says it. The only time she is able to escape her own mind, her own life, the only time she is in control of her world, is with a pencil in hand.

"Then you must devote yourself to it," Charlotte says. And when Charlotte says it, that which had felt amorphous and impossible is suddenly simple. Of course she must. It makes Emily's head pound. Someone is approaching, keys clanging, and she hurries to stand.

"I'd better get on," Emily says, already halfway down the hall as a guard begins unlocking the nearby cells. Once per day, the prisoners are permitted to walk in the yard, trailing one by one in a wide circle like a tired band of circus animals. It is then that Emily most pities Charlotte.

She feels almost like a long-lost sister when they chat through the bars of the cell. But when the guards lead Charlotte out to walk handcuffed around the well-trodden circle of dirt, Emily is reminded that they aren't the same. Still, even under the guards' apathetic gaze, a kind of radiance emanates from Charlotte, an undimmable light.

"Em," Thomas says when she walks in that evening. The kettle sits humming on the stove, and the kitchen is bathed in the glow of candlelight, a welcome change compared to the near-total darkness to which she is accustomed.

"You're home early," she observes aloud.

"Don't sound so surprised," he says, pulling out a chair. "Come sit."

She takes off her scarf and sits down, trying to conceal her puzzlement. She can count on one hand the number of times her father has filled up the kettle, and now he is inexplicably offering her a teacup and settling down beside her. His eyes are clear; he hasn't been drinking tonight, for a change. A heavy silence hangs between them, and Emily suddenly becomes transfixed by a small chip on the rim of her cup, one of the last relics of the cheap china set her parents inherited upon their marriage. At last Thomas speaks.

"Your mother and I—" He clears his throat. "We had discussed you pursuing your education." The low tone of his voice sounds so pitiful Emily wants to hug him then and there. But instead she keeps her eyes on her teacup and listens. "Your mother wanted you to become a teacher."

Emily nods.

"You were always good in school," Thomas says, reminding them both of happier days. This she remembers distinctly—her parents' pride when she brought home an essay with top marks. "It was meant to be a surprise," he continues. "Your mother and I were saving for quite a while and we nearly had enough for your first term."

Emily does not dare look up now. Her fingers trace the rim of the cup, waiting for the *but*.

"With the doctors and the funeral . . ." His voice hitches. "Well, I'm afraid our savings aren't what they were. And I can't say I always agreed with your mother that more schooling would be worth the cost. But I've worked it out, and if you take on extra hours here and save your wages, we can look into the teachers college for next year. Unless you'd rather save the money for something more practical. A wedding, perhaps. A future home."

Shocked, she finally looks into her father's face. He grins, the skin around his eyes crinkling into little starbursts like the rays Emily used to draw around the sun when she was a child. "Every generation has it a little better than the one before. My father came over from Ireland with nothing, and he faced a lot of prejudice. Here I am, with a government job. And you've got a bright future ahead of you." He looks proud. And for the first time in ages, almost happy.

"Thank you, Papa," she says. "I'll work and save up for . . . something. I'm . . . I'm so grateful."

She holds her breath as the final sentence she wants to utter disappears into the air—that she wishes her mother were here. That promise returns to her now. *Don't follow some fellow down the aisle before you've got your teacher's certificate.* Emily squeezes her father's hand, and he pulls her into his shoulder. She inhales the familiar mustiness of coffee and tobacco in his shirt.

The first person she wants to tell is Charlotte. But when Emily shows up the next morning, Charlotte is already gone.

CHAPTER SIXTEEN

BEATRICE

Beatrice's father named the horse himself when he presented the chestnut mare to his daughter on her tenth birthday. "July," he declared, slapping the horse's rear haunch with a wide hand. "She's bright as the sun and quick as lightning, just like you."

She was a beautiful horse, with doleful chocolate eyes and a star-shaped blaze on her forehead. Beatrice fell in love with her at first sight. As soon as the governess closed the afternoon lesson book, she'd race outside and into the garden, running beyond the pastures, leaping over the stream, and arriving breathless at the stable. If her mother caught her, Beatrice was made to don her riding habit. But when she escaped the house unnoticed, she merely hiked up her skirts and climbed astride July bareback, launching out into the meadow with a quick kick and a click of her tongue.

Beatrice loved her horse, and she loved the barn. She spoke to July in half sentences, half songs, stroking that long, coarse mane as July's large ears twitched pleasurably. Beatrice would have slept out in the barn every night if she was allowed, curled up in a sweet-smelling bale of hay beside July, her sentinel. But it wasn't proper. It wasn't right.

As a child, many things about Beatrice were not right. She had too many questions. A distinct memory, at the age of four, saw Beatrice and Nan at bath time—it took years for Beatrice to realize that not all nannies were also named Nan, but that was another story.

"Are Mama and Papa friends?" Beatrice had asked, popping an iridescent bubble on the water's surface.

"Of course," Nan said.

Even at age four, Beatrice had a hard time believing this to be true. She saw how rarely her parents spoke to each other, let alone spent time together. Papa mostly stayed in his study or went away for long hunting trips. Mama spent her days in the morning room or upstairs with a headache.

"You must be sure to marry your best friend," Nan added, gently massaging soap into Beatrice's white-blond curls. "Then you will be happy." Nan must have been in her thirties, then, dreaming of some lost love from years ago.

"My best friend is Grace," Beatrice said, thinking of the little girl who lived on the neighboring estate. Nan laughed and helped Beatrice out of the tub.

The next day, Beatrice told her mother that she wanted to get married.

"How wonderful, darling," said Helen, peering at her daughter over her needlepoint. Helen never spoke to Beatrice like a child. They shared the same angular nose and pink lips, though Helen's blond hair was dark like caramel, while her daughter's was as light as straw.

"I must ask Grace straight away."

"Why is that?"

"I am going to marry Grace."

Without glancing up from her work, Helen said, "Nonsense, dear. You'll marry a gentleman from Kent."

Beatrice wanted to explain that she was supposed to marry her best friend. And she didn't know anyone in Kent. But her mother had begun to rub her temples, a sure sign of the onset of a migraine. Beatrice slipped out of the room.

Over the years, Nan and Helen forgot all about the bathtime conversation. Beatrice grew up to be graceful and pretty and obedient. Her father's pet, she developed a taste for whiskey and a sharp sense of humor. She was a respectable flirt and just spoiled enough. Though her parents had been unable to have another child, they got over the disappointment as soon as Charles worked out how to change the entail so that his daughter could inherit the estate upon her marriage. They were satisfied without a son, so long as they had an heir.

Her mother's only complaint was about July. Why, Helen demanded, did Beatrice feel the need to ride the beast every day? It wasn't good for her posture or her health. And though Charles turned a blind eye, Helen could not abide a young woman—for Beatrice was no longer a girl—to ride astride a horse. Sidesaddle during the symbolic seasonal hunt would be acceptable, but daily bareback rides, disappearing for hours, were inappropriate. Whenever she saw him, Helen begged her husband to stop indulging their daughter. But then again, Helen and Charles rarely interacted.

The summer before Girton—the summer of the incident—Beatrice spent long hours brushing July, getting her hands as dirty and calloused as she could, defiant. By then, the stable needed a fresh coat of paint, and July had lost her youthful exuberance. Still, with a click of her tongue, Beatrice sent them both galloping out of sight of prying eyes and flying over the meadows. She never intended to disobey her parents that summer. And soon she regretted it, deeply.

When Beatrice returns home after Charlotte's expulsion and Daniel's proposal, July whinnies at the sound of her voice. Later, Daniel will come to Champney House and request her hand in marriage, which her parents will, of course, agree to with enthusiasm and relief. But until then, she wants to forget. She needs to forget. She runs toward her old horse, tears swollen in her eyes. Every tension that had built in her body over the course of that autumn melts away at the sight of July's nostrils flaring as sunlight streaks through the stable windows, illuminating motes of powdery dirt suspended in the air like fairy dust.

With a push and a kick, she heaves herself onto July's back, and bending forward, she wraps her arm around the horse's warm neck, burying her face in July's mane. The side-to-side lull of the horse's broad back under the sun, her mane shimmering amber, puts Beatrice at ease when everything else seems so confused, so wrong. The steady rumble of hooves beneath her, the second-nature head duck under low-hanging tree branches, knees and thighs gripping as July leaps over logs, return Beatrice to her body.

At the end of term, she finished up her examinations seated alone in a classroom, just Beatrice and the proctor. A dozen young men took the same exams in a building across campus. She knew she was kept out of their exams for fear that she would create a distraction, but she didn't care. The degree is meaningless. At least it ruffles her mother's feathers. Beatrice wishes she was miles away, in London. Every day she scanned the newspaper for reports of the WSPU's latest activities. She even snuck a copy of *Votes for Women* when she could, though she was embarrassed to purchase an issue from any of the volunteers she used to know.

There is action in London. It makes everything in Cambridge seem hollow. She can recite the common law dictates, memorize Blackstone's commentaries, but what use is any of that when the WSPU is whipping up a storm with their protests and publicity campaigns? She read the coverage breathlessly while she should have been revising for her final examinations. Photographs of women in their jail uniforms, a map of

Hyde Park detailing an upcoming march, thousands of women intentionally erased from the census. Apparently Adeline Hurston delivered a rousing speech at a recent rally, but Beatrice couldn't find a single quote in the paper. She missed her chance.

Beatrice doesn't have to think when she is on horseback. She is an animal in motion, at one with July, whose flawless footfalls know every stone and stream. She never stumbles. In childhood, Beatrice taught herself how to leap on July's back while the horse was already trotting, swinging onto her saddle at a run. She learned how to steer with a gentle tug of July's mane, rarely bothering to put on a bridle. She even figured out how to tumble safely off July's back and land with a splash into the pond when she fancied a swim. It has been years since Beatrice attempted a running mount or a backward ride, but she knows she could still do it if she wanted. She feels more comfortable on and with horses than anywhere.

Her body never betrays her when she is riding.

CHAPTER SEVENTEEN
CHARLOTTE

At last, Charlotte has earned her prison badge, and just in time, too. It's dawn on Sunday morning, and she would have cursed herself forever if she missed today's march. She'd been publicizing this very event when she got arrested. Now, at last, the day has come. Sadie is outside the gates, there to greet her with a hug and the promise of a warm cup of tea as she steps out of Holloway a free woman.

"Come on, I'll fill you in," Sadie says.

In the last two weeks, the Union had worked harder than ever before, publicizing the upcoming march to attract women not only within London but from all around the country. "Women's Sunday," as Adeline has coined it, will be an organizational feat. They are anticipating at least one hundred thousand participants, all of whom have been instructed in *Votes for Women* to dress in white in order to stand out in the black-and-white newspaper photographs. As they speak, women are pouring into the city from trains and carriages and even on foot, guided by maps hand-drawn by members of the Union, and arriving at specific entrance points around Hyde Park. When the march officially commences, the park will become a sea of white, the women a flock of swans—dignified and elegant with their demands.

At headquarters, they bump into Adeline, Isabel, and Jessie—Isabel's best friend and one of the Union's longest-serving volunteers—all three wielding large, hand-sewn banners. Adeline wears a simple white dress with a cluster of violets pinned to her hat. "We'd better get going. Welcome back," she says, clasping Charlotte's shoulders briefly. Tears spring into Charlotte's eyes, and she blinks them back.

The others leave for Hyde Park to set up speakers' platforms and coordinate the delegates from the local Union branches. Sadie and Charlotte stay behind so Charlotte can have a nap and a proper meal, but soon enough they've gathered up their six-foot banners and are hurtling west together, hopping off the lorry near the Marble Arch.

"Hurry up!" Sadie calls.

Charlotte hikes up her skirts and hastens her pace. "Hold one of these, will you?" Charlotte says. She's running on pure adrenaline now, and fading fast.

Sadie relieves her of one of the banners and flings it over her shoulder. "Do you want to talk about Holloway? The first time is always hard," Sadie asks. They slow to a more manageable walking pace a few blocks from the park. "Actually, every time is hard."

Charlotte shrugs. "It was bleak. Freezing and damp. Itchy. I'm afraid this cough is all I've gained from the experience."

Sadie nods. To the rest of the world, describing one's prison experience might take hours. Charlotte cannot imagine explaining it to anyone from her previous life. But Sadie understands. All the suffragettes do. A few words suffice to paint a thorough picture.

"Oh, I did get to chatting with the warden's daughter."

"Can you imagine?" Sadie groans. "I thought it was bad enough when my father tried to tamp down the newsboys' strike. I didn't speak to him for weeks until he bargained with them."

"I know. It's awful."

"If my father were the warden in charge of imprisoning political activists as common criminals, I'd run away."

"Easier said than done, I suppose," says Charlotte. She thinks of her mother, from whom she has not received a single letter in all the time since she left school. It was easy enough to cut off her mother, but somehow she'd hoped that Sarah would protest the estrangement. Shouldn't there be something biological that tethers a mother to her daughter?

"Here we are," Sadie says.

For a moment, Charlotte cannot catch her breath. Her vision is blurred by bodies in white. Surely there is some mistake. But no, she blinks and there they are, stretching out in every direction as far as the eye can see: women. Women wearing white dresses and hats bedecked, like Adeline's, with beautiful flowers. Women singing and laughing and ambling from the sidewalks toward the center of the park, adjusting their tricolor sashes. There is a giddiness in the air, like children let out early from school. Charlotte and Sadie link arms, maneuvering through the crowd together.

"I've never seen anything like this," Charlotte says.

Sadie's eyes are wide and glassy. "This has never been done before."

They take it all in. Charlotte can feel the energy around her, the vibrations of possibility from the crowds to the trees to the terrifically blue sky. It's Sunday, so even working-class women are here, identifiable by their threadbare aprons and simple straw hats. Everyone looks beautiful.

"We'd better find the others," Sadie says, guiding Charlotte by the elbow. They make their way through the winding park paths, finding pockets of space to squeeze between the ever-unfolding population of suffragettes. "Ooh, look who's here," Sadie whispers. "There's Adeline's friend, Maggie Andrews."

Charlotte follows Sadie's gaze toward a woman seated in a wheel-chair. She's draped a WSPU flag over the back of her chair like a one-woman parade float.

"And over there," Sadie says, pointing a gloved finger, "is Lady Constance Cunningham, wife of an earl."

"Since when do you read *Burke's Peerage*?" Charlotte teases.

"I don't care for titles," Sadie says. "But even *I* know that an earl has a fat checkbook."

There appears to be no start or end to the profusion of women. As Sadie and Charlotte weave deeper into the park, it becomes harder to identify where they are at all.

"An impressive showing, don't you agree?"

Charlotte and Sadie turn to see Adeline standing behind them, her hands clasped in front of her stiff bodice.

"Ripping," Sadie says.

"I cannot keep up with your Americanisms." Adeline laughs.

"It's wonderful," Sadie translates.

"You really pulled it off," Charlotte adds.

"We all did," says Adeline.

"And the papers are eating it up." Sadie gestures to a gaggle of reporters who stand out like an ink blot against the current of women in white.

"Yes, well, this ought to prove to society that women who want the vote can organize themselves the same as men, in a manner both effective and beautiful. When the men's Reform League gathered here in the sixties, violence broke out, and men *still* expanded the franchise. But today, look around—peaceful, refined, determined—and double the men's turnout."

"Unimpeachably appropriate," Sadie agrees.

Somewhere in the crowd, a three-note melody sounds from the all-female marching band.

"Time for us to march," Adeline says. She rolls back her shoulders and disappears into the crowd, where she will join Isabel and lead the masses. Somewhere in the din, Isabel links arms with her mother. Charlotte can hardly imagine having a mother like that.

All at once, women begin to move forward. They are swept into the crowd, surging together on the tide. Someone starts to sing, a solitary voice, and quickly everyone catches on. Lyrics had been printed in advance in *Votes for Women*, and even though Charlotte hasn't had time to memorize the words, she joins in as much as she can. There is something euphoric about singing all together, everyone's voices blending unselfconsciously, resonant in the crisp air.

> *Shout, shout, up with your song!*
> *Cry with the wind, for the dawn is breaking!*
> *March, march, swing you along,*
> *Wide blows our banner and hope is waking!*

As Charlotte and Sadie take tiny steps, keeping pace with the movement of the crowd, they spot signs identifying all sorts of women by trade and by origin. A delegation from Liverpool is toward the front; schoolteachers walk together in the rear; Jessie leads a group of mill workers from Lancashire; even college graduates, all wearing caps and gowns instead of white dresses, though accessorized with suffrage sashes, promenade beneath an Oxbridge banner. A twinge of something pulls at Charlotte, not quite envy but identification.

Every so often, someone will introduce herself, sharing where she's from and how she came to be here today. They are all connected, a symphony of stories. After an hour or so of marching, the crowd gathers at the Marble Arch. Adeline climbs atop a small wooden stage to deliver her remarks. From their position hundreds of people back, Charlotte and Sadie cannot make out her words. But the women around them applaud nonetheless.

"I can't quite believe it," Sadie whispers. Charlotte looks back over her shoulder. The expanse of women stretches farther than they can see, thousands of faces and dresses and voices. Every woman hangs on Adeline's words, every woman dedicating her time, her day, her pride, to the cause. Charlotte shakes her head, still in awe.

"We did it."

When the sun begins to set, Charlotte realizes how badly her feet ache; she's hardly stopped moving since her release, and her limbs feel like lead, far too heavy for her body. She wouldn't have missed this, though, not for the world. Her heart surges with emotion, a thrumming, desperate sense of hope. All she's ever wanted was to be a part of something. And now, to be a part of *this*, this momentous, beautiful, remarkable gathering—it is more meaningful than she ever could have hoped. Surely, it will inspire change. All of London's eyes will be upon them tomorrow, when the papers will report on the massive crowds, the elegance and eloquence of hundreds of thousands of women demanding, in unison: Votes for women.

When they return to Park Lane that night, Charlotte is so exhausted she wants to weep. Sadie draws a bath and helps her into the tub. She lifts her limbs gingerly; her body feels tender.

"Would you like me to stay?"

Charlotte is grateful to Sadie for knowing that she needs company right now.

"It's alright to cry, you know," Sadie whispers. "We've got each other now. You can lean on me."

Charlotte's eyes well up. It's been so long since she allowed herself to cry in front of anyone. With a ragged breath, she lets it out, no pillow or closed door to muffle the sound. The sheer desolation of Holloway, the euphoria of the march, and unequivocal exhaustion release as Sadie pours pitchers of warm water over Charlotte's back and she curls into herself, tears cascading into the murky water.

The next morning, Charlotte and Sadie scour the daily papers for reports of the march.

"Here, look at the *Morning Post*," says Sadie, holding up a section of thin newsprint. "'Estimates of over two hundred thousand suffragettes gathered in Hyde Park yesterday. The women have certainly given the prime minister something to talk about. Whether they will ever show that there is any overwhelming feeling among women as a whole to have a vote is another matter—'"

"What's that supposed to mean?" Charlotte interrupts.

"'Women are less strong in persistence and in physical power than men,'" Sadie continues, her voice rising. "'We believe that it would weaken the moral fiber of the nation if the supreme decision of the State were determined by women.'"

"No!" Charlotte shouts. "Let me see the *Daily Mirror*." She riffles through the pile of papers on the table. "'Thousands of females made their presence known in long-suffering Hyde Park yesterday afternoon . . .' The *park* is long-suffering? Christ. 'People should not get votes simply because they say they want them. The distribution of the vote should, if possible, be based on some principle.'"

Charlotte slams down the paper. "How about the principle of equality?"

"This is mad," says Sadie. "I can't believe after all that—the largest showing in Hyde Park history—*this* is the only coverage we've gotten."

"What does this mean for the movement?" Charlotte asks.

Sadie rests her chin in her hands and sighs.

"I can't just sit here today," Charlotte insists. "Let's go make speeches. Let's get arrested."

"But you were only just released—aren't you tired?" Sadie asks.

It's true. Charlotte's neck is sore from shivering for so many nights in the cold Holloway cell. Her legs ache from walking all of yesterday in the park. But why waste momentum in prolonging the inevitable?

"I'm only tired of sitting around." Charlotte is standing, her mind already spinning with new strategies. The old ways do not work. Waiting patiently won't do. "Come on."

It takes only a few hours to set up a soapbox near Oxford Circus. And then it takes only a few minutes of chanting "Votes for women" at top volume for the bobbies to arrive. The officers grab Charlotte's arms so tightly that weltlike bruises blossom on her skin almost instantly.

"Be a good girl and go on home," one officer whispers into Charlotte's ear. "You *are* a good girl, aren't you?" She feels his hot breath on her neck and his hand reaches up to her breast, giving her a sharp, painful squeeze.

Sadie slumps her body, allowing the other officer to remove her from the soapbox. But Charlotte's patience is thin. She is exhausted and frustrated and now her breast aches. Without thought, she curses in the officer's face and stomps on his foot.

"I thought so," the man says with a snide smile. "That'll be an assault charge, that will."

Sadie grows smaller and smaller from Charlotte's vantage point out the back window of the lorry that barrels toward Holloway. This time, her sentence will surely be longer. This time, she will have to try something different.

CHAPTER EIGHTEEN

EMILY

Emily hates to admit it, even to herself, but Holloway feels emptier without Charlotte. Lonelier. Martin appears around corners, grinning like a hopeful puppy each time he catches her eye, but she isn't in the mood to talk in circles with him. And Thomas, despite his plan to save up for Emily's future, retreats once more to his office and his drink, taking his meals alone. The days are exhausting, waking before six in the morning to start a twelve-hour shift, sometimes adding more hours to simply avoid the empty cottage. She disappears to sit on the cold Holloway floor sketching, studying the lines and shadows that make up her small world.

When Charlotte returns so soon after her release for another sentence, Emily conceals her happiness. She knows it is wrong to take joy from a friend's imprisonment. And perhaps it is wrong to consider Charlotte a friend at all, when they've known each other for only two weeks, during which time iron bars kept them apart. But Charlotte is the only person who takes Emily seriously, the only person who has bothered to inquire about what lies within Emily's heart. She isn't sure of the answer herself. But it triggers something in her, it lights a wick she never knew was waiting there.

As Emily comes to realize that she does, indeed, consider Charlotte a friend, the sinfulness of her pleasure is magnified. Still, Charlotte is like the beginnings of a sketch—the outline is there, but even the artist herself does not yet know what details will emerge. That's her favorite part, the moment when blankness, possibility, starts to mean something. The drawing takes on a life of its own. Emily is desperate to find out what lies within.

"Assault, my arse," Charlotte says to Emily after recounting the tale of her arrest. "As if *I* was the one doing the assaulting." She massages her breast unselfconsciously. "Two hundred and fifty thousand of us showed up in Hyde Park in support of women's suffrage. That's more than any men's group, more than anyone ever! And do you know what the government said in response? Nothing."

Emily slips a blanket through the gap between the bars. Unlike the guards, she has no right to a key.

"I'm so sorry."

"One day down and twenty-nine to go." Charlotte's voice is bitter.

Emily hesitates, then says, "I know it's wrong to say, but I'm glad you're here."

"You're the only good thing about this place," Charlotte says darkly. "A political prisoner is, by definition, a person protesting for fair treatment in the political sphere. As such, they have the right to writing materials and their own clothing. And yet look at me." Charlotte pulls at the itchy brown Holloway uniform. "They lock us in solitary, cut us off from the outside world, and treat us like common criminals. This can't go on."

"What do you mean?" Emily asks. It isn't as though Charlotte has a choice in the matter.

"You'll see." The glint in Charlotte's eye, one that Emily recognizes from stories of childhood mischief, is unsettling. It seems as good a time as any to change the subject, and Emily has been bursting to tell Charlotte her news.

"I'm going to school to become a teacher."

"Is that so?" Charlotte asks. "I thought you were going to be an artist."

"I never said that," says Emily, crossing her arms over her chest. She has only spoken of drawing as a daydream. "My mother always wanted me to be a teacher. I'm saving for the training course."

"So you want to become a teacher, or your mother wanted it?"

Emily digs her nails into her palms. Now Charlotte is warping her words, and inexplicably, Emily is feeling defensive. "I . . . we both want it."

"Good then," says Charlotte.

"If you ever return to college, we could go together," Emily adds, hating the eagerness in her voice but unable to suppress it. Charlotte told her all about her escapades at Girton. Emily knows, of course, that she could never afford to go all the way to Cambridge, to study along-side the daughters of barons and earls. But Roehampton, in London, admits women and offers a teachers course. Perhaps, for Charlotte, it could be a compromise.

"Oh, Emily, I'm never going back," Charlotte says. "But I'm glad for you."

"Well, I still have to work for a year to save up. When all this is over, won't you want to return?"

"All this," she says, waving an arm around her tiny cell, "is not going to be 'over' anytime soon. And frankly, when we do win the vote, there'll be more important things for me to do than gossip in the dormitories."

"That's not fair," Emily says quietly. Charlotte had been born into middle-class privilege by sheer luck. Few are as fortunate. "I'm working really hard for this."

"I'm sorry." Charlotte exhales. "I just think you could do more than be a teacher."

It takes every ounce of willpower Emily has to bite her tongue. Charlotte simply does not understand. For all the stories she told of the snobbish Girton girls, Emily sees now that Charlotte is as bad as any of them—and worst of all, she doesn't even realize it. In Charlotte's world, there are opportunities and connections and second chances. In Emily's, however, life is a constant struggle. Becoming a teacher is the pinnacle, it is the dream. There is no *more than*. And it's callous, really, and cruel for Charlotte not to realize this.

"Good night," Emily says. She wipes her hands on her apron and hurries down the corridor. The night guard tips his cap as she slips through the courtyard.

The next morning is one of the coldest since the previous winter. The cells have no hearths or heating, and Emily shivers in anticipation of her day sweeping and scrubbing the drafty corridors. She ties her apron snug around her waist and tosses a shawl over her shoulders. Now on the official Holloway payroll, she strides into the building ready to work. The previous night's conversation with Charlotte cemented her resolve. She cannot continue this life of drudgery. And teaching is her only way out. Still, the conversation niggles at her more than she cares to admit.

The prisoners' breakfasts have just been delivered when Emily arrives. She hears the disembodied echoes of slurping and scraping as the inmates eat their gruel and drink their lukewarm tea inside their cells. When Emily stops before Charlotte's grate, her ears stinging from the cold, Charlotte is still in her cot, huddled beneath a blanket.

"Good morning," Emily says briskly. She's decided she won't mention last night's discord. It's not worth it. "Having a lie-in?" Her tone is light and, she hopes, conciliatory.

Charlotte peels back the blanket just enough to expose her face. "Hello."

"Look, your breakfast is here," Emily says. "I have a moment if you want to come eat it." Emily slides onto the ground, crossing her legs to sit in their usual picnic position, and waits for Charlotte to join her on the other side of the bars.

"No thanks," Charlotte murmurs, without stirring from bed.

"Look, I'm sorry things got rather tense last night."

Charlotte must have heard the crack in Emily's voice, for she finally sits up. "It's not that," she says. "Don't worry about it. I'm just—" She sighs. "It's going to get hard from here on out."

"Why?" Emily asks. "Will you please come here so we can talk about it?" She glances over her shoulder. Despite her mother's kindnesses, Emily knows full well that employees are not meant to fraternize with the inmates.

"No," Charlotte says.

"But your breakfast is getting cold. Well, colder."

"I'm not eating it."

"Why not?"

"I'm not eating anything," she says. "At all."

Blinking in annoyance, Emily stands. "Fine. I have work to do." With that, she picks up her bucket and hurries away.

Emily proceeds to clean, turning over their conversation in her head in an endless, rankling reel. Why couldn't Charlotte just be happy for her? Here she was, trying to accomplish the one dream Marianne had harbored for her only daughter—while Charlotte, whose stepfather had tossed buckets of money at whatever whim she wanted, was throwing it all away with a grating air of condescension. And it isn't enough for Charlotte to keep her judgments to herself; she has to thrust them upon Emily, too. Yet it cannot be quite so simple. Emily is missing something; she just isn't sure what.

Emily is kneeling down before a grate in the early evening, swiping at cobwebs as thick as lace, when Martin taps her on the shoulder.

"Heading home soon, Emily?" he asks.

"Oh, I must've lost track of time," she says. "I suppose so. And you? Or are you on the night shift?"

"No, no, I'm heading out as well. But I wanted to tell you," he says, lowering his voice. "I'd keep an eye on your friend Charlotte Evans."

Emily stiffens. She does not like how he used the word *friend*. Her relationship with Charlotte is a complicated, private thing. "Why is that?"

"She didn't take any meals today. Hope she isn't, well . . ." Martin makes an odd gesture toward his stomach, ballooning his hand out from his waist and raising an eyebrow. It takes Emily a moment.

"Oh," she says. "Oh no. No, no. Of course not." Prickles of sweat puddle beneath her arms. Martin shuffles in place, his overlarge feet scraping the floor.

"Just thought you should know. Good night, Em."

"Good night," she says, though she is already turning away. She takes the stairs two at a time, clattering down to the level of Charlotte's cell. Charlotte will hear her coming—everything echoes in Holloway—but Emily slows before an empty cell a few doors down, catching her breath.

It is not terribly unusual for an inmate to skip a meal. The food is widely acknowledged to be abhorrent. Prisoners discover maggots in their meals almost as frequently as rats claw through the corridors and lice creep into the women's hair. For that reason, Charlotte's breakfast-time abstinence did not raise any eyebrows. But now . . .

"Charlotte?" She walks at a purposely slow gait, willing her voice to sound normal. Charlotte doesn't respond, and Emily peers inside the cell. Like all of the others, it is already dark. Why waste fuel to light a prisoner's evening? Outside the door, three tin trays of food sit untouched. Emily thinks she can see something crawling in the morning's gruel, though the rest of it doesn't look terrible. She can just make out Charlotte's form in her cot, in the same position as that morning, a bulbous shadow beneath the threadbare blanket. "Are you . . . are you feeling alright?"

Charlotte shifts in bed so that she can see Emily's face in the dim light of the corridor, though she does not sit up.

"I'm fine," she says.

Emily could swear that Charlotte winks at her, though it is too dark to tell.

"I'm going home," Emily says. Lowering her voice to a breath-like whisper, she adds, "Would you like me to bring you something? Bread? Soup?"

Charlotte bows her chin. "No, thank you."

"Is anything the matter?" Emily tries not to assume the worst, but how well *does* she know her? They had laughed and gossiped and bonded between bars. They had told each other stories of their lives and their families. But there were gaps in Charlotte's tales, chasms during which Emily didn't know where she'd lived or with whom she'd spent her time. What if Charlotte is—well, Emily does not want to think the word, but Martin's graceless gesture toward the stomach had said it all. If Charlotte is ruined, then Emily knows all too well the pathetic story that will play out. She's seen it so many times before—an infant's mewling cries, a woman in primal distress as the child is ripped from her arms and taken to the orphans' asylum, the breasts leaking into the sodden fabric of the Holloway uniform.

Charlotte's eyes widen. "Oh no," she says. "No, don't worry, Emily. I'm not—"

Emily holds her gaze, pleading. "Let me bring you something. You must be so hungry."

"No." Charlotte is firm. "I'll just go to sleep. But I'll see you tomorrow, alright?" Somehow, Charlotte twists the conversation, taking control, giving Emily an out. She is good at that—maneuvering a discussion. Sometimes it helps Emily feel more comfortable. But other times, like now, she feels manipulated and lost. The hall light winks, the night guard's signal that soon the entire jail will go dark. It is barely seven o'clock. But for the rest of the night, the inmates will have only the pinpricks of stars through slit windows to illuminate their solitude.

"Alright," Emily whispers.

She stumbles into her father in the courtyard, both heading home at the same time.

"Did you have a good day?" he asks.

"Fine," she says. Does he know about Charlotte's condition? Usually Thomas's position keeps him at a remove from the daily drudgery of the jail. Though, on the other hand, word travels fast.

"I saw you," he says, holding open the cottage door. "Talking to Martin Jennings."

Emily exhales with relief. If he'd seen her talking to Charlotte, or God forbid, offering her food . . .

"Are you laughing?" he asks, misreading the reassurance on her face. "Heavens, do you fancy him?"

"Papa!" Emily says. "No, I don't fancy him."

He sits down at the table and pulls off his hat. In the yellow light, his hair looks much grayer than usual.

"He's a nice lad," Thomas says, grinning now at Emily's flustered expression. "And we never talked about him taking you to tea."

"It was nothing," she insists.

"You don't like him, then?"

"Well, I don't not like him."

"Aha!"

"Oh, stop," Emily says, striking a match to light the stove.

"Let your old man dream a little," Thomas says.

When Charlotte refuses to eat the bread Emily brings her in the morning, turning her wan face away and into the shadows, Emily knows something is very wrong. "Please," she whispers through the bars. "You're unwell."

"I'm fine," Charlotte insists, her voice reedy and weak. Even her jug of water remains untouched.

The prison doctor is called in on the third day. He is middle-aged, with a full beard and a permanent grimace. The silk of his vest is taut across his belly, and Emily sees him check a gold pocket watch before knocking on the door to Thomas's office.

"How do you do, sir? Please, Dr. Bainwright, do come in," Thomas says, shaking the doctor's hand and performing an odd sort of bow. Emily feels embarrassed for him. Her father treats everyone of a higher status with a humiliating obsequiousness that must have been learned back when he still spoke with an Irish accent.

"Mr. Brown." The doctor speaks tersely, gripping Thomas's hand for a fraction of a second, barely a handshake, before pulling away.

She watches her father close his office door and she stations herself outside it with a broom she has no intention of using to sweep. She strains to listen over the thumping of her heartbeat. Oh, if Charlotte is very ill, if she were to die—Emily couldn't bear it. Charlotte may be selfish and even a little snobby, but she is also idealistic and courageous, and now she's been reduced to a weak thing, slumped over in that dreadful cell.

"How many days has it been?" The doctor sounds bored.

"Let's see, nearly three days?" Thomas replies.

"Is that a question?"

"No. No, sir. Three days."

"Has she taken water?"

"Not a drop."

"Hmph."

Emily jumps away from the door at the sound of a chair scraping the stone floor. She barely manages to duck around a corner when the door swings open and Dr. Bainwright emerges, Thomas shadowing behind him.

"Where is her cell?" the doctor demands.

"Wouldn't you like a cup of tea?" Thomas offers.

"No, of course not. I'll see to the patient."

Thomas nods, as though the two had determined this course of action together. "Right this way then, sir."

With quick steps, Thomas starts down the corridor. The doctor lags behind him, but soon both pass by. Then someone taps Emily's shoulder.

"Hello there." It's Martin.

"Oh, hello."

"Spying, are you?"

Her cheeks instantly redden. "No," she says. "I've been . . . sweeping."

"Right. Your friend's not doing so well, is she? It's not every day we call in the doc."

"She's not my friend," Emily says. Her voice quivers unconvincingly, and she instantly regrets the words. Why should she lie to Martin? Why should she care what he thinks at all when Charlotte is ill and possibly dying down the hall? "I mean—"

Martin places a finger to his lips. "C'mon," he says. "Let's see if we can get a closer look."

Emily follows him up the back stairs, used only by the guards, to the sentinel post. They creep around the corner and find it empty. "The prison is a panopticon," he begins.

"I know," she interrupts. "I've been here longer than you."

"Right," he says. "I guess you already know, then, but this is the optimal position for surveillance. We should be able to see into her cell from here."

Emily realizes that he is being kind. Despite her frequent rebuffs, Martin is still trying. She attempts to soften her voice, though the sound comes out with a crack. "Thanks."

He pats her hand, just once. Then he walks away, leaving Emily to squint down toward Charlotte's cell. There she is, a figure huddled in shadow. And there is Thomas, his keys jangling as he unlocks the door and holds it open for the doctor. Dr. Bainwright steels himself for a moment. Emily forgets how much the prison reeks; she is immune to its odor. Then he ducks inside.

CHAPTER NINETEEN

CHARLOTTE

A man wearing a long white coat enters Charlotte's cell, breathing only through his mouth, and he does not introduce himself. It hardly matters. Charlotte is curled into herself, a nest of frozen bones. Her mind is a haze of hunger and thirst. Her heart beats far too quickly in her chest.

"Well, well, well." The doctor clicks his tongue, leaning down toward the cot. His face is round and he has a long beard that reminds her of a twisted Father Christmas. "Somebody's in a spot of trouble."

Charlotte won't speak. She won't deign to answer him.

"Let's see, then." He pulls the blanket off her body in one fell swoop, sending ice up her spine. She clings to the itchy uniform, desperate for warmth. The doctor presses two fingers below her pelvic bone, then reaches up into her skirt. "Have you been a good girl?" he murmurs, his fingers searching. Charlotte clamps her eyes shut. "Hmm, not pregnant, then?" He drops the skirt and she tucks her legs up to her chest. "Well, then. What's the problem? You're trying to make some sort of political statement?" His laugh is languorous. "But you are mistaken.

You think that someone out there will care if you live or die." He leans so close that she can feel the heat of his breath on her neck. "Pity."

What if he's right? Charlotte wonders. What if this impulsive decision not to eat, to draw attention through starvation, will be met by blind eyes? What if no one cares at all? For all her independence, her desire to set out on her own, Charlotte has never before felt so completely alone.

"You are a good girl, aren't you?" the police officer had whispered as he groped her breast. The doctor, too. And so, as desperately as Charlotte would like to toss up her hands in resignation, she cannot. These horrid men in their powerful positions, they believe they can control women's bodies: shackle them with wedding rings, legislate away their existence so they have no more autonomy than a child, and lock them up if they disobey. The only option left for a woman like Charlotte is to take control herself. She must put her very survival on the line, make her body the site of the protest.

The thought had come to her as she rode in the clanging police lorry to Holloway, seething, the glow of their incredible demonstration in Hyde Park fading fast. If that did not make a difference, that peaceful protest with singing and marching and speeches, white dresses everywhere one looked, what would? The protests cannot merely occur outside the jail. She must protest imprisonment itself.

There is only one way forward, and though it is at once unprecedented, even absurd, and utterly, incapacitatingly terrifying, she shall not—cannot—back down. She will not eat or drink until she is free.

The metal door clangs shut behind the doctor.

When Charlotte was ill as a child, her mother brought soup and tea to her bedside. It only happened two or three times that she can recall; she was a healthy child. But she secretly loved those few days when she was ill, for she had her mother's complete attention—no little sisters competing for affection and, later, no stepfather incapable of lifting a finger on his own. Sarah would sing to Charlotte, little nursery rhymes unuttered anywhere except her daughter's sickbed. The lilting lull of her mother's voice, those gentle fingers combing through her curls, sent Charlotte straight to sleep no matter how wretched the fever or aching her throat. If only she could remember the words to those songs, she thinks now. But they are gone from her memory, if ever she knew them at all.

Hours or days after the doctor leaves her cell—time is meaningless, a clawing chasm of hunger and thirst—a woman appears in silhouette outside the door. Charlotte's eyes well with tears. *Mama!* she wants to cry, choking on the word. Her mouth is so dry. Her throat sears. The figure moves and she wonders if it is a ghost or a hallucination. But then she sees that it is not Sarah at all. It is Emily. Emily is crying.

"Please," she begs. "Charlotte, please." A scraping sound. She slides a plate through the bars. Charlotte does not dare move, not even an inch. The ache of hunger thrums within her, though it seems tired now, like a starving bear resigned to hibernation rather than hunting.

When George told Charlotte, Sylvia, and Anna that he was going to marry their mother, their father had been dead for only a year. Charlotte felt his absence every day, like an oozing flesh wound that refused to heal. She still glanced twice at the rocking chair each time she walked by, still hoped, by some stroke of luck, that she'd find Papa, pipe in hand, inviting her to sit on his lap and read aloud from *Alice's Adventures in Wonderland*. It still broke her heart, every time, to discover the chair empty. How could her mother cover such a gaping gash with a flimsy piece of gauze like George?

Soon they moved into a new house, his house, leaving behind the few remnants of her father that had not already been sold off—the worthless items, his sweaters and socks and wool scarf. Charlotte snatched the scarf, which still smelled like his tobacco, before they left home for the last time. In the new house, George presented his stepdaughters with store-bought cloaks, oxblood wool with matching muffs. It was his Christmas gift to them. The younger girls squealed, rubbing their cheeks on the rich fabric. Charlotte stood stony-faced, refusing to relinquish her father's scarf, and wondering at how quickly their world could turn upside down.

"Say thank you," Sarah hissed, pinching Charlotte's upper arm. Later, a mottled blue bruise formed on Charlotte's bicep. By the new year, her father's scarf had disappeared.

The doctor returns; she does not know when. Testing, tongue-clicking, a firm grip around her wrist. Her eyelids feel so much heavier than she has ever remembered them feeling. But perhaps she simply never noticed before. Have they always been this leaden? She hears words like *running out of time* and *heart* and *pulse*. Are those words spoken to her? About her?

As her body seizes with shivers, she remembers last summer, the days she spent in the sunshine, stringing Jack along with illicit kisses. Her body had been so hot that summer, never more so than when she let him press her onto the floor of the cellar, their skin sweat-damp and electrified. She felt both reckless and rather bored as she lay beneath him. How naïve she'd been to think that she had any power at all, to believe that her body was anything more than an object, an instrument used for someone else's pleasure. A pawn for someone else's pain. When Sarah confronted her in the dark bedroom later, with that pleading look in her eye and the warning to be virtuous, Charlotte had felt invincible and wise. Her mother had no idea what her daughter had already done. But now, she wishes for her mother's worry. For anyone to know or care what she's put her body through. That look in Sarah's eye, searching and despairing, calls to mind Beatrice on the day they said goodbye at Girton. How anguished Beatrice had seemed then, like she had something she desperately needed to say. And now, Charlotte will never know.

Sometime later, the memories stop. Charlotte's mind is flooded in blackness, an inky midnight sky. In a daydream (or a night dream, time is untrustworthy) she imagines that she is dead. And wouldn't that be easier? If she was dead, she would not feel so weak. Her stomach would not pain her so. The flutter in her heart, too fast, like a moth approaching a fatal flame, would cease. And her fingers would not shake as she tries to pull the thin blanket tighter around her body.

She hears someone banging on the bars of the cell. She does not open her eyes.

CHAPTER TWENTY

EMILY

Papa, *please*."

"Emily, what's all—"

"She is going to die!"

Emily bursts into her father's office. It is so small, she realizes, perhaps for the first time. The walls seem to lean in, coffin-like. How can he bear to sit here all day in this tomb? He looks up at her from the intake papers, an expression of genuine confusion on his face. He does not know about her friendship with Charlotte. He does not understand why she should care.

"The doctor was just here—" he begins.

"I heard what the doctor said." She'd listened outside the door. She'd rushed in as soon as that impotent old man left. "He's not going to do anything. She will sit there and starve. He doesn't care."

Now Thomas is angry. She can tell by the twitch of his lower lip, the way he grips the corner of his desk with his hands, once calloused by labor, now as smooth as he's always wanted. Still, the scars remain. He cannot erase them. Not from her.

"You should not be eavesdropping," he says, his voice tense and slow.

"It doesn't matter!" Her face feels boiling hot and she knows she is going to cry. She must tell him what she feels before she bursts into tears, before he can attribute her words to the irrationality of emotion. "Papa, please, isn't there something you can do? We could . . . we could take her back to the cottage. No one would have to know. Please, you can't just . . . she's going to die here! I can't lose her, too—"

Her shoulders ache from the effort of staunching her sobs, but they finally come, tears raging down her cheeks. There is no sympathy in her father's eyes.

"Pull yourself together, Emily," he commands in a loud whisper. His eyes dart to the door, and she knows he is praying that the doctor hasn't lingered to overhear his disgraceful daughter forgetting her place. "You cannot cavort with prisoners," he hisses, his face growing redder by the breath. "And you shall not speak to your father in this way. I work for the government. You talk of treason."

"You take yourself too seriously! If you had any real power, you could actually do something."

Thomas takes a step toward her, but the desk stands between them, unrelenting. She does not know what he intended to do. Would he grab her? Shake her? He's never touched her in anger in her life. But Emily has never before seen him this angry. She whirls out of the cramped office, knocking files to the ground as she rushes along the corridor. She does not consider the direction of her steps until she has run nearly straight into Martin. She looks wild, her face streaked with tears and her chest heaving with ragged breath.

"Emily," he says. She tries to push past him. "Wait! What's wrong?"

"Unless you can free Charlotte, I have nothing to say to you."

He opens his mouth to speak but says nothing. She flees.

Thomas comes home late, though Emily does not wait up for him. She can hardly eat, her stomach is so unsettled imagining Charlotte's hunger, and so she shuts the door to her bedroom and does not emerge until morning. Dawn glows an eerie cerulean the next day, as though the entire prison is submerged in the Thames. She wakes before Thomas and slips out of the cottage unnoticed.

"Charlotte." Emily crouches before her cell, whispering. The lump in the cot is unmoving. Emily squints; is she breathing?

"That you, Emily?"

She turns. It is not Charlotte speaking, but another prisoner, whose cell is diagonally across from Charlotte's. Hannah, a prostitute, had been admitted last week. Her eyes were outlined in smoky black kohl when she arrived, and Emily's first thought had been that she looked like an Egyptian queen. Since then, the black has faded, and she simply looks tired. It is remarkable how the prison strips all individuality from its inhabitants. They enter as unique persons, with striking features and expressions. But they emerge flat, ashen, drained.

"She was crying in the night," Hannah says as Emily approaches.

"When?"

"Few hours ago, I reckon. Couldn't really tell the time."

"Did the night guard come by?"

She shakes her head and lifts an eyebrow. Emily follows her gaze up to the guard station at the center of the panopticon. Martin appears to be asleep. But he must have heard her cry. Or hadn't he cared?

"When the doctor came by yesterday, he gave her twenty-four hours," Hannah says.

"Until?"

Hannah shrugs.

"Until what?" Emily's voice pitches higher than it should. Twenty-four hours until starvation? Death? How long can a person survive without food or water? It has been almost four days.

A clanging sound startles them both, and Emily relinquishes the bars of Hannah's cell. Above them, Martin judders awake, sitting up from his slumped position. Emily ducks around a corner as Thomas appears, still in his nightcap, followed by the doctor.

"Can't let her die here," the doctor mutters. He moves decisively toward Charlotte's cell. "Damn it," he says as Thomas fiddles with the key. "Damn it."

They both enter the cell. The doctor lifts Charlotte's wrist. Her skeletal shadow crawls across the wall.

"I need a stretcher," the doctor orders.

Martin's footsteps echo overhead, and he and another guard soon appear with the stretcher. They lift Charlotte as easily as if she were a doll. Emily winces as Charlotte's hand flops from the edge. She looks dead. *Oh, God*, she looks dead.

"The ambulance is waiting outside," the doctor directs. He groans impatiently as the guards move ahead toward the mouth of the main entrance. "It was good you called," he adds to Thomas. Thomas perks up at the praise, and Emily feels a tingle of hope. Maybe her words yesterday had meant something to him. "Would be an awful look if she died in here," the doctor continues. "These bloody suffragettes are enough trouble as it is. They certainly don't need the sympathy."

"Right you are, sir," Thomas says.

The doctor shakes his hand and then follows Charlotte's stretcher outside. Emily's blood runs cold. Thomas does not care about Emily or Charlotte or anything, only about saving his own arse and the reputation of his precious government. Thomas spots her from where she stands around the corner. His eyes narrow, the pride from the doctor's compliment evaporating.

"Emily," he growls. "Get home. Now. And don't go anywhere else."

"But I have chores to do here."

"Your shift doesn't start for two hours. You are not permitted on the premises until the start of your shift. Go."

Emily bites her lip. She could protest. But what good would that do? Charlotte isn't even here anymore. She turns and stalks out of the building toward the cottage. She is exhausted. She may as well sleep for a couple of hours. Charlotte will be in hospital; Emily can stop worrying.

Don't go anywhere else. Where does he imagine she would go? She hardly ever leaves Holloway. But then she realizes, she *can* go. She can go get help. She can make sure Charlotte is not alone. Emily is already in the courtyard. She turns on the spot and flings open the back gate.

Emily has never walked the city alone, never ventured beyond the route to the market. *Dangerous*, had been her mother's warning; *improper*, her father's. Now she is passing through unfamiliar neighborhoods, crossing teeming streets farther from home than she's been, perhaps, in years. She trains her eyes straight ahead, not permitting them to stray. She feels stares, the eyes of men upon her. Workers on their way to shifts crowd the streets; she sidesteps their wide stances, walking in what she hopes is the right direction.

The gate of Clement's Inn rises before her. It is an unpretentious brick building situated in a quiet square. Emily realizes she is not wearing gloves, but she knocks on the door anyway. She feels so exposed out on the street; it is too late to lose her nerve.

She can hear the clattering of feet from within. Muffled voices shout and then the door swings open.

"I've got it!" a young woman yells over her shoulder and then faces Emily on the stoop. She has an American accent and rosy, freckled cheeks framed by auburn hair. Her vaguely familiar eyes narrow at the sight of Emily.

"You're the warden's daughter," she says in greeting. "Can I help you?"

"Charlotte, Charlotte Evans—"

"She isn't here."

"I know. She's—" Emily feels her breath catch. She'd hardly noticed that she ran most of the way here.

"Come on in, it's cold outside," the woman says, leading Emily in by the arm. "I'm Sadie, by the way. We've never properly met."

Sadie brings her to a small sitting room. Every inch of space besides the couch cushions is stacked with papers. Suffrage banners hang on the walls, and the surfaces drip with ribbons of violet and green. It looks like the jolly, if cramped, backstage of a theater.

"Tea?"

"No, thanks."

"Just as well." Sadie shrugs. "I don't much care for it myself. Why are you here? Is Charlotte alright?"

"She's been taken to hospital," Emily says. "She refused to eat or drink for days. She was very weak when she left."

Sadie's face falls. "When was this?"

"This morning. Just now, I came straightaway."

"I must go to her at once," she says, standing abruptly. "Jessie!" Sadie shouts up the stairs and soon another woman emerges, thin and gangly. "Charlotte has been taken to the hospital. She's unwell."

Emily recognizes Jessie, of course. They both recognize each other. Emily tenses. Why has she come here? These women must despise her. But Jessie nods, curt yet polite, as she reaches for her coat by the door. Sadie turns back to Emily. "Thank you so much for coming," she says. "You're a doll."

Somehow she emerges back out on the street. The two women race down the block in the opposite direction. A part of her wishes she could have gone with them. But then again, who is she to sit at Charlotte's bedside? These women are her real friends, not Emily. She is simply an acquaintance of convenience. If Charlotte never returns to jail, Emily will probably never see her again. She is turning away from Clement's Inn and starting back toward Holloway when she hears a shout.

"Wait!" It is Sadie, jogging in her direction. "Come to my house, will you? When Charlotte's back? We'll thank you properly then."

"I . . . I will." Emily knows she does not deserve this kindness. But she is grinning as she memorizes the hastily whispered address.

It is midmorning when she arrives back at the jail. She is late. As she strides down the long central corridor, she is struck by the sudden image of being swallowed down a dark throat. When she was little, she used to imagine the jail was a dragon, with a great wingspan reaching to the tips of the east and west wings, its gaping mouth the front gate. Her eyes well with tears, relieved that Charlotte is safe and no longer in this tortured place. The door to Thomas's office is closed as Emily sneaks past and heads to the cottage.

She changes her pinafore and braids her hair. The little house feels empty, and its disrepair appears starker in the midmorning light. That eerie, familiar sensation returns. It feels like Marianne ought to still be here. Like she's gone out, but she'll return. Emily pokes her head into her father's bedroom. The bed is rumpled on his side only, and the windows are coated with dust. Still, her mother's drawers appear as though she'd never left, her stacks of pressed and folded handkerchiefs as meticulous as ever. Emily rummages around for her mother's rosewater. She finds the bottle and inhales deeply—a sudden and instinctive urge to breathe in that maternal scent.

"Martin, bring in the buckets, will you?" Thomas's voice echoes from just outside the cottage. She leaps out of the bedroom, closing the door behind her. By the time Thomas enters the cottage, Emily is at the kitchen table, neutral territory.

"And now you've overslept?" Thomas says, shaking his head when he sees her. Emily tightens her jaw. "It's been a stressful few days." He sighs. It is not an apology, but it is something.

"I was just going to have a bite of breakfast," she says. "I'll work late if I need to. Would you like me to make you something?"

Thomas nods. "S'alright," he says. "Can you put some tea on?"

Emily stands and reaches for the kettle.

CHAPTER TWENTY-ONE

BEATRICE

Helen is giddy at the news of Daniel's proposal. She would probably encourage a whirlwind weekend up to Gretna Green if only to ensure the deal was done, but thankfully, Daniel still has another term remaining at King's.

"What'll you do between now and then?" Charles asks over breakfast. Helen rarely emerges before noon, so it's just Beatrice and her father at the table.

"It can't possibly take me six months to prepare my trousseau," she says snarkily.

"Your mother could find a way," Charles jokes. "Ah, thank you, Whitney," he says as the butler brings in the stack of letters from the post. "And here's one for you, Beatrice."

Beatrice opens the letter quickly, eyes scanning the page of unfamiliar handwriting. "Father," she says. "I know exactly what I'll do until the wedding. I'll go to London."

She did not have to convince her father. He left the decision entirely up to her mother, who would never have permitted it if Beatrice didn't already have a ring on her finger. But Beatrice, for once, dug her heels in. "My Girton friend needs me in her convalescence," she insisted. And so Helen relented.

The stranger who'd written to her, an American girl by the name of Sadie Lawrence, is waiting on the stoop when the chauffeur pulls up to the house on Park Lane. Hair flame red and eyes shining, Sadie nearly yanks Beatrice out of the car. "Thank you for coming! I'll explain everything inside."

Over slightly burnt scones, for Sadie does all the cooking herself, Beatrice learns with horror about Charlotte's imprisonment.

"She'll be released from the hospital later today," Sadie says. "Will you stay to help take care of her? I'm sure Charlotte would love that."

"Sadie, has Charlotte ever mentioned me?"

"Well, no, I don't think so." Sadie frowns, her pink lips in a knot. "But she kept all of your letters in her room. I thought you must be close. She doesn't speak to her family. You're the only person she seems to be in contact with."

Beatrice's heart sinks. "She never responded to any of my letters."

"Oh," Sadie says. "I see."

They sit in silence, Beatrice wondering if she's made a mistake in coming. But then Sadie reaches out and squeezes Beatrice's hand.

"I think she'll be glad to see you. She needs familiar faces around. And yours is a very pretty face."

Beatrice's cheeks burn. "That's very kind. But she won't be thrilled to see me. At least, not at first. But maybe I can explain myself. I want to help," she says. "And I want to work with the WSPU again, as much as I can until I have to get married."

"Married? What a bore!"

"Do you always speak your mind?"

"If I can help it." Sadie smiles.

"No wonder Charlotte likes you so much."

"Yes, we have that in common. And you, Beatrice, do you speak your mind?"

"I try to," Beatrice says, after a pause. "I will try even more so now."

Sadie grins, her smile warm like sunshine. "Good. Well, then, let's bring our girl home."

"I think you'd better get her," Beatrice says, a knot of worry in her chest. "I'll wait here."

Beatrice twists the ring on her finger. In a way, this ring is the key to everything she's ever wanted, if only for a short time. She is engaged but not yet married—no longer under her mother's thumb, but not yet under her husband's. She is ideally situated to do, for the first time in her life, exactly as she wants.

And Beatrice wants to use her last months of freedom to make up for lost time, with both the suffragettes and with Charlotte. Although Charlotte never responded to her letters, at least she kept them. Now she can tell Charlotte in person how dearly she wants to use this time to make a difference, to be braver than she ever felt she could be back at Girton. To be as brave as Charlotte has always been.

Even if Charlotte is angry at Beatrice, Sadie will help. The thought of Sadie's confident smile as she reached across the table for Beatrice's hand warms her. They'll make a good team, she is sure. If only Charlotte will have her.

CHAPTER TWENTY-TWO

CHARLOTTE

After several days in hospital, Charlotte is released, frail but stable. "You clever little minx," Sadie says when they return together to Park Lane. "A hunger strike? What were you thinking? The Hurstons are in a tizzy."

"Are they angry?" Now that the wooziness of hunger has worn off and she can see and think clearly again, Charlotte wonders if the Hurstons will punish her for going rogue. No one had authorized this kind of rebellion, not in any of the planning meetings or strategy sessions. Sadie's phrase, *hunger strike*, isn't something she's ever heard before; clearly, the Hurstons have been talking.

"Don't worry about it now," Sadie insists. "You need rest." And though Charlotte wants to protest, Sadie manages to put her to bed, and Charlotte falls into a deep sleep almost instantly. A few hours later she wakes to whispering outside the door.

"Is she awake?"

Charlotte stirs, rubbing her eyes. Then the door opens, just a crack, and she spots a halo of blond hair.

"Charlotte?" Beatrice whispers from the doorway. Sadie seems to give her a shove, and Beatrice walks up to Charlotte's bedside. "Oh, Charlotte, can you ever forgive me?"

Charlotte blinks, almost expecting Beatrice to disappear like a mirage. "How . . . Why are you here?" Her voice is raspy, but the note of accusation is clear.

Beatrice glances back toward the door, where Sadie's smile twitches with doubt. When Charlotte catches her eye, she blushes.

"I hope you don't mind," Sadie says. "But I looked through some of your things when you were in the hospital. I wanted to know if there was anyone I could contact, since you're not really in touch with your family. Anyway, I saw Beatrice's letters and—"

"I'm so sorry," Beatrice interrupts. Bea looks as lovely as ever, though perhaps a little thinner since they were last together at Girton. "I was haughty and foolish. I cannot tell you how sorry I am for abandoning you, abandoning all of this." She gestures toward the banners strung up on the walls, the VOTES FOR WOMEN pins and sashes scattered about the room.

Charlotte thinks about everything she has sacrificed since leaving Girton. Her education, her family, and now her health. She finds she has to will her eyes to focus; she is still exhausted to the bone.

"You'd be wise never to trust me again," says Beatrice. "But that is what I'm hoping you can do."

"Trust you?" Charlotte feels her resentment froth. The truth, which she hates to admit, is that it's *good* to see Beatrice again. "Why now?"

"Because," Beatrice says, taking a deep breath, "I'm joining you all. In the WSPU. At least until the spring. After that . . ." She holds up her left hand, revealing the twinkle of a silver band.

"You're engaged?"

She nods. "Daniel proposed after the King's College ball."

"Shouldn't you be with him, then?"

"We won't marry until after he graduates. I finished my law degree in the Michaelmas term. But I told my parents that I won't return to Kent to wait for Daniel. I'll work here in London until the wedding."

"But where will you stay? Surely your parents don't approve of the Union."

"They most certainly do not. But when I told them about a respectable house in Park Lane, teeming with Girton girls and chaperones, I managed to convince them. Sadie and I worked it all out while you were in hospital. I'll stay here with you two. That is," she adds, "if you'll have me."

Charlotte locks eyes with Sadie. All that secret planning while Charlotte was ill and Sadie didn't think to mention it? It's a welcome change to see Beatrice take her life into her own hands, at least for a little while. But Charlotte remembers the sting of Beatrice's rebukes, the burn of abandonment. Back in Cambridge, perhaps the stakes weren't as high. But now, now there is no turning back. If this last brutal stay in jail revealed anything, it's that there is no space for doubt, not even an inch.

"I'm serious about this," Beatrice says quietly, intuiting Charlotte's concern. "Please, will you give me a second chance? I want to prove myself to you. I know I owe you that. I promise I won't let you down again."

"Alright, Bea," Charlotte says, allowing herself to smile. "But we've got a lot to discuss."

"I'd say a discussion is best served over tea," Sadie interjects. "And for what it's worth, the kettle's about to boil over." She regards them both sternly, schoolmarm at the ready to wrangle her unruly pupils. "Well then," Sadie says, "that's settled. Now, Beatrice, let's put you to work."

The following day Sadie and Beatrice bundle Charlotte in blankets and prop her up on pillows in the parlor. She struggles to keep food down and finds that her fingers tremble uncontrollably, but it is comforting, after all, to have Bea here. She tries to focus on her friends, watching them buzz around preparing supper. Beatrice seems freer and lighter than she ever did at Girton. Charlotte wonders what has changed.

"Say *particular*," Beatrice demands of Sadie.

Sadie feigns insult but obliges in her American accent.

Beatrice squeals with laughter. "Par-tick-u-lar," she mimics, as Sadie slaps a chicken leg out of her hand.

"The damn Yankees!" Sadie shrieks, making fun of herself with an exaggerated drawl.

Both women have flour on their foreheads when a knock sounds at the front door. They look at one another and then Sadie scurries to answer it. A chilly gust of wind accompanies Adeline, Isabel, and Jessie into the house. A tightness crawls up Charlotte's throat as she anticipates Adeline's impending reproach. What if Mrs. Hurston expels her from the Union for the hunger strike? Then another thought, perhaps even more fearful, creeps into her mind. What if Mrs. Hurston asks her to do it again?

"Charlotte," Adeline says, approaching her at once. She still wears her traveling cloak, and her gray hair is swept into a stern bun at the nape of her neck. "How are you feeling?"

"A bit better, Mrs. Hurston," Charlotte says quietly. She can see Sadie and Beatrice holding their breath. "Thank you."

"Good," Adeline says, patting Charlotte's hand. "You showed those bastards in Holloway not to mess with us."

Charlotte blanches, her tongue caught in her throat. But Isabel bursts out laughing first, and then everyone joins in. Soon, they're all howling riotously, weeping with tears of laughter and relief.

"It smells delicious in here," Adeline says, straightening at last. "What's on the menu?"

"Roast chicken," Sadie says. "With buttered potatoes for our invalid."

"And who are you?" Adeline asks, turning to Beatrice.

Highborn Beatrice stands proud before the Union's leader and extends her hand. "Beatrice Piper, ma'am."

"Beatrice has volunteered to work with us until she gets married," Sadie explains, giving Beatrice's arm a light squeeze.

Beatrice rests her head on Sadie's shoulder for a moment before returning to the chicken. Adeline nods, a flare of amusement in her eye. Sadie's cheeks grow pink. Jessie and Isabel offer to set the table just as another knock comes from the door.

"Are we expecting anyone else?" Adeline asks.

Isabel opens the door, and there on the stoop stands a shivering Emily Brown.

"I'm so sorry to intrude," she begins, searching through the faces before landing on Charlotte.

Charlotte would have raced to the door if she could, but still too weak, she extends her arms wide.

After a moment's hesitation, Emily walks toward her and leans in for a hug. "Thank God you're okay," she whispers.

Charlotte breathes into her shoulder, eyes brimming with tears.

"Everyone, this is my dear friend Emily Brown," Charlotte announces. "But I think most of you have already met her, in one way or another."

Sadie introduces everyone and quickly pulls another chair toward the table.

"You must stay for dinner," Adeline insists.

"I can't stay long," Emily says.

"You didn't tell your father that you came here, did you?" Charlotte whispers.

Emily shakes her head.

"Well, I'm afraid you have to stay. We can't let the roast go cold. I'm rather hungry, you know."

At that, Emily breaks into a grin. "Oh, hush, Charlotte," she says. But she takes off her coat.

As everyone busies themselves with setting the table, Emily and Charlotte sit on their own. Emily is staring, her blue eyes narrowed with concern.

"What?" Charlotte says. "I'm doing better now, really I am."

"It's not that. It's just . . . well, I've never seen you *not* behind bars."

Charlotte laughs aloud. "I suppose not!"

"It's nice," Emily adds.

"I do hope so. It's quite preferable for me, too."

Emily bites back a rueful grin, her lips curling at the corners.

"Why are you here?" Charlotte asks.

"To visit you, of course."

"Sadie told me that you came to get her when I was taken to hospital. Thank you."

"I was so afraid for you. You really bloody scared me."

Charlotte locks eyes with Emily. "I'm sorry."

"I'm sorry, too," Emily insists.

"And thank you for helping me."

"Anytime."

"Promise?" Charlotte clasps Emily's hand.

Emily knits her brows together, puzzled. Then Adeline calls everyone to the table. Emily and Sadie help Charlotte up, and they all settle in around the modest feast. Adeline raises a glass. Everyone has wine, except for Charlotte, who drinks only a cup of milk. They've even convinced Sadie to indulge in a small glass, in spite of her commitment to temperance.

"To Charlotte's recovery," Adeline says.

"And to this meal," Isabel declares. "Thank you, Mayflower. Who ever said suffragettes don't know their way around a kitchen?"

Emily regards Isabel in confusion. Charlotte opens her mouth to explain the name, but Sadie interrupts.

"Hear, hear!" Sadie shouts. She takes the most burnt portion of the roast for herself.

The sounds of clinking and cutting ring through the room, creating a cozy and pleasant din. Charlotte feels stuffed after only a few bites, and though Sadie leans over and encourages her to eat, her stomach clenches uncomfortably. She pushes food around her plate, taking shallow breaths.

"I've just heard from Downing Street," Adeline says. "They are not pleased. Not pleased at all." She is smiling.

"Do you realize what a difference this has made?" Isabel asks, turning to Charlotte.

"Has it?" she manages to say. Dread creeps into her fingers and toes, cold as ice.

"From the start, we've been willing to push beyond the bounds of traditional protest," Adeline says. "Militancy is in our very constitution. But our militancy—our public marches and speeches and campaigns—has landed us in jail. And that is *all* it has done. Even Women's Sunday in Hyde Park, our grandest showing, had no result at all."

"Right," Jessie says, nodding vigorously. "They shut us up and lock us away. Treat us like common criminals and give us long sentences—"

"Which take us off the streets," adds Isabel.

"Now, however," says Adeline, "we have a new strategy. Why should we waste our time in jail, sacrificing our forces to endless sentences?"

"You're going to stop getting arrested?" Beatrice asks.

Adeline and Isabel chuckle.

"We couldn't stop getting arrested if we wanted to," Isabel explains. "It doesn't matter what we do—they invent crimes to lock us up."

"But we won't sit quietly in jail anymore," Adeline says.

"You don't mean," Emily says slowly, "more hunger striking?"

Charlotte feels as though she's going to be sick.

"That's precisely what I mean," Adeline says. "Charlotte was sentenced to a month, and she got out in four days. This is the next phase of our campaign."

"Mrs. Hurston, I don't think this is a good idea—" Charlotte begins.

"We'll all take turns," Adeline insists. "It is imperative that we keep the government's eyes upon us. We must keep causing disruptions and getting arrested. But we can't stop there. They cannot forget about us when we're locked away. We must protest our imprisonment, too."

"Good! I'll do it next. I'm happy to," Sadie exclaims.

"But Charlotte could have died," Emily says.

The table is silent for a moment.

"She didn't die," says Adeline. "And next time, we'll be prepared. We'll have eyes on the inside."

"Who?" asks Beatrice.

Six sets of eyes burn upon Emily. "Me."

PART TWO

WINTER 1912–1913

CHAPTER TWENTY-THREE

EMILY

Winter creeps into London, damp and cold, with frozen breath, raw skin, aching bones. The arrests continue, and the women of the Union fill Holloway's cells. Sadie arrives one bitter evening, sentenced to a month for heckling MPs outside Parliament. Emily is mopping the entry hall when they bring her in, and Sadie grins at her, her flaming hair illuminated in the sunset visible from the mouth of the corridor. Sadie asks loudly whether she will receive the privileges of a political prisoner as she jostles against the grip of the guards. They do not respond.

Emily averts her eyes as she strips off Sadie's clothes. "I'm sorry I have to do this," she mutters.

"Me too," Sadie whispers, before heaving one of the putrid prison boots against the wall with a feral shriek. Sadie goes on hunger strike immediately, leaving her very first serving of lukewarm broth to freeze. The guards catch on soon afterward and report to Thomas. The silence between father and daughter has been deafening since Emily's attempt to save Charlotte. His odd expression when he passes her in the corridors, a strangled, hesitant half smile, seems to ask whether or not Emily has heard, whether or not she will care, about this next woman's struggle. Emily has perfected a blank expression, rendering her emotions invisible. She lets him writhe, wondering.

The guards are not so silent.

"She says she'll eat if she can have her own clothes and what back."

Emily hears them talking in the courtyard, kicking at the dirt in the cold air. Martin takes a long drag from his hand-rolled cigarette as the other guard continues to expound.

"She says she ain't a common criminal. Well, I'm sorry, but she ain't bloody Queen Vic, neither." The guard spits on the ground.

After dark, Emily takes the torch and sneaks out of the cottage. Thomas's drinking has gotten worse, and at night he is as good as dead, passed out beneath the now-stained blankets he once shared with his wife. Emily hardly needs the light, so familiar is the path across the courtyard and through the labyrinth of cells. Her breath balloons before her and then dissipates into the darkness. Silent footsteps lead her straight to Sadie.

"Are you alright?" she whispers through the bars.

"Happy as a clam." Sadie's voice is flat but resolute.

"You sure I can't bring you something to eat? No one will have to know." Emily hates to watch her wither away in here, hates it. All of a sudden, she has a role, albeit a secret one, in this women's union—and yet she has never felt more helpless.

"No," she insists. "It has to be this way."

When the guards carry Sadie out on a stretcher after ninety hours, nearly four days, it's Emily's cue to let the suffragettes know. It feels cruel to knock on the door at Park Lane and explain that she watched with her very own eyes as their friend starved herself, weakened to the brink of death. Even though it is all part of the plan, and no one blames her, a small part of Emily blames herself. She is the only witness. When she explains what's happened, Beatrice, who opened the door, bursts into tears. Emily does not stay long.

That night she finds a note on the windowsill outside her bedroom, tucked beneath a stone and wedged into the corner. It's a single sheet of paper, with a ragged edge as though it had been ripped from a diary. Tiny handwriting spells out what appears to be, perhaps, a shopping list for a florist or gardener. She reads the items and quantities in confusion.

Mayflower - 10
Fern - 15
Foxglove - 17
Feather - 20

She grips the paper so tightly her fingertips turn white. Even as she wonders what it could mean, a sinking feeling tells her she already knows. Didn't Isabel call Sadie "Mayflower" at the dinner? Emily had been perplexed in the moment, but then they'd begun discussing more hunger strikes and she'd forgotten all about it.

Her pulse thrums with icy dread as she realizes what she holds in her hands. Emily closes the window and folds the paper, smaller and smaller until it is the size of a stamp. She guesses that the suffragettes have some kind of code, and if she is right, then Mayflower must be Sadie. Sadie, who appeared at Holloway four days ago, on the tenth of December.

The next day, Isabel arrives in the jail, arrested for interrupting an MP's speech from behind the grates of the Ladies' Gallery. Isabel is Fern, then, on the fifteenth of December. Over the course of the next week, the suffragettes appear on cue. The note, presumably from

Charlotte, though signed at the bottom simply Ivy, is like a stage play, a notation of characters in their order of appearance. Jessie, Foxglove, arrives on the seventeenth; Adeline, Feather, on the twentieth. It is sickening, the transformation of the innocent list into a schedule of the women's impending starvation. Sickening, but effective.

Thomas makes every effort to not mention the chorus of hunger striking suffragettes who come in and out of Holloway. But she listens as he and the doctor discuss it angrily behind his closed office door.

"They're making a fool out of me," Thomas says. "Of the government, of all of us."

She cannot hear the doctor's reply. He seems to speak softer every time Thomas erupts. Emily is embarrassed for her father, even as she resents his actions, even as she despises the doctor. Nearly every other day a suffragette is admitted to Holloway and another exits by stretcher, her pulse too fast, her stomach empty. But a month's sentence becomes just a few days. And so, they persist.

Meanwhile, Emily scrubs the cells until her skin is raw and her knees bruise beyond purple to a deep, indigo-tinged gray. She is saving money, preparing for her future. But the walls of Holloway close in around her. It is hard to imagine a world outside, a world in which she stands before a classroom instead of beside these cramped cells. The only contact she has with the outside world comes from Charlotte's notes, though they are infrequent and appear mysteriously on her bedroom windowsill. She does not question the network of women who somehow maintain these communiqués, but Emily learns to leave her replies and trust that they will get back to Charlotte. She provides short updates on the Union members in the cells, and asks questions that Charlotte never answers. Everything Ivy writes is urgent, brief, and coded.

The doctor comes and goes again, right on cue, to carry a weak and wan Adeline Hurston into the cold night of Christmas Eve.

"These bloody women can't just decide the length of their own sentences!" Thomas shouts, his face red, the vein in his temple leaping.

Emily scrawls a note to Charlotte. *I'm worried*, she writes. *The government is humiliated. I don't know what they'll do next.*

On Christmas, Emily wants so badly to hug her father, to return to those days when her parents made the holiday feel warm and lovely, even when they had so little. Marianne loved Christmas. She used to decorate their small cottage with berries and branches that she collected herself, strewing holly on the table and looping vines of ivy around Emily's bed. It wasn't much; they usually couldn't afford presents. Emily was lucky to receive new trim for an old dress, and perhaps some drawing pencils. But it is the warmth she misses most. The wonder. How at midnight on Christmas Eve, Marianne would lead Emily by the hand to step outside and watch their breath dissipate beneath the stars. The raw skin of Emily's grief is torn anew. The absence, the ache, is an open wound. Tears threaten all day, and when a knock on the door comes that evening, she is grateful for any distraction.

"It's for you," Thomas says.

Emily steps out to find Martin puffing hot breath into his hands as he shifts his weight from side to side on the stoop. He holds a package, fist-sized and wrapped in brown paper.

"Oh, Martin, you didn't have to—"

"I wanted to," he says. They stand awkwardly.

"Shall I open it?"

"Yes, yes, go ahead."

She unties the rough string. It's a miniature cake, only the size of a few bites, but decorated with colorful sugar and frosting. A Christmas scene is painted on its palm-sized surface.

"Thank you," she whispers. A tear rolls down her cheek, and she wipes it clumsily. There is no reason for her to be crying right now, absolutely not. But her emotions have been so close to the surface these last few days, too close. She feels constantly on the brink of shattering, like in storybooks when children go skating on frozen ponds, and one step too far sends them plummeting beneath the icy waters. She is crying in earnest now, and it is almost a relief to allow herself, finally, to be submerged.

"Here," Martin says, taking her cold hand into his own. "Shh."

He brushes his lips against her temple, gentle as a breath. Her whole body shudders.

"Happy Christmas, Emily."

CHAPTER TWENTY-FOUR

BEATRICE

Sadie returns from hospital thin and ashen faced. The sight of her makes Beatrice feel ill. Both of her friends have gone on hunger strikes now, returning battered and weakened. Still, when Sadie lights eyes on Beatrice, her whole demeanor changes, joy and warmth spreading across her pale face. And when Sadie insists on a proper Christmas tree, Beatrice and Charlotte leap to the task, haphazardly stringing popped corn around a rather scrappy branch of spruce.

"I'm sure it's nothing like the great evergreens of Massachusetts," Beatrice says as they prop the lopsided branch in the parlor.

"It's even better," Sadie says.

Beatrice's parents send a hamper full of gifts; they've decided to spend the holiday with relatives in Scotland, and as a result, Beatrice is able to stay in London. She unwraps a dowdy shawl from her mother and places it over Sadie's shoulders. Even in her weakened state, Sadie manages to throw it across the room with a shriek.

"That," she moans, "is the most hideous shawl I've ever seen!"

"My mother sent it for my 'chaperone.'" Beatrice giggles, reading the card. "Who, I may have implied, is somewhere around the age of seventy." Daniel sends a gift, too, in the form of a small velvet jewelry box. Beatrice regards the gift impassively and then tucks it away upstairs without another word.

Beatrice has been bunking with Sadie ever since her arrival. At night they take turns telling stories, and Charlotte piles into the other girls' bed. When the candles have burned down to the stubs, Charlotte at last drags herself down the hall to her own bedroom, whispering, "Good night and happy Christmas."

"Finally," Sadie whispers.

Silently, Beatrice rolls over so they are facing each other. Sadie reaches out to twirl a strand of Beatrice's hair in her fingers. Beatrice shivers, but she doesn't withdraw, and Sadie runs her hand down Beatrice's arm, goosepimples erupting beneath her touch. She aches beneath her thin nightgown.

Beatrice can hear her heart hammering in her skull, radiating from the place where Sadie's touch lingers. She inhales, a ragged breath, and closes her eyes.

"I have a story," Beatrice says, her voice soft. "This one is just for you." Sadie nods.

"It was the summer before Girton, and I had spent the previous year away at finishing school." Beatrice speaks quietly, but the words tumble out of her mouth in a hurry, like she's been holding them in for too long. "When I returned home, I bumped into Grace, my childhood friend. Every day that summer, Grace would visit me in the stables, and we'd go for rides as far from my parents' house as possible.

"One afternoon we were racing up a hilltop, edging the horses faster and faster. Then, well, I'm still not quite sure how it happened, but there was a branch hanging lower than we remembered. I heard an awful sound, *thwack*.

"It was too late for me to slow down, but it was like time stood still for a split second as I watched Grace fall to the ground, and I remembered a piece of advice my father gave me years before: if you ever fall off a horse, keep rolling and you won't get trampled. I screamed it to her then, 'Keep rolling!'"

Sadie's eyes are wide.

"My horse July's hooves narrowly missed her head. A few yards up I slowed enough to leap out of the saddle and I ran back to Grace, still flattened in the mud, so silent, so still. I was terrified. But then, she started to laugh."

"Thank God!" Sadie whispers.

Beatrice, her expression morose, forces herself to keep speaking, her voice like an automaton, emotionless as she wills the words out of her mouth.

"In that moment, with twigs in her hair, Grace had never looked so beautiful. And—" Beatrice squeezes her eyes shut. "I kissed her."

Sadie swallows.

"Grace slapped me across the face and stormed away. I wanted to die. I swore I would never give in to temptation like that again. Later that summer, Grace began spreading rumors in Kent society. Which, of course, got back to my mother, who came home from a game of bridge having learned that her daughter suffered from unnatural tendencies, was mentally unstable, and should perhaps explore a stay in a sanatorium should the symptoms persist. My mother forced me into my bedroom and barred the door until the doctor arrived."

"Bea, I'm so sorry."

Beatrice shakes her head, unable to meet Sadie's gaze.

"No one mentioned Grace directly, or even what *symptoms* were implied in the rumors. But the doctor's assessment of my so-called horse-riding obsession led to his prescription of the rest cure. For the remainder of the summer, I was forced to stay in my room and avoid any mental or physical exertion. No reading, especially novels. No riding. Nothing. It was just terrible."

Deeply bored and profoundly ashamed, Beatrice had watched the shadows arc across the walls. She'd watched the wooden furniture glint gold in the afternoon light. She watched the wallpaper curl and peel in the corner by her bed. She thought about the sinful impulse that had ruined her friendship with Grace, that look of shock and revulsion marring her friend's face. She alternated between being angry at Grace and simply hating herself.

"At last," Bea said, "autumn arrived, and it was time to go to Girton. There had been a few weeks over the summer when I had thought I'd lost my chance at college, that the doctor would insist on bedrest for months or even years more. I considered ways to kill myself."

"No," Sadie breathes.

"But for the first time in years, my parents agreed on something, and that was to let me go to Girton."

Before she left, Helen whispered to Beatrice that the housemother, Mrs. Pennington, would keep an eye out should any *symptoms* arise. And that if she was not engaged to be married by graduation, Beatrice would be admitted to a sanatorium. The notion sent ice through Beatrice's veins, but when she arrived in Cambridge, she finally felt free.

"I think of it as *the incident*," Beatrice says, meeting Sadie's gaze. There is compassion there, in Sadie's eyes, and something else, too. Recognition. "I think it explains a lot. About me."

"Thank you for telling me," Sadie says. She squeezes Beatrice's hand tight, and for the first time, Beatrice does not recoil.

The incident was an admission, a confirmation. The incident was why Beatrice did not remain by Charlotte's side after Mrs. Pennington caught them hawking *Votes for Women*. It was why she agreed to a hasty engagement with Daniel Rosseter.

That night, when Beatrice finally closes the space between them and reaches out to stroke Sadie's cheek, her hands are trembling.

CHAPTER TWENTY-FIVE

CHARLOTTE

A deline Hurston sends a note to Park Lane written in code, which Charlotte puzzles over at the breakfast table. Recently, postal workers had been accepting bribes from the government in exchange for information on the whereabouts of the WSPU's leadership, according to information gleaned by a suffragette spy, hence the need for this elaborately coded missive. Charlotte deciphers the letter, smiling to herself at the thought of bewildered postal workers reading about what seems more like a description for a flower arrangement than a plan of action.

Adeline has arranged a meeting for Charlotte to attend on her behalf, as Adeline is still recovering from her last hunger strike. She is older, and it takes longer for her to regain her strength. Rather curiously, Adeline has suggested that Emily should accompany Charlotte. The letter gives Charlotte pause, but she does not question orders from the Hurstons. And so, one windy morning in January, she walks to the back gates of Holloway.

It is strange to see Holloway from behind. It looks no less imposing, with its blood-red bricks and high towers. But somehow, from this vantage point, Charlotte can look it in the eye without fear. She is a free woman, at the moment, and she can go wherever she wishes. It feels like a pleasant little rebellion.

Emily appears at the gate and tugs a cap off her head, setting loose her wispy curls. She glances over her shoulder once before stepping out into the street, and Charlotte knows instantly that Emily has not uttered a word of this to her father. Which is a good thing, of course. When Emily turns back to face Charlotte, certain that the coast is clear, she blinks rapidly in the bitter air.

"You look much better."

"Thanks. I feel better, too." In a quiet voice Charlotte adds, "Mrs. Hurston thinks I'm nearly strong enough to do it again."

Emily grimaces. "And how is Sadie?"

"Much improved. But I'm glad you're coming with me today."

"And where, exactly, are we going?" Emily asks.

Charlotte could not risk putting any more information than was necessary in the note.

"You're going to like it." Charlotte links her arm through Emily's, but Emily doesn't move. "Are you alright?"

"It's just . . . well, I said I could be your eyes on the inside. But I . . . I can't afford to get into trouble."

"I know," Charlotte says. "I promise you won't." She thinks: *Not today.*

They walk toward the station, boarding the Northern Express. The train car is far cozier than the one she rode in, alone and terrified, when she left Girton nearly three months ago. The seats are plush, and deep wooden panes outline the frost-coated windows. The train lurches to a start with a great puff of smoke, and soon the rattling lull of motion begins.

"I know it isn't my place to judge," Emily begins. "But I'll never forgive myself if I don't say something."

"Go on, then."

"I have to say that I think the hunger strikes are a mistake," Emily says, speaking in a fast whisper. "I hate to see the pain you all endure. Starving yourselves, depriving your bodies. I . . . well, I consider us friends, and it's horrible to watch you suffer like that."

"We *are* friends," Charlotte says, squeezing Emily's hand. "And it's no picnic for us, believe me." Charlotte is tempted to confess that she despises the hunger strikes. She hates to watch her friends and allies suffer, and that vertiginous faintness she felt in the final hours of her own strike was so terrifying she refuses to think about it if she can help it. Death loomed in her cell that day, an arm's length away, bearing down on her with rattling breath.

But Emily is searching Charlotte's face for weakness, and Charlotte won't let it show. The cause is bigger than all of them. And they need Emily's help—more, perhaps, than Emily even realizes. Charlotte had better keep her doubts to herself.

"But four days of suffering is much better than weeks or even months behind bars," Charlotte insists. "It hurts, and it's hard, but we get back to our work so much faster. Until the government is willing to treat us like political prisoners instead of common criminals, we must resist our unlawful imprisonment."

"But nothing is changing," Emily argues quietly. "And the government is getting frustrated. My father can't stand it. I worry that things will get worse before they get better."

"We're worried, too," Charlotte admits. "Which is why I've brought you today."

London has faded to a gray speck on the horizon. They hurtle past brown fields frosted with a thin layer of snow that sparkles like sugar beneath the crystalline sky.

"Lady Constance Cunningham is one of the wealthiest supporters of the WSPU. She's been funding our campaign for several years now. Did you hear about our meeting at the Royal Albert Hall?"

Emily shakes her head.

"Well, we were able to let the hall, which seats six thousand, thanks to Lady Cunningham's donation. She and Mrs. Hurston were friends years ago when Mrs. Hurston worked for the village almshouse. I've met her a few times now."

"So, we're visiting Lady Cunningham today?"

"Yes. With an important message."

"What is it?"

"Just follow my lead."

Sunlight creeps over the stone façade of Hazelwood Hall. The windows gleam milky white, opaque and impenetrable. Manicured gardens encircle the drive, and the leaves of the hedgerows and shrubbery are tinted silver with frost. At the grand front doors, liveried footmen stand like toy soldiers. For such a large place, it is remarkably quiet, as though the manor itself projects a hush upon all who approach, compelling visitors to admire its imposing splendor in silence. The manor is a mile's walk from the train station, and puffs of hot breath escape from their lips into the still air. Their frozen toes crunch into the gravel just as the great oak doors swing open. The footmen's faces remain impassive as their mistress strides past.

"Miss Evans," the woman murmurs.

Charlotte dips into a deep curtsey. "Lady Cunningham, may I present my companion, Miss Emily Brown."

Lady Cunningham's eyes are a translucent blue, almost eerily clear, and ringed with delicate smile lines that deepen as she studies their faces. Emily curtseys clumsily.

"Miss Brown. A pleasure," Lady Cunningham says, rolling each word slowly off her tongue. "Please, do come inside."

They follow the petite woman through the foyer and toward the drawing room. Her hair is streaked with silver, but she walks briskly. Charlotte catches Emily staring as they float between lush carpets and marble tiles. Her eyes dart along the halls of ancient portraits, up the broad mahogany staircase, and to the tables laden with exquisite trinkets. It reminds Charlotte of visiting the ornately decorated rooms of the other students at Girton. She had felt as though if she looked too close, she would never be able to tear her eyes away.

"Thank you for your hospitality, Lady Cunningham," Charlotte says as they sit down.

Emily is silent, eyes wide.

"It is a pleasure to see you again, Miss Evans. How is Mrs. Hurston?"

"She is recovering well, thank you, and will soon return to work."

"Of course she will. I'd expect nothing less from her," Lady Cunningham says fondly.

"She always speaks so warmly of you," Charlotte adds.

"And who exactly are you, Miss Brown?"

"Emily, if you please. I am . . ." Emily glances at Charlotte, who nods. "I am the daughter of the warden of Holloway." She keeps her eyes fixed on her folded hands.

Lady Cunningham's face is impassive, but she inhales sharply before saying, "Tea?" She gestures to the fine silver teapot at the side table. Emily stands to retrieve it and nearly bumps into a footman. Her whole face turns bright red. Charlotte winces.

"How kind of you, Miss Brown," Lady Cunningham says gently. "But Alfred will pour our tea."

"Of course," Emily mumbles, returning to her seat, her cheeks still burning. *Perhaps*, Charlotte thinks, *bringing Emily was a mistake*. But no, it was Adeline's decision. And Lady Cunningham, for all of her pomp, is smiling at them benevolently.

"So," she says, nodding as the footman fills her dainty cup. "How can I be of service to you?"

Charlotte smiles. "As you know, Lady Cunningham, we have begun a new tactic in our protest campaign—the hunger strike. Already several of our members, myself included, have refused food when the jailers deny our rights as political prisoners. As a result, we've been released from our sentences after only a few days."

"Indeed, I have read about your efforts," Lady Cunningham says. "When Mrs. Hurston comes to visit, she usually asks me to lend my purse. I have a feeling, however, that such is not the case today?"

"No, your ladyship. We had hoped, as it were, that *you* would participate in our new line of protest. As you say, you've read about the hunger strikes. But soon, the press will move on to another story. And we need to keep hold of their attention. We thought perhaps—"

"I would be worth writing about?" Lady Cunningham finishes. She leans in conspiratorially. "I was wondering when you'd ask. I shall consider it. But first, can you promise me one thing?"

Charlotte doesn't even glance at Emily. They will make whatever promises she requires. "Of course."

"Please, just call me Constance."

Charlotte grins. "Thank you, Constance. I certainly will."

"Good," she says. "Crumpet?"

Constance Cunningham is a remarkably well-humored woman considering that she was brought up in what was essentially a castle. She'd gone out into society in the seventies and had been presented to Queen Victoria herself. It is as though they live in entirely different worlds. Charlotte can only imagine how overwhelmed Emily must feel. But they find themselves laughing at Constance's rather lewd jokes and easing into her velvet cushioned chairs as though they have known her forever. Constance is warm and funny, but she is also sharp. She knows the weight her words hold, and she wields them bluntly.

"Emily," she says. "What exactly are you doing with the WSPU? The daughter of the warden—doesn't that sound like a conflict of interests?"

Emily's fingers tremble and she quickly sets down her teacup. "Well, my lady," she begins.

"Constance."

"Right. Constance. I . . . I don't entirely know. Charlotte is my friend. We got to know each other when she was in Holloway, actually. I just came to accompany her today."

"I see."

"Emily is our eyes on the inside," Charlotte explains. "A double agent, so to speak. She passes information to the prisoners from the outside world, and vice versa."

Emily shifts in her seat.

When the dinner bell rings, Constance sits up straighter. "Ah, my husband must be back," she says. "I'm afraid I can't invite you to stay. Lord Cunningham has a few gentlemen guests, and I daresay they wouldn't take kindly to sharing their table with suffragettes."

"I'm not—" Emily begins.

"Of course," Charlotte cuts in. "Thank you for your hospitality, Constance. And please do think over what we've discussed."

"I will," she says, leading Emily and Charlotte to the door. "I'll have our chauffeur deliver you to the station."

Together they climb into the automobile, waving to Constance through the window, and the fairytale splendor of Hazelwood Hall fades behind them.

"I'm so sorry," Emily begins. "I know I sounded daft. Interrupting and, I just, I don't know what came over me in there—that house was enormous!"

"You don't have to be sorry," Charlotte says, settling against the leather seats. "I think it went really well."

"You don't have to lie to me. Lady Cunningham didn't even agree to a hunger strike. And, I'm sorry, but I don't think you understand how insignificant I am. I'm not your eyes on the inside. I just happen to be there, but I couldn't do anything to save you even when I tried."

"Emily! Enough with the apologies. Constance agreed to consider the strike. She is a very strategic woman. This is *good*. And as for you, I think you'll find you are more capable than you realize."

The car sweeps past fields of frost-covered grasses and Emily dares to smile. "Really? Oh, I thought I'd ruined it all." She laughs aloud. "I mean, the teapot—I was so nervous!"

"You'll get better with practice. That wasn't so bad, really."

"That house, though . . . It's the kind of place you imagine, perhaps look at from afar—but to go inside . . ." Emily clasps Charlotte's hand.

"I know." Charlotte laughs. "I kept waiting for Mr. Darcy to come in from around a corner."

Charlotte raises Emily's hand to her lips and plants a kiss upon it.

"My lord," she intones in a low, manly voice.

"My liege," Emily replies in turn, and they both burst out laughing.

CHAPTER TWENTY-SIX

EMILY

In the days following their trip to Hazelwood Hall, Emily alternates between feelings of awe and ire, imagining what it would be like to live there. Constance had been a gracious hostess during their brief visit, and kind in spite of Emily's missteps. But something about the encounter makes her skin crawl. It had to be the manor itself—so vast, so lavish. Every surface was gilded. She tries not to calculate how much even the teacup from which she sipped might be worth. The sum would make her vomit. Charlotte seemed unfazed by the encounter. Still, how could anyone grow accustomed to that kind of wealth, immune to the splendor? Emily knows she never could. In some ways, she feels like she hardly knows Charlotte at all.

Thomas grumbles about the suffragettes' new routine, and Emily admits—only to herself, of course—that perhaps her doubt had been misplaced. Charlotte's idea is still working well. Overall, the women are spending far less time locked up in Holloway. The hunger strikes have become a standard procedure: three days starving, summon the doctor on day four, send them home. But that does not mean Emily finds it any less upsetting to witness. Nor does it mean that she has any less work to do. The skin on her hands is permanently chapped, her fingers stiff and sore from the cold by the time she returns home each evening, depleted, to make their supper and go to sleep.

In these stupors of exhaustion, she cannot help but wonder how the great Lady Cunningham spends her days—wandering the corridors of her mansion, servants always tiptoeing around to light her fires and bring her furs. Emily invents the bit about the furs on a particularly frigid night when no number of shawls piled on top of each other can stop her teeth from chattering. For all of Call-Me-Constance's promises, Emily has not seen her enter Holloway like the rest of the volunteers.

Charlotte keeps her word and keeps Emily out of trouble. Since their trip to Hazelwood Hall, no future missions have been mentioned. The silence is unsettling. Not that she wants to be more involved. Or to get caught. But it's a strange, liminal place in which Emily finds herself, disconnected from the Union's activities and yet somehow also at their beck and call. A week passes, then two, without any word. Has she done something wrong? Charlotte did say they were friends—an admission Emily finds both buoying and terrifying—but what if the suffragettes found a better ally elsewhere? It would be easier, she thinks sometimes, if the suffragettes moved on without her. But the thought of more meaningless sweeping and mopping while her friends continue their work is no comfort. When at last a note arrives in the beginning of February, excitement surges in her chest even as it mingles with dread.

The hinge is almost too frozen to raise the window, but at last she manages to retrieve the small slip of paper wedged into the corner of the sill, and she rips it open at once.

> *I do apologize for my silence; I know it's been some time since we were last together. I've made an appointment later this week and I expect I'll be seeing you after. Wishing you well.*
>
> *Ivy*

Emily feels cold as ice, hardly because of the temperature outside. She knows that Charlotte's "appointment" is some kind of protest. One that will lead to her arrest. Emily tosses the note into the fire, and it spits tiny sparks. The note is burnt to gray ash by the time Thomas opens the front door. He steps inside, his face stretched into a smile. It catches Emily off guard, that unexpected giddiness.

"Hello, my dear," he says.

She winces. That is the greeting he had once reserved for Marianne. She still remembers crawling under the kitchen table and watching her parents embrace upon her father's return from work. "Darling," Marianne always replied as she kissed his cheek.

"Good evening, Papa," Emily says, turning away from him. She busies herself with the kettle, subtly assessing how drunk he is tonight.

"That Martin is a good lad," he says, slurring only slightly.

"Oh?"

"We've just been talking with Dr. Bainwright, you know?"

"Yes, of course." *The bastard.*

"He's been here to discuss some new developments. Martin had some clever ideas of his own. I was impressed. That young man is going places, mark my words."

"Is that so?"

"You know he fancies you, Emily. You ought to give him some encouragement, now and again."

Perhaps, Emily thinks, *Thomas is a little more than tipsy.* She finally turns to face him, and he gazes at her with such affection that she pities him, forcing a smile across her cheeks.

"He could be your way out," he adds, taking Emily's hand.

"What do you mean, Papa?"

"That's a promising young man who will be able to take care of a wife and family. Unlike me." Thomas is definitely drunk. His eyes well with tears and his voice grows gravelly. "Your mother died because she worked too hard in those mills. And even here, the labor in the cold cells—it killed her. You don't have to live like that. It's all I want for you. Marry somebody who can keep you safe."

"Papa," she murmurs, prying her hand out of his insistent grip. "I don't need to marry right now. I'm only eighteen. I'm going to do the teacher's course."

"But you wouldn't have to," he says, eyes shining. "You wouldn't have to work at all."

"It's what Mama wanted, remember? I promised her."

Thomas waves a hand gracelessly. "Just—" He clears his throat. "Think about it."

"I'm going to bed, Papa."

"Please." His voice cracks.

"Fine." Emily walks to her bedroom as though moving through molasses and only when the door is firmly closed does she crumple. What would Marianne say to this? Would she agree, and want her daughter to be cared for above all else? *No*, Emily thinks. Marianne wanted her to be a teacher so that she could take care of herself. Nonetheless, she feels the weight of her father's hope. He may be misguided. But he is the one who is here now, not Marianne.

Emily thinks about the Christmas cake. She cannot deny that Martin is, as Thomas said, a good lad.

CHAPTER TWENTY-SEVEN
CHARLOTTE

Rush the House of Commons!" Charlotte shouts into the crowd. From where she stands, at the mouth of the lion statues in Trafalgar Square, the bodies in the street below writhe like a mass of crawling ants. "Next week! Come demand votes for women!"

"Votes for women!" Isabel repeats.

Beatrice beams at Charlotte from the opposite lion. The audience echoes their chant.

When Charlotte, Beatrice, and Isabel left headquarters together early that morning, she felt a new sense of closeness in their shared purpose. Charlotte had been asked by Isabel and Adeline specifically to help train Beatrice as a public speaker.

"You're one of our very best," Adeline had said.

Charlotte tried not to show it on her face, but her chest warmed with pride.

Of course, Beatrice is a quick study. By the afternoon, when they've been in the square for a few hours, the three women are completely attuned to each other. They take turns shouting, so the others can rest their voices, and when aggressive hecklers yell or grab at their skirts, the others are always ready to assist. There is a pleasure, too, in imagining Isabel telling her mother about today's rousing protest. Adeline's pride in her will be worth every insult flung at them.

Isabel nods, giving Charlotte her cue to begin another speech. She never feels as alive as she does in this moment, right before she begins to speak. She always starts jittery, no matter if she is speaking to a small crowd on a street corner or an audience of hundreds like this one. But then there is a moment when suddenly her anxious energy melts into a blissful state of calm. It is like being underwater, transported. All of the noise melts away and it is just Charlotte and her words.

That is probably why she doesn't notice the arrival of the police at the square, at least not at first. She doesn't notice the jostling in the crowd. Only when she catches sight of the expression on Beatrice's face does she realize something is wrong. Beatrice's jaw tightens, and with a quick glance toward Isabel, the two women hop down from the platform. Charlotte continues the sentence she'd been midway through delivering, keeping an eye on Beatrice and Isabel as her friends camouflage into the crowd. There is a fraction of a second in which to make this decision. Charlotte is tempted to descend from the ledge and disappear into the throngs of people. Her brain knows what is next, knows all too well the pain of the hunger strike to come, but her body roots her in place. And then the window has passed. Charlotte stays.

The officers approach, elbowing through the crowd. From her perch, still high up on the lions' platform, the officers are several feet below. Charlotte knows she could kick one straight in the mouth if she wanted—and, admittedly, she considers it—but of course, she does not. As Adeline has said thousands of times, the suffragettes are nonviolent activists, rousing the citizenry with democratic remarks. *Peaceful protest*, Charlotte repeats to herself, even as her blood boils. *At least until Holloway.*

"Get down from there," a wide-set, mustachioed bobby demands.

She approaches the edge of the stone edifice. Deep within the crowd, Isabel gives the faintest nod before she and Beatrice disappear entirely, swallowed into the mass of bodies.

"You're under arrest," the other officer sneers.

Charlotte extends her hand, as though a gentleman is escorting her out of a carriage and not taking her into police custody. Through gritted teeth, she allows them to lead her toward the street. She will save her resistance for jail, though she cannot help stiffening, just a bit, when the officer digs his nails into her shoulder. *Let the strike begin*, she thinks, strapped into the back of the police wagonette, jostling through the crowded Westminster streets. Her stomach is already clenching. She wills the memory of her weakened body being lifted onto a hospital stretcher out of her mind, but her last hunger strike is seared like flame onto the backs of her eyelids.

The city flashes past along the bumpy road. The spire of Big Ben casts a shadow over Parliament Square, and then they weave through neighborhoods where filthy children sit on stoops, looking out at the passing vehicle with orb-like eyes. Sentencing at the Old Bailey is a blur of bureaucratic jargon. And then she is back at Holloway, with its familiar, menacing towers. The officers hand their captive off to the guards, who drag her down the long throat of the central passageway and into the belly of the jail's main holding area. She is stripped of her clothing and forced into the prison uniform. The process is no less humiliating than it was her very first time. She throws a standard-issue boot at one of the guards, but she misses.

"I want to write a letter," she says, even though she knows—everyone knows—that it is futile. "I demand the privileges of a political prisoner."

The guards drag her deeper into the prison than she has ever been before, locking her away in a cell far from the other inmates. *They're wising up*, Charlotte thinks.

The letter had warned Emily of Charlotte's arrival, and so it is no surprise when Emily finds her cell that first night.

"Isabel and Bea escaped," Charlotte says, gripping the bars.

"But you couldn't?" Emily whispers. Her eyes are ringed with shadow.

"I wouldn't." Charlotte tries to ignore her racing pulse. It's only been a few hours without food, but her body anticipates the impending deprivation. Her heart pounds in preemptive protest. *I will make the sacrifices that are required of me*, she thinks, the words from Isabel Hurston's very first speech in the meeting hall in Cambridge thrumming through her mind like a mantra.

"The doctor is already here, talking with my father," Emily says. "I don't know why. It's too early for you to get discharged."

"Maybe he's here for another inmate?"

"There is no one else," Emily says. "You'd better get some rest."

"Thanks for stopping by."

Emily nods, just once, then disappears into the darkness. The first day of the hunger strike, Charlotte fixes her mind on reliving the excitement of yesterday's speeches. They managed to speak to hundreds, if not perhaps thousands, of passersby and supporters alike. A photographer captured her image, her arm raised as she stood before the great lion statue. When she closes her eyes, Charlotte can still see the flashbulb.

On the second day of the hunger strike, when she can no longer replay the demonstration in her mind, and her own stomach's protest grows too loud, she begins to feel faint. The walls seem to close in, and she stretches out her arms to reassure herself of the cell's size. It is so cramped she can nearly touch both walls at once with her arms extended. It feels like a coffin. And soon, she can no longer stand up or stretch out her arms at all. She can hardly swallow. Her hands shake just trying to pull the blanket around her sharp shoulders.

By midafternoon, when it has been nearly forty-eight hours, the doctor arrives. "Charlotte," he says, drawing out the syllables with relish. He has dropped all pretense of propriety. She is not *Miss* Evans to him, but Charlotte. Still, channeling the Hurstons, she addresses him politely.

"Good afternoon, Dr. Bainwright." Her papery tongue is too dry for her mouth. She wonders why he is here, and hopes, perhaps, that he will release her even earlier than last time, saving them both the trouble since he already knows of her resolve to carry out the hunger strike.

"You're coming with me," he says as Thomas Brown approaches with jangling keys. He unlocks the cell and steps back so that he and a rough-handed guard can enter.

"Where are you taking me?" Already her brain is muddled, her vision blurs. No one answers, and each man grips one of her arms. Charlotte chances a sidelong glance at the guard, pleading, but he refuses to meet her eye. They pull her out into the corridor and she looks back toward Mr. Brown. His eyes are trained firmly on the ground.

CHAPTER TWENTY-EIGHT

EMILY

N ow, isn't this grand?" Martin and Emily emerge from the Under-
ground and blink in the sunlight. Bond Street bustles with shop-
pers and somewhere in the distance a street performer plucks at a
violin. "This way."

Emily holds Martin's hand tentatively, allowing him to guide her
through the crowd until they cross the street.

"Where to now?" Emily asks. She met Martin outside the Holloway
gates this morning, her day off. She hadn't planned to leave the few blocks
surrounding the jail, but Martin tipped his hat, said he had the day off, too,
and invited her on an adventure. "Sure," she'd said, too surprised to object.

"My lady," he says now, in a posh accent, tucking her hand into the
crook of his elbow. "Shall we admire the . . . er, offerings?"

"You mean, good sir," she plays along, "peruse the wares of these
fine establishments?"

"I do, indeed." Martin's ears pinken.

They stride together, arms linked, toward the billowing banners
of Selfridges department store. The shiny windows reveal displays of
sumptuous dresses, elegant hats, a man's silk suit.

"I suppose this shall suffice," Martin says, still in his accent.

"What do you mean?"

"For my wardrobe, of course. Though the silk is a tad excessive. But it shall keep me cool in the summer."

Emily giggles; she can't help it.

"And you, darling, will look positively dashing in that gown."

She looks into his eyes, framed by wispy lashes. Martin grins and drops the accent.

"This way, now."

He guides her through narrow streets, and all of a sudden Emily is aware of the heat between their clasped hands. For a fleeting moment, she wonders how Charlotte is doing at Holloway. She'd forgotten her day off entirely until Thomas reminded her last night, too distracted by Charlotte's hunger strike. But Emily pushes the thought from her mind. Martin looks over his shoulder at her and catches her eye, and something in the pit of her stomach swoops pleasantly.

They've stopped at the Marble Arch entrance to Hyde Park.

"Oh," Emily says.

"What is it?"

"I used to come here with my mother."

"I'm sorry, Emily. I didn't realize. We can leave if you'd like."

"No, it's alright. It's nice, actually. I've missed coming here."

Martin leads her to a bench and they sit. He releases her hand and she weaves her fingers into his.

"You must miss your mum," he says.

"I do. Every single day." Emily sighs. "Where is your family? I'm sorry I've never asked."

Martin smiles. "I rent a room in Clerkenwell with my two older brothers. They work in the shipyards. I also have three younger brothers, still at home with my parents on the East End."

"Six boys? Your poor mother," says Emily.

"Ha," Martin laughs. "Too right. I try to send some money home each month, for food and such." He looks down, adding, "I wish I knew for sure it fed my brothers, but I'm afraid most of what I give my parents ends up in the pubs."

Emily is quiet, watching as Martin's brow softens.

"I like spending the day with you," he says.

"Me too." She is aware of how close they are, hip to hip on this bench. She could rest her head on his shoulder if she tilted only a few inches. Martin leans closer and then, suddenly, his lips are pressed against hers.

Martin's lips are so much softer than she imagined, warm and ringed by tufts of scratchy stubble. One of his hands comes up to cradle her head, while the other circles around her to rest on the small of her back, pulling her close to his body. Her mind goes blank and she relaxes into his embrace for just a moment. Then she withdraws, staring at him. A small smile creeps across his face.

"Was that alright?" he asks.

She nods. Her lips tingle with the taste of him. Scarlet rises up Martin's face and he laughs.

"I've been wanting to do that for a long time, Em."

"Have you, now?" She finds her voice. "And did it live up to your expectations?"

He lets out a ragged breath. "Even better."

On the way back home, they stop a few blocks from Holloway to say goodbye.

"I've had the best day," Martin says. "I hope we can do this again sometime."

"I'd like that," Emily says. "What are the chances our days off align again?"

"I'm sure it can be arranged. I actually—" Martin blushes. "When your father told me he had given you the day off, I asked if I could have today, too."

"My father told you? Why?"

"I reckon he thinks you've been working too hard."

Emily thinks back to last night, when Thomas reminded her not to come to work today. Something niggles the back of her mind.

"I should get going," Martin says. He leans in and Emily offers him her cheek; it's too close to home, to the neighborhood where everyone knows her, to allow him to kiss her properly. He seems to understand, squeezing her hand before heading in the opposite direction.

Emily unlatches the iron gate and enters the prison courtyard. The building is dark for the night, though the sunset still streaks pink in the sky. The windows of the prison glow a menacing onyx.

CHAPTER TWENTY-NINE
CHARLOTTE

S hrieks echo throughout the jail, guttural, animal. Her body is flattened against a hard-backed wooden chair and someone's screams ricochet off the cinderblock walls. It doesn't sound like her own voice. It doesn't even sound human. It's a disembodied wail, a ghost, a fury. Thomas and a guard each hold an arm until they can secure the leather straps that bind her in place, and together they force her into a seated position. The knobs of her spine smash against the wood; her coccyx crunches. As soon as they withdraw, she bucks her hips up, refusing to sit still. They slam her back down again, a grotesque waltz.

Then, from the shadows, Dr. Bainwright emerges with an unfamiliar wardress beside him, one of those few female employees like Emily whose job is usually to strip the prisoners and put them in the Holloway uniform. They never stay long, these women, for it is unforgiving labor. Strange instruments clatter in her hands, something long and tubular, and another conical piece, like a funnel.

Charlotte lets out another wail, and the wardress claps a hand over her own mouth, horrified. Dr. Bainwright fixes the woman with a look of daggers, and her eyes dart between the doctor and the prisoner.

Meanwhile, Charlotte kicks as the guards hold her firmly in the chair. The woman hands the doctor a metal instrument with quivering hands and he forces it into Charlotte's mouth. She can taste his fingers on her lips, sweaty, hairy, as he cranks open her jaw. She is frozen, mouth open unnaturally wide, like a pig for slaughter. Then, with a nod to the wardress, the doctor takes the arm-length tube and begins to snake it down Charlotte's throat. She instantly gags, her whole body thrashing reflexively in revolt.

Balancing the tube with the funnel on top, the doctor holds out his hand to the wardress. The woman steels herself and passes him a pitcher. He begins to pour. Charlotte's entire body convulses. The men grip harder in their effort to hold her in place and the doctor leans on her knees as though taming an animal. Charlotte pleads with her eyes, feeling them bulge from her head as she gags and coughs. Her eyes burn. Her throat burns. Her nostrils are on fire. No one meets her gaze. Ceaseless waves of pain course through her body as Dr. Bainwright pours and pours. *God*, Charlotte thinks, *I am going to choke! I am going to suffocate!*

Suddenly it is over.

They remove the tube and the guards step back. She slumps in the chair, limp, her neck bent back at an abnormal angle. They no longer need to hold her still; she is too weak to move even if she wanted to. Everyone begins clearing up around her, moving past Charlotte as though she is an empty chair, gathering the instruments that had, moments ago, scraped and prodded the inside of her body.

"Should we take her back, then?" the guard asks.

The doctor pauses. She can barely see; she is only looking at him through her lashes. He studies Charlotte, surely, she believes, about to pronounce her dead. He bends down to her face, so close his beard scratches her cheek. She can feel his hot breath on her neck and she wants to bite him. She is a beast, primal and furious. If she had any strength left at all, she would lodge her teeth in the bulbous flesh of his nose until she drew blood. Oh, she would lick that metallic spittle from her lips and hack it back at him. But Charlotte cannot move. She can hardly focus enough to see his face, though all her other senses feel unnaturally heightened, every hair on her arms standing up, electrified.

"That didn't hurt a bit, did it?" he whispers.

Charlotte cannot tell whether he believes her distress is feigned, or if he derives some sadistic pleasure from her pain. She would have given anything to be able to protest. But her throat throbs, a screaming ache from her sore jaw down to her cramping stomach. She can already feel bruises blossoming where the guards strapped down her arms, and on her back where she had resisted with all her might, throwing herself against the chair in her futile attempt to escape. When the doctor withdraws, his teeth oddly pointed, vampiric, she slumps down.

Then he slaps her. The sound is like a shot.

"Take her back," he says, turning away.

Charlotte finds herself back inside her cell. Her head spins. Her cheek stings. She vomits.

She does not sleep. Cannot sleep. Everything hurts. Her skull throbs with terror, hunger, and the sheer pain of her body being forced open against her will. *Invaded*, she thinks. *Raped*. She wants to cry. To think that she once took the simple act of crying for granted. But now she cannot indulge in that catharsis, cannot relieve her pain through heaving breath and gushing tears. It would be excruciating.

"Charlotte!"

She rouses to the frantic whispering of her name. During the hours she lay in the cot, a lump had formed in her throat from where the metal tube had scraped her skin. It hurts to swallow, even to breathe.

Emily's shadow blocks the dim light of the corridor as she stands in the doorway of the cell. It must be dawn.

"Oh, Charlotte," she whispers. "What happened to you?"

Could it be that Emily does not know? Where has she been? Where was she? Charlotte wishes she could feel betrayed, but she simply aches. Her throat is too sore to speak. After a while, faced with Charlotte's stony silence, Emily disappears.

It is hard enough to measure the passage of time while on a hunger strike, how the hours spool out endlessly, punctuated only by hallucinations and stomach cramps. But now, with feedings twice each day, time is cruelly delineated. Charlotte hardly has time to settle her heart, to quell the tremors in her limbs, before the doctor returns to probe her, to rip her open again and again. As they drag her down the corridors she catches sight of other prisoners clinging to the bars, watching her go. They gape at her, curious to catch sight of the woman whose bloodcurdling screams resound throughout the building.

After the last forced feeding, Charlotte thinks she would be better off dead. What is the point if her own body has become the battlefield upon which the war is waged?

She wonders if all the suffragettes will have to endure this torture from now on. Or is this a special punishment reserved for Charlotte alone, the narcissistic bitch who thought she could cheat the system? The voice in her head turns shrill and cruel, taunting in her exhaustion. She hates herself, and everyone, and the world.

"I'm so sorry," Emily whispers.

Charlotte hadn't noticed that she'd come again. The night guards are gone.

"I didn't know. God, Charlotte, I'm so sorry."

It isn't Emily's fault.

"My father gave me the day off work. I can't believe—do you think he planned it?" She is speaking maddeningly fast, her hands tugging at her hair and then gripping the bars. Charlotte won't waste a breath indicting Thomas Brown when they both know that's exactly what happened. "What can I do?" Emily pleads. "Let me help you. We have to tell the truth somehow. The world has to know how you've . . . how they've been . . . hurting you."

"If you tell, you'll be sacked," Charlotte breathes. The effort burns. She wonders how she will ever be able to give a rousing speech again, how she could ever again shout from street corners if it hurts so much just to whisper. She feels like Philomela, silenced, her tongue cut out to absolve her rapist's guilt.

Emily gulps. "I . . . I don't care if I'm sacked. I'll tell the whole world, just tell me how."

Charlotte thinks. Her brain feels too large for her skull. Everything is pounding. She cannot let Emily give herself away. They still need her on the inside. "There's something," Charlotte says slowly, "that you can do." She pauses to swallow, and shakes off the pain. "Without getting caught."

CHAPTER THIRTY

EMILY

Damn it!" Thomas's face is a mottled red. He slams the newspaper on the kitchen table and runs his hands through his thinning hair, pacing and cursing. Emily silently pours the tea. Then he grabs the paper again and, knocking over his cup without an apology, he hurries outside, slamming the door behind him.

When he is gone, Emily exhales. She slowly cleans the spilled tea and wrings out the rag. Her father hadn't said what's bothering him, but she knows. It has been less than a day since she ran from Charlotte's cell in the dead of night, devising a plan. In the moment, it seemed not just the right thing to do, but the only thing. Charlotte looked so pained, so weak, but she insisted she had the strength to carry it out, as long as Emily could hold up her end of the bargain. How could she refuse?

Now that bargain, that plan, has landed on the front page of the London *Times*.

Oh, yes, Thomas is furious. And Emily's mind thrums with uncertainty. Hold the government to account or save her father's job? Help her friend or plan for her future? Not that she weighed those choices in the moment. She only realized after the fact, after she had slipped the illicit pencil and paper into Charlotte's cell and held a candle aloft, after she collected the forbidden words and smuggled them out of the jail. Only then did she realize that she was risking her father's position, and with it their home, their livelihood, her own chance to escape this life. *Damn it,* indeed.

There is a rap at the door. She cracks it open and finds Martin standing on the stoop.

"D'you see this?" he asks. He bites his lower lip and in his slender hands he holds a copy of the newspaper.

"My father just took our copy out with him," she says, avoiding the question.

"Right, yeah. I saw him leaving his office with it. The board of governors telegraphed this morning and called him in for an inquiry. Shit."

She catches Martin's eye, expecting to see anger there. But no, she realizes, recognizing that flit of emotion that passes across the faces of so many of the inmates—it's fear.

She feels oddly calm.

"Shall I read it to you?" he says.

She nods instinctively and he begins to read aloud.

Letter from a Suffragette in Holloway

I did not eat or drink for two days, protesting my treatment as a common criminal when I should have received the privileges of a political prisoner. I was sitting in my cell when the guards entered. They grabbed me and I struggled as hard as I could, but there were two of them and each was much bigger and stronger than I. They dragged me down the hall, holding me by the shoulders, the arms, the knees, and the ankles.

Emily swallows, watches Martin's face.

In a dark room far away from the rest of the prisoners, someone seized me from behind and the doctor tried to force my mouth open with a steel gag. I tried to resist, clamping my mouth shut, but with two of them holding me down and prodding the tube around my gums, feeling for gaps in my teeth, they forced its way in, slowly prying open my jaw with the turn of a screw. Cutting into my flesh, my gums bleeding, I tried to tighten the muscles of my throat but they forced the tube down. My breath was ragged, my body convulsed, and I felt like I was going to suffocate. I lost consciousness, until I heard them say, "That's all," and the tube came up.

They left me there, tied to the chair, sobbing convulsively and gasping for air as blood dripped from my mouth. I vomited. That night, it all happened again. Morning and evening, over and over, the same excruciating struggle of the tube scraping my stomach, my throat, my mouth, sometimes through my nostrils. I don't know how to breathe. There is so much blood, so much pain, my insides are screaming.

Martin stops reading. His face has gone white. Though Emily had memorized the words when she collected them, the fragments of paper slipped between the bars in Charlotte's wobbly scrawl, they still sting in Martin's mouth, the visceral pain, the humiliation, the hopelessness.

Martin stares and Emily realizes that she is meant to react. She is not supposed to have known that any of this even happened. It is not difficult to feign emotion, for Emily feels it rise up in her, but her response is delayed. She covers her face with her hands.

"Oh, it's horrid."

Martin places a hand on her shoulder, and surprising even herself, Emily dissolves into a sob. He draws her nearer until they stand in a tight embrace. She presses her face against the worn fabric of his coat;

it smells like earth and something sweet. His shoulders shudder along with her own, his breath quickening. He is crying, too.

"I didn't know," he whispers feebly.

She isn't sure how long they stand in the frigid doorway, gripping each other through tears. At last she draws back, just a few inches, and looks up at his face. His cheeks are streaked red and his eyes glisten.

"Have you got snot on my shirt?" he asks. His voice cracks as he tries to smile.

She sniffs, and he tucks a loose curl behind her ear. Suddenly their faces are so close she can feel his breath on her skin. He kisses her deeply, with more urgency than when they sat in the park together. She pulls away to catch her breath.

"I'm sorry," he says.

She shakes her head and takes a step backward into the house. He follows her and at last she closes the door against the morning's chill. The cottage feels like it is being heated by something far stronger than the hearth. Emily's back is to the door and he pushes her against it as his lips return to hers, magnetic and fiery.

She hates to think how much she enjoys it. Until two days ago, she had never been kissed, and now, suddenly his hands are in her hair, unfurling the long braid down her back, and his lips are warm and insistent on her neck, her cheeks, her eyelids, her mouth. He wants her. And she wants him, too. Dizzily, she allows him to press her against the wall, and she pulls him closer until, though standing, their legs are intertwined. She feels lightheaded; she feels alive. Then, somehow, they are in her bedroom. Every inch of her skin tingles, electrified, and blood thrums through her body to the place beneath her belly. Her shawl is off, her lips in Martin's teeth, and then she pulls back, panting. They must stop.

"What is it?" Martin wipes his mouth with the back of his wrist.

Emily steps away. "I can't."

"Oh no, I wasn't . . . I wouldn't—" He stutters, stuffing his fists into his pockets.

She isn't listening to him. Marianne's voice has entered Emily's brain, as unwaveringly clear as if she were standing here in the room. *Be good.*

"You have to leave." She picks up her shawl from the ground and wraps it tightly around her chest, feeling around for the yarn that must have slipped out of her hair.

"I'm sorry," Martin begins.

"Don't be," she says. "You just . . . you have to go."

They are by the front door now. She braids her hair with clumsy fingers. Martin looks at her, eyes searching for meaning. She gives him none and looks down at the floor. He leans in and kisses her cheek.

She makes sure Martin doesn't see her leave the jail complex a few minutes later, unlatching the back gate to race down the street. In her hand, she grips the newspaper he left behind.

CHAPTER THIRTY-ONE

BEATRICE

B eatrice opens the door when Emily arrives at the house in Park Lane, cheeks red, her lips swollen. "Sadie!" Beatrice shouts up the stairs. "Emily's here!" The clattering of feet precedes Sadie's arrival.

"Oh, Emily," Sadie cries, wrapping a dressing gown around her waist.

For a moment, the sight of Emily almost makes Beatrice forget how disheveled she and Sadie both are, having tumbled out of bed at the knock on the door. Now, Bea twists her tangled curls into a knot, wincing at the sight of Sadie's bare feet leading Emily to a chair in the parlor. They have to be more careful. And yet, when the letter from Charlotte had arrived, it was all they could do to cling to one another. In that moment, nothing else mattered. Not Daniel's letters from King's, oblivious to his fiancée's brushes with the law. Not even the fear that she and Sadie could be arrested any day during their activities for the Union and face the same horrific treatment, which she herself had escaped by only a hairsbreadth. No, they just had to hold each other.

"We have news, Emily," Beatrice says. "Thank God Isabel escaped, because she had a connection with an MP who was willing to help publish the letter. Next week, he plans to bring Charlotte's testimony to the floor of Parliament."

"Thank God you *both* escaped. You managed it all brilliantly," Sadie says, though her usual smile is gone. "It was precisely the publicity we needed."

"What will happen next?" Emily asks.

"Well, no one knows. This has never been done before."

"And what about Charlotte?"

Beatrice and Sadie exchange a glance.

"We don't know that either," says Beatrice.

"How is she?" Sadie asks.

"She's being so strong," Emily begins. "But—"

They've all read the letter. There are no words left to say. Charlotte is trapped, in agony, with no end in sight. Beatrice reaches out a hand and squeezes Emily's.

They sit around together for the next hour or so, and Beatrice feels gratefully unburdened to be among people from whom she does not have to hide her secrets. Well, not all of them.

The trembling in Emily's hands subsides, and Sadie sidles up beside Beatrice on the couch, leaning over to kiss her on the cheek. It all appears perfectly friendly, of course. But Beatrice stiffens, and all of a sudden, Emily starts to cry.

"Oh, honey," says Sadie, sitting up and reaching out a hand. "What's the matter?"

Emily shudders, wiping a tear. "I'm sorry," she says, sniffing. "I just can't stop thinking of Charlotte."

"We know."

"And even though the letter's been published, she's still . . ." She can't finish the sentence. Still alone. Still being tortured. Starving. Possibly dying. "What can we do?"

Beatrice twists her finger around her lower lip. "I have an idea."

CHAPTER THIRTY-TWO
CHARLOTTE

C harlotte loses count of the times she has been fed. Every inch of her body aches. Her shoulders and knees are bruised from where they held her down. Her cheeks sting, gums metallic and swollen. Her fingertips bleed from futile clawing in defense. Her head throbs from hunger and dehydration. Her stomach roils. She cannot see the point of the ordeal; on top of everything, she ends up vomiting after every meal, as her body rejects that which had been forced inside her. She prays to a god she does not believe in, prays for the reprieve of death. *Let me die, oh, please.* And she cries out for her mama, her papa, her sisters. *Mama, Mama.* She had tried to be a good daughter. But she had failed. Perhaps she deserves this. She hears voices in her head, feverish and cruel. Evil echoes shout at her, lashing her skull with their words. *Worthless, useless, pointless, selfish. You bitch. You cunt. You whore. You selfish, useless whore.* This is all worthless, pointless, meaningless. She hears someone whimpering in a strange high voice. She realizes it is her. *Bitch. Mama, Mama, please. Oh, please.*

Shout, shout, up with your song!
Cry with the wind, for the dawn is breaking!

When the singing starts, she buries her head in her flea-riddled pillow. *Make it end. Make it stop, oh please.* But it doesn't stop. And she realizes that the voices are no longer screaming at her. She hears her own name over and over, clearly, in shouts and in song.

March, march, swing you along,
Wide blows our banner, and hope is waking!

Could it be angels? But if this is heaven, why hasn't the pain gone away? Summoning her last ounce of strength, Charlotte climbs up on top of the cot and pushes onto her toes so that her sight line is just at the level of her slit window. She clings to the metal bars and peers out. There are bodies huddled in the courtyard.

Song with its story, dreams with their glory,
Lo! They call, and glad is their word!
Louder and louder it swells,
Thunder of freedom, voice of the lord!

"There she is!" someone cries.
Who?
"I see her, too!" says another.
"Charlotte!"
"Charlotte!"
She realizes slowly, groggily, that these are her friends. They came to see her. She nearly collapses from the relief of it and begins to weep. But she holds on to the bars, her eyes feasting on the faces

outside, the voices that sing gently and clearly, lifting like birdsong to her prison cell.

Firm in reliance, laugh a defiance,
Laugh in hope, for sure is the end,
March, march—many as one,
Shoulder to shoulder and friend to friend.

CHAPTER THIRTY-THREE
EMILY

It is dusk, and her surroundings appear in gradations of smoke and slate. As soon as she unlatches the gate, Emily goes inside the cottage to prepare supper for her father. He enters a few minutes later and they settle into their usual routine, with Emily at the stove and Thomas, grim-faced and taciturn, at the table. He hasn't mentioned anything about the newspaper article or the forcible feedings, and as always, Emily says nothing.

About thirty minutes later, the suffragettes sneak in through the gate. By then, Emily is serving the stew and Thomas never glances toward the window behind him. If he did, he would see a dozen or so women file in silently, skirts flapping like a flock of birds, led by Sadie and Beatrice. From the corner of her eye, Emily catches them counting the slit windows and easing around the corner, just like she had explained, to find the cell belonging to Charlotte. They are out of sight by the time their voices lift in song, and Emily can only detect the sound because she knows to expect it. Between the roar of the fire and the hum of the kettle, Thomas does not hear anything at all.

It is the guards' shouting, not the suffragettes' singing, that finally alerts Thomas to the intrusion.

"What the hell are you doing?" the men are shouting. "Get out! Get out of here!"

The scuffle unfolds out in the courtyard, but Emily pretends not to hear.

"Mr. Brown!" Martin bangs on the door, and when Emily opens it, he is red-cheeked and irate.

"What is it?" Thomas asks, pushing back from the table. His spoon clatters to the floor.

"Come and see," Martin demands. Emily grips her apron, hiding her shaking hands within its folds.

"Sorry, Em," Thomas says. "I'll be back shortly."

He grabs his jacket from the hook by the door and follows Martin outside. The men round the corner, and then the women begin to flee, running in all directions, no longer in any elegant formation. Some race for the open gate; others head toward the shrubbery. One girl catches Emily's eye through the window and Emily points toward the back garden, through which the girl will find a break in the fence.

All of Thomas's dishes have been cleared and washed by the time he returns, huffing and sour, an hour later.

"What happened?" Emily asks, surprising herself with how easily she can feign ignorance. Their whole relationship has become playacting; they each say the line the other expects to hear, performing a character distinct from reality.

"Security breach," he mutters. "Don't worry about it." He slumps into his armchair, resting his forehead in his palms. She has never seen him so sullen, so still. A strangled sort of cough emerges from Thomas's throat.

"Papa?"

"It's nothing, Em."

She kneels beside him on the threadbare carpet. Thomas blows his nose into his handkerchief.

"Oh, Em," he whispers. "What have I done?"

"What do you mean, Papa?" Could it be remorse at last?

"The board of governors won't be happy about this. And, Jesus, they're going to want someone to blame." Thomas mumbles on, as though musing only to himself. "This house isn't ours. It's the government's. If I lose this job, we lose this house. We lose everything." He emits a low, tired laugh. "We'll be out on the streets."

Emily's heart hammers.

He regards her with exhaustion in his eyes. "Go on to bed," he says.

The next morning, Charlotte is carried out on a stretcher, discharged on the brink of death. Dr. Bainwright insists that no hospitalization is necessary, but it's only to save his own skin, not to save Charlotte. Later, the guards will install a new padlock on the back gate. But it is like using a rag to stanch the flow of a waterfall.

CHAPTER THIRTY-FOUR

CHARLOTTE

H ow's my favorite invalid?" Sadie asks, shimmying out of her sash after another afternoon out selling papers.

"Ripping," Charlotte replies in a hoarse voice, employing Sadie's adjective of choice. Charlotte's convalescence is slow, much slower than after a hunger strike. The sores inside her mouth from the metal instruments are taking too long to heal, and though the bruises on her limbs have faded from purple to a putrid celadon, everything still hurts. There is peace in the house, though, in the air that they breathe and in the words that they do not need to say. They are all together; they are all alive.

"As I should bloody well hope," Sadie says, flinging the unsold copies of *Votes for Women* onto the side table and approaching Charlotte, who sits on the chintz chair nearest to the fireplace, wrapped in a wool blanket. Sadie pats her shoulder and then crosses the room to greet Beatrice.

"My lady," Sadie says.

Beatrice rolls her eyes and puts down her needlepoint.

"The lady doth protest? She seweth day and night, this lady!"

"Oh, stop. It's for the new banner," Beatrice explains, shaking out the fabric to display WSPU, emblazoned like the Roman SPQR in bold violet letters.

"That looks great, Bea," Charlotte whispers. She cannot help but think, however, that the symbolism is eerily accurate. She feels like she's just crawled out from the arena, escaping only narrowly from the torture her captors viewed as amusement.

"Thanks, love," she says. "My thumb is twice its size from all the pinpricks, but I daresay it's come together rather well."

"My poor lady has wounded her nimble fingers!" Sadie cries, fainting onto the couch and sprawling across Beatrice's lap. Beatrice attempts to shoo her away, but Sadie snuggles in, and soon they are cuddled together, the banner abandoned on the floor.

"It was a lot quieter before you arrived," Beatrice says, stroking Sadie's hair.

"Just admit it," Sadie insists. "You missed me."

Beatrice's cheeks grow red.

"Of course we did," says Charlotte. Her voice is rough as sandpaper. These past few days since her return from Holloway, Charlotte has been grateful for her friends' company. She can hardly eat, and the broth they diligently bring her sears with every swallow, but she feels cared for, loved. She has, perhaps, never felt this safe.

They have not heard a word from Emily, not since Charlotte left Holloway. A part of Charlotte misses her. And yet it is like the distance between them has somehow, very rapidly, widened. The comfort of knowing that Emily was on the other side of the bars during Charlotte's torturous nights in Holloway made all the difference in the world, but at the end of the day, Emily knew, in more barbaric detail than anyone else, exactly what had happened to her. She isn't angry with Emily, not quite. But Charlotte senses that Emily might be avoiding her.

Adeline and Isabel drop by later that evening.

"Your courtship with danger continues, my dear Miss Ivy," Adeline says, placing a hand on Charlotte's shoulder. "Now, you have not done anything I wouldn't do myself—but do not be reckless." The maternal concern brings tears stinging to Charlotte's eyes. Adeline shows her the letters they've printed from doctors in America, all of whom wrote to condemn the forcible feeding procedure. "*We* knew it was ghastly," Adeline says. "But now we have medical proof of it."

Charlotte reads quickly, disbelieving the fact that somewhere across the world, doctors are decrying what happened to her. She can't help but notice, however, that the only newspaper printing the condemnation is *Votes for Women*. The London dailies have been silent.

Before they leave, Isabel pulls Charlotte aside. "I'm so sorry," she says, gripping Charlotte's hand. "I shouldn't have left you in Trafalgar Square. I should have been there."

"Nonsense," Charlotte insists. "You and Bea were right to escape when you had the chance."

"Well, if it comes down to it, I'll take my turn next time," Isabel says with a tight smile.

Charlotte won't dare say it, but her heart sinks with dread. She cannot survive a next time. If that means leaving the Union, so be it. She cannot endure this torture twice.

That night, Charlotte can't sleep. She tosses and turns in her bedroom, unable to drift off despite her exhaustion. It feels wrong to be swaddled in soft sheets when every time her eyes close she pictures her torture chamber in Holloway and feels the phantom pain of that terrible tube down her throat. At least she knows her friends are right down the hall. It is reassuring to feel their presence, the quiet creaks in the floorboards that remind her she isn't alone when she wakes from a nightmare. Still, she is grateful for the privacy of her own bedroom. She can cry without fear of disturbing anyone.

Tonight, though, she isn't crying. Perhaps, she thinks, she has finally spent all of her tears. Over the past few days, she has cried for her pain, for the terrors that come back to her when she least expects them—the leering face of the doctor is branded in her memories. She cried for the father she lost and the mother she both resents and misses. She cried for the vote and all that it promises, and for the fact that she cannot fathom fighting like this ever again. And Charlotte cried because tears cascaded from her eyes, in burning salty streams, whether she wanted them to or not.

The moon shines bright through the window. Sadie's father had left the decorating to Sadie's brother, Sam, who never got around to putting up drapes for the spare room. Charlotte doesn't mind. She has a clear view of the sky. Though usually hazy from the factory smoke, tonight it is clear, and the moon glows like a pearl. She stands tentatively and walks to the window, bringing her face so close to the glass that the tip of her nose presses up against it, and her breath casts clouds upon its surface. Then she hears a whisper.

Trailing a fingertip through the condensation, she turns toward the door. Yes, there is definitely whispering. If the others are awake, Charlotte wouldn't mind company. She tiptoes into the hall, pausing in front of the door to Sadie and Beatrice's bedroom, listening.

"Do you think she suspects?"

Charlotte cannot tell whose voice it is, low and quiet as air.

"Would it matter if she did?"

Ah, that's Sadie.

"It's just—if anyone were to find out . . . I wonder if we shouldn't anymore, now that she's back," Beatrice whispers.

"Shhh. Of course we should, if we want to. Only if we want to. And no one needs to know. Do you still want to?" Sadie's voice cracks.

There's only silence. Charlotte wonders if Beatrice is nodding her head yes or shaking it no. Are they keeping a secret from Adeline and the rest of the Union? She hears movement, the creak of the bed. But no feet on the floor. The door remains closed. Charlotte backs away, vibrating. She pulls her own door shut as quietly as possible.

CHAPTER THIRTY-FIVE

BEATRICE

Beatrice cannot say for certain when exactly it happened. She cannot pinpoint a precise moment, though surely when Sadie returned from jail looking weak and pale all those weeks ago, she knew there was no going back. But she'd been down that road before. The summer before Girton. The summer of the incident. And so, she resisted, fortified her walls.

For the first time in her life, someone cared enough to try to scale them.

Now that Charlotte is back from jail, all three of them living in the house together, she tries to keep things as normal as she can. Sadie, however, is less willing to compromise. Beatrice just barely convinces her to maintain an outward veneer of propriety, but only because of the promises she makes behind their closed bedroom door.

"How did you find me?" Beatrice whispers, her face centimeters from Sadie's under the covers. "How did I get so lucky?"

"You know how. I came here to see the world. And my father didn't care where I went as long as Sam kept an eye on me."

"Sam's done a very good job keeping you out of trouble, then." Beatrice's hand creeps toward Sadie's skin, but she doesn't touch. Not yet. Heat radiates toward her.

"Oh, sure," Sadie sighs, arching closer. Her eyes flutter closed. "I suppose there is another reason why I came."

"Tell me."

"I was afraid."

"Sadie Lawrence, afraid?"

"Say it again."

"Sadie." Beatrice extends the syllables soft and slow. "Lawrence." At last, she allows herself to touch. Her hand cups the smooth curve of Sadie's hip bone. Sadie swallows hard.

"I was afraid of my feelings."

"You fell in love?"

Sadie nods, eyes still closed, leaning into Beatrice's touch. "I was engaged to be married." Bea's hand moves over her waist. "But he wasn't the one I loved."

"Who was?"

Sadie cracks a smile, shrugs. "It doesn't matter anymore. But that's why I came. I had to get away. It was all so messy over there, so complicated. But here, none of that matters. Here, everything is clear." Sadie takes Beatrice's hand, weaving their fingers together. Her thumb traces a circle on Beatrice's palm, and even that soft, chaste touch makes Beatrice want to cry. "Have you ever been in love?"

"Are you suggesting that I'm not in love with my fiancé?" Beatrice jokes.

Sadie stiffens. Anytime Daniel comes up, her face turns to granite.

"Sorry." Bea presses her lips to Sadie's earlobe. The skin is delicate and feather soft. "I don't believe I've ever been in love. Lust, yes. Long ago. But not love, not until . . ."

Beatrice cannot finish the sentence. On the other side of that admission is a sheer face of rock, a deep drop into the unknown, into terror and euphoria and a bliss that cannot possibly last. Sadie knows that. And Sadie doesn't care. She says it for both of them. "I think I might be. Falling in love, that is."

Warmth spreads through Beatrice's chest, settling somewhere beneath her stomach. And suddenly everything is urgent. Hair, limbs, lips. Bea wants to warn Sadie to hush or Charlotte will hear, but she can no longer see straight. She is blinded by the curve of bodies and the intoxicating warmth of skin that is smooth and smells of soap, by kisses that take her breath away, by Sadie Sadie Sadie.

For once, she does not have to hide. She comes truly, ecstatically alive.

In the daylight, she has to stifle all this. One glance at Sadie's shining red hair, and Beatrice's cheeks are on fire. She wishes she could hold Sadie's hand, wishes they could dance together in the streets. She settles for linking arms as they walk, sitting near each other, whispering. But even those simple pleasures are punctuated by the persistent thrum of fear beneath her bones.

No one can ever know.

CHAPTER THIRTY-SIX

CHARLOTTE

M y mother's written," Beatrice groans into her tea. Charlotte stifles a twinge of jealousy. Even the most irritating missive from her mother would be more welcome than these sad months of silence.

"What does she say?" Sadie asks.

"Oh, just wedding things."

The wedding to Daniel—Charlotte has nearly forgotten. "Do you write to him often?"

Beatrice shakes her head. "Not really," she says. "He's busy finishing up at King's. I don't like to bother him. And I suppose I've been busy, too," she adds, her neck flushing pink as she looks anywhere but at Sadie.

"Well, if you're going to get married, you should probably keep in better touch with your husband-to-be," Sadie says sharply.

Beatrice suddenly appears fixated on something inside her empty teacup. With a knock on the door they all turn toward the foyer, grateful for a distraction to cut through the strange tension hanging in the air.

"It's me," Emily calls, opening the door before anyone can rise to greet her. When she catches sight of Charlotte, she pauses, a stricken expression on her face. Even if Charlotte hadn't seen the dark circles around her eyes and the jutting collarbone in her own mirror, she can read it all on Emily's face.

"It's our secret messenger!" Sadie says. "Come sit." They pull up a chair and pour a cup of tea. "How are things on the inside?"

Emily bites her lower lip. "I'm just so glad you're safe," she says, squeezing Charlotte's hand.

"Thank you for getting my letter to the press," Charlotte says. "I hope you didn't get into trouble."

"I don't think so," Emily says. "Not yet. Was it worth it?"

The women glance at one another. They have all been thinking it. But only Emily dared to ask aloud. All that pain, that torture, for what? Charlotte made the headlines, at least for a day or two. But then the world moved on. The suffragettes were forgotten in favor of the next news story. And the government has said nothing at all about forcible feedings. As far as they know, all hunger-striking suffragettes will continue to receive that brutal treatment. That is, if they dare to continue.

"Things don't change overnight," Beatrice says. "But it's a start. Thank you, Emily."

"Yes, thank you," Sadie adds. "So is it official, then? Will you finally admit that you're one of us?"

"Oh," Emily stutters. "Well, Charlotte thinks it's important for me to remain in the shadows, so—"

"I'm not so sure anymore," Charlotte interrupts. "As you said, even my letter didn't help."

"I can see the headline now!" Sadie's eyes flash. "Jail keeper's daughter condemns unjust imprisonments."

"Well . . ." Emily twists her fingers. "The truth is, I don't know if I can take on much more. I can keep an eye out, of course, but I can't be, you know . . ." She lowers her voice to a whisper. "A suffragette." The word is sticky with shame.

Charlotte's blood runs cold, like ice water, like spiders. She doesn't want to quit the Union; it's the only family she has. But she also will not, cannot, face Holloway again. Something has to change drastically. That something could, perhaps, come from Emily. But one look at Emily's face quashes her hope. "What do you mean? Is this about the teacher's college?"

"Well, yes, somewhat. You know it was my mother's dream for me."

"I didn't think you really wanted that."

"I do," says Emily, a note of defensiveness creeping into her voice.

"Well, I don't see why that would stop you from joining us."

"Wouldn't it?" Emily's voice catches. "Look what happened to you, Charlotte. You couldn't stay at Girton. And you, Beatrice, had to finish school before joining the Union. Sadie, you had a whole life in America before you came to London, isn't that right?"

"But you said yourself, nothing else has made a difference," Charlotte says. She realizes she is speaking far too loudly. She wants to provoke someone, anyone, Emily. Someone has to hear her. Someone must listen. Her throat throbs, but she doesn't care. Beatrice glances at Sadie. "Think about how much *I've* already suffered. You said you didn't care if you got sacked."

"Well, things have changed at home," Emily says.

"Look, Emily," Sadie begins. "I know that college seems like a valuable opportunity. But honestly, I've learned more campaigning for the WSPU than I ever did in a lecture hall."

"That's easy for you to say," Emily says. "You've already had the opportunity. And you all made your own decisions about whether to stay or leave. But I've never had this chance. This is my *only* chance."

"It's not your *only*—" Charlotte interrupts.

"Yes, it is. It very well may be," Emily insists.

Charlotte flicks her tongue across her teeth. "Is that really what you want? To be a teacher? Because I think—" She narrows her eyes, boring into Emily. "I think you just want to marry that prison guard and please your father. You don't care about teaching. You want to make other people happy. We're too risky, too messy. You want your neat little life, and you'll follow the rules straight to your grave."

Emily blinks rapidly, and rather too late, Charlotte realizes she is fighting back tears.

"Well," Emily says, "if that is what you think of me . . . You have no idea, do you, how much I've already risked to help you? I've risked not just my own future, but my father's job—"

"The father who let them stick a tube down my throat and nearly choked me to death? Oh, pity!" A burning fury rises up in Charlotte's chest, spawned from frustration and futility and days and days of agony. Does no one care? She poured her heart, her pain, onto the pages of that newspaper, and not a single MP blinked. And now, even Emily, the friend who helped her in her darkest moments, is a stranger, staring the establishment in the face and welcoming it in. "Thanks for all your *help*," Charlotte spits, "but if it's such a burden, I don't need you anymore."

Charlotte and Emily stand up at the same time. Emily turns swiftly from the table and runs toward the door. It slams behind her with a thud.

"Shit," Beatrice mutters.

Charlotte buries her head in her hands. "That was too far, wasn't it?"

"Are you kidding?" says Sadie. "What was that about?"

Charlotte shakes her head. "I don't know," she says. "I don't know."

CHAPTER THIRTY-SEVEN

EMILY

E mily storms out of Park Lane and weaves through the manicured Mayfair streets, pulse pounding in her ears. How dare Charlotte suggest that she has not sacrificed for them, that she hasn't done enough? She's risked her home, her father's livelihood, her own future. How can Charlotte still consider her a docile little daughter, a good girl without the gumption to disobey? She could scream. Instead, when she at last arrives back at the grim stone cottage, crumbling in the corner of the Holloway courtyard, she kicks the door to her bedroom, pain shooting from her big toe straight up her shin. Unsatisfying, but at least her pain has a location.

Charlotte and the others have had every chance for a good life—no, a great one—and they threw it away, for what? To be political rebels? The truth is, they have hardly thrown anything away at all. Beatrice and Sadie can return home to their mansions at any moment, where presumably large dowries and inheritances await. Charlotte's situation, she knows, is more complicated. But her stepfather gave her a chance at prosperity, at mobility, and Charlotte squandered it. That was her choice to make. And Emily is making a choice of her own.

She has already risked her father's position—his job, his home, his pride. And though the flash of the thought bloats with guilt, she thinks, too, of the life her mother wished for her, a fantasy that seems more distant than ever.

Her thoughts spiral. What would a vote offer anyway? She would still be sweeping floors and wiping up shit. Thomas would still be cramped in his dingy office, cowering before the board of governors, cutting corners to keep the blasted prison afloat. Isn't an education more valuable than a vote? With a teaching certificate she can cling to the middle class like her mother always wanted. Is it really such a sin to want a life without hunger, a life where one can peer into Selfridges' windows and actually buy something once in a while?

But what makes Emily seethe the most is how thoughtlessly Charlotte dragged Martin into the argument. Suggesting that Emily wants to marry him? Her father clearly wants it—and God, if she did too, would that be so terrible? Martin warned Emily about Charlotte's hunger strike, he turned a blind eye when Emily snuck in the writing materials and smuggled out the letter. He risked his job to help them both. Now Emily is responsible for the precarious state that both her father and Martin find themselves in. How ungrateful could Charlotte be?

Martin comes to the cottage that evening, his face tense, his eyes wide and looking so much younger than she had noticed before. He looks like a boy. "They suspect me," he says without preamble, furtively glancing behind him before stepping through the doorway of the cottage.

"What do you mean?"

"Your father. The board of governors. They've summoned me for questioning about Charlotte Evans. He thinks I—they think I smuggled her the writing supplies and let the suffragettes in through the back gate." Martin's gray eyes probe Emily's. She tries to maintain a blank expression, though her insides are roiling. Her father had said they would need someone to blame. "I didn't do it," he continues, pulling at his hair distractedly. She has never seen him this upset. "I don't understand. I've never done anything. I *need* this job." He won't ask the question, but it's there, in his searching gaze.

"I know," Emily says quietly. Her hands begin to sweat. She cannot admit to Martin her own involvement—but surely he already suspects.

Martin scuffs his foot back and forth across the floor. The heel of his shoe is so worn that grayed fibers drag along behind him. When was the last time he'd bought a new pair of shoes—had he ever?

"The meeting is this afternoon," he says.

Emily grabs his wrist impulsively, holding him still, trying to communicate some reassurance. Veins snake purple-blue up his forearms.

"My father is fair," she begins.

He nods, swallowing thickly. "I can't afford to lose this job. My brothers need me, and I don't know how to do anything else. This is my only chance to join the Yard. This is it for me—"

"Shh," she whispers, as his voice pitches higher. "Please. It'll be alright."

Martin grabs her hand and she releases his wrist, easing her fingers between his own. *He's going to ask*, she thinks. He knows she gave Charlotte the papers, and he is going to ask her to confess. They lock eyes and Emily thinks, dizzily, that she ought to run away. Then he squeezes her hand.

"It helps knowing you're here, Em," Martin whispers. He bends and brushes his lips against her cheek. Then he drops her hand. They stare at each other for a moment, eyes locked, faces expressionless and yet taut.

"My father shouldn't find you in here," she says, breaking the silence. "He's fair, but to a point." She'd wanted it to come out as a joke, but it sounds threatening. A strange sort of exhalation, not quite a laugh, escapes her lips.

"I'll go, then." Martin turns to leave and she lets him, but before closing the door she leans her head against the threshold and watches him cross the patchy dirt of the courtyard.

"Good luck," she whispers. He is too far away to hear, already disappearing into the dark archway. Later, she summons the moment in her mind's eye and, hand flying over the page of her sketchbook, she captures Martin on the page. His too-short pants barely skim the top edge of his worn shoes. His face is masked in shadow.

CHAPTER THIRTY-EIGHT

CHARLOTTE

C harlotte knows the argument with Emily is stupid and spiteful. Why should Emily sacrifice anything more? Just because that's the choice Charlotte made—fatefully, and perhaps even senselessly—it shouldn't have to be everyone's choice. And, with a pang of jealousy, she knows that at the end of the day, Emily has an alternative that Charlotte does not: the ability to simply go home.

These empty hours make Charlotte dwell on her own discontent. She hasn't been able to do much of anything since the forcible feeding. It is too painful to stand for long, and her throat is tattered with sores that make everything taste metallic. Worse, in the back of her mind there is a persistent ache, one that plagues her most when her body is still. Its dull drumming at the base of her skull asks, over and over, *Is this worth it?*

She silences its thrum for now, heading into the printshop in response to a summons from Adeline. At last, a day with purpose, before she has to tell Adeline the truth she's been keeping from everyone—that she will not protest again. The stuffy storefront smells like ink and paper. A half dozen heads glance up from piles of newsprint as Charlotte enters with a cool breeze from the street.

"Close the door," Adeline orders. "Have you seen this?"

She holds up a newspaper. It's not an issue of *Votes for Women*, but the latest from *The Times*. The cartoon takes up half the page. The title, in bold block letters reads: FEEDING A SUFFRAGETTE BY FORCE. It is an ugly caricature of a woman lying supine on the ground, clearly in a jail cell, while two men wrestle a funnel over her mouth. The woman's eyes bulge.

"They've made it into a joke," Charlotte says, disbelieving. "Even after my letter—"

Adeline crumples the paper and throws it to the ground. "No one cares," she says. "Why would they? Who are you to them, anyway?"

Charlotte knows not to be offended by Adeline's bluntness. She is right.

"You asked to see me?"

"Not here," Adeline says. "Come with me."

Charlotte follows Adeline past stacks of back issues, stepping over crumpled papers, mock-ups, and towers of empty ink bottles. Adeline's makeshift office is barely the size of a broom closet, but she shuts them both inside before starting to speak.

"No one can know," Adeline whispers, handing her a letter on a thick square of paper, addressed to the Union in smooth, jet-black ink. Even before reading it, Charlotte knows this was sent from Hazelwood Hall.

"Are we expecting another donation?" she asks, thumbing the ruby wax seal, her finger catching on the Cunningham family crest.

"Read it," Adeline instructs.

Charlotte reads silently. "Is she serious?"

Adeline nods.

"This could change everything," Charlotte says. "Will it?"

"Who can be certain? If Constance is willing, we must try. But *no one* can know. Not even the volunteers out there, bless them. These volunteers skip home after their shifts and open their mouths to who knows who. Don't tell Emily, either. She could wreck everything. I appreciate her, of course, but she cannot know."

Charlotte is grateful for the dim light, because her cheeks turn crimson. "I don't think Emily is going to be much of a help to us anymore."

"Why is that?"

"It's nothing." Charlotte shifts her weight backward, trying to find some space away from Adeline, but the older woman merely leans in closer. "I just don't think she's serious about any of this, that's all."

"Do not underestimate her," Adeline says sharply.

"Alright," Charlotte says. "So when is it happening?"

"Tonight."

"Tonight?"

"She's on the train to London as we speak."

CHAPTER THIRTY-NINE

EMILY

The guards bring in the last round of inmates for the night. Cells clang and the dim Holloway corridors are steeped in shadow. Somewhere beyond the brick walls and metal grates, blackbirds swoop through the watercolor sunset. Emily sweeps lazily in the courtyard, pushing the dust back and forth in swirls of soot and debris. She turns at the sound of footsteps to find Martin leaning against the stone wall, waiting for her shift to conclude.

"Evening," he murmurs, voice low.

Emily takes his hand in hers. Both are cold and chapped. When her father called him in a few days ago and asked questions about how Charlotte acquired writing materials, Martin stayed stony faced. He covered for her. He repeated it over and over and finally, Thomas really believed that Martin was a loyal, lowly guard who knew nothing of the matter. Emily has not forgotten, however, the fear on Martin's face. Nor can she ignore the truth—that her own actions nearly sent him out on the street. Now, holding hands, they walk in a circle around the courtyard in the waning light, savoring the few minutes they have until Thomas locks up for the evening and expects to see Emily stoking the hearth fire in the cottage.

Their shared minutes in the shadows, their stolen evenings in secret, give Emily a distraction, if not a thrill. When Martin kisses her, pressing his body against hers, her back to the cold brick wall, she can shift, if not suppress, her gnawing guilt. She can make amends to Martin, if not to Charlotte. He wraps his arms around her waist and exhales onto her neck.

"How was your day?" she whispers.

"Pretty dull, till this evening."

"I brightened your evening?"

"Right, yeah of course," Martin says. "But I actually meant that the day was dull until we brought in a new woman."

"Oh. Anyone interesting?"

"Eh, some poor older lady called Jane. She's a suffragette." He pauses, an unacknowledged beat between them. "I hear she spit on an officer at a by-election rally this evening."

Emily smirks. That had been Charlotte's tactic, spitting to ensure an arrest. It isn't funny, of course, not at all. But she is relieved that she does not know this Jane person.

"I'd better go," she says.

Martin leans in once more, his lips cold but soft on her mouth.

"I have to get home."

"Someday," Martin says, "we could go home together."

She smiles, appeasing. His eyes light up at even the smallest encouragement. Walking away, she feels his eyes on her back. Her stomach churns.

On Sunday, Emily brings her sketchbook to the park. It's still chilly to be spending the day outside, but it is no colder in the park than in the corridors of Holloway. With a spare shawl wrapped around her shoulders, she inhales the pleasure of being alone. The scratch of charcoal against paper, her fingertips blackened, the distant sounds of children playing—these sensations conjure a familiar, comforting satisfaction. Long gone are the days of picnics in the park with her mother, the sun-dappled summer afternoons. Marianne wanted her to be an independent woman, with a career that could support her without the help of a man. But Marianne never knew what it was to truly be taken care of. And Thomas knows what Martin can offer.

All her life, Emily wanted to be a good daughter. But now, with one parent's last wish weighing heavy and the other's dream for her pressing on her shoulders, there is no single way to be good. She will inevitably disappoint one of them. Lost in her sketches, time suspends and melts away.

The evening is gray and oddly bright when Emily crosses the courtyard back at Holloway. There is so much smog in the sky that she cannot see the moon or stars. Everything appears drenched in dishwater. When she opens the door, Emily is surprised to find Martin seated at the dinner table, at Thomas's invitation. Though she scrambles to scour the charcoal from her fingertips and scrape together a decent meal, the dinner itself is pleasant. Martin brought a small bouquet of flowers, and Thomas's cheeks are rosy with candlelight instead of ale. Their home is, after so long, jolly. After supper, Thomas goes to check in with the night guard, leaving Emily and Martin alone.

"Let me help you," Martin says, as Emily begins to clear the table. "How'd that go, d'you think?"

"You mean with my father?" She grins. "Quite well, I expect."

"I thought so too," he says, plunging his hands into the soapy water.

"Oh, you really don't have to wash up—"

"It's my pleasure," he insists.

"Wait, your shirt." She approaches him from behind and begins rolling up his sleeves. "They're a little wet already," she says, smoothing the fabric up Martin's forearms. His skin is delicate, fair beneath wisps of wheat-colored hair. Impulsively, she stands on her toes and kisses his cheek. Martin's ears grow pink. Hands still in the water, he turns to face her, and then he is kissing her deeply, insistently, pulling away just as Thomas reenters.

"Everything alright in there, Mr. Brown?" Martin asks, with a wink at Emily, who begins quickly drying the clean plates, turning away to hide the rising color in her face.

"It's fine," Thomas says, though his smile is stiff.

"And the issue we discussed earlier—"

"Will be taken care of tomorrow," Thomas says. "Well, thank you for joining us, Martin. You should get home now."

"Yes, sir." Martin hands the last plate to Emily to dry.

"What was that about?" Emily asks after Martin leaves.

Thomas chuckles. "Never mind that. What are *you* doing, making our guest do the dishes?"

"He insisted!"

Thomas shakes his head. "Let me finish up at least."

"I've got it," Emily says.

"Would you stop arguing and get some sleep, love?" Thomas's eyes crinkle with his smile. "I need you up early tomorrow. The quarterly report is due to the board of governors first thing, and I can't spare one of the lads."

"Well, alright," she says. "If you insist." Under the covers, with the candle extinguished, she replays her kiss with Martin in her mind. The whole evening felt, for the first time, like the start of something real. Warm, and promising, and hopeful.

Emily stifles a yawn as she delivers the report to the sallow-faced secretary across town in the morning. She'd woken in the night thinking about the cryptic words that passed between Martin and her father. *It will be taken care of tomorrow,* Thomas said. An odd turn of phrase, but at the look between the two men, a tacit understanding, Emily has begun to think about a proposal. Martin, surely, is not yet ready to marry. His rented room in Clerkenwell isn't exactly a home. But the glow of their shared dinner made anything seem possible. What a relief it would be to finally stop trying so hard, to finally accept someone's help. Maybe it isn't what her mother would have wanted. But doesn't it matter what Emily wants? God, if she could finally feel less alone in this world, wouldn't that be worth it?

If Martin asks, Emily thinks she might say yes.

It's midafternoon when she returns to Holloway. She walks cell by cell down the corridors, checking in on the inmates with extra care like her mother once did. It is relatively empty, but the long-term prisoners remain.

"Hello, Hannah," Emily says.

"You look happy," the woman replies, pushing knotted strands away from her face to get a closer look. "Let me guess. There's a boy."

"Now, now." Emily giggles. When has she ever giggled before? It is an embarrassing admission. She checks over her shoulder to make sure none of the guards—least of all Martin—are lurking nearby.

"Oh ho!" Hannah's gravelly laugh echoes until it turns into a cough. "Don't tell me it's somebody in here. Girl, you need to get out more."

"That may be true," Emily says. "Then again, so do you."

"Fair enough," Hannah says. "Though with everything going on, you really *should* get out and be done with this place, if you can."

"What do you mean?"

"Didn't you hear her this morning? The screams . . ." Hannah shudders, holding her hands over her ears.

Emily speaks slowly and calmly, though her stomach lurches. "What are you talking about, Hannah?"

"The suffragette they brought in two days ago. Jane Warton. She started hunger striking first thing, and then this morning, they dragged her out for feeding. Lord, she's older than any of us. I can't stand the shrieking, Emily, I really can't. This place echoes like hell."

"Who dragged her out? My father?"

A man's heavy tread reverberates in the hall. She turns to see Martin approaching, and she feels her heart catch in her throat. Hannah nods and leans in to whisper, "And him."

Emily whirls away from Hannah's cell and races toward Martin. "Where is she?" For a split second, she watches Martin's face contort, deciding whether to feign ignorance or tell the truth.

"Upstairs."

Emily takes the rickety metal stairs two at a time. She doesn't know where to turn in the labyrinth up there until the shrieking begins. It is as though a bolt of electricity shoots up her spine. She is seized with a sudden urge to cover her ears and run away, and yet her feet cannot move. Within seconds she gets a grip on herself. How many times has she heard screams in the halls of Holloway? Countless. For a moment, she is transported to the day she and her parents arrived, back when she was barely seven years old. They had stood nearly in the same spot as she finds herself in now, clutching their belongings, taking in the dim, cavernous space around them. Emily had been worried about her doll, Geraldine, and had gripped the familiar, calloused skin of her mother's hand. Then someone had shrieked, a desperate, primal wail. It was frightening for Emily, but worst of all was the fact that no one else had seemed to notice. Marianne's jaw had tensed, barely perceptibly. But the guard showing the Browns around had not blinked an eye at the disturbance.

The scream she hears now, however, is unlike any sound she has ever perceived from a human throat. She has heard women in varying states of agony, anger, insanity, even childbirth. This is different, near continuous, an unrelenting cry for mercy.

Sprinting down the hall, she follows the sound. Her feet take on a rhythm, *please please please*. She does not know why she is begging. Not until she arrives in a formerly abandoned corridor and sees the bodies pushing and writhing does she realize what she is witnessing. The doctor lifts his black leather bag off the ground and disappears down the back staircase, trailed by Thomas. They do not see her. Emily runs to the woman, abandoned and curled up into herself on the floor, her strength so sapped that she cannot climb onto her cot. At the sound of footsteps she flinches, but then she sees Emily.

"It's you," the woman whispers.

Emily cannot make out the woman's features in the dim light through the grates of the cell. And then, all of a sudden, she can.

"Lady Cunningham?" Emily gasps. "What are you doing here?"

"Shh," Constance hisses with a shuddering breath. "No one can know who I am." Slowly, she raises herself to her hands and knees and crawls feebly to the grate, coming as close as she can to Emily. Silver strands of hair frame pupils as large as marbles. Blood is crusted around her lips.

"Jane Warton?"

"An alias," Constance breathes. "It's all part of a plan. Please. You must not tell anyone."

CHAPTER FORTY

BEATRICE

S adie stirs the batter with something like ferocity.

"Would you stop that?" Beatrice yanks the bowl away. "We're baking scones, not bashing brains."

"Oh, ha-ha," Sadie says in a flat voice.

Beatrice sighs, dropping the telegram into the hearth. "I thought you'd think it was good news."

"That you're not needed at home until the wedding?"

"Yes, Daniel is finalizing business with his father, and my mother will take care of the planning at Champney House. That gives us plenty of time."

Sadie scoops dough from the bowl and, with equal vigor, begins to pound it on the table. "Plenty."

"Yes, well. As much as I could have hoped for. My mother is rather irritated that I won't be involved in the preparations. But I didn't think you'd be. Heavens."

Sadie blinks back tears.

"What more can I do?" Beatrice's voice breaks. "I don't understand what you want from me."

"I don't think *you* understand." Sadie finally looks up at Beatrice. "Just hearing you talk about Daniel and the wedding," she lowers her voice to a whisper. "It's agony for me." Sadie wipes tears with the back of her wrist. "It's just prolonging the pain. I mean what I said, Bea. I'm in love with you."

The words crack open Beatrice's chest like a raw egg. She wraps her arms around Sadie's stiff back, nestling her cheek into the space between Sadie's neck and shoulder. How is it that Sadie always smells of roses?

"I'm in love with you, too," Beatrice whispers. They are both trembling now, hearts hammering and hands unsteady. Is this what love feels like? Dizzy and desperate? Beatrice breathes into Sadie's skin.

"I really, truly love you," Beatrice says. "I don't know what else I can do or say. But if I don't get married, you know what my mother has threatened." The edge of Beatrice's voice trembles. The unspoken threat hangs between them. *The sanatorium.*

"I'd never let that happen to you," Sadie says.

"How could you stop it?"

"We could run away, leave the whole world behind. I don't know, Bea. But there's always an alternative."

"I don't want to think about that now," Beatrice whispers. "I don't want to think about that or Daniel or my mother or anything. I just want to be with you. Can't that be enough?"

It's right there on her face, Sadie's belief that it will never be enough. But her resolve crumbles.

And then they are kissing, magnetic and fervent, like the churning of ocean waves. It's like the story Sadie told her about coming to England, crossing the Atlantic on a steamship accompanied only by a dotty old chaperone who spent the entire journey seasick in the cabins, and Sadie could not take her eyes off the vast sea. It had made her feel small to see the world extend in every direction, relentless and all-consuming. But it also made her feel, somehow, herself. Her truest self was among those waves, when everything but the integrity of her own heart was reduced to insignificance, when all that mattered was how she felt surrounded by the great, expansive blue.

Beatrice understands that feeling now, wrapped in Sadie's arms. How can anything else possibly matter? Life is too short, their problems arbitrary and small, compared to the vast and overpowering emotions of their love. So what if it swallows her up? She would rather drown in love than never feel its pull at all. They hold tight to each other, anchored.

CHAPTER FORTY-ONE

EMILY

For the first time in a decade, Emily finds herself thinking, again, of the Invisible Lady. Except this time, it isn't a fiction. It isn't a circus act, a spectacle. There is a very real woman, in a very real cage, suffering and struggling in very real pain. And once again, no one can see her. The Invisible Lady had an answer to every question, and people paid good money just to listen to her. What a wonder, a woman with knowledge! But now those words she uttered in a little girl's ear return, like a spectral whisper from the past: *They choose not to see me.*

That day at the fair, when her mother was alive and her father was young and the world was full of magic, Emily thought that she had learned life's greatest secret. Just be quiet. Just be good. There is a mystique in remaining unseen. And so she had; she had been a good girl, a docile daughter, dutiful and quiet.

Suddenly, ten years later, those words take on new meaning: *They choose not to see me.* People rendered the Invisible Lady unseen because it made them more comfortable. They accepted her voice, her knowledge, only because she did not get in their way. Outside of the circus, society did not want to hear a woman's opinions or thoughts or ideas. Which was why a woman who did speak, who did know, became a gimmick, an oddity, a spectacle.

All these months she has watched women just like herself—Charlotte and Sadie, Jessie and Isabel and Beatrice—who dare to be seen and heard. And now, even Lady Constance Cunningham chooses to don the disguise of a commoner to prove how brutal the treatment is at Holloway. Constance could have kept safe. She could have continued donating funds and observing from the sidelines. But she didn't.

Meanwhile, Emily has remained in the shadows, safe and unseen. But what has that achieved? Her halfhearted attempt to be a spy, a double agent, feels silly in comparison to what her friends sacrifice. That's what they are, her only true friends. She sees how their prison uniforms scratch spidery rashes up and down their stomachs. Their plank beds crawl with lice as they shiver and starve in their cinder block cells.

And yet, the MPs sleep comfortably in their beds, pillows plumped by unnoticed maids, their wives stiff beside them so as not to take up any extra space. The MPs do not bat an eye at the protests, do not blink when the bobbies grip the women's wrists and asses and breasts as they shuttle them back and forth from Holloway like cattle. The women shout from the tops of their lungs about rights and justice, but no one listens.

Emily herself has been complacent. That's the thing about invisibility. It isn't a passive choice. It's an everyday commitment. And she realizes, for the first time, that she is no longer willing to commit. Life's daily struggles won't cease when the vote is won, but if Lady Constance Cunningham, whose life is blessedly simple, is still willing to put herself through torture, there must be a reason. That's what Marianne never understood, what Emily sees now. Even though the drudgery and struggle of daily labor won't end with the vote, women will no longer be at the mercy of men. The Thomases, Martins, and

Dr. Bainwrights of the world will not operate behind closed doors. Women will have a voice.

Marianne never had choices. She worked in the mill until it nearly killed her, and then she worked in the jail until she died. But what if she could have advocated for herself? What if she could have made the mill a safer place? What if she did not have to marry at eighteen, still a child but already a burden to her parents?

The pencil bites into Emily's palm, staining her skin black. She is drawing, fearless and furious. Her fingers fly across the paper, slashes of charcoal, lines and shadow. A woman, thin, frail, shackled, her figure prostrate, protesting. The men, looming, holding her down, forcing their instruments inside of her.

The door to Thomas's office is closed. Dr. Bainwright will not return until the night feeding. In a few hours, the evening paper will go to press. It is Emily's second time carrying an illicit message out of Holloway. But this time, the message is her own.

If society chooses not to see—well, Emily will give them no choice. She will make herself visible, and with her, the truth.

Knuckles raw and cracked, Emily knocks ceaselessly on the door at Park Lane until it flies open. Charlotte stands framed in the doorway.

"What are you doing here?"

Emily tries not to read into the bite in Charlotte's voice. She presses the missive into her hand wordlessly, watching as Charlotte unfolds the paper and studies the image. A tear spills down her cheek before she wipes it away and grabs Emily's sleeve.

"Come inside."

They hover awkwardly in the foyer, waiting for the other to speak first.

"I know it's Constance," Emily says.

"We couldn't tell you. It was Constance and Adeline's idea. We had to make sure she wouldn't be recognized." Charlotte's tone is brisk now, but not hostile.

"Why?" Emily already suspects.

"So that they'd treat her like the rest of us. The plan is, after she is released, Constance will expose the whole thing, do a big interview and tell the truth of the brutality happening in Holloway. Even if no one listened to me or cared about my letter, we think they'll care about the wife of an earl."

Emily swallows the bile rising in her throat. "It was a fine plan," she begins. "But, listen, Constance is old. She isn't as strong as you. I saw her just now and . . . she looks weak. I'm afraid she's really quite ill."

"She knew what she was getting into—"

"I know. But I don't think she can take much more. Don't you see?" Emily points to her drawing. "Can't we take this to the papers right now, reveal her identity along with the image? The whole city will know in a few hours and Constance will . . . well, I don't know if they'll stop the forcible feedings. But we have to try."

Charlotte searches Emily's face. "If Constance is doing as poorly as you say, I suppose it's the best chance we've got. But I have to speak with Adeline first."

"Can she get it to press in time?"

"If we hurry. But, Emily, you realize that if we publish this, there'll be no doubt it was you. It's not just my words in a letter anyone could have smuggled out. Your father will know that the drawing is yours."

The fairytale family dinner, warm and full of laughter, almost like when her mother was alive, flashes before Emily's eyes. Her stolen kisses with Martin and the future he offered. Her father's efforts, misguided as they may have been, to make her dreams come true. The opportunities her mother had envisioned, and the promises she made.

Charlotte is right. There will be no going back. Her father will be furious, Martin betrayed—but then, they betrayed her first.

Emily thinks about the overheard conversations, the exchanged glances that she half heard and half ignored. They think her a fool. And she let them make her one. Both Martin and her father had a hand in Constance's torture, and Charlotte's, too. She has no doubt now that they will do it again and again, without remorse. Would they do it to her if they had the chance?

"Are you sure?" Charlotte asks.

"I'm sure."

"I'll tell Adeline, then." Charlotte pauses only to insist that Emily stay a few hours, and then she races out to find Adeline at Clement's Inn.

CHAPTER FORTY-TWO

CHARLOTTE

Well, I'll be damned," Adeline says, Emily's drawing in hand. Charlotte is still panting from running nearly all the way to headquarters. "Didn't I tell you not to underestimate Emily Brown?" She exhales with a whistle. "This is better than we could have planned. It really is. I just hope it works."

Charlotte winces at Adeline's words. *Better than we could have planned.* Even though she is accustomed to Adeline's bluntness, the ugly truth of the words is painful. They are all pawns in this brutal game.

"Will you be able to get it printed in time?"

"I'm going to find my man at *The Times* right now. It'll make the evening papers, I guarantee."

Charlotte gnaws her bottom lip.

"There's going to be fallout," Adeline adds, as she pulls on her coat.

Back at home, Charlotte finds Emily staring into her murky teacup and the other two communicating something unspoken, something she can sense but not name.

"Will you stay here overnight?" Charlotte asks. "It might be safer for you than staying with your father."

Beatrice and Sadie exchange a glance with raised eyebrows, but Charlotte does not clarify.

"No," Emily says. "My father will be furious. But I have to be at home."

"I thought you'd say that. Remember, the door is always open here, if you need it."

Tears well in Emily's eyes, and Sadie nods in agreement, despite the fact that she doesn't know what is happening.

"I'd better go," Emily says, pushing away from the table.

Charlotte walks her to the doorway. Standing there once more, the tension is palpable. Then Charlotte flings her arms around Emily and hugs her.

"I'm sorry for being so unfair to you," Charlotte whispers. "I was wrong. You've already risked so much for us."

"It's alright," Emily says, holding tight to Charlotte's back.

When Charlotte pulls away, she gazes at Emily through tear-rimmed eyes, but she is smiling. "You're one of us now, you know," she says, her own doubt supplanted by a whisper of newfound hope. "A suffragette, whether you like it or not."

Emily nods, and with a laugh that sounds more like a choked sob, she steps out into the dusky street.

CHAPTER FORTY-THREE

EMILY

E mily begins to walk home, but her limbs feel like they've been torn off and haphazardly reattached. They are not quite moving as they should. Somewhere, a clock chimes seven o'clock. She steels herself at the sight of a newsboy, wiry and red-haired, probably only ten years old. She glances at the cover; it's the evening *Times*. She digs into her pocket for a few coins, and the boy tosses her the top paper from his pile. Walking and reading at once, she flips one page, then two, and then—there it is. Her image. Her art. A drawing to refute the care- less cartoons that had littered the pages of this very publication, of ugly women, caricatured figures deserving of ridicule. Her drawing is alive—the pain, the horror, the reality of it all. And then, above it, a headline: LADY EDWARD CUNNINGHAM FORCIBLY FED.

The uproar at Holloway is worse than she predicted. From the court- yard, the rumbling shouts of men—the guards, the warden, the doctor—echo through the halls along with the high-pitched shrieks and whoops of the female prisoners. Old Hannah's husky laughter rings out. Emily feels the hand clasp around her shoulder before she even registers the sound of anyone's approach.

"How dare you?" Martin growls. "How bloody dare you?"

"How could *you*?" Emily cries. "I thought you were—let go of me."

Martin's fingers dig into her collarbone. She struggles to shake him off, but he holds on tighter.

"I covered for you—"

"Let me go!"

Martin leers in her face, his eyes wide and raging. The sweet boy she kissed in the park is nowhere to be seen. "We were supposed to have a life together!"

She wants to explain it to him. What kind of life would that be? One built upon cowardice and complicity, selfishness and lies. How can they stomach a life like that? The tears begin to flow, wet and hot on her cheeks. She wishes she could put it into words, the betrayal *she* feels, the anger at herself for her naïveté. She had been humiliatingly, shamefully close to swallowing her principles for the comfort Martin promised. God, just this morning she had thought that last night's whispering foreshadowed a proposal of marriage. How blind she had been, watching them both conspire torture right before her eyes. She had thought Martin was different, or maybe she had been willfully blind. But now she knows, without a doubt, and she cannot unsee what he has done.

"You brought this on yourself!"

"I was just doing my job—"

"Let go of my daughter." Thomas pushes Martin away, a seething anger radiating from his every pore.

She gasps, heart surging with gratitude toward her father. Martin stumbles away and Emily stands alone with Thomas. She presses her hands to her thighs, trying to catch her breath, but the flash in his eye, red-hot rage, sends her reeling backward.

Thomas's voice is slow and grave as he speaks, enunciating each word with a quiet fury. "How could you?" He does not touch her, but Emily feels as though she's been punched in the gut. It does not matter that he has been drinking, though she can already smell it on his breath. After what she's done, his face would be this red, his eyes this fiery, no matter what. Her ears ring, a strange, sibilant hissing in her brain, and she takes a step back, finding herself against the exterior brick wall, cornered.

"I had to!" Her throat is tight, but she won't cry. She refuses to collapse.

Thomas has never raised a hand to her in her life, but now, suddenly, his calloused hand grips her shoulder, his thumb creeping close to her neck. Her pulse leaps against his hand.

"Papa," she gasps. "I had no choice! You knew what they were doing in there. You knew and you didn't care. I had to stop it! If Mama knew—"

"Do you take me for a fool?" he pants. His teeth are bared inches from her face, and as her breath comes in short, shallow spurts, she can see the spot where he is missing a molar. Marianne had yanked out the rotting tooth when Emily was a child. Emily had watched with a mixture of fascination and horror as her father downed whiskey and held a bloody cloth to his mouth. Now that missing tooth revolts her. Who is this man? He is no one she knows. No one she could have ever loved. "Did you think I wouldn't know it was you?"

"I knew you would know," she breathes, leaning back as far as she can. Her skull presses into the wall behind her. His grip on her shoulder remains viselike. "So what? What if it had been me instead of Charlotte and Constance?"

"If it had been you?" he repeats. "You'd never." Emily wonders if that is a threat. "I've given you everything I could," Thomas rages. "The food you eat, the bed you sleep in. The roof over your head. Do you think I wanted this to be our life? *Do you?* How bloody dare you humiliate me like this?"

In the moment it takes Emily to pause, to assess what to do next, she sees her father's eyes glaze over with such fury that he is unrecognizable. There is no sympathy, no reason left in this man. And hadn't she decided, the very moment she put pencil to paper and made that sketch, that she did not care what her father thought anymore? That some risks were worth taking?

She reels back, sucking in her cheeks, and then spits. It's the shock, more than the wetness, that does it. Thomas's eyes widen in astonishment, and his hand instinctively loosens around her neck as he wipes the saliva from his scruffy cheek. It's all she needs—that millisecond of opportunity. She runs, veering around the corner and sprinting past the cottage. Out in the courtyard, yellow pools of light from the electric lamps are stained in shadow. Then she is at the gate, hands fumbling with the latch, and at last it sings its squeaky protest as she flings it open. Her ribs ache and her breath, already stifled from her father's chokehold, comes in desperate gasps as her lungs fight against her whalebone stays.

Emily makes it three blocks down Parkhurst Street before she turns to look back. A scarlet sunset surrounds the black silhouette of Holloway Prison, like she set the place on fire.

PART THREE
WINTER–SPRING 1913

CHAPTER FORTY-FOUR

EMILY

E mily shivers in bed that first night, uneasy, an arm's length from Charlotte but so very far from home. She has never slept on a real woolen mattress, wrapped in blankets as fine as these. But no amount of luxury can keep out the chill that permeates every inch of her body, from her numb toes to the bruised tips of her fingers. She refuses to regret the choices she's made. Still, it's terrifying, this new life. She is completely untethered.

"Shh," Charlotte whispers, jostling Emily's shoulders. "You'll wake the others."

Emily blinks. It's still dark out, sometime before twilight. "I'm sorry. Was I . . . ?"

"Shouting, yes," Charlotte says. "Here, shove over."

Emily inches to the side and Charlotte climbs into the bed. The feeling of another warm body, another heart beating beside her, is so comforting it makes her want to cry.

"You had a nightmare?"

Emily nods.

"My father always said that if you tell someone else your nightmare, it gets it out of your head. Do you want to tell me what it was about?"

"That's just it," Emily whispers. "I don't remember. All I know is that I tried to scream, but no one could hear me." It's hard to put into words that horror, how real it felt when she opened her mouth in desperation, producing nothing more than breath. Charlotte rubs Emily's back gently and stifles a chuckle.

"Oh, Em," she says. "Trust me, I could hear you."

Suddenly, it's all rather funny and they're both laughing.

"I'm proud of you," Charlotte says. "I know this isn't easy."

"No," Emily admits. "But it also feels inevitable, do you know what I mean?"

Charlotte smiles. "Yes, I know exactly what you mean. But tell me, what changed your mind?"

"Besides my father kicking me out and leaving me with no choice?"

"Yes, besides that."

"It was Constance." They are silent for a moment as Emily collects her thoughts. "I think seeing her in there, treated like . . ."

"Like scum?" Charlotte offers. "Like shit?"

"Like she was less than human. And knowing that as soon as they found out she wasn't Jane Warton, everything would change. It made me furious—at the system, yes, but also at myself. I'd been so caught up in the idea that if I could just do a bit better, get myself to a solid, middle-class life, you know, that somehow I'd be safe. That would be all that mattered." Emily shakes her head. "But going to teacher's college or getting married—none of that would protect me or any woman. I realized we've got to reform the system from the inside out. Otherwise, it's all just a lie. Any happiness I ever felt would be built on the back of someone less fortunate."

"You know who you sound like?" Charlotte asks.

"Who?"

"Your mum. Everyone used to talk about how she treated the prisoners like we mattered. Maybe she didn't agree with us. But she still knew we deserved human dignity."

Emily breathes deeply. A part of her knows that she will always have disappointed her mother. She failed to achieve her dying wish. And yet Charlotte is right, even though each word scrapes at the wall Emily so carefully constructed around her heart.

"Mama always said, 'They're all someone's daughter.'"

"And we are." Charlotte squeezes Emily's hand.

Nearly every family rejects the daughters that choose revolution over duty, Emily learns in the days to come. It takes time to adjust, but all of the full-time volunteers go through it. Except, of course, for the Hurstons. Lucky Isabel—her mother not only supports her suffrage activism but stands by her side.

"It's about time we give you a code name," says Charlotte.

"Do I get to choose the name myself?" Emily asks.

"Well, as you might have guessed, we've already been using one for you. For a while," Sadie says.

Emily shakes her head, feigning annoyance, but of course it makes sense. "Alright, then, what is it?"

"Just wait," says Charlotte.

They guide Emily to a high-backed chair in the sitting room and instruct her to close her eyes. Emily hears tiptoeing footsteps and whispers.

"Iris, step forward."

Emily opens her eyes to find Beatrice striding toward her. She places a hand on Emily's left shoulder.

"Mayflower of Massachusetts," Charlotte cues.

Sadie steps up to Emily's right.

"And now, Ivy, with the ceremonial sash," says Sadie.

Charlotte emerges from down the hall with the violet, white, and green suffragette sash in her outstretched arms. She bends one knee in front of Emily.

"We welcome you to our ranks," says Charlotte. "Hollyhock, our warrior."

Emily giggles as Charlotte drapes the sash over her head; it's silly, but it means more than she can articulate.

"One, two, three!" Sadie shouts, leading them into a rousing, off-key rendition of "The Women's Marseillaise."

Then the work begins. Adeline assigns Emily jobs at regular intervals—it is essential to keep the new recruits busy as they adjust. In addition to the usual cooking and sewing, with which everyone takes a turn, she is given the responsibility of sketching layouts for new issues of *Votes for Women*. Emily is grateful for Adeline's maternal presence whenever she visits the headquarters at Clement's Inn. It is a relief to feel that someone older and wiser is looking out for her, even from a distance.

Jessie, too, keeps an eye on Emily. "I hope you're adjusting alright," she says after a long strategy session. Jessie offers Emily her good hand, pulling her up off the floor, where she'd been finishing the sketch Adeline requested of the meeting.

"I'm trying." Emily puts on her bravest smile.

"Look how far you've come."

"I remember when we first spoke when you were in Holloway. When I saw you again here, I thought you'd hate me."

"Hate you? Of course not. You were kind to me then."

"But I worked in that terrible place."

Jessie laughs. "I've worked in too many terrible places to count. I would never judge you for doing what you had to in order to feed your family." Jessie tilts her head to the side, a smile playing on her lips. "What is it?"

"It's just so nice to know that you understand," Emily says.

"Believe me, I do," Jessie says. "And I'm here for you. Now, these other women are some of my dearest friends and most admired colleagues, but I understand, too, how shocking it must feel for you to be dropped into this new life like a fish in a strange pond. One moment you're scraping by, the next you're living in a grand house on Park Lane with, well—"

"Rich girls," Emily says.

"Your words, not mine!" Jessie laughs unselfconsciously, a more vibrant version of the woman Emily once spoke to behind the bars at Holloway. Even then, though, Emily could tell that Jessie wasn't a person whose light could be easily dimmed. "We working girls have to stick together, alright?"

CHAPTER FORTY-FIVE

BEATRICE

No one has heard from Constance "Ladybug" Cunningham since her husband retrieved her from jail. Even the papers have been conspicuously silent on the topic, though Adeline suspects that Lord Cunningham has something to do with that. The earl was aware of his wife's suffragette involvement, at least her financial contributions over the years. But they can only worry and wonder about how he has reacted to her newly public status. And even though Emily's sketch sent shockwaves through London, no one knows whether it will make any difference. What if, once again, all their sacrifices have been for nothing?

Then, about a week after the publication of the sketch, Beatrice races into the Park Lane parlor with a newspaper clutched in her hand.

"What is it?" Sadie runs toward her and reads over Beatrice's shoulder.

"It's . . . an apology." The paper trembles in her hand.

Charlotte grabs it and begins to read aloud, hiccupping through her mixture of anguish, fury, and downright frustration. At last, the government issued a public apology to Lord and Lady Cunningham.

Beatrice feels the slap on behalf of her friend. After everything Charlotte endured and all she had publicly testified to in her smuggled letter, no one batted an eye. But as Constance and Adeline predicted, when *Lady* Cunningham underwent the same treatment, the government was compelled to revamp their investigation into Holloway Prison's governance and reconsider the question of votes for women.

"Parliament is putting it to a vote," Sadie breathes in disbelief.

"After all this time." Tears well in the corners of Charlotte's eyes. "After everything."

"We must go to headquarters straight away!" says Beatrice.

"Will this really change things?" Emily asks.

Beatrice and Charlotte exchange a glance.

"Em," says Charlotte. "This changes everything."

When Isabel opens the door at Clement's Inn, she is positively beaming. Beatrice has never seen her so happy. Isabel can be imperious and captivating and charming and strategic, but giddy—never.

"Come in," she chirps. Stepping into the hall, it sounds like someone is singing upstairs. "Mother!" Isabel calls. The singing stops and Adeline bounds down the stairs like a Labrador. Even Emily raises an eyebrow.

"Ladies," Adeline says, her typically impeccable chignon replaced by a loose mass of gray-blond curls. "A Conciliation Bill has been introduced to the House of Commons, one that includes women's suffrage in its text. The bill is poised to pass."

"It's just a start—only partial suffrage, for certain women," Isabel interjects. "But it's an enormous step in the right direction!"

"Oh." Charlotte clasps her hands together. "If even some women could vote—"

"We could begin to stand for Parliament," Adeline says. "And extend the vote to the rest."

Emily bounces her legs beneath the table. It's finally happening.

"This is the closest we have ever come to success," Adeline adds, though they all know this already. "I'm calling off all protests we had planned from now until the vote. All militancy is suspended. From here on out, we are the government's very best friends."

Isabel nods so vehemently, Beatrice thinks her neck might give out. "I'm planning a celebratory parade," she says. "For after the vote." She claps once, then stands. "Oh, I can't take it! I have to tell Jessie and the others." Isabel excuses herself, leaving Beatrice, Charlotte, Sadie, and Emily with Adeline at the table.

"So, I take it you don't need our help today?" Sadie asks.

"Well, you know how these things go. Nothing is settled until it's settled. You should await further instruction." Adeline's dancing eyes belie the caution in her words. "But take the day off. Go sit in the park. Have an ice cream!"

The four women burst out laughing. Adeline appears as though she might launch into a jig. "I'll be in touch," Adeline promises as they say goodbye.

Outside, the sun breaks through the cloud cover, and shards of light glitter in the puddles like melted mirrors. "Perhaps," says Beatrice, "we *should* have an ice cream."

"I think I joined the suffragettes at just the right time," Emily says.

For three weeks they await news of the Conciliation Bill. It is hard to imagine that everything they've fought for might at last come to fruition. If property-owning women are granted the vote, it will only be a matter of time before it is extended to all women. And until then, women like Adeline Hurston could stand for Parliament and usher in reform right away.

The house on Park Lane is taut with anticipation. Every morning, Sadie wakes first and snatches the newspaper from the stoop, scanning the political section for updates before slamming the door as she steps back inside.

"Nothing!" she shouts up the stairs, waking the whole house but saving them the suspense of wondering.

The four women spend days poring over the bookshelves in Sadie's brother's library, reading Henry James and Jane Austen to distract from the lack of news.

"Imagine if . . ." Sadie says, folding down a corner of *The Portrait of a Lady*.

"Don't!" warns Beatrice. It's too painful to fantasize about victory; the possibilities are too tantalizing.

They cannot jinx it, cannot risk getting their hopes up. And yet it is irresistible. "When the bill passes," Charlotte muses.

"Shhh," Emily insists. But her sketches these days are exuberant and hopeful, sunshine piercing through clouds, abundant gardens.

"Did you know that since the 1860s, women have circulated over nine thousand petitions for the vote, containing over three million signatures?" Beatrice asks, apropos of nothing.

"Oh, Bea," Sadie says, squeezing her hand.

Then one morning, Sadie reads the paper, and as the door slams shut behind her, she doesn't say anything at all. Upstairs, Beatrice is in bed, the empty spot beside her still warm from Sadie's body. She listens, waiting. Down the hall, Emily and Charlotte are awake, too. As the minutes pass, they hold their breath. At the sound of Sadie's footsteps thudding upstairs, all three women walk silently to the landing. Sadie meets their eyes and shakes her head.

The Conciliation Bill collapsed. Squabbling MPs with their eyes on the next by-elections turned their backs as the bill floundered, then died, leaving women in the lurch once again. The first and only hope for the suffragettes in the decade since Adeline and Isabel first organized the Union in 1903 had failed. Not miserably, not spectacularly—it had just plain failed. Sadie cries. Beatrice kicks herself for hoping. Charlotte and Emily stand still, stunned.

CHAPTER FORTY-SIX

EMILY

The protest is not meant to be anything out of the ordinary.

Adeline gathers her closest recruits at Clement's Inn on the morning of February 28, 1913. She wears a somber navy dress and pins violets to her hat. Isabel matches her mother and sets her jaw with unbending resolve. Charlotte, Emily, Beatrice, and Sadie huddle in the entryway beside the familiar faces of women they have gotten to know over the past months. There's Constance Cunningham, leaning on a cane in the corner. Maggie Andrews sits at attention in her wheelchair to Adeline's left. Jessie stands up front beside Isabel, straightening her sash.

With vague and then startling recognition, Emily spots women she has glimpsed only through the bars of Holloway cells and others whose faces she has seen in the newspapers. The buzzing room settles to silence as Adeline raises a hand. Emily holds her breath.

"These men," Adeline begins, eyes steel gray and gazing toward a hazy future that she, somehow, can still conjure in her imagination. "They little know what women are."

"Hear, hear!" Sadie says. Beatrice grips her hand.

"Once roused, women are determined. Nothing on heaven or earth will make women give way." The small crowd murmurs in agreement. "Failure is impossible," Adeline says with a sharp nod. "When we win this hardest of fights, we will pave the way for women all over to the world to win *their* fight, too. We must not give up."

"And so," Isabel adds, her spine straight to match her mother's. "Are you going to play the woman or the coward?"

Emily feels her heart thrum in her chest. Isabel's words ignite some ember inside her.

"We are made of sterner stuff," Isabel continues. "Say it with me: I will be a woman!"

Emily's voice catches in her throat. It emerges sounding strange and unfamiliar. Strong. Loud. She is no longer invisible. She doubts that she ever will be again.

"I will place myself in line with the great forces of womanhood that are stirring in the world today! We shall stand before these lawmakers, peaceful, unarmed, demanding the most basic of democratic principles: a voice."

Their heartbeats set the pace for their footfalls as the women file out the door and into the midday gray. They walk slowly at first, measured, with a silent energy, as they pass along the Strand. Then quicker, steadier, as Trafalgar Square comes into view. The great lions grin down at the women and Emily shudders. Suffragettes have been trampled, she knows, beneath the lions' gaze. Her first protest is suddenly becoming very real.

"Don't be nervous," Sadie whispers. She follows Emily's gaze and then sticks out her tongue. "They're only cats. Women are the real lions."

By the time they reach Downing Street, several hundred women have joined their ranks. It is not the largest march of suffragettes, nor is it the smallest. Emily feels a firm resolve settle in her chest. Around her, women begin to sing "The March of the Women," and Emily's own voice lifts with the melody that she once heard sung in the prison yard, a beacon of hope in a place of utter despair.

March, march, many as one,
Shoulder to shoulder, and friend to friend

At last, they reach Parliament Square. Black iron gates, tall and foreboding, separate the women from the Gothic chambers of government. Policemen stand stationed around the entrances. As usual, Adeline and Isabel lead the group, so they approach the officers first. In her gloved hand, Adeline holds a handwritten petition for the prime minister.

"Please, sir, we wish to enter the Strangers' Gallery," she says, her tone crisp and polite.

The officer, a stocky middle-aged man with graying sideburns, ignores Adeline entirely. He looks down his nose and past her, as though she does not exist. Isabel steps forward, directly into the man's line of vision, and repeats her mother's words.

"We wish to enter the Strangers' Gallery," she says.

The officer's upper lip twitches, but he does not speak. Isabel stands her ground, a mere foot from the man's face.

Another officer appears. "Is there a problem here?" he addresses the first guard, ignoring, again, the two women in front of him, and the hundreds more holding their collective breath beyond.

"We have a petition to deliver to Prime Minister Asquith, sir," Adeline says firmly. "As citizens, we have a right to present it in the Strangers' Gallery."

The second officer sweeps his gaze over the crowd. Nearly three hundred women freeze, straining to hear his reply. It is one syllable. "No."

As he utters that singular grunt, he grabs Isabel by the shoulders and pushes her aside. Hard. The force of the shove, and the shock of his response, sends Isabel reeling backward. She regains her balance before slamming to the ground, but only just. As she steadies herself, her eyes flicker with anger. Adeline steps forward to defend her daughter, but Jessie cuts in first.

"Don't you dare touch her," Jessie snarls.

Thin but muscular from so many years of physical labor, Jessie stands unflinching before the officers, her eyes blazing. The first officer realizes then that he can no longer pretend not to see the women. He lunges at Jessie, grabbing her by the shoulders and whacking his kneecap into her chest. There is a loud crack. The silence that follows, a split second in which Jessie gasps for air, rings in the square like a shot.

Then, mayhem.

"Come on!" Charlotte leads the charge as the women plunge toward the entrance. Other officers, stationed along the length of the fence, converge around the crowd of women. Emily quickly loses sight of the Hurstons. Charlotte's hand is on her wrist, and grateful for her friend's iron grip, she does her best to follow.

When the gate is nearly in reach, Emily feels a hand on her waist. She turns, expecting to see Sadie or Beatrice beside her, but a strange man's face leers in her vision. His rough hands tighten around her. Cold panic shudders through her body. She shakes Charlotte loose in order to have both hands free and tries to wrest herself from the man's clutches. She knocks the police hat off his head. He bends down, and instead of picking up his hat, the officer grabs Emily's skirt hem and yanks it up. She hears a rip, and she is shrouded in darkness.

Fabric presses against her nose and mouth. Coughing and clawing, she realizes he has lifted her skirt up over her head. Between her legs, the man gropes at her knickers. Emily screams louder than she ever has in her life. But in the din of the mob, it is like shouting into a pillow. It is her worst nightmare come true—screaming soundlessly.

The officer's hands move from between her legs to her waist and up to her chest. With one hand squeezing her breast, tight and unrelenting, the other clenches her wrist. Can one human hand shatter the bones of another? Such brutality should defy some law of science. But as her flesh begins to pulse, angry red splotches of skin purpling in his unyielding grip, Emily stops wondering. She goes limp. Limp to the pain she never sought, the situation she stupidly agreed to after years, after a lifetime, of playing it safe, of saying no.

For a singular dissociative moment, she allows herself a pointless wish. She wishes she could shut her eyes and disappear. How satisfying it would be if she never said yes to Charlotte's mad plan all those months ago. How relieving it would be to wipe the slate clean with the edges of a damp rag and say *no*.

When had she stopped saying no?

In the sudden stillness, it all comes rushing back: a lifetime of deference, silence, submissiveness. The role of the dutiful daughter had defined her and molded her, and just as irrevocably, it had brought her here. And there it is. The choice that was never really a choice at all. There is no one to save her. No father to swoop in and defend his daughter. No husband to whisk her away. No mother to shield her from life's tragedies.

But somewhere out there, in the writhing mass of bodies, she senses her friends. A whoop in the distance sounds like Charlotte's voice, and beyond, Sadie and Beatrice battle their way across the square.

The noise of the crowd returns with a roar. Emily kicks backward and flings herself to the ground, wresting free. She wipes her mouth with the back of her wrist, breathing hard. A flash of surprise passes over the officer's face, almost indiscernible, before he replaces that irascible mask of malice. Looming, he launches an arm out and grasps at the back of her dress. A splitting sound rings in her ears, the tearing of fabric, as he pulls her in close. Then her back is up against his chest, and hot breath floods her ears, zinging down to her toes as he whispers words as incomprehensible as they are revolting.

"You've been wanting this for a long time, haven't you?"

She is flushed and chilled all at once, sweating even though her blood runs cold. Emily hears a bone-splitting crack, and she winces, preparing for the pain. It is strange, this separation between sound and sensation. But the crack was not her body. The officer stumbles away, clutching his nose. It runs with blood. And then, there is Sadie, cradling an already bruising fist.

"Jesus Christ." Emily limps toward Sadie.

"You're alright," Sadie says. They look around for Charlotte and Beatrice, but the bodies surrounding them blend together, a throng of arms and legs and voices raised in fear. Emily spots a flash of blond.

"Bea!" she cries, and Sadie follows her gaze. With slow motion terror, they watch another police officer grab Beatrice by the neck. With swift precision, he rips the bodice of her dress and twists her breast forcefully. Her screams dissolve into the air. Sadie runs toward Beatrice, and Emily loses them both in the crowd. She turns around herself, spinning, terrified, jostled, and alone.

"What the hell is happening?" Emily whispers, willing her body to stay upright, her whole being alert to the next attack from any of the hundreds of officers who seem to pour in from every direction.

"Watch it!"

Emily ducks just in time. A wheel the size of a bicycle's soars past where her head had been seconds before. She whirls around and there on the ground sits Maggie Andrews, tears pouring down her face. Emily drops to her knees beside her.

"Bastards," Maggie growls. Her wheelchair is decimated. Only the seat remains. The other pieces, like the wheel Emily narrowly avoided being decapitated by, have been cruelly disassembled. They have only moments before both she and Maggie are trampled.

"Help!" they cry. "Help!"

Through the forest of legs and skirts, she sees a man in plainclothes stumbling through the crowd. Somehow this passerby, caught in the fray, meets her eye.

"Please, sir," Emily yells. She crouches beside Maggie on raised knees. The man steps toward them. "She can't walk. Can you help me carry her to safety?"

The man edges closer and leans in toward Emily. Then he rears back and kicks her square between the legs. She crumples, smacking her head against the pavement. Maggie hurls herself on top of Emily's back like a protective shell. A searing pain, like something broken and burning all at once, ripples from her core out to each and every fingertip. Emily thinks she will die. Now is the time. Whistles blow in her ears and she is vaguely aware of Maggie's heartbeat pummeling on her back. But perhaps the shrill sound is a breeze whistling through trees. Perhaps the heartbeat is her mother's, curled beside her in bed.

When Emily comes to moments later—*or has it been minutes?*—her vision is blurred. Strong hands grip her arms. Through unbelievably heavy eyelids, she can just make out Maggie being lifted up onto a stretcher.

"Get in," says a gruff voice. Emily blinks once, twice. She feels a hard slab of wood beneath her aching groin, and her body lurches with the motion of the wagonette. She is packed, shoulder to shoulder, beside other women.

"Where"—Emily's breath is shallow, her whole body throbbing— "are we going?"

A woman reaches for Emily's hand, holding her tenderly. "Holloway."

CHAPTER FORTY-SEVEN

EMILY

It is sometime near midnight when they arrive. There is no clock, of course, but the night guard has already extinguished the lamps, and so only the dim glow of the torch illuminates their way to the cells on the lower floor of the hold. The sounds once so familiar—the echo of footsteps along a cement corridor, the creak of metal stairs—have become foreboding and strange. Emily strips off her clothes, regarding her legs with an abstract curiosity. These purple bruises must belong to someone else. Only the jolt of pain she feels when she touches the largest one convinces her that the angry indigo welts are not a stranger's, but her own.

Once in the cell, Emily cannot make it to the cot. She curls her aching body into herself on the cold floor. The sensation inside the cell is infinitely more claustrophobic than she ever imagined. How many times has she been in these cells before? Sweeping, cleaning, replacing worn pallets and lice-riddled blankets. But the door always remained open. What a difference a door makes.

When she wakes, the sky has changed from black to gray. It is nearly dawn. Something clenches in her chest, her heart beating like a caged bird. That anxious fear, that flapping of trapped wings, brings back a hazy memory. Her childhood bedroom in the cottage. Her mother's soft footsteps. Marianne slipping beneath the quilt beside her.

"Another nightmare?" Mama had whispered. Emily nodded. Beneath her cheek, the pillow was damp. "It's alright, my darling. I'm here."

"But my heart is beating so hard."

Marianne pressed her palm to Emily's chest.

"Do you know what that feeling is?"

Emily shook her head.

"It's hope."

"Hope?"

"Hope is like a little bird that lives in your heart. It's within you, always. Why, you are feeling its wings beating in your chest right now. Don't you feel it?"

Emily wasn't sure. She felt a tightness in her rib cage, a queasy flutter. Marianne stroked Emily's hair, feeling her daughter exhale beside her. "Hope is always inside you. Even—and especially—when you feel most afraid. That flutter in your chest is hope, reminding you to never give up."

Metal scrapes cement, like nails against slate. Emily jolts awake. Everything hurts. Not in the way that one feels sore after a hard day's labor, or even the fuzziness of waking up to a bad cold. It is a relentless, full-body ache.

Someone slides a tray inside the cell. Even the stench of maggots in mush cannot quite disabuse Emily of the rumbling in her stomach. She cannot remember the last time she'd eaten. She crawls to the tray, fingers twitching above the food, before she remembers to stop.

She lifts the tray, and summoning an inordinate amount of strength, she hurls it at the metal slats in the door with a guttural moan. Gruel drips to the ground.

At the sound of her own primal cry, Emily begins to laugh. She has become one of the raving women she grew up alongside—a screaming, throwing, groaning, and now cackling witch. She laughs and laughs until tears stream from her eyes and her aching rib cage forces her to stifle herself.

No one speaks to her for hours. No one comes to clean up the mess. She vaguely wonders where her father is, whether he's been fired from his post or is somewhere in the building right now. Does he know his daughter is locked in his own jail? Does he care? Yesterday's disastrous protest comes to her in fragments, but mostly she cannot believe what happened. Police, in uniform and plainclothes, had attacked. Why? How? Poor Maggie, her wheelchair ransacked. Sadie, Bea, and Charlotte swept away into the riptide of the pulsating mob. What happened to the others?

CHAPTER FORTY-EIGHT
CHARLOTTE

In the afternoon, one of the guards enters the cell and clamps Charlotte's hands in cuffs, leading her out into the yard to walk in a circle. Exercise time. She tries to catch his eye, but he refuses to look at her directly.

"No talking," he grunts, releasing her into the shuffling ring of women.

It is frigid outside. Puffs of breath escape her mouth in gossamer wisps. Her knuckles are chapped and bleeding. Across the courtyard, she spots a figure hobbling, her face so smashed and swollen she is almost unrecognizable.

"Emily!"

"No talking!" the guard yells.

Charlotte limps toward her, her whole body burning in protest. She feels the guard's eyes upon her as she approaches Emily. Straining against the metal handcuffs, Charlotte squeezes Emily's little finger.

"No touching!"

Together they traipse slowly around the circle. Once out of the guard's earshot, Charlotte whispers rapidly. "They arrested over a hundred of us. Bea is somewhere in here. Isabel and Jessie, too. Sadie escaped and so did Adeline. Are you alright?"

"I'm fine," Emily says, though she winces with each step. "I refused breakfast."

"Me too," says Charlotte.

The repercussions of this choice are too terrifying to think about. When the Conciliation Bill failed, did the government's sudden concern about suffragette welfare in jail end too? Likely. They won't know for sure, though. Not until the doctor arrives.

"Yesterday—" Charlotte finds she has no words for what happened. "I can't believe it."

They pass the guard again, staying silent until they are far enough away to speak once more.

"Did you hear what happened to Maggie Andrews?" Emily asks. "They wrecked her chair."

"I haven't seen her. Maybe she's in hospital. Have you seen your father?"

"No. Have you?"

"No."

The low hum of women whispering dies down. It is so cold. And they all look so much worse than Charlotte has ever seen in Holloway or following a suffragette demonstration. Every woman is bruised, beaten, limping. Few are bandaged properly, although some look to have makeshift slings. Almost everyone has a splotch of dried blood somewhere on her body.

Isabel's scream pierces the still air.

A body is crumpled on the ground, perhaps twenty yards from where Charlotte and Emily stand. Isabel shrieks, dropping to her knees. Everyone runs toward them, moving much slower than they ought to have, fighting the current of their cuffs and injuries. A guard whistles wildly, but the women ignore him until at last he pushes through, heaving up the woman's inert form.

Charlotte catches sight of a wisp of dark hair. Jessie. Her neck lolls at a strange angle as the guard carries her away. Someone reaches for Isabel, and though they cannot free their arms to hug her, they huddle around her as she cries for her friend.

How long do they stand there after the guards remove Jessie's limp body? Long enough that Charlotte's fingers and toes lose all color. Long enough that Emily's sallow cheeks and bruised face give her an almost lavender pallor. And then, a quiet, reedy voice quivers in melody. It doubles, then triples, and soon, everyone is singing. The guards shout for silence, but the women sing and sing, their voices together louder than Isabel's sobs, louder than the guard's commands, until they are as irrepressible as an ocean swell, as lilting and free as birdsong.

CHAPTER FORTY-NINE
EMILY

Time loses all meaning. And it happens so quickly—that is the real surprise. Without access to daylight, save for the narrow-slit window too far overhead to see through (for the prisoners have lost their yard privileges), and without meal intervals, Emily loses all sense of day or night, time passing in minutes or hours or days. She does not know how long it has been since she arrived when she hears the jangle of keys on her cell door and the sound of a voice that makes her want to cry.

"Em." Thomas enters the cell, tentative as he approaches his daughter's cot. For a moment he pauses, observing her—the bloodstains still on her sleeve from someone else's nose, the bruises on her wrists. The stench inside the cell, even for a man inured to the odors of the jail, seems to give him pause. Then he kneels on the floor beside her.

"Papa." In her hunger, her confusion, Thomas's face is a welcome sight. It has been weeks, the longest time they have ever spent apart, since she left home. Thomas looks worn, tired. The wrinkles around his eyes, which Marianne once teased were signs of past smiles, simply make him look old and sad now. He speaks quickly, a rush of rehearsed words.

"Em, I know we've had our disagreements. But please, let's put this all to rest. You've proven your point. Your mother and I wanted you to have a better life, and sweetheart, this isn't it." He pushes his hair from his forehead, eyes pleading. "I'm going to pay your bail and you'll come home. It's expensive, almost everything we saved for your future, but we can start over." His hand hovers over her shoulder, and finally, tentatively lands. She shudders.

It would be so easy to say yes. With a single nod, he would carry her in his arms, like when she was a child—her papa would carry her to safety.

"No." She says it fast so she doesn't change her mind. "I'm staying." Emily hardly has the energy to raise her head, but she uses every ounce of strength to keep her voice clear and level.

"Emily, dear, you don't know what you're saying. Let me pay your bail and take you home."

"I am home."

Thomas stands and begins to pace the cramped cell, two steps one way, two steps another, his impatience rising.

"I *have* to get you out of here," he snaps. "It's been two days already. You will be forcibly fed, and there is nothing I can do about it."

Emily's chest clenches, blood cold. They couldn't have known for sure, after the government's inquiry, if forcible feedings would continue. Yet again, it seems, a different set of rules apply to the poor. Emily tries to control her breathing, but panic rises in her, making every sip of air somehow less substantial than the one before. She remembers Charlotte's broken body on the stretcher; her mind is imprinted with the echo of Constance's primal scream.

"Your mother would never forgive me," Thomas adds, his voice breaking. Emily glares up at her father through the strands of hair that fall across her face. A man she once believed could save her from anything admitting to his own impotence. It would have been heart-breaking, if not for the terrible irony.

"Oh, Papa," Emily whispers. "Mama will never forgive you for what you've already done. Remember what she used to say when she did her rounds? *They're all someone's daughter.* You're only seeing that now, because of me, but it has always been true. We are all someone's daughter."

"Marianne wanted you to live a better life, an independent one, outside this place—"

"That's what I'm doing. Just go, Papa. You can't save me." She rolls over, her back to her father, her face to the wall.

Thomas means to argue, to convince his daughter, but then there is shouting in the corridor.

"Mr. Brown! Come quickly!"

A woman screams and Thomas touches Emily's shoulder once more before he runs out into the hall, locking her inside. Emily swallows hard. She has no energy for tears, but that doesn't stop her soul from aching.

Time passes. She cannot say how much. Then, another voice at her door. Male. Familiar. She shudders with fear, until—

"Emily?" It is Martin.

She winces, something churning in her gut. How, in spite of everything, can her body still long for him? The angry red hatred in her mind does not translate to the rest of her. She doesn't stir from the cot, but she listens as he speaks through the grates.

"I wanted to tell you, er—" Martin clears his throat. "One of your, uh, friends—she's died."

There is a moment of disconnect as the blood rushes to her head. "Who?"

"Jessie. The doc said she had some kind of internal bleeding."

Emily closes her eyes. A hot tear rolls down her cheek. Sweet Jessie. She'll never forget the stoicism on Jessie's face when she recounted the story of her childhood in the mills, the determination with which she laughed. *I choose joy*, Jessie had said.

Emily is numb.

CHAPTER FIFTY

CHARLOTTE

C harlotte's cell is next to Isabel's. This she knows because of the wailing. Poor Isabel, and poor, poor Jessie. The fierce friend who welcomed Charlotte into the campaign, who lost a finger in the mills and worked every day to make life better for the women she left behind—vibrant, resilient, unflinching—how can she be dead? Jessie had stepped in to defend Isabel outside the gates of Parliament. And the policeman's violent thrust must have shattered her rib cage and punctured something inside of her.

Word spreads fast, whispers exchanged like pollen on a breeze, until the wrenching truth arrives through the slits in Isabel's cell. Throughout the night, the hold echoes with strains of song and the swell of sobs. Charlotte wonders how long it will take for Adeline to learn Jessie's fate. Perhaps she already knows.

CHAPTER FIFTY-ONE

BEATRICE

Beatrice is covered in blood. She has no rags to stanch the flow, and so she is soaked, the brown uniform a sickly, scarlet rust. She counts her breath. She counts to a hundred, to a thousand. She pictures Sadie's smile in the glow of candlelight, her skin like a pearl against the pure white of clean sheets. But the image twists, distorts. The sheets are blood-spattered. She conjures up images from her childhood, long rides in the meadows where the only sound is the whisper of wind, the hum of the insects, and the steady footfalls of July's hooves. But this is no comfort, either.

She is flooded with shame.

A man's hand up her skirt, against her skin, inside of her. The gasp of pain, the terror of immobility, the futility of her screams.

And now the blood. Her monthly courses, yes, and something worse, darker, clotted.

Her parents were right. She is troubled. She is bad. There is, and has always been, something wrong with her. What would they think if they could see her now? Would they pity her, or be too ashamed to even look? Would they think she deserved it?

She probably does deserve it.

To cry is to admit to it. To speak is to acknowledge its reality. And so she rocks herself silently, curled on the cold, hard floor, covered in blood.

CHAPTER FIFTY-TWO

CHARLOTTE

On the third day, no one brings Charlotte breakfast. She steels herself for the forcible feeding to come. She is grateful for the hunger, for the way it fogs her brain. If not for that haze, she could not face what is to come. The other women are afraid, but they can only imagine the pain. She has suffered this before, and it is worse than any description. No one can be that brave twice unless she is not quite in her right mind.

Still, the confusion of hunger is not enough to suppress the phantom choking sensation that has haunted her ever since that first time she was tied to a hardback chair with leather straps that cut at her wrists. The sharp metal tube had been inserted down her throat. When her body had bucked reflexively, expelling the foreign object and slicing the back of her tongue, blood dripped out of her mouth and down her neck. They had forced a rubber tube down her nostril instead, and then she thought for sure that she would asphyxiate, for she could not breathe through her nose nor her mouth. *Stop stop stop—*

A guard opens the door. Charlotte goes limp. Someone carries her out of the cell. She closes her eyes, and bright light shines through her lids. Not the dim corridors, nor even the artificial bulbs, but daylight. She opens her eyes. The hundred suffragettes from the march are blinking beside her at the Holloway entry gate. She finds Emily, and beside her, Beatrice, whose blond hair has become a matte, ashy gray. Beatrice regards the ambulance nearby with hollow eyes.

"You are free to return home," a man reads from a piece of paper. "If you require assistance, these ambulances will transport you. You must return to your homes and recover your strength, after which time you shall be re-arrested to serve the remainder of your sentence."

No one cheers; they are too weak. Jessie's absence is a gaping wound. There will be more questions later. But slowly, they hobble toward the vehicles, survivors. Beatrice is silent when they arrive at Park Lane and does not speak even as Sadie sobs into her chest; she is stiff and impassive, her eyes unfocused. Despite her own bruises, Charlotte wonders what happened to Beatrice. She shares a glance with Sadie. They all wonder.

"You've been served," Sadie says, reading aloud from a piece of paper clutched in her hand. "'You have been hereby charged with conduct likely to provoke a breach of the peace.' It says you're to appear at Scotland Yard in two weeks' time, at the police court."

"They're adding insult to injury," Charlotte says, rubbing her temples. Emily and Beatrice share a glance, but before they can respond, Sadie interjects.

"No—this could be good. It's an opportunity to plead your case. We could get the charges dropped before you face re-arrest."

The mention of the re-arrest drains the faces of the women around the table. They are still trying to understand what this means. Rather than forcibly feed a hundred women, the government decided to let them go—but when they are well enough, they'll have to come back to finish out their sentences. If they continue to hunger strike, how long will it take? How much longer will they be willing to take it?

During their first week home from jail, Charlotte's heart beat far too fast in her chest. The glazed look on Emily's face thawed as her bruises faded, and Beatrice started speaking again after days of eerie silence. Sadie tried to tend to all of them, but she, too, seemed stricken by the pain on all of their faces and the sheer dumb luck and the police force's dysfunction that had allowed her and Adeline to escape arrest.

After a few days of recovery, word had arrived from Clement's Inn: Isabel and Adeline are grieving. Charlotte can't help but think how narrowly they all avoided Jessie's fate. There was no time for a proper funeral.

By the end of the week, the patients are strong enough to shuffle around the flat and sit up at the table to sip broth. It is during one of those slow mealtimes—to eat fast causes terrible digestive pain—that Sadie reads the telegram aloud.

"I've discussed it with Adeline already. We have a plan." Sadie sounds firm, even confident. "You will be represented by one of the finest legal minds in the country."

"Who?" asks Charlotte.

"One of the preeminent scholars to earn a Cambridge diploma."

"Who?" asks Emily.

Sadie's eyes dance to Beatrice.

"Someone you already know and trust."

Beatrice buries her face in her palms.

"Miss Beatrice Piper, LLB," Sadie says.

"But how can that be? I mean, sorry, Bea, I know you studied it, but women can't practice law," Charlotte scoffs.

Sadie folds her hands on the table. "Tell them."

"But . . . I—" Beatrice looks confused. Then recognition washes over her face. "Oh," she breathes. "Women are not permitted to practice law—but we may appear before the bar as defendants . . . and defend ourselves."

Sadie nods. "Precisely. And not only is Beatrice truly a genius legal mind—"

"You don't know that," Beatrice objects.

"—she will also captivate the press with her wit, strategy, and beauty! The papers will eat her up."

"Sadie," Beatrice protests, suppressing a cough. Emily chuckles in disbelief over her bowl of broth, but Charlotte smiles.

"It's a brilliant idea," Charlotte says.

"Are you serious?" Beatrice asks.

Charlotte takes a beat. "Deadly."

Soon they set about developing their legal strategy. Once she overcomes her initial hesitation—"Do you really trust me to represent us, when this is the first and *only* case I have ever officially argued?"—Beatrice sets about the task with remarkable fervor.

"This reminds me of our Girton days," Charlotte teases, as she delivers a late-night cup of tea to Beatrice, who remains hunched over her law books, her face scrunched in concentration.

"Ah, yes. The good old days of me revising enough for the both of us, while you climbed out the window."

Late-night messages arrive by courier from the Hurstons. Isabel will be on trial, too, and both she and her mother have ideas and concerns. Beatrice tacks their notes on the wall, weaving a strategy like a spiderweb.

"Do you really think this will work?" Emily asks Charlotte the night before they are to appear at Scotland Yard.

For all the strength they have regained in the past few weeks, simply imagining a re-arrest is excruciating. Beatrice's argument will be their only chance to avoid an endless cycle of hunger striking to the brink of death and re-arrests as soon as they are well enough to do it all again. Public sympathy since Constance's revelation has put the government in a bind. Forcible feeding made martyrs of the women. Thus, the Prisoners Temporary Discharge for Ill-Health Act. Now, interrupting hunger strikes with returns home avoids public martyrdom and keeps the suffragettes off the streets. Adeline calls it more bluntly the Cat and Mouse Act. The women are, of course, the tormented mice.

"It damn well better," Charlotte responds. Everything hurts. Their bruises have barely faded, merely changed in color from inky purple to a jaundiced yellow. The specter of Jessie's death hangs over everything, present in every silence, unspoken in every conversation. They whisper until they cry, cry until they fall asleep.

CHAPTER FIFTY-THREE

BEATRICE

In the morning, the ground glimmers with a sheen of recent rain. Beatrice wakes at dawn as streaks of pink illuminate the sky. The world is so still, so silent, as she watches Sadie sleep. She wishes they could stay exactly as they are, wrapped in the warmth of blankets, legs intertwined, while outside, the world is stilled by the hush of dawn. Beatrice nuzzles her head back into the pillow, splashed with Sadie's hair. When Sadie finally starts to stir, Beatrice kisses her awake.

A tiny moan escapes Sadie's pink lips as she stretches her legs, her toes, and leans in to Beatrice's mouth. Eyes still closed, Sadie reaches out, feeling, rather than seeing, the golden threads of Beatrice's curls.

"Look at the sky," Beatrice murmurs.

"Beautiful." Sadie does not glance out the window but fixes her eyes upon Beatrice's face.

A cold fist clenches in Beatrice's chest. How numbered are these mornings together? Sadie had taken such loving care of her after Holloway, back when her breasts were so bruised that anything more weighty than a loose slip made her cry out in pain. Sadie had crawled into bed with Beatrice that first night home, and except for when she checked in on Charlotte and Emily, she never left Bea's side. She washed the caked blood from Bea's limbs, blood in places that Bea wouldn't talk about. She kissed away the tears that fell not like rain, but slowly, like dewdrops suspended on rose petals.

Every night, she swears this should be the last that she clutches Sadie close and breathes in her skin. It is like a punishment to herself, knowing how little time they have left and clinging to it anyway. Maybe it's a punishment she deserves. All she knows is she can't let go. Not yet.

The imposing stone façade of Scotland Yard belies its shoddy interior. The ruby-brick exterior gleams with all the authority of the empire, while the inner chambers crumble. The women pass through a dank, dimly lit corridor. A uniformed officer meets them at the end of the hall and wordlessly motions for them to wait by the door. Beatrice slows her breath. Even the sight of the policeman's uniform makes her palms sweat. The hall remains eerily silent, but for the *drip-drip-drip* of some unseen pipe leak. Isabel's eyes are bloodshot, her face raw with grief. Somewhere beyond the bowels of the building, Sadie and Adeline make their way from the public entrance to the police court chambers.

She fidgets with her hat. The pins dig into her scalp, but she cannot adjust them without removing the whole enterprise—and the last thing they need today is a photograph of a disheveled suffragette in the papers. The faint clang of Big Ben marks the hour even deep within Scotland Yard, and as the eleventh chime rings out, the officer leads them into a small courtroom that smells of damp and perspiration.

The room is packed with spectators stuffed onto wooden benches and reporters lining the walls. The officer brings the four women, Beatrice, Isabel, Charlotte, and Emily, arbitrarily deemed the leaders of the WSPU's protest march on Parliament, to the elevated defendant's box in the center of the room. A wooden railing encircles the box like a cage. Beatrice cranes her neck, searching the faces in the crowd. At last, her shoulders soften as her gaze lands in the room's back corner, where Sadie and Adeline stand watching. They both wear black mourning dresses.

"Order, order," one of the officers demands as the magistrate enters the room. Smoothing his rumpled front, the magistrate settles into his chair. His white sideburns, reminiscent of the fashion of the previous century, creep down his cheeks like caterpillars, and his eyes scan the women's faces, lingering on the famous Isabel Hurston and the exquisitely beautiful Beatrice Piper, while barely glancing at Emily and Charlotte. Beatrice stands and suddenly the room is silent.

"Sir, on behalf of the defendants, I would like to enter a request." Beatrice's voice is soft but firm. Only those who know her could detect the faint tremor in her vowels. The press table erupts in whispers and the scratching of pens. *Who is she?*

"So you may," the magistrate says.

"I request that the case be removed from the police court and sent to trial before a judge and jury. We desire—" She clears her throat. "We demand the right to a jury of our peers."

The magistrate does not blink. "Denied," he mutters, licking his lips.

Beatrice turns to the desk before her. They did not expect success with her first request. But they know, legally, that they will succeed with their second. Beatrice scans her notes but does not lift the paper so that no one will notice how much her fingers tremble.

"Motion to call witnesses, sir."

"Proceed."

"The defense calls Prime Minister Herbert H. Asquith."

The crowded press table quavers with the frenzied scribbling of reporters. The spectators forget decorum, and the room erupts in chatter. This is Beatrice's coup, the realization, two nights before the trial, that she could subpoena members of the government as witnesses.

"Why not? They were at Parliament that afternoon," Beatrice had said, cracking her first smile in days as she compiled her witness list to submit to the police court.

"The papers will go mad!" Sadie had said gleefully, planting a kiss on Beatrice's cheek. "You bloody, bloody genius."

The magistrate bangs his gavel. "Order!"

At last the room settles down, just as the doors swing open. The prime minister enters the room. Asquith's angular, clean-shaven face is almost handsome, though his eyes dance with mocking amusement.

The room falls silent as he takes his seat. Beatrice's heart pounds in her chest, but her mind is clear, crystalline. There's a lightness haloing her, like the swooping sensation she feels while riding—the motions are arduous at first, but then, in one beautiful instant, the flow of the gallop unfolds, elegant and unstoppable. To think she studied for years without ever imagining she would practice the law, and now the weight of their freedom rests on her shoulders. It should be terrifying, but she is calm. She knows exactly what to say. If their lives were not at stake, this might even be fun. She takes a deep breath.

"Lord Asquith," Beatrice begins. "Is it true that you were at the House of Commons on the twenty-eighth of February?"

"Yes, that is true," the prime minister responds slowly, as though speaking to a child. He reclines in his chair, legs spread just wide enough to suggest a certain lack of respect for the ordeal.

"And so," she continues, "is it correct to say that you saw our group of women approaching Parliament Square?"

The prime minister puckers his lips in patronizing amusement, raising an eyebrow at the magistrate.

"It has already been established that the PM was present and a witness to the proceedings of the twenty-eighth of February," the magistrate interjects. "Move on, Miss Piper."

"I asked whether the prime minister *saw* us approach," Beatrice says. "But my next question is whether he *heard* us."

The magistrate moves to object but Asquith raises a hand.

"Yes, yes, I saw *and* I heard," he responds, grinning toward the press table as if to say, *See how I handle this silly little woman?*

"What did you hear exactly, sir?" Beatrice asks. "Did you hear any speeches? Any words that were likely to incite violence?"

Asquith leans slightly forward in his seat. "No. I was inside the building. So I didn't hear any speeches. That being the nature of walls."

"Right," Beatrice agrees. "Nor did you hear any words used that were likely to incite violence?"

"No," Asquith says. He taps his fingers impatiently.

"Not even when you stepped outside to get a closer look? What, if anything, did you hear then?"

"I . . . well, I think I heard . . . singing."

"You *think* you heard singing?"

"Yes," Asquith says. His cheeks redden slightly.

"What song did you hear?"

"I don't know. Just some suffrage song, lots of harmonies. I'm no musical expert."

"I see," Beatrice says. "You did not hear any speeches nor any words used that were likely to incite violence. All you heard, on the twenty-eighth of February, was the faint sound of harmonious singing outside the gates of Parliament. Is that correct?"

Asquith shrugs.

"Your honor, please direct the witness to answer with a yes or no," Beatrice says politely.

"Yes, alright, that's correct," Asquith says.

"Very good. Now, I would like to turn to a prior statement that you, sir, once made on the subject of women's suffrage. Is it not fact that you yourself have said, and I quote, that 'Women could never get the vote because they could not fight for it as men had fought'?"

"I did say that," Asquith admits.

"What did you mean by 'fight as men had fought'?"

"Well, when the franchise was extended to men, it was because men came out in great numbers to show a widespread demand," he says, relaxing once more into condescension. *How easy it is to explain away these women's ridiculous little notions*, he must be thinking—just as Beatrice knows how easy it will be to trap him in his own words.

"Such as the 1867 demonstrations that led to the Reform Act?" Beatrice prompts. "I believe your own father was a leader of that reform movement."

"That's right," Asquith says. "Men, like my father, assembled in the tens of thousands. Of course, it cannot be expected that women can assemble in such masses. But you see, Miss Piper, power belongs to the masses, and through this power a government can be influenced into more effective action." He smiles, satisfied with his own turn of phrase.

"Do you know, sir, just how many 'tens of thousands' of men assembled in 1867?"

"No, I don't know off the top of my head—"

"According to contemporary estimates, between sixty and seventy thousand members of the Men's Reform League protested in Hyde Park in 1867, which led to the extension of the Reform Act within that same year."

"Miss Piper, you are not the witness. Stop testifying and ask a question if you have one," the magistrate warns.

"Very well. Lord Asquith, do you know how many *women* have demonstrated to achieve votes?"

The prime minister leans forward, locking eyes with Beatrice. His carefree veneer is cracking.

"Not precisely," he says through his teeth.

"The defense hereby introduces Exhibit A, a copy of *The Times* from last autumn." Beatrice holds a large piece of newsprint out to the prime minister. "Surely you read *The Times*, sir. Will you please read aloud from this headline?"

Asquith nearly tears the paper in his grab, no longer attempting to hide his agitation. He reads silently, his ears turning purple as he reaches the bottom of the page.

The magistrate shifts uneasily. "Your lordship, please read aloud," he directs at last.

Asquith grimaces. "'Women assemble in Hyde Park,'" he recites.

"Yes, and below that, please read the first sentence," Beatrice says.

"'Estimates of over—'" Asquith swallows. "'Over two hundred thousand women were present, and more than two-thirds of the women taking part wore white dresses, giving the streets of London through which they marched under their silken banners a richness and refinement of color such as the grandest of military pageants has never supplied.'"

"I wonder, Prime Minister, if you could describe the manner by which the men's Reform League demonstration conducted itself in Hyde Park in 1867?" Beatrice asks.

"That's enough about 1867," the magistrate says. "This trial concerns only the events on the twenty-eighth of February."

The prime minister smirks.

"As you wish," Beatrice says. "I thought it relevant to illustrate the difference between the peaceful women's marches of late and the violent men's uprisings in the past. For instance, in 1867, the railings of Hyde Park were torn from the earth in a destructive demonstration by the Men's Reform League. The prime minister has already testified that the Men's Reform League succeeded in extending the franchise after that very assembly."

In the time it takes the magistrate to splutter, Beatrice continues to speak.

"How curious it is that women assembled in numbers that more than tripled the precedent set by men and gathered in a peaceful fashion, rather than a violent one. Yet the Reform Act of 1867 passed within weeks of the men's destructive assembly, whereas it has been over six months since women gathered peaceably in Hyde Park."

"Do you have anything else to ask his lordship? The prime minister has better things to do than listen to your recitation of ancient history," the magistrate steams.

"One final question. Did you, sir, on the morning of the twenty-eighth of February, upon hearing the faint sound of singing in Parliament Square, order your home secretary to intervene, to the best of his judgment?"

"I did."

"No further questions." Beatrice turns toward her friends as Asquith stands and swiftly exits the room. As the crowd chatters, she gives her friends the slightest hint of a grin. Then, turning once more toward the magistrate, she says, "The defense now calls Home Secretary Winston Churchill to the box."

Churchill enters the room and removes his hat to run a thick hand through his thinning hair. Tall and ruddy-cheeked, he sidesteps the press table and positions himself in the chair just vacated by the prime minister. Beatrice's mind is in total focus now—she sees her line of questioning clear as sunlight.

"Sir, as home secretary, you are responsible for the conduct of the Metropolitan Police, are you not?"

"Yes," he grunts, tapping his right foot.

"And so, since we are currently in a police court, is this technically a continuation of your jurisdiction?"

"I suppose so."

"Thank you." Beatrice pauses and takes a breath. "Are you aware, sir, that of the one hundred and fifteen women arrested on the date in question, more than half of them report sustaining physical abuse at the hands of police officers?"

"Ah," Churchill says.

"And are you aware, sir, that upon their admission to Holloway Prison, these one hundred and fifteen women, including over fifty who suffered physical injury, were denied medical attention?"

"Well, ah . . ."

"Is it your customary practice to permit your subordinates to go against your direct orders?"

"I beg your pardon. No, it is most certainly not," Churchill splutters and his foot stops tapping. Beatrice hit a nerve.

"So, do your police officers always follow your orders?"

"Of course they do!"

"And did you order your officers to physically assault the women in Parliament Square on the twenty-eighth of February?"

Fury washes over Churchill's round face as he realizes he has been boxed in. Even the magistrate cannot interject to spare him embarrassment.

"Mr. Churchill, one of the women assaulted on the twenty-eighth of February died, subsequently, from injuries sustained that day. Her name was Jessie Morgan."

The audience murmurs. Behind Beatrice, she can hear Isabel suppress a sob.

"'The price of greatness is responsibility,'" Beatrice quotes. "Do you know who said that, sir?"

"Yes," Churchill mutters.

"Will you tell the court please?"

"I did."

"Indeed, you did. *Responsibility*," Beatrice repeats. "I ask, sir, that you take some. No further questions."

After a moment's pause, Churchill stands.

"Blasted shrew," he snarls. Then he storms out of the courtroom, the door swinging behind him.

The magistrate clasps his palms and closes his eyes as though in prayer.

"Do you have any more witnesses?" He finally asks.

Someone mutters, *shall we summon the king?* Soft chuckles emit from the galley.

"No, sir," Beatrice says.

"Proceed with your closing statement then."

The room seems to hum and Emily, Charlotte, and Isabel lean forward, as if willing their love and confidence in Beatrice's direction.

"Ladies and gentlemen, today's proceedings have been taken in malice and vexation in order to incapacitate a political enemy. From the very outset, this case has been a sham. My colleagues and I were summoned here today on the basis of 'conduct likely to provoke a breach of the peace.' This practically hypothetical charge, based on a centuries-old statute from the time of King James, is simply absurd.

"Now, I acknowledge that under the law, the charge which might *properly* be brought against us was that of illegal assembly. But the government has not charged us with this offense, because they wish to keep the case in police court. We have therefore been deprived of a trial by jury and deprived of the right to appeal." Beatrice paces confidently toward the press table, where the reporters are hunched over, scribbling breathlessly. Then she turns once more to face the magistrate.

"You have heard the testimony of Prime Minister Asquith. His lordship made clear that we have assembled hundreds of thousands of peaceful women to advocate for reform. What a contrast between the far fewer, and far more violent, protests held by men in the past. In spite of this, we have faced hostile mobs at street corners. We have been told that we could not have representation for our taxes. We have been misrepresented and ridiculed. We have had contempt poured upon us by ignorant mobs incited to offer us violence. And on the twenty-eighth of February, unarmed and unprotected, we endured the violation of our safety and our bodily integrity by members of the Metropolitan Police—the very institution in which we find ourselves today.

"You have heard the testimony of Secretary Churchill, a man complicit in the violence enacted by his own police force against women demonstrating in a peaceful assembly. The only complaint made against us has been the fact that our voices were lifted in song. And yet over one hundred women were arrested, and more than fifty women were brutally assaulted. And one among us lost her life. This last fact, this tragedy, is not in dispute.

"We are here today not because we are lawbreakers. We are here in our efforts to become lawmakers. And therefore, we ask the court to dismiss all charges. The defense rests."

Beatrice walks stoic-spined to her seat beside Charlotte, managing to sit down just before her knees give out from beneath her.

CHAPTER FIFTY-FOUR

EMILY

The magistrate leaves the room to deliberate. No one else dares to move. A few minutes pass and Emily reaches out to squeeze Beatrice's hand. *What if what if what if.* This is not only a matter of principle, not merely the rhetoric of justice, it's also their fates. Where will they sleep tonight? At home or back in Holloway? As the adrenaline of the trial dissipates into the cold and damp of Scotland Yard, Emily cannot help but think of the cell that awaits her if they've failed. She cannot shake the image of her father's face through the bars—the leaden weight of fear and shame.

By the time the magistrate returns to his seat, Emily, Charlotte, Beatrice, and Isabel all grip hands, entwined like a daisy chain of steel.

"Order," says an officer. The magistrate shuffles his papers and peers down at the women.

Charlotte stiffens beside Emily, the vein at her throat cord-like. Emily's fingers are slowly turning blue in Beatrice's grip, but she clings back, squeezing tighter.

"Let the record show that the conduct likely to provoke a breach of the peace, with which Misses Emily Brown, Charlotte Evans, Isabel

Hurston, and Beatrice Piper have been charged, has been hereby dismissed by the Metropolitan Police."

A moment of silence is followed by exclamations of euphoria. Beatrice stands stunned as Isabel, Emily, and Charlotte envelop her in their arms. "We bloody well did it!" Sadie shouts from the stands. The magistrate is long gone by the time the women collect themselves and make their way back onto the street, free.

"I heard someone say that the PM himself told the magistrate not to pursue charges," says Adeline as they stand outside.

"Well, it would be fairly unfeasible to corral all one hundred and fifteen women back to Holloway," Beatrice points out.

"No," Sadie insists. "It was Beatrice's legal brilliance alone."

"I'd just like to go to sleep now," Beatrice demurs, but she is smiling and holding tight to Sadie's hand. Soon a cab arrives, and they all pile inside. Emily holds the door for Beatrice, the last to climb in.

"Thank you," Adeline whispers to Beatrice, with tears in her eyes, as she helps her into the cab. "For defending my daughter. And honoring Jessie."

When they return home, Sadie draws a bath and Beatrice goes straight to bed. Charlotte and Emily stay up late, too elated to sleep, replaying every moment of the trial over and over.

"This changes everything," Charlotte says.

"You always say that."

"Well, this time I don't mean about the cause. This changes everything for Bea. She'll be all over tomorrow's papers. You saw how those reporters ate her up. *Beautiful blond gentlewoman cross-examines the prime minister!*"

"I wonder how her family will react," Emily says. She thinks of her father. He must have known about their trial, if only through the whispers in Holloway. What will he think when the papers appear on his doorstep tomorrow morning?

"I wonder how her *fiancé* will react," Charlotte says with a shudder.

They do not have to wait long to find out. In the morning, Beatrice receives two letters. She holds them between pinched fingers, as though they smell of something rotten. The first envelope contains a telegram from Daniel. Beatrice studies it for a moment and then groans. "I can't read it."

"Let me," Sadie says, reaching across the table.

Beatrice grimaces but hands it over.

"Hmm . . . this isn't so bad." Sadie's voice sinks. "He says not to tell his father, but the truth is, he is one of the few members of the landed gentry who actually sympathize with the socialists and the suffs. 'I'm a modern man,' he says, and the whole thing gave him a good laugh."

"Really?"

Sadie deepens her voice and reads aloud. "'When we're married, you won't have time for all this, so enjoy yourself with the girls.'" She pretends to gag.

"*Enjoy* yourself?" Charlotte repeats.

"It gave him a *good laugh*?" adds Emily.

"We're having so much fun, aren't we *enjoying ourselves*!" Sadie shrieks. "On trial and in prison and, oh, what else, avoiding rape on the street!"

"Stop," Beatrice protests. "Please."

"That was a ridiculous thing for him to say," Sadie insists.

"I suppose," Beatrice says. "And now for my mother." She opens the second envelope with a wince. "She says that I am a disgrace. Oh, and that this was not the intended use of the education for which my father paid."

"Interesting. I wonder what they thought you'd use your law degree for if not to practice law." Sadie rolls her eyes.

"Anyway, she is furious and—oh." Beatrice bites her lip.

"What?" Sadie asks.

Beatrice's face is suddenly drained of color. She reads the words with a shaky voice. "'*The Times* reports that our daughter rushed into the arms of a red-haired companion, sharing an embrace to celebrate their victory.'" She clears her throat.

Emily and Charlotte exchange a glance.

"So if I've squandered my marriage prospects, they will have no choice but to resort to an alternative solution for my errancy. Lovely." Beatrice blinks rapidly, turning away from the table.

Sadie reaches for Beatrice's hand, but she shakes it off. "Bea—"

Head down, Beatrice walks determinedly out of the kitchen, pocketing Daniel's telegram, while tossing her mother's letter into the fire.

CHAPTER FIFTY-FIVE
BEATRICE

Spring arrives too soon. As the bitter rains begin to warm, so too does Helen Piper. Since Daniel stands by their plans to wed, the Pipers take it upon themselves to ensure that Beatrice is married and off their hands by the end of April. Money is sent for the dressmaker. Lists are made for guests, menus, decorations, and so many elaborate details that Charlotte suggests Mrs. Piper ought to consider offering her services to the Royal Navy.

It's all anyone can do to laugh at Charlotte's mild jokes. The tension in the house is oppressive. Beatrice is grateful for Charlotte's humor and Emily's offers to help with this or that small task. But it's Sadie whose reactions matter—and hurt—the most. Sometimes it's too much to take. Perhaps if Sadie's absolute radiance were just a bit further out of reach, Beatrice could better . . . control herself. But what is control when it is gravity drawing them together? What force is strong enough to escape sheer magnetism? If anything, the attraction between them grows by the day. And despite Sadie's passive-aggressive barbs about the wedding plans that increasingly interrupt their suffrage activities, at night in their bedroom, there is no distance between them. There is only skin and beating hearts.

At last, an invitation on thick, creamy paper arrives by post, just as Beatrice is packing to return home to Champney House for the wedding.

"You're all invited, of course. But the Hurstons can't come. They're too controversial. My mother doesn't want my 'little friends' making a scene at the wedding."

All four women are crammed into Bea and Sadie's bedroom. Beatrice's valise sits on the bed, half-packed.

"How rude," Charlotte says. "Doesn't she know that making a scene is among our greatest talents?"

Beatrice balls up a dress and shoves it into the valise.

"Wait," says Emily. "Let me fold that."

They work steadily in silence, interrupted only by Sadie's heavy sighs. At last, Beatrice stomps her foot.

"Spit it out, Sadie," she demands.

"What?"

"You clearly have something you want to say."

Charlotte and Emily exchange a glance. Sadie's cheeks, as bright red as her hair, glint in the small looking glass that hangs above the chest of drawers.

"Nothing," Sadie says. "It seems like you have all this under control. Packing, the wedding—everything." She excuses herself from the bedroom. Beatrice blinks in frustration before following Sadie down the hall.

"Wait," she calls. "Sadie, stop!"

Sadie whirls around, her eyes blazing. "What? What more can you possibly want from me?"

"I . . . I need you." Bea's voice cracks.

"Don't you think I know that?"

They stand in the hallway, frozen and staring.

"What are you going to do about it, then?" Sadie asks.

"Sadie," Beatrice breathes. "I—"

"Choose *me*."

"It's not . . . I can't—"

Sadie shakes her head, tears blooming in her eyes.

"Will you come with me? Home to Kent?" Bea whispers. "I don't want to be without you."

The words are out of her mouth before she can stop herself. In only a few weeks, she will be married. It would hurt less to sever ties with Sadie now, to say goodbye when everything that's happening can be brushed off in her memory as a passionate friendship, the heat of the suffrage campaign mystifying her senses. But Beatrice cannot get her tongue to cooperate; it will not curl around the words. She cannot send Sadie away when those hazel eyes, framed with long lashes and a smattering of freckles, are pleading with her.

"Come with me," Beatrice whispers. "I need you."

And so, Charlotte and Emily wave goodbye to both Beatrice and Sadie the next day. On the train, Beatrice cannot stop staring at Sadie. It's as though the impending deadline has made every unsaid word irrelevant, and all she can do is absorb every breath and blink of this beautiful woman, capturing every beat in her memory. At least they have this time together now. At least Daniel isn't arriving for another week. At least, at least.

But in Kent, Helen Piper and the endless staff of Champney House servants pull Sadie and Beatrice in different directions all day. Beatrice tries to catch Sadie's eye to apologize, but Helen's hawklike gaze catches their every exchange, interrupting and pulling Beatrice away the moment the two women find themselves briefly alone. Only at dinner are they in the same room for more than a few minutes, but there's no privacy to talk. Charles drones at the head of the table, and

Beatrice sits stiffly in some silk confection her mother has insisted she wear. Worst of all, her parents make no effort to suppress their dislike of Sadie, either ignoring her or muttering backhanded criticisms of all things American in her presence.

Their bedrooms are separate, which was not a surprise given the size of the rambling mansion, but Helen seemed to have chosen the guest room farthest from the family's quarters for Sadie. When Sadie, in a fleeting moment of privacy, says she'll come find her in the night, Beatrice shakes her head no. They cannot take the risk.

The bed feels cold and vast without Sadie beside her. She's grown accustomed to the cadence of Sadie's breath, a soothing rhythm against the clamor of the city beyond. Now she feels trapped by the silence of the countryside, the emptiness of the bedroom. Beatrice digs her nails into her palms until pink crescents form in her skin, holding back the tears that lie waiting just beneath the surface.

At last, Beatrice sneaks a note into Sadie's bedroom late one evening. Together, they tiptoe down the back staircase and out to the garden. Beatrice has recounted many stories of this place to the suffragettes, tales of childhood antics and stuffy parties. But there have been stories just for Sadie, too. The story of Beatrice's first kiss, the stolen minutes behind the hedgerows with her best friend, the escapades riding July bareback in the summers. And, of course, the incident.

They make their way silently toward the stables, the hems of their dressing gowns dragging along the dew-damp grasses.

"Finally," Beatrice whispers, holding a lamp in the doorway of the stable, breathing in the scent of hay and earth. The sight of Sadie framed by the wooden beams and dressed in her simple white nightgown like some kind of angel makes Beatrice want to weep. "Come sit," says Beatrice, taking Sadie by the hand and guiding her to a back corner, where a blanket has been spread out on the soft ground. At first, their motions are fast and needy. Then they slow, savoring each other. And then they cease, lying still, side by side, in near-total darkness. The tears fall fast, and Beatrice feels them on Sadie's cheek before she hears the hitching of her breath.

"Oh, love, what is it?" Beatrice whispers.

Sadie shuts her eyes, squeezing out the hot tears. "I remember," she whispers, her voice a hairsbreadth from a sob, "when I was on the ship, crossing the Atlantic to come here. The captain told us when we were equidistant from both shores, each horizon as far away as the next."

"What are you saying?" Beatrice asks, searching Sadie's face.

"I thought then that I was as alone as I would ever be. But—"

She pauses, and Beatrice wants to stop her right there, wants to capture this moment in amber and keep things exactly as they are. But she cannot stop time. She cannot hold Sadie tight enough to stop the words they both know she is about to say.

"I can't do this anymore," Sadie says.

"What?"

Bea hears. They both know it.

"I can't."

"Please."

In the silence, they can hear the slow, snuffling breaths of the horses, and the crickets in symphony outside in the meadows.

"You said you need me," Sadie whispers. "But I . . . I can't need you like this."

"I'm sorry," Beatrice says. "I'm so, so sorry. But please, stay until the wedding. You're the only thing keeping me sane and there's nothing else I can—"

"Nothing you can do? That's not true. You know it isn't." Sadie stiffens. "There's always *something* you can do."

"We can't all move across an ocean to escape our problems."

"Don't, Bea. You're brilliant. You saved our lives. You cross-examined the prime minister. Don't tell me there's nothing you can do."

"Sadie—"

"I don't understand you, Bea. I really don't. You say you need me, but you won't sacrifice anything for me. Your perfect life's plan, laid out by Mummy and Daddy—you've chosen to accept it. But you can't have it both ways. You can't have me, too."

Beatrice clasps a hand over her mouth. Her heart beats, blood thunderous, in her head. Somehow, they stumble separately into the night.

The next morning, Sadie is on a train back to London.

CHAPTER FIFTY-SIX

EMILY

C harlotte and Emily wake up in the bright bedrooms of Champney House. It is a glittering green spring day, the perfect weather for a wedding.

"Poor Bea," says Emily, parting the curtains to reveal manicured gardens outside. A songbird swoops past the window and tall grasses sway like dancers. Charlotte groans as she rolls over in bed, a pillow across her face to block out the sunlight. Sadie remains in London. She says Adeline gave her an important task, but they all know the truth, or at least some version of it.

"Poor Sadie," Charlotte counters.

Emily drags Charlotte out of bed, and the two dress hastily, helping to lace each other into corsets. Charlotte attempts to follow directions from *Lady Waltingham's Style Suggestions* to do up Emily's hair, but when the tongs they'd heated over the fire make the whole room smell like burnt toast, and the tips of Emily's limp curls begin to sizzle, she tosses the entire manual into the hearth. They both settle on simple buns and steal flowers from their bedroom's vase to decorate their hats. Pulling on gloves, they dash down the great staircase to meet the wedding party outside.

Days like this, which simply sing with the promise of a new season, remind Emily of her mother so much it aches. She can just hear Marianne insisting on a walk in the park. She links arms with Charlotte, and they follow the group of guests down the country road toward the little stone church. It is picturesque, like a Constable painting or a scene out of an Austen novel, with all the townspeople dressed in their finest and the smattering of daisies that smile among the ancient stone pathways of the old churchyard.

As the party approaches the great Gothic door, Charlotte notices a figure standing off to the side, plucking at the petals of a daisy. She breaks into a grin at once and races ahead of the group, dragging Emily behind her.

"Sadie!" Charlotte flings her arms around her.

"You made it," says Emily, searching Sadie's face.

Sadie reddens. "Of course I made it. I had to be here. Even if"—she holds up the bald stem of her petal-plucked daisy and gives a small, sad smile—"she loves me not."

"I'm so glad you're here," Charlotte whispers. "And Bea will be, too."

They enter the church together with linked arms and find a pew near the back. Even the servants from Champney House have come to honor the daughter of the estate; they sit apart from the guests, distinct in their navy-blue uniforms. Emily catches the eye of a young housemaid, then looks away. It feels wrong to sit with the members of the fancy house when she knows she's more similar to the servants.

Sadie and Charlotte poke fun at an old lady wearing what looks like a bird of prey perched atop her hat, and a man with a flaming mustache. Charlotte plays patty-cake with one of the flower girls, and Sadie feigns deep interest in Emily's description of their train ride. But when the first notes of the organ break through the chatter, with a foreboding finality, everyone falls silent.

The doors open to reveal Beatrice in her bridal gown. A layer of ruffles at the neckline melts into a cream silk bodice that cascades to the ground. She clutches a bouquet of violets and lilies, the white and purple flowers a subtle homage to the suffragettes. Beneath her beaded lace veil, Beatrice's blond curls are swept into an elaborate chignon, a few loose strands escaping to frame her pale face. Sadie squeezes her own wrists so tightly that she leaves a mark.

The ceremony is efficient, and Miss Beatrice Piper becomes Lady Daniel Rosseter in a matter of minutes. Sadie holds up remarkably well, suppressing her sobs until the bride and groom have left the chapel as man and wife.

In the grand mirrored ballroom of the Piper estate, Daniel greets family and friends gregariously as his wife stands stiff beside him. After hours of mingling, Beatrice stumbles out onto the balcony for a breath of air. Sadie notices immediately, leading Emily and Charlotte out with her. Beatrice's cheeks are flushed from dancing and champagne, a bright pink against the ivory of her wedding gown.

"You came," Beatrice murmurs. "Thank you."

Half of Sadie's face remains in shadow, the other half lit only by moonlight. Sadie nods, looking off into the distance, so close and yet so far.

"I'm sorry to have to leave you," Beatrice says. She is looking at all of them, but it's clear her words are meant for Sadie alone. "I always will be. And," she whispers, "I'll try to visit, whenever Daniel allows me to go to London."

Emily and Charlotte slip away, granting Sadie a precious moment alone with Beatrice before they'll all be missed inside. Emily hears the words they whisper and her heart shatters.

"I'll always love you," Sadie breathes, pressing a tender kiss to Beatrice's cheek. Then she pulls away and disappears into the din of the party. Emily and Charlotte follow her, leaving the bride alone on the balcony, empty-handed, fighting tears.

CHAPTER FIFTY-SEVEN
CHARLOTTE

After Beatrice and Daniel depart for their honeymoon in Italy, activity at Clement's Inn grows busier than ever.

"Tonight, we'd like to announce a new course of action," Adeline says during a gathering at headquarters.

Charlotte and Sadie take notes at the table, while Emily sits on the floor, leaning against the back of the sofa with her sketchbook on her lap.

"Years ago, when we set about forming the Women's Social and Political Union, we decided on a motto: *Deeds, not words*. For decades, women's groups advocated quietly and patiently for the vote. We set out to be radical by making ourselves visible: out of the Victorian parlor and into the streets. But that has not been enough. We have suffered bodily and emotionally. We have endured jail time without the rights of political prisoners. We have been assaulted at the hands of the police. We have been all but forgotten by the press, our most vital tool. And we have suffered the greatest loss of all—a loss of life."

Adeline looks to Isabel, still dressed in her mourning clothes. Grief has etched itself into Isabel's face, in the lines between her brows and the circles beneath her eyes.

"The press and the public are tired," says Isabel. "And so are we."

"But we can't stop," says Sadie.

"No, of course not," Isabel says, adding in a low voice, "Jessie wouldn't have wanted that."

"We used to make headlines. But now the announcements of deputations and arrests have been shunted to the back pages—if they're even reported on at all," Charlotte says.

"What else can we do, then?" Emily asks.

"We are all women," Adeline says, standing. "So you'll know what I mean when I say this. You have two babies, both very hungry and wanting to be fed. One baby is a patient baby and waits indefinitely until its mother is ready to feed her. The other baby is an impatient baby and cries lustily, screams and kicks and makes everybody hear her.

"We know perfectly well which baby is attended to first. That is the whole history of politics. You have to make more noise than anybody else. You have to make yourself more obtrusive than anybody else. You have to fill all the papers more than anybody else. In fact, you have to be there all the time and see that they do not snow you under."

"What do you suggest?" Sadie asks.

"How many men's groups, in the history of this country, have taken violent action against the government? Countless. But we value human life, don't we? We are women. We do not want to hurt anyone. But we must be loud. We must be visible. We can destroy property without hurting any people. Smash a window and make a statement—a time-honored tradition in English politics. That is what I suggest. A tour of the West End, throwing stones through shop windows."

"Throwing stones?" Charlotte repeats. It sounds rather barbaric. "But aren't those shops our primary advertisers in *Votes for Women*?"

"Deeds, not words," Adeline repeats.

"Rather broken panes than broken promises," Isabel adds. "And those shops rely on our business even more than we depend on their advertising."

"We'll just get arrested again," Sadie argues.

This is how the strategy meetings always go: a proposition, a debate, a counterargument, a consensus. The room thrums with energy, everyone testing the bounds of a new idea.

"Most certainly we will," Adeline says. "But we'll make sure it means something."

"Imagine walking through the West End streets and seeing shop windows boarded up for days or weeks because of us," Isabel explains. "Even when we're locked away, they won't be able to forget us."

The thought sends a tingle through Charlotte's fingertips. The suffragettes will be indelible.

"We won't let them make us invisible," Emily says.

"As always, it is your choice whether or not to participate," Adeline says. "But we rely upon each and every one of you to fight for women."

Charlotte, Emily, and Sadie walk back to Park Lane, talking over one another in excitement. They all agree that the Hurstons presented a brilliant, if controversial, idea.

"I do pity the shopkeepers," Emily admits.

"But they capitalize on our business! Their entire profit model is based on convincing women to buy things we don't need," Sadie counters.

"I know," says Emily. "But they're hardworking people, too."

"They're complicit," Charlotte says. "That's what matters."

When the sound of shattering glass rings out through the West End, some will say that the screams of mythical sirens sang out that night, seductresses whose voices sent men to madness. Others will declare that Jack the Ripper's victims descended for one last haunting of the streets.

The truth is far more earthly.

Adeline Hurston, middle-aged, a mother, grips a rock in her fist and smashes the panes of a Selfridges window display. Cries of "Votes for women!" echo in the streets as slivers of crystal ricochet into the night.

It is strangely pleasurable to pierce the glass—to feel the thwack on impact and then hear the rainfall of fractured shards a millisecond later. The same women who hold tea parties, who work in factories, who are mothers and neighbors and friends, who have for so long kept quiet, spared others their feelings, and held the weight of their families on their shoulders, let loose now. They laugh and shriek and dig their nails into the rocks before letting go. These women are stronger than anyone suspected. Strong from kneading dough and carrying babies and cleaning homes and giving birth. Their arms are strong and their aim is true. The women flee on foot, skipping through a city of shattered glass. That first night, everyone escapes except Adeline. She gives a nod to Charlotte, hidden in a darkened corner on Oxford Street. *It's alright*, she says with her eyes, *leave me*.

"Well, if it isn't Mrs. Hurston," the bobbies croon as they cuff her wrists. Adeline pants, a small stream of blood curling toward her elbow, her smile satisfied.

At Holloway, she instantly begins a hunger strike. In three days she is released, with a decree of re-arrest awaiting her upon her recovery in two weeks' time. If she leaves her house before the deadline, she will be arrested immediately. Adeline is sentenced to three months. At such a rate, her sentence will take years to serve.

The newspapers are giddy with their self-important condemnations. "Hyenas in petticoats," the women are called. If only they asked politely for the vote. If only they were patient. And, by all means, if only they were more ladylike. But all press is good press, according to Adeline. Charlotte puts the clippings in her scrapbook.

By the light of day, the three friends walk through the West End, as street cleaners sweep the remaining shards and shopkeepers board up the storefront windows. The women squeeze each other's hands. No one will be able to forget them anytime soon. Jail may put the suffragettes out of sight and out of mind, but now, these storefronts serve as a signal to the entire city: *We are here. We are still waiting for justice.*

✎

Emily, Charlotte, and Sadie visit Adeline the day after she comes home from Holloway. The older woman looks small and frail in her bed, her skin drawn and tinged greenish gray.

Adeline raises a spindly hand. "Thank you for coming," she says. Her voice is hoarse and weak, like a poorly played reed instrument. "I wanted to see you all before I go."

"Where are you going?" Sadie interrupts.

"Oh, goodness, dear, you look like you've seen a ghost." Adeline chuckles softly. "I am not going to die, if that was what you thought. No, no. We need funds. As you know, I can usually collect quite a sum when I go out on speaking tours. However, my latest sentence makes such an endeavor impossible—at the local level. But I've been corresponding with some friends internationally, and I've been assured that there is an appetite for our voices overseas."

"So you'll go to the continent?" Charlotte asks. Adeline has had invitations to speak in Paris for years, and she is fluent in French from her finishing school days. Someday, Charlotte herself would love to visit Paris, following in the footsteps of the revolutionaries.

"Actually, I am going to America."

Charlotte's breath catches in surprise.

"Yankee Doodle!" says Sadie, her whole face lighting up.

"Yes, my friend Harriot Stanton Blatch invited me to stay with her. I'll travel to Ellis Island at the end of the week. I have to make my exit, you see, before my re-arrest."

Charlotte's thoughts begin to race. How can Adeline make it to the port before the police realize she's gone? Will the Americans let her into their country knowing she is a wanted woman back home? And how will the WSPU fare with their leader an ocean away?

"I'll need your assistance," Adeline says. "I'm afraid Isabel won't be able to leave this house without attracting police attention, so it'll have to be you three."

"Of course," Emily says, with Charlotte nodding alongside her.

"Will you travel in disguise?" Charlotte asks.

"I think I shall have to until we reach the port. But in America, I'll need to reveal myself. What do you think, Sadie?" Adeline asks. "Will the Americans let me in on the other side?"

Sadie is silent for a few moments, chewing on her lower lip with a look of deep concentration.

"I think so," she says at last. "But it would help if you had an American escort."

"Well, I'll have Mrs. Blatch on the other side, but . . ."

"I can come with you."

"What?" Emily gasps.

"Sadie—" Charlotte begins.

Sadie shakes her head, her long auburn braid bouncing over her shoulder. "I . . . I've actually been wanting to go home. I've thought about it a lot lately, as a matter of fact. It's been two years now since I've been home, but my family is back in Boston. And, well, I think it's about time that I return."

"But we need you here," Charlotte argues. "London needs you."

"I think Sadie is right," says Adeline, silencing Charlotte's protest. "We can spare her here in London. The Americans need leadership, someone with Sadie's experience who can bring the campaign to American cities in full force. We can spark an international women's movement. Why, Sadie, you can organize among the attendees at all of my speeches. By the time my tour is done, you'll have hundreds, perhaps even thousands, of American women newly interested in the cause."

Sadie nods. "It's been the privilege of my life to serve here with you all," she says, squeezing Charlotte's hand tightly, once, and then clasping Emily's. "But I think my energies will be better spent back at home. I am needed there. And I can help you travel, Mrs. Hurston. It would be my honor."

"Are you sure you're making the right choice, Sadie?"

"Charlotte. I haven't been home in almost two years. It's time for me to go."

"But we need you here."

"The movement at home is stuck in the nineteenth century. They need me more than you do, even Adeline said so. We need an international coalition, and I can help build it."

Sadie folds her clothing meticulously on the bed, making small piles with straight edges. They have been talking in circles for hours. Charlotte wants to kick those perfect piles and send them spilling to the ground.

"How can you leave *us*?"

Sadie pretends not to hear the accusation in Charlotte's subtext.

"Dinner!" Emily calls up the stairs.

"Tell her I'll be down in a moment," Sadie says.

"Fine." Charlotte closes the door behind her. In the kitchen, Emily ladles soup into bowls, her hairline frizzed from the steam. "I don't know where Sadie's mind is right now," Charlotte mutters. "She's going to regret this."

"I'll miss her, too," Emily says. "But she wants to go home. I can understand that."

"It's not that. She is going to regret leaving Beatrice. She hasn't even written to her!"

"Bea doesn't know?"

Charlotte clucks her tongue.

"That's a shame." Emily sighs.

"It's more than a shame," Charlotte insists. "It's a travesty. We have to write to her ourselves. She'll be devastated if she returns and Sadie is gone forever."

"It's not our place to tell."

They hear Sadie's footsteps on the stairs, and Emily moves to set the bowls on the table.

"Mm, it smells delicious, Em!" Sadie plops down into her chair, shooting Charlotte a look that says *don't even try.* Charlotte spoons a large bite into her mouth so she won't be tempted to argue.

"So, Sadie," says Emily, speaking through the tension. "Did your mother receive your telegram?"

"Yes, she's really happy. Surprised, but happy. She will take the train down from Boston to meet me in New York when Adeline and I arrive. And my little sister, who's at Wellesley College, will join us, too."

"That's wonderful."

"So everyone's heard the news, then?" Charlotte asks pointedly. Emily scrapes the side of her bowl with her spoon.

"Is there any bread?" Sadie asks.

"I'll get some." Emily dashes into the kitchen.

"Stop," Sadie hisses at Charlotte. Her eyes are wide and brim with tears.

"You are going to regret not telling her," Charlotte shoots back.

Emily returns with a loaf of bread. "You know, the baker actually told me . . . Wait, are you crying?"

Sadie buries her face in her hands, her shoulders heaving over the abandoned bowl of soup. Emily glares at Charlotte and begins to pat Sadie's back.

"Shh," Emily whispers. "It's okay." She widens her eyes questioningly, but Charlotte looks away.

"I just need a minute," Sadie says, pushing out her chair and running upstairs.

Emily turns to Charlotte. "What did you say to her?"

"Damn it." Charlotte tugs at the neckline of her dress. "I pushed her too hard. But I think there's something she's not telling us."

"Should we check on her?"

"Let me."

Charlotte walks upstairs slowly, wringing her hands. She didn't want to make Sadie cry. But Charlotte knows the feeling of regret, that hard, cold stone that lodges itself in one's chest and weighs one down forever. It is an intimately familiar sensation, one that began the day Charlotte left Girton without telling her mother. Little did she realize back then, but Sarah—a widow, a mother—was the kind of woman the suffragettes fight for. Charlotte spent so much time resenting Sarah that she hardly stopped to realize her mother is the reason she fights for women's rights in the first place. Now, the chasm between them has grown insurmountably great, and that heavy regret sometimes makes it hard to breathe. Not that Charlotte has ever told anyone. But she can't let Sadie make the same mistake.

She takes a few deep, slow sips of air, and then knocks gently on the door. When Sadie doesn't respond, Charlotte lets herself in. Sadie is on the bed with her face buried in the pillow. The piles of folded clothes are rumpled beside her.

"Sadie," Charlotte whispers. She perches on the edge of the bed and begins to stroke Sadie's hair. "I'm sorry. I shouldn't have pushed you like that."

Sadie's body tenses.

"You can make your own choices," Charlotte continues. "I was just thinking about how I never really said goodbye to my mother, and now we don't speak at all. I miss her. And I . . . I don't want you to make the same mistake."

Sadie sniffles and turns her head so that her tearstained cheek faces up.

"I know you're not trying to make it worse," she says. "But I'm frightened."

"Frightened of what?" Charlotte offers Sadie a handkerchief to wipe her streaming nose.

"I'm afraid that she won't care. I mean, what can she do? She's not due back from her honeymoon for weeks. So what's the point of telling her at all?"

Sadie burrows back down into the pillow and mutters something under her breath.

"But she does love you," Charlotte whispers. Sadie shakes her head, her shoulders shuddering with sobs.

Later, Charlotte and Emily scrub the pots and whisper heatedly.

"I did all I could," Charlotte says. "She's afraid. She thinks that if she never tells Beatrice she's leaving, then she'll never have to feel Beatrice's abandonment. It's just that if Sadie doesn't reach out—"

"—then she'll bring the same fate upon herself, because Beatrice will never forgive *her* abandonment."

"Exactly." Charlotte dries her hands and unties her apron. "Bea's married, but she isn't dead. She said she would visit. We could even try to convince her to volunteer with us again someday. But Sadie won't allow herself to hope."

"It's not our place to tell," Emily says again.

"I know you're right. But what if we just write to Beatrice and ask her to come home to us, without explaining why?"

"It's too late. She'd have had to leave from Italy today in order to get back in time."

Charlotte groans.

"I just hope Beatrice can forgive her," Emily says.

"I hope Sadie can forgive herself."

CHAPTER FIFTY-EIGHT

EMILY

Their time together that had, for so long, seemed to stretch indefinitely is nearly over. Sam writes to say that Charlotte and Emily are welcome to remain at Park Lane without Sadie. At first they protest, insisting that they can camp at Clement's Inn or find a boardinghouse. It is hard to imagine the house without Sadie's echoing laughter, the doors unslammed and the staircases no longer battered by her stomping feet. But the Lawrence siblings won't take no for an answer. And it would be harder still to leave, so Emily and Charlotte agree to stay on by themselves.

On Sadie's last night, the three friends pile onto the sofa, knowing that they do not need to say anything at all. Being together is enough to communicate the triumphs and frustrations, the hopefulness and the helplessness, the giddy joy and the devastating letdowns of these last many months. And most of all, the love that lives in this room. The feeling of their bodies curled together, someone's arm resting on someone else's leg, heads cradled in each other's curves; still, the absence of Beatrice is palpable.

Emily's heart swells and she swallows a lump of emotion, turning her head just slightly to catch Sadie's eye. "Remember when we first met? When I came to tell you that Charlotte was in hospital?"

"I nearly ran into the street with my pin curls in," Sadie says, misty-eyed.

"Remember when you tried to bake us an apple pie?" says Charlotte. "And the whole thing caught fire?"

"Bloody hell. I'm going to miss you both."

"We'll miss you, too," Charlotte says, her voice soft. She nuzzles closer.

In the pink dawn, all three women wake to say goodbye in a flurry of hugs and promises to write. Sadie dons her traveling cloak and heaves her valise down the stairs. Charlotte, too, wears a cloak to escort Sadie, and she replaces her usual simple hat with a large flowery thing, reminiscent of Adeline's millinery excess. Its wide brim casts a shadow across her face. If anyone is monitoring the house, Charlotte will give them a diversion and, hopefully, provide the real Adeline Hurston time to make her escape. "Disguised in plain sight," Adeline always says.

Later, Charlotte will abandon the hat and meet Adeline and Sadie on a street corner near the Strand, where Constance Cunningham's chauffeur will drive them in his automobile all the way to the port in Southampton to stay overnight in an inn before boarding the ship. It will be a safer route than to attempt any of the transportation within London. Emily is to stay in town so as not to arouse suspicion. After Charlotte deposits Adeline and Sadie at the ship, she will take a circuitous route back to London, just in case they were followed.

After Charlotte and Sadie leave, Emily wraps her dressing gown closer around herself and pours a cup of tea. The house is eerily silent. She holds tight to her mug, watching curls of steam rise from the muddled liquid, though her hands still feel frozen.

Two days pass in which Emily is alone. Then, on a misty morning when the sun begins to creep through the clouds, she is startled by a knock at the door. It's too early for Charlotte's return, and Isabel is still in hiding at Clement's Inn. She peeks out the front window and regards a hooded figure standing on the stoop. The woman tilts her head skyward, and a beam of sunlight slices through the fog, revealing a bright blond curl.

"Beatrice?" Emily opens the door. "I thought you were on your honeymoon!"

Beatrice steps inside, her face ghostly.

"Charlotte wrote to me," is her only explanation.

"Here, sit down," Emily says, pulling Beatrice into the kitchen and silently cursing Charlotte's impetuousness. She quickly refills the kettle, hands quivering.

"I told Charlotte it wasn't her news to tell," Emily begins.

Beatrice furrows her eyebrows, and Emily notices the dark circles under her eyes.

"What news? Where is everyone?"

"I'm sorry . . . What did Charlotte write to you?" Emily asks, her voice tightening.

"Here." Beatrice pulls a folded slip of paper from deep within her skirt pocket. "She said: 'Come at once. Find any excuse you can. We need you.'" Beatrice refolds the paper and places it on the table between them. "I really did have to find an excuse. Daniel was quite angry about it."

"Shit," Emily mutters, using one of Sadie's choicest words. "Shit, shit, shit."

"What is it?"

Emily presses her fingertips against her eyelids, waiting to speak until her vision splotches with yellow. "Sadie," she says sadly, "has gone back to America to accompany Adeline on tour there. Charlotte escorted them to Southampton two days ago."

Beatrice stands up to leave, as though she could outrun the trains and the automobiles and make her way to the port in time. Then she catches herself and stills, slumping against the wall. With some coaxing, Emily moves Beatrice upstairs, guiding her to her own bed to rest. It feels inappropriate to put her in the bedroom only just vacated by Sadie, where the two of them had slept for so long together. But Emily cannot think what else to do. Beatrice is stricken, numb. Until she isn't, and then Emily wishes for a return to that dreadful silence, if only to stop the sound of racking sobs.

A few hours later, Beatrice descends the staircase, her eyes red-rimmed and tearstained, but she has fixed her hair and holds her back stiff and straight. Emily looks up from her sketchbook, where she has been tracing lines of swirling nothingness, and motions for Beatrice to join her on the sofa.

"I'm sorry for my outburst," Beatrice says. "Obviously, this came as a shock. But it's not just that," she adds. "I've been so emotionally drained lately. My honeymoon was . . ." Beatrice searches for the words. "It was overwhelming."

Emily nods.

"It's funny," Beatrice says, her monotonous voice sounding not funny at all. "My favorite Austen novels always ended with the wedding day. I was stupid not to consider that there's a whole lifetime afterward. And no one prepares you for it." Beatrice twists a strand of hair around her finger until the tip of her thumb turns bruise-colored.

"Perhaps you need time to adjust," Emily says.

"Yes. Well. I'm sure you're right. That's all there is to it." Beatrice's forced laughter trills like the rattling of chains.

"You can tell me the truth. Why are things so bad?"

"Oh, no, they're not so bad," Beatrice says. "It's only that, well—" She leans forward and at last her mask slips. Her green eyes lock with Emily's, baring the truth. "He's so controlling," she whispers. "Daniel.

God, when I insisted I had to return to London because of an emergency concerning my friends, I had to beg him, truly beg him. Not that we'd been having such a grand time together, either! Perhaps it would be easier if I hadn't spent so long here, living independently. Because now, he must know where I am and what I'm doing every moment of the day. And he spends all day with *his* friends. I have to sit with the wives, the most *dull* and conservative women." Beatrice's voice is high and breathy. "During the whole honeymoon, we only spent time alone together at night," she adds, reddening. "And that was rather . . . unpleasant."

"I'm sorry," Emily says.

Beatrice waves the apology away like an incessant gnat, wiping at her tears. "He's meeting me in a few hours, and then we're going back to Kent. Even during the season I doubt I'll be able to see you all very much. Remember how Daniel reacted so well when he found out that I had defended us in court? To him, it was all a grand joke, apparently. And now, it's like he's a different person. He doesn't want me to have any independence at all. If he even hears a whisper about suffragettes in conversation, he starts spluttering. I've never seen this side of him before."

Emily's mind conjures up Martin's two sides, the aggression she uncovered behind his seeming sweetness.

"God," Beatrice says, biting hard on her lower lip. "I guess this is my life now. I'm Lady Daniel Rosseter. Beatrice Piper is dead."

"No," Emily says, gripping Beatrice's hands. "Don't say that. You're still you. Look at Lady Constance; her husband lets her work with us."

"Only because her family's fortune is tied to his estate," Beatrice says darkly. She looks around the damask-papered walls of the parlor, a place that only weeks before she had called her home. It is as though she is seeing it all anew, and she crinkles her nose as if a foul smell passed beneath it. "Anyway, there's nothing for me here anymore," she says. Sadie, though unnamed, looms large in their minds. "I should go."

"Wait," says Emily. "Won't you stay with me until Charlotte returns?" *Until,* she thinks, *you're in a better state of mind?*

"I must get back to my husband." Beatrice stands and retrieves her cloak. One of Sadie's scarves still hangs by the door. Emily pretends not to notice as Beatrice leans toward it, breathing in the scent of the woman who left it behind. "She didn't leave me a note or anything, did she?" Beatrice whispers thickly, ashamed but desperate to grasp for this last shard of hope. It pains Emily down to her very core to shake her head no.

Beatrice kisses her on both cheeks, makes a flat joke about etiquette on the Continent, and then leaves. Through the window, Emily watches as Beatrice hails a black cab, the car slow and hearse-like as it carries her away. She shudders, as Beatrice's ominous words echo in her mind—*Beatrice Piper is dead.*

PART FOUR

SUMMER 1913

CHAPTER FIFTY-NINE

CHARLOTTE

My dearest Ivy and Hollyhock,

Feather and I arrived at Ellis Island to what we Americans call a slight hiccup. Apparently, the United States government was informed that a certain woman aboard our ship was wanted for arrest back home in Jolly Old England. Feather was detained for twelve hours—a dreadful arrival, since my own mother and sister were awaiting us in Manhattan. I feared she would be deported, but at last they let her in. I think some of our friends in New York lent their assistance.

Anyway, we managed to make it onto solid ground, and I cannot express what a relief it was to feel the firm earth beneath my feet. Feather agreed; seasickness did not suit us. You must forgive me for saying that I am glad to be back in my homeland. My little sister has grown so much—she is taller than I am! And my dear mother has forgiven my recklessness now that I have returned to her welcoming arms. As I could have predicted, my father was too busy at the newspaper to make the trip to greet me. It is reassuring, you know, how some things never change.

So far, our business in New York is going well. You will likely read reports in the papers. We've met some of the most sparkling women in New York society (does the name Alva Belmont ring a bell to you? I'm certain our Ladybug knows her well). I'm afraid these women would faint if they knew all the trouble we've kicked up back in London—so send over the smelling salts, dears, because I intend to bring the revolution back to New York!

I am not entirely alone in that enterprise, thankfully. You remember the tragic fire at the shirtwaist factory back in March? I've now got the chance to meet with a young organizer, a woman by the name of Rose Schneiderman, who is working to get the vote and improve labor conditions in New York. I intend to assist her when Feather's tour is complete.

I already miss our laughter, and believe it or not, I even miss the muddy taste of tea. Still, it is a thrill to be back home and seeing my country through new eyes. Please tell Fern that Feather sends her love, and feel free to pass along this missive to any of our friends back in London. I am on my way now to Hartford, and after a sojourn in Newport, we will be back home in Boston by week's end.

All my love,
Mayflower

Any of our friends'—She wants us to pass it along to Beatrice," Emily says when Charlotte finishes reading the letter aloud.

"Obviously. But she's too proud to say so."

"Poor Bea. Well, it sounds like Sadie is becoming quite the radical in the eyes of her countrymen."

Charlotte cracks a smile. "God save the president."

Although Sadie keeps them apprised of her activities through frequent letters, Emily and Charlotte hear almost nothing from Beatrice.

"She must be busy with her wifely duties," Charlotte says.

Despite her gratitude to have escaped Martin, someday, Emily confesses, she would like to find a man, a partner, with whom she could build a life. Charlotte, on the other hand, declares that she will never marry. The idea of tying herself to another person forever holds no interest. Not that she wouldn't enjoy a man's company. At night, when her hand slips beneath her nightgown, she finds herself thinking of last summer with Jack, of inviting his body into her own. But she never, ever wants a life dominated by a man's will. And the deafening silence they hear from Beatrice serves merely to prove her point.

"I wonder if Sadie will ever marry," says Emily.

"I doubt it," says Charlotte. "She and I are aligned. I'd rather be a free spinster than a wife and paddle my own canoe."

"You're so independent. But I think Sadie would like to have a companion."

Charlotte raises an eyebrow. "A companion, not a husband?"

Emily shrugs.

Perhaps Emily is right. In another world, another life, she could imagine Sadie and Beatrice growing old together. They would invite Emily and her children over for tea, and Charlotte would use their parlor to host literary salons when she wasn't gallivanting around the world. But in the world in which they live, right now, Sadie is alone overseas. And Beatrice, though married, seems terribly lonely, too.

CHAPTER SIXTY
BEATRICE

F eeble light streams onto her skin, tepid and dull, through the
  sheer drapes that surround the canopy bed. It illuminates her blue
veins and the bone that juts out like a marble in her wrist. Peering
through long lashes, her eyes still mostly closed, she can tell that it
is late afternoon, but still she wears her white nightgown. And she
has not combed her hair in days, or perhaps even weeks. Everything
around her is soft: the mattress is stuffed with fine goose feathers,
the quilt is creamy satin, and even the voices in the hall are hushed,
as the maids wonder aloud what has happened to their mistress. But
her heart feels like a block of sharp, cold ice. Beatrice sinks deep
into her pillows, willing the world away.

The summer blossoms of 1913 are in full display, redolent and brightly
colored. It is, they say, an excellent year for rose gardens. But Beatrice
will not—cannot—leave her room to see for herself. It is hard to believe
how much time has flown since the little church wedding in Kent.
According to letters from Emily and Charlotte, there have been dozens

of arrests, countless smashed windows, signed petitions, coordinated parades, and soapbox speeches during campaigns all around the country. The weeks passed in a frenetic blur, though despite the maelstrom of activity, there grew a gnawing sense of fatigue. How much longer would it take to win the vote? The Union's numbers grow as more working-class women are recruited to join the movement, and Emily leads the charge in reaching out to women who work in mills and factories. But at the same time, their coffers are running low, and the stance of Parliament remains unrelenting.

For Beatrice, these last many weeks presented their own strange challenges. Even her education in law and diplomacy could not prepare her to negotiate the fine balance of her husband's moods, the expectations of the household, and the crushing, clawing loneliness that pervades her life. For a while, Beatrice would read the newspaper religiously to learn what the suffragettes were up to and whether Parliament would budge. But Daniel has taken to tossing the paper into the fire after he reads it at breakfast, sparing his wife, he claims, the agitation.

A few weeks after Sadie left, Beatrice caught sight of an article about American suffragists. A group had organized a massive protest against anti-suffrage president Woodrow Wilson. For the first time in American history, tens of thousands of women paraded down the avenues of Washington, DC. Beatrice knows Sadie was behind the march—not that she heard directly, but she could intuit Sadie's dramatic flair from the few lines of newsprint she glimpsed before Daniel disposed of the paper. Rather than fish it out of the flames, Beatrice resigned to watching it burn.

Beatrice takes to bed, and at first she is almost content with her confinement. At least she is alone. A cesspool of melancholia drags her under, and it's no use fighting now. She doesn't have the energy to get up. And why should she, when she is already drowned? She has nothing to do. No purpose to serve. No matter what Daniel says, she cannot bear the thought of having a baby. God, just the idea of Daniel's seed squirming inside her makes her want to retch.

Their wedding night had been a disaster. When Daniel tried to touch her, Beatrice had collapsed on the ground, her whole body trembling. In an instant, she was in the damp cells of Holloway, where a strange man forced his fingers inside of her. Daniel simply stared as she wept on the floor.

That night they slept back to back. The next night, too. Each time he reached for her, she shuddered uncontrollably. During a nightmare, she called out Sadie's name. When Daniel's patience eroded on the third night of their honeymoon, she found herself on her back, eyes squinted shut, tears burning her cheeks as he thrust dryly between her legs.

The worst part was, once the pain subsided and the numbness crept in, there was absolutely nothing she could do about it.

So she disengaged. She didn't write to her friends. The weight of lies she was forced to tell, the smiles she was forced to fake, crushed her. And with Sadie gone—she can never forgive herself for letting Sadie go—what is the point? Even the vote, that glittering idea that had given her the courage to subpoena members of Parliament and march through the streets of Westminster, feels utterly meaningless.

The physician takes one look at her and diagnoses a case of neurasthenia. She hears her husband and the doctor discussing her condition outside the bedroom in barely disguised whispers.

"The female is a sensitive animal," the doctor explains. "There are plenty of likely causes of her distress. Does your wife like to read?"

"Yes," Daniel says. "Newspapers, novels, anything really—though I've tried to dissuade her."

"Ah, yes. With such a fragile constitution, she ought not read anything that will excite her nerves. I suggest only the Bible, though even that, in excess, should be discouraged. Now, I believe you mentioned that you and Lady Rosseter both attended Cambridge. Would you say that your wife harbors any unnatural aspirations?"

"Such as?"

"Any range of symptoms—career ambitions, interest in politics, a passion for physical exercise—"

Even through the door, she feels her husband's jaw tighten.

"I see," the doctor says, reading Daniel's expression. "Lady Rosseter is clearly prone to hysteric morbidity. She needs rest and no excessive stimulation. She must stay in bed, and she should not read, write, or see visitors. I'll check in on her again in a month."

"Thank you, Doctor," Daniel says. "One more thing. I wonder about . . . conception?"

"Lady Rosseter remains resistant?" The doctor tut-tuts. "Perhaps, after a month or two of the rest cure, she will change her mind. If not, I can always arrange a stay at a sanatorium. That will often do wonders to rid a woman of her obstinate tendencies."

Beatrice imagines them grinning, their shared language of Cambridge dons and pressed shirtsleeves and patriarchy conveyed through a handshake. She wants to scream. She married Daniel to escape her parents' threat of sending her away, choosing the shackles of marriage over a straitjacket in an asylum. But it was all for nothing. Something has always been wrong with her, hasn't it? She should have stayed with Sadie, should have run away and risked it all. Now it is too late.

A week passes. Then two. She feels as if she is in jail once more, because she is not permitted to read or write, let alone to take in the fresh air or ride her horse. She has no contact with the outside world, no amusement beyond her haunting thoughts, her mind playing a reel of regret over and over in a torturous cycle.

Her brain is a fog, until it isn't. Until images from Holloway creep through her thoughts, memories of pain in her abdomen, blood on her legs. How she never told anyone what really happened in there. Not even Sadie. Sadie's face when she saw Beatrice's skirts drenched in blood, a blazing look of love and fury, was enough to silence her for good. She has always strived to spare others the pain she feels. But lately that pain is overwhelming. It isn't something she can button away in a box in her brain. It seeps into every breath. She wishes she could sleep forever.

But that light—it streams in, unrelenting. She feels its warmth on her skin, the fine hairs on her arms glinting gold. The heavy diamond on her finger winks like sunlight on the sea. The sea, blue and expansive and wild and endless. She would like to dive into it, to swim out as far and as deep as she can, and then when she runs out of breath, she would like to let go. She dreams of mermaids and sirens, whales and dolphins, currents and tides. Ships. Like the ship that carried her back from Italy. Like the ship that took her love away.

At last, Beatrice creeps out of bed, standing on gelatinous legs for the first time in weeks. Daniel is out for a ride. She corners her chambermaid and demands paper and a pen.

CHAPTER SIXTY-ONE

EMILY

t's a letter from Beatrice!" Emily feels a wave of relief as she retrieves the envelope from their stack of post. It has been worryingly long since they last heard anything from her, and despite Charlotte's thinly veiled contempt for what she assumes is Beatrice's luxurious married life and intentional abandonment, Emily harbors a quiet concern that Beatrice's silence has a more insidious cause.

"Read it, please!" Charlotte shouts. Her hands are black with ink as she pores over an article she is working on for *Votes for Women*. She recently took up the mantle of co-editor alongside Isabel.

"Dear Ivy and Hollyhock," Emily reads aloud.

> *I apologize for my negligence these many weeks. I assure you, married life is not all that you might think. I find myself in a state of confinement—no, not with child, but rather with a case of neurasthenia. Even writing this letter is forbidden, but as we have said before, sometimes we must be lawbreakers ... Needless to say, my chambermaid is under the strictest orders to send this to you without my husband's knowledge. Should you like to send*

your reply, please do address it to Daisy Smith rather than myself;
she will deliver it to me personally.

"What is neurasthenia?" Emily asks.

Charlotte looks stricken. "It's a complete sham. A blanket diagnosis for women who won't conform."

"So she isn't really ill?"

Charlotte sighs. "She is probably quite poorly. And heartbroken. But no, not ill."

> *This is rather difficult for me to put into writing, and so I will keep it brief. I have struggled since my marriage. I feel myself in a state of impermeable gloom, and I truly do not know how to lift the veil. I am twenty-two, but I feel about a hundred years old. I turn to you, my dearest friends, as my last hope. I am not permitted to receive visitors, but my bedrest ought to be lifted at the month's end if I make an adequate enough recovery. I will do all that I can to feign my improvement in the hopes that I can see you at that time.*
>
> *The truth is, and perhaps you have surmised as much already, I miss our Mayflower more than I can bear. I punish myself for failing to say goodbye before her departure, and now I fear that my silence has been unforgivable. As trying as it is to write this letter to you, it is impossible for me to write to her at all. I tell you this although I know that there is nothing to be done, but I fear that if I do not tell you the truth and put these words on paper, they will eat me alive.*

"Poor Beatrice! I had no idea how much she was suffering."

"How could we have known?" Emily shakes her head. "But what can we do?"

Charlotte nibbles at the end of her pen. "We must get her back to London. There's no life for her in Kent. If she could only come back to town—"

"If she could convince Daniel to let her rejoin the Union—"

"I do think she would feel considerably better," Charlotte says. "Beatrice Piper is not a person suited to feeling useless."

"It sounds like Daniel is really strict." Emily paces the room, still gripping Beatrice's letter. "We need an excuse to get her here."

Charlotte gasps, pointing to a square box on the newsprint in front of her.

"What is it?" Emily reads over her shoulder. It is an advertisement; they have dozens of advertisers in their journal every week. Even the major West End retailers have forgiven the suffragettes for smashing their windows; capitalism trumps all.

"It's an advert for the King's Derby. I'd forgotten all about it. That's just the type of posh event that I could imagine a man like Daniel Rosseter attending."

"The derby?"

"Yes," says Charlotte, smiling up at Emily with a glint in her eye. "We could stage a protest there, appeal to the aristocracy, the House of Lords, and the king himself. The press will be there already, so it's perfect for publicity. I bet Beatrice could convince Daniel to attend—they could even attend as a couple—"

"And then she could sneak off and join our demonstration?" Emily suggests.

"We'll be able to see Bea, make sure she's alright," Charlotte says, nodding. "And she'll feel much better if she gets the chance to be involved again. We can unfurl a great big banner across the track! It's the perfect site for a spectacle, I can't believe we haven't thought about demonstrating at the derby before."

"It's perfect," Emily agrees. "Write to Beatrice."

CHAPTER SIXTY-TWO
CHARLOTTE

Incandescent blue sky breaks through the clouds on the morning of the Epsom Derby. The stands are crowded and jostling with bodies. Gentlemen in their top hats, their wives hanging limp from their arms, stand in the private boxes up above, while on the ground, young boys run about, shouting and weaving between the legs of the horses and the jockeys. Charlotte shades her eyes. Somewhere in the stands, King George himself surveys the racecourse.

"I see the Cunninghams," Emily says, pointing upward. There is Constance's overlarge, flower-bedecked hat in one of the boxes. Charlotte waves, and Constance acknowledges her with a subtle nod.

Beyond the gates of the fairgrounds, Isabel is stationed in the cottage of a supporter. She has become too famous, too conspicuous, to arrive at an event such as this without causing a stir. And as they all decided, a stir will be more effective if it is raised by the spectacle itself, not merely the women in attendance. Better that Isabel stand at a distance but remain on hand to choreograph the press attention in the aftermath. The unfurling of a suffragette banner before the king himself, in front of crowds of journalists and the landed gentry, will surely make the front page of the evening papers.

Charlotte searches the crowd for Beatrice, scanning the sea of faces for a shock of blond. Someone blows a whistle, and children shout in the din. Young boys holding placards sell ribbons and tokens; men line up to cast their bets.

"Oh! Look, I think I see her," Charlotte says.

They wind their way through the humming crowd and approach Beatrice and Daniel as the couple maneuvers toward their private box.

"Lord and Lady Rosseter," Charlotte says primly. "How do you do?"

Beatrice turns to face her friends, and the first thing Charlotte notices is how tired she looks. Her eyes are rimmed with bruise-colored circles, and her skin is pallid and pocked with gray blemish scars. Still, she smiles at the sight of her friends.

"Miss Evans, Miss Brown," Beatrice says, her voice quiet.

Daniel smiles, gripping his wife's forearm tighter. "What brings you to the derby today, ladies?"

"We're here to watch the race, of course," Charlotte says.

"No funny business, then?" He speaks with a teasing lilt, though behind his joviality, Charlotte spots something serious in his eyes.

"I'm sure we don't know what you mean," Emily says. She holds up their tickets and gives a little shrug of her shoulders.

"Ah, I see what's going on here," Daniel says. "You've been conspiring."

Beside him, Beatrice freezes. Charlotte maintains a practiced, impassive expression, and Emily cocks her head innocently.

"You've been conspiring to socialize with my dear wife," he finishes. "Yes, I was curious why you were suddenly so insistent upon attending the derby, dear Lady Rosseter. Especially when so little has interested you as of late. Now I see." He taps his finger against the bridge of his nose and raises an eyebrow. The gesture is both playful and somehow sinister.

"I wonder, Lord Rosseter, if you could advise me on placing a bet," Emily says, diverting Daniel's attention as planned.

"Now, now, proper ladies do not gamble," he chides.

"Oh, sir, I only wonder whether you could tell me *your* predictions. Surely you can hazard a guess?"

"Well, I suppose I can do that. His Highness's horse, Anmer, is a beautiful beast. That black steed with the star, over there," he says, pointing. As Daniel instructs Emily about what to look for in a race-horse, Charlotte slips a sash to Beatrice. She stuffs the violet, white, and green ribbons into the folds of her skirt. Emily coughs.

"Thank you, Lord Rosseter. This has been most instructive. I suppose we should let you get to your box before the race begins."

As Emily speaks, Charlotte whispers in Beatrice's ear. "We'll be positioned at Tottenham Corner, the bend before the home straight. Join us when you can." She motions with her chin and, but for a minuscule nod, Beatrice's expression remains vacant.

"Come, wife," says Daniel, extending his arm. With a tip of his hat, he leads Beatrice away. She does not look back at her friends.

"Good work," Charlotte mutters when they've escaped the Rosseters' earshot.

"What an arse," Emily says. "He explained everything to me as though I was an imbecile. The horses *run* round and round in a *race*," she repeats in an exaggeratedly slow voice. "Explaining, explaining! He's such a . . . a . . ."

"A man?" Charlotte says.

"Quite right. How did Beatrice seem to you?"

"She didn't say much," Charlotte admits. "Her eyes were dull, almost glazed over."

"I noticed that, too."

"She's like a ghost of herself," Charlotte says sadly. Even in the sunshine, her skin prickles with a chill. "I hope this will be worth it."

They approach the corner just as a whistle blows to signal the approaching start of the race, and they duck beneath the fence to station themselves safely off the track.

"I hope so," Emily says.

CHAPTER SIXTY-THREE
BEATRICE

The derby is one great drum, beating, beating incessantly. The horses' hooves pummeling the track, the clapping spectators, the thrumming anxiety in her chest. Beatrice spots Emily and Charlotte waiting, as agreed, near the final bend of the course, their carefully sewn VOTES FOR WOMEN banner tucked out of sight among the folds of their skirts.

"Hello," Beatrice whispers.

"Oh, thank goodness you found us!" Charlotte says, making space for her against the fence as the horses fly past.

Beatrice draws her shoulders back, standing tall. She looks at Emily and Charlotte, studying their faces. It's like the last six months, her life in London, are right there in her mind's eye, as clear in her memory as running water.

"What is it?" Emily asks.

Beatrice bites her lip, a small smile creeping across her cheeks. "It's just so good to see you both."

Charlotte wraps an arm around Beatrice's shoulder and plants a kiss on her cheek. "Alright, m'lady, let's get into position."

"You're sure you want to do this?" Emily asks.

Beatrice nods. She's told them over and over that she can do it, that this is her only chance. She is as calm as she was on the day of the trial, when all her frenzied thoughts distilled into crystalline certainty—still, the horses are already on the course, barreling along at top speed like a train on a track. Everything is happening so fast.

Emily and Charlotte exchange a glance.

"It's all in the timing," Beatrice insists.

The crowd shouts over the thunder of hooves as the horses whip past the bend. A rush of wind blows back their hair.

"Look, it's the second-to-last lap, isn't it?" Charlotte leans forward.

"Come on, get ready now," Beatrice says.

There is no time for second-guessing. Emily pulls the banner out from where she'd sewn it into her skirts, handing one end over to Charlotte. Beatrice digs her sash from within the folds of her dress, fingering the smooth violet ribbon, the satin seam between the white and green. Dignity, purity, and hope. Dignity is lacking these days. And even purity feels compromised. But hope remains. It must.

"Here they come," Emily says.

The leading horses grow larger with each second until they whip past the corner, kicking up dirt in their wake. The king's horse, Anmer, lags behind by a few paces. All three women duck under the guard rail. The hammering of hooves rumbles nearer and nearer, rhythmic. It sounds to Beatrice like an incantation. *Sadie. Sadie. Sadie.*

"Trust me," Beatrice breathes.

CHAPTER SIXTY-FOUR
EMILY

Time slows to a painful, wretched standstill as Beatrice slips the tricolor sash over her shoulder and runs out onto the track just as Anmer rounds the bend. Even as Emily and Charlotte unfurl their banner as planned, something feels wrong. Now that they are here, the plan seems far too dangerous, even mad. Beatrice is a few steps ahead, all blond hair and delicate bones. So breakable.

Why did they ever agree to this harebrained plot? Beatrice's wrists are right there, an arm's length away, and it would be so easy for Emily to grab hold of one, to root her in place.

But it is too late. Anmer was a speck on the track. Now he is a boulder. Arms lifted, as though wielding Joan of Arc's invisible sword, Beatrice lunges at the beast. There is a horrible sound on impact, like the smacking closed of a book. *It's all in the timing*, Beatrice had said. And there she lies, crumpled on the ground. The horse and jockey both crash and tumble, a pile of writhing bodies in the dirt. *No no no no no—*

A collective intake of breath from the crowd.

A bloodcurdling scream.

Emily is on her knees, and there is Charlotte beside her, both reaching for the limp and crumpled form that is Beatrice. Her body is motionless. Her arm is bent in the wrong direction. Her blond curls fall loose from her hat pins, powdered with dirt from the track.

This was a mistake. A reckless, desperate, foolhardy mistake. It takes every fiber of strength to stand when Constance appears on the track and takes Emily and Charlotte by the hand, leading them out of the fray as the medic carries Beatrice away on a stretcher. The Cunninghams' chauffeur leads the women swiftly through the crowds, the bodies pushing and shouting and pulsing, tauntingly, with life. If Emily were not so stunned she would have screamed.

Somehow, Emily and Charlotte climb into the ambulance. Charlotte vomits into her hat. They drive away.

It is a story that will grip the world, splattered on the front page of two-pence papers like something out of a tawdry novel: Beautiful young woman trampled by the king's horse. The captions sensationalize freely—lusty suffragette gets what she deserved; hysterical neurasthenic meets her tragic demise. But those newspaper reporters, and the insatiable audience that gobbles up the stories—they do not really know her. They do not know the whole story. Or any of it really, any of it at all.

Emily wakes with nightmares, her thin cotton gown clinging to her sweat-damp skin. Across the room, she hears Charlotte writhe and whimper, too, both scarred by that day. The mistakes they could have made or avoided. The words they could have chosen more carefully. It was too close.

And yet, when she remembers that she is dreaming, she feels relief.

They both cry at the inquest, when the police question them in the dank back rooms of Scotland Yard. The memory of Beatrice, battling bravely at their trial, is present everywhere in that place, in the stained walls and the scent of the officers' stale breath.

"Did you know of Beatrice Rosseter's plan to interrupt the race?"

"No."

"Are you aware of any conspiracy between Beatrice Rosseter and any other members of the Women's Social and Political Union?"

"No."

"Did Beatrice Rosseter exhibit any signs of insanity in the moments leading up to her death?"

"No."

They cry real tears, and the police let them go, exhibiting, for once, a genteel sense of pity. More likely, it is not pity at all, but rather Daniel's insistence on discretion. Sweep it under the rug as an accident, a tragedy—Emily imagines his instructions are accompanied by a signed cheque slipped under the desk. Plead madness, plead insanity, just not suicide.

And so Emily and Charlotte weep, but behind their handkerchiefs is joy. For as they speak, they know that a young woman stands on the bow of a steamship, the cold Atlantic wind whipping her blond curls, her eyes on the horizon. Her left arm is bound in a sling, but she stands otherwise unscathed, feeling freer than she ever has. Emily imagines Beatrice unpinning her hat and letting it flutter into the sea. It swoops upward first, like a bird taking flight, before plummeting down; she does not watch it drown, for though she grips the cold steel railing of the ship's edge, that piece of her is already gone.

If anyone were to ask how they pulled it off, Emily would not know where to begin. But no one asks. No one has any reason to wonder. Every so often, she catches Charlotte's eye, and her friend shakes her head in disbelief. They do not need to utter a word to know how close it all came. But then again, they did it for Beatrice. They could not fail.

When she collapsed on the racecourse, the puffs of dirt rising dark around that waxen, still body, like the soot from a train's engine, Emily's heart stopped beating, frozen in panic. *What have we done?* Her mind shrieked. But she and Charlotte ran blindly into the chaos. The jockey lay on the ground, flung a few feet from where Anmer had fallen, though the great beast already stood, righting himself, his haunches quivering.

"Trust me" were Beatrice's words as she dove headlong into the race.

No matter how long they had planned it in secret letters and coded missives, no matter Beatrice's assurances, they could not be sure that she would survive. Beatrice had grown up with horses, she reminded them over and over. She had leapt from them, fallen from them, rolled beneath their thundering hooves to avoid being trampled a hundred times. She could do this with her eyes closed. And she wasn't afraid. But that, to Emily, was the most chilling part. Beatrice was not afraid of death, for a part of her had already died—or it had, at least, been buried. On their own, Emily and Charlotte had debated the plan, argued over Beatrice's tearstained letters and cryptic instructions. But the truth they could not avoid was that they had to help her, even if it was against their better judgment. They had to help Beatrice risk her life in order to survive; if she stayed, she would surely die, but if she ran, there was a chance she could live.

But who could guarantee it? As Emily dashed out onto the track, pulling Charlotte with her, and caught sight of Beatrice's body crumpled and contorted, she thought they had made a terrible mistake. The wails, the screams, that escaped from Emily's and Charlotte's throats were not feigned at all. Someone got a stretcher and hoisted Beatrice onto it, one arm limp and lifeless hanging from the side. Emily hissed into Charlotte's ear to calm down, to pull it together, and helped her up into the back of the ambulance.

And there, as the cart pulled slowly through the clogged streets of Epsom, Beatrice sat up.

"Bloody hell," Charlotte cried, tears streaming down her cheeks.

"I told you to trust me," Bea said.

They'd had only a few moments together and they quickly tried to wrap Beatrice's injured arm as best they could. Soon, Lady Constance's automobile pulled up beside them, and in the chaos of the derby streets, no one noticed as a young woman, her clothing dirty and her hair askew, swung from the back of the ambulance and into the open door of the shiny blue Siddeley.

In the hours that followed, through all the commotion, no one asked to see the body. All it took was the ambulance driver's declaration of dead upon arrival, induced by a fat wad of cash from Lady Constance. The press gave her grieving husband privacy—a courtesy for the upper classes, for it would be improper to pry.

The dawn sky is the color of a spring rose when New York's horizon comes into view, pale and pink and bright. Etched against the sky, a beacon of liberty raises her arm in welcome. Later that day, pulses cross the sea, and back at Park Lane the telegram arrives. Five words: Iris in bloom with Mayflower.

HISTORICAL NOTE

I t would take another five years for some women to gain the right to vote in Britain. During the First World War, the Women's Social and Political Union suspended all militant activity in order to support the war effort. Four long years passed in which women (including many suffragettes) worked in munitions factories, served as nurses, drove vehicles, worked on farms, and connected essential telegraph wires at the front and at home, before Parliament passed the Representation of the People Act on February 6, 1918, extending the franchise to women over the age of thirty who owned property, and eliminating all property requirements for men over the age of twenty-one. It took until 1928 before men and women could vote on equal terms in the UK. In the United States, the Nineteenth Amendment granted women the right to vote in 1920. Jim Crow laws and terrorist tactics left many Black men and women disenfranchised well into the 1960s, and other racist laws like the Chinese Exclusion Act limited nonwhite suffrage long after 1920. Throughout the United States, voter suppression tactics remain in effect today.

This novel takes place over the course of one year, yet the events I depict in fact occurred over a nearly five-year time span. I condensed the Women's Sunday march of 1908, the first hunger strike and forcible feeding in 1909, Black Friday in 1910, the Cat and Mouse Act of 1913, and the infamous Epsom Derby of 1913 into a much shorter time frame.

Adeline and Isabel Hurston are stand-ins for Emmeline and Christabel Pankhurst, the mother-daughter duo who led the Women's Social and Political Union. In reality, Emmeline had two other daughters, Sylvia and Adela, and a son, Harry, but alas, I could only cram in so many characters. Christabel trained as a lawyer, and though she was unable to seek employment in her field, she did successfully defend herself and fellow suffragettes in court and even subpoenaed Prime Minister Asquith and Home Secretary Winston Churchill. Lady Constance Cunningham is very much influenced by Lady Constance Lytton, an aristocrat who went undercover to publicize the horrors of forcible feeding.

Many working-class women participated in the suffrage campaign, and characters like Jessie were inspired by Annie Kenney, a former mill worker who became a leader in the WSPU and a trusted friend and collaborator of the Pankhursts. Beatrice and Charlotte are completely my own invention, though of course educated upper- and middle-class women made up a significant contingent of suffragettes. Sadie was inspired by Alice Paul and Lucy Burns, American women who spent years volunteering in England with the WSPU and learning the tactics of mass marches, public demonstrations, and hunger strikes before returning home to reinvigorate the American suffrage campaign with those unprecedented forms of protest. I wanted to note Sadie's involvement in the first women's march on Washington, DC, when suffragists demonstrated against President Wilson, although I took liberties with the timing. (For more on Paul and Burns, I highly recommend the Tony Award–winning Broadway musical *Suffs*, created by Shaina Taub.) As for Emily, female wardresses working in Holloway were often intimately close with the suffragettes imprisoned there. Some were complacent or cruel to the prisoners, but others were, in fact, allies. A poem written by a suffragette describes one of the wardresses as "one we'll ne'er forget, / She says she's not—and yet and yet / We feel she is a Suffragette" (Caitlin Davies, *Bad Girls*, 72).

I tried to encompass a wide breadth of classes into this novel. While earlier and more conservative suffrage groups, like the National Union of Women's Suffrage Societies led by Millicent Garrett Fawcett (represented by Matilda George Foster in early chapters), tended to skew more wealthy, the WSPU represented a diverse range of economic backgrounds. Save for a few notable exceptions, including Queen Victoria's Indian goddaughter Sophia Duleep Singh, we have scant evidence of women of color participating in this movement. In the US, many women of color, especially Black women, participated in the women's rights movement, encountering racism and white supremacy among white suffrage leaders.

We also know that romantic relationships occurred between suffragettes. Some (mostly male) historians have, over the years, denigrated and pathologized these relationships. Not only was that harmful (and based upon negligible archival evidence), but it also forced women historians to dispute those claims, which may not have been untrue but were made to cast aspersions over the suffrage campaign as a whole. More recently, historians of gender and sexuality have begun to reveal a fuller portrayal of the relationships that took place among suffragettes, relationships that included profound friendships, mentorship, and also romance.

My research took me to the British Library, where I spent days poring over crumbling original copies of the suffragette newspaper *Votes for Women*. Included in this novel are excerpts from real speeches, newspaper reports, and suffrage songs. Parts of Isabel's speech in the Cambridge meeting hall and Adeline's speech before the window-smashing campaign were extracted from real speeches by Emmeline

Pankhurst. Charlotte's letter from jail about her experience enduring forced feedings is based on a letter written by Sylvia Pankhurst. The song the suffragettes sing at marches and in jail is a real song from 1911 called "March of the Women," composed by Ethel Smyth with lyrics by Cicely Hamilton. The newspaper excerpt that opens this novel is based on real reports of the 1913 derby, as are the newspaper articles reporting on the Women's Sunday march in 1908.

During my research, I visited Parliament Square, the site of the Black Friday protest where over 115 women were arrested, many of whom suffered physical and sexual assault, for peacefully submitting a petition to the House of Commons. Just outside the gates of Parliament, separated by a wrought iron fence from the place she so ardently tried to change, is a statue of Emmeline Pankhurst. I visited that statue back when she stood on her own, and then a few years later, when the first statue of a woman, the moderate suffragist Millicent Garrett Fawcett, was erected across the street in Parliament Square. I was heartened to see that both times I visited the Pankhurst statue, violet, white, and green flowers were strewn by her feet. However, there is a reason why Fawcett stands in the celebrated square alongside Winston Churchill, while Pankhurst is tucked away on her own. The militant branch of the women's suffrage campaign, Pankhurst's WSPU, dared to be seen and heard, demonstrating publicly and using increasingly radical tactics after the government ignored their years of peaceful protest. The WSPU remains misunderstood, characterized as radical and violent, when the women's militancy was only ever enacted in reaction to the government's abuses.

I first started researching the WSPU in 2016, as an undergraduate at Brown University. Since then, I've grown up in a political system that is at times inspiring but so often infuriating. At a lecture given by Jill Lepore in the fall of 2019, I learned about the Invisible Lady, a real feature of nineteenth-century carnivals. Our society's distrust of women with knowledge, of female leaders seeking power, is not new. Nearly ten years since my research for the college thesis that would eventually inspire this novel, the suffragettes' story—a story of persistence in the face of defeat, and a reminder of the exigent need for more women in power, to safeguard our rights and promote our equality—remains as urgent as ever.

It is inevitable that I bent history as much as I tried to depict it accurately, and I take full responsibility for any errors and omissions, intentional or accidental. The most apparent alteration is, of course, that fateful day at the Epsom Derby. On June 4, 1913, a woman named Emily Wilding Davison, who had been involved with the suffragettes for many years and had undergone arrests, hunger strikes, and forcible feedings, ran out onto the racecourse just as the horses rounded the bend. Davison collided with a horse and later died as a result of her injuries. Her story instantly became sensationalized, and newspapers around the world reported on the tragic spectacle. Her demise epitomized, for the press and the public, the irrationality of suffragettes, who had at last got their just deserts. In the first draft of this novel, my character Beatrice also died. However, I am fundamentally convinced of the brilliant strategizing of these women, their courage, their gumption, and their daring. I decided to allow Beatrice to survive, rewriting a more hopeful history.

RECOMMENDED READING

Beard, Mary. *Women and Power: A Manifesto*. Profile, 2017.

Davies, Caitlin. *Bad Girls: The Rebels and Renegades of Holloway Prison*. John Murray, 2018.

Lytton, Constance. *Prisons and Prisoners: Some Personal Experiences*. William Heinemann, 1914.

Mackenzie, Midge. *Shoulder to Shoulder: A Documentary*. Penguin, 1975.

Marlow, Joyce. *Suffragettes: The Fight for Votes*. Virago, 2015.

Pankhurst, Emmeline. *My Own Story*. Eveleigh Nash, 1914.

Purvis, June. *Christabel Pankhurst: A Biography*. Routledge, 2018.

Purvis, June. *Emmeline Pankhurst: A Biography*. Routledge, 2002.

Tickner, Lisa. *The Spectacle of Women: Imagery of the Suffrage Campaign 1907–1914*. University of Chicago Press, 1988.

ACKNOWLEDGMENTS

Thank you to my agent, Shannon Hassan, for your belief in me. I'm so grateful for your vision and persistence in helping me enhance this story and find its home. To my editor, Victoria Wenzel, thank you for your immediate passion for this project. Your keen insights helped immeasurably to bring these characters to life. Thank you for the enthusiasm of your margin notes and the detailed attention you paid to characters that had only ever existed in my head. To the entire team at Pegasus, including Julia Romero, Jessica Case, Claiborne Hancock, Maria Fernandez, Emily Torres, Meghan Jusczak, and Lori Paximadis, thank you for all of the time, care, and energy you put into every stage of this book's production.

I'd like to thank the teachers and mentors who have inspired me throughout my life, some of whom were integral to the writing of this book, and others of whom will never fully know the extent of their impact. In particular, my heartfelt thanks to Kelly Colvin—your classes at Brown changed my life. I am immensely grateful for the passion you brought into your classroom, for the encouragement you gave me from day one, and for your humor, candor, and guidance during my years at Brown and beyond.

Thanks also to friends and mentors in the writing and publishing world, and especially my wonderful colleagues at St. Martin's Press, who have helped me grow as an editor. To my authors, thank you for checking in on me, laughing knowingly as I described being "on the other side" of the editorial process, and for energizing me with your creativity and brilliance. To Julie Sarkissian at the Westport Writers Workshop, thank you for building my confidence and sharing your thoughtful feedback in the early stages of drafting this novel. And of course, thank you very much to the authors I so admire who supported this novel, including Fiona Davis, Madeline Martin, Caroline Woods, Jenni Walsh, Adriana Allegri, Henriette Lazaridis, Jessica Mills, and *Suffs* star Ally Bonino. Your time and care are deeply appreciated.

I'm overjoyed to thank my friends and family who encouraged me from the very start to fulfill my dream of publishing a novel, even when the sign on my door while writing said "Do Not Disturb" and my superstitions around this dream coming true meant I avoided all inquiries into my progress. You have helped me, held me, built my confidence, made me laugh, and made me remember why this story matters. To Allie Dolido, thank you for reading extremely early drafts, for giving me excellent feedback, and for being the best cheerleader and friend. To Tessa Duke, thank you for taking me seriously as a writer, from one writer to another, and for sharing your boundless optimism in the face of rejections. To my sister, Juliet Dale, who inspires me with her infectious enthusiasm, love, and friendship.

It's hard to put into words how to thank my parents, who are without a doubt the reason this book exists. Eric Dale, my dad, believes in me with his whole being. I am the luckiest daughter to have a father who is exuberantly supportive, who cares about every detail large and small, and whose mantra to make the most of each day has always guided me. To my mom, Pamela Dale: this book is dedicated to you. Thank you for reading to me every single night of my childhood. Thank you for teaching me the power of my words, for believing in my talent, and for encouraging me to pursue my wildest dreams. Thank you also for instilling in me a fierce sense of feminism, equality, and justice; for modeling what it means to advocate for yourself and settle for nothing less than what you deserve; and for telling me that my voice matters, that women's history matters, and despite my doubts, that I could achieve whatever I set my mind to do.

To David, who heard about this novel on our very first date. Thank you for reading drafts and meticulously helping me sharpen and shape this story. Thank you for being my partner in every stage of getting this book published. It was a journey involving many, many tears—you hugged me and let me cry, and then helped me see that I could do it anyway. I love you.

Finally, thank you to the women who fought for our right to vote, both in Britain and at home in the United States. May we remember their sacrifices, tell their stories, and use the power they earned us for good.